SKYLARK
DANCING

OLIVIA GODAT

SKYLARK DANCING

A NOVEL

atmosphere press

Dedicated to my family for their support
and encouragement. Thanks guys.

PROLOGUE

The cloaked rider reined his horse in the dark shadows of the cottonwoods. He bent his head and listened, heard only leaves rustling in the wind and the call of a distant night bird.

"What is it, Papa?" the little girl cradled in his arms asked.

"Hush, my little skylark. We must be very quiet, and from now on no more English. Where we're going, they speak only Spanish."

"While we're there, you'll call me Alondra then?"

He chuckled. "Yes."

"Will Mama be there?"

The man sighed. He had explained before, but his daughter was only four years old. "No. Remember? You will wait for me with the nuns while I go for your mama. My ship sails over the waves swift as a skylark, so before you know it I will return for you, and once again we will all be together."

The little girl smiled, wrapped her arms around his neck and kissed his cheek, her trusting eyes bright with tears. "*Vaya con Dios*, Papa. Tell Mama I love her."

It tore his heart to leave his small daughter, but he couldn't take her with him. The dangerous mission to rescue his wife would require all his skill and cunning. Fighting a war to gain its independence, the Mexican government distrusted all Spaniards and was holding his wife, a famous dancer from Seville, prisoner in Mexico City, and, as her American husband, he was watched closely by Mexican bounty hunters.

Across the open space, candlelight shone from one of the village huts. A few more minutes and his daughter would be safe.

From his pocket, he pulled a leather pouch stuffed with silver coins meant as payment for the child's care. He opened the bag and took out a small dagger with a jeweled handle that had been in his family for generations. "Keep this safe for me until I return." He wrapped the knife in buckskin and returned it to the leather bag.

"And here are your *castanets*," he said, "so you can practice your dancing. And this," he showed his daughter a theater playbill with a drawing of a dancing woman, "so you can see your mama's face whenever you like." He tucked the paper in with the other items and handed the bag to her.

She looped the leather ties around her wrist and snuggled against him. "I'll take good care of these things, Papa."

"Now, we must be very quiet." He kissed the top of her head, inhaled her sweet child scent.

Once more he peered into the darkness and listened. He heard nothing and guided his mount out of the safety of the trees and into the moonlight. The jangling bridle irons, the creaking saddle leathers, and the horse's shod hooves clopping on the dusty road broke the stillness. Every few yards, the man glanced over his shoulder at the empty night.

He heard the gunshot before he felt the bullet's sting. Blood oozed from his left side. Spurring the horse to a gallop, he hunched over his daughter to protect her. He felt her frantic heartbeat, but she made no sound and he held her closer.

Again, a gun blasted and then another. A bullet slammed him in the back. He swayed in the saddle. His vision blurred.

He clutched the little girl tighter. Together, they fell from the galloping horse and crashed to the ground.

Bianca, a poor widow who lived in an adobe hut on the outskirts of the village, heard the gunshots and peeked out her window. She saw the riders race away, and when she finally heard a cricket chirp she ran to the huddled form lying in the dirt. She could do nothing for the man but picked up the unconscious child and tenderly carried her to the house.

She examined the little girl for wounds and found nothing but a small bump on the head. Carefully, she folded the child's pale blue dress which was made of soft cotton with lace on the collar and fine embroidery on the bodice. Bianca peeked inside the leather bag and slumped to the floor. Never had she seen so much silver at one time. Surely this child came from a wealthy family and the authorities would soon come looking for her. Bianca did not trust the authorities. Until the parents arrived, she, Bianca, would care for the child as her own.

The little girl did not speak for three days. Then one morning while they sat in the sunshine, a bird swooped overhead. After a moment, the little girl answered Bianca's often asked question. "They call me Alondra."

"Where are your parents, little one?"

Her brown eyes wide in puzzlement, Alondra whispered, "I don't know."

CHAPTER 1

Alondra drew water from the village well and set the bucket on the ground. Swiping a forearm across her brow, she pushed black curls off her face. Her empty stomach rumbled, and she tried to remember when she'd eaten more than a bite of stale *tortilla*.

With a hollowed-out gourd, she dipped water from the pail and sipped, hoping to stave off her hunger for a bit longer.

The thick dust muffled the rider's approach. "My horse and I also thirst, *Señorita*. May I trouble you for a taste of that water?"

Alondra looked up into the smiling hazel eyes of a *vaquero* riding a beautiful black horse. No, he was not an ordinary cowboy, but a *caballero*. He wore buckskins, but, from the proud way he sat in the ornate saddle and his manner of speaking, he was no doubt a gentleman. She dipped fresh water and handed him the gourd.

The horse plunged his nose into the pail and, snorting and blowing, drank. Both Alondra and the *caballero* laughed. The light in his green eyes flustered her; she had never seen anyone's eyes change color before.

Led by a man in a splendid uniform, a group of soldiers on horseback cantered up the street.

"Captain Baca," the *caballero* murmured. His voice held a note of disdain.

"*Señor* Felipe Montez, eager to sample the flesh of San Antonio's fairest, I see. Although only a peasant, she is ripe for sharing." The captain reached out a hand to Alondra. "Come with me, my little beauty, and I will delight you in ways you never dreamed of."

She backed away, bumping into the black horse.

"Don't be shy," the captain said. "My pockets are heavy with silver."

Felipe leaned down, picked Alondra up by the waist, and set her across his lap. Struggling to get free, she muttered through clenched teeth, "Put me down."

Felipe held Alondra tight. "You're safe with me," he whispered and turned to the captain. "She's mine, Baca. Go find your pleasures elsewhere."

The captain barked a laugh. "She does not appear too willing."

"Be that as it may, she stays with me."

"Bah, you can keep the ragged trollop. I'll take the black horse instead."

Felipe's green eyes turned hard. "We have discussed this same subject at every campfire between here and Mexico City. For over six hundred leagues, I have heard your same arguments. For the last time, I will neither sell you my horse nor give him to you." He spurred the horse and started him at a trot. "And now, *Señorita*, show me to your house."

"What are you going to do?" Alondra heard the panic in her voice.

He chuckled softly. "Not what I'd like to do. I'm taking you home."

"I can get there on my own."

"I am sure you can, but I will escort you anyway."

"Put me down. I can take care of myself. I am not a child."

"I agree. You are definitely not a child."

The huskiness in his voice sent an unfamiliar tingle through her body. "My house is over there, but I have to go back to the well. I forgot my water."

"You want to go back there among all those soldiers just for a wooden bucket?"

"No, for my water jar."

"You should get a tin pail. They are easier to carry."

With his fine horse and silver on his saddle, what did he know of hunger, of poverty? "The captain called me a... a trollop. I'm not one. If I were, then maybe I could afford to buy a tin bucket."

Without saying a word, Felipe turned the horse around and galloped back to the square.

Alondra saw the soldiers lounging around the well, her *jarro* on its side in the dusty street. She hoped it had not cracked.

Felipe flipped the reins. "Now, El Moro."

The horse leaped forward so swiftly Alondra's hair streamed out behind her. "What are you doing? Put me down."

"Hold on tight, *Señorita*," Felipe said in her ear. He leaned from the saddle, scooped up the clay jar by its handle, and straightened, holding it high. The soldiers clapped and shouted, "*Olé!*"

Three times they galloped around the well before Felipe reined in. "*Oye,* Lalo," he shouted, "Fill this with water for me, please."

His face creased with laughter, a burly soldier took the ewer and filled it from the well.

Felipe carried the jar carefully so as not to spill and walked El Moro at a sedate pace to her house. He helped Alondra slide off the horse and handed her the jar of water.

"Thank you," she said.

"Bar your door and keep it barred," Felipe commanded. "Don't leave your home until tomorrow morning. The soldiers should be gone by then." Without another word, he cantered away, leaving Alondra angry and frustrated.

She probably should be grateful that he'd gone back for her jar, but he didn't have to show off at her expense in front of his soldier friends. And ordering her to stay in her house until the next day. Well, she couldn't do that. She had to find work or starve.

Alondra set the water jar on the adobe bench and, as usual when entering the one-room adobe hut, turned her gaze to the playbill of a dancing woman dressed in a ruffled skirt and posed with *castanets* in her hands. Tacked on the mud wall with a bent horseshoe nail, the picture had hung over her bed since she'd come to live with Bianca, her foster mother. It kept alive a fading dream in which Alondra danced with the woman in the picture.

There was writing on the back, and years ago Bianca had taken the picture to the mission priest in hopes he could read the strange marks. He narrowed his eyes and held the paper up to the window to gain more light. "I cannot read this, *Señora*," he said. "It is written in the American language, but I do recognize the words Saint Louis."

He could not tell them what it meant but suggested that perhaps they should pray to the blessed saint for guidance. Bianca took the suggestion to heart and had added Louis to the list of saints she petitioned daily, saying that he probably was the patron saint of dancers.

Alondra poured water into a clay basin and, as she bathed with a cloth and piece of soap plant, wondered if she could find work dancing and sent a prayer to Saint Louis.

As a child, she had made up her own dances. Bianca told her that dance steps were meant to tell a story and sent her to Ignacia, a woman bent and stiff with age, who claimed to have danced with the gypsies. She taught Alondra the *flamenco*, ancient folk dances, and the proper way to use *castanets*. "Bend your arms just so," Ignacia would say, "cup your hands, but your wrists must never move."

To pay for the lessons, Alondra had done the old woman's laundry. Ignacia had been dead three years, but Alondra practiced dancing every day until five months ago.

That's when Bianca became ill with a painful sickness that no number of prayers, or herbs, or incantations would cure. Her death had been a blessed relief for Bianca and a heartbreaking loss for Alondra. She had nursed her foster mother with loving care and, when the last of their meager horde of coins had been spent, she sold everything of value to pay for the medicines, except for a small dagger with colored glass stones set in the handle.

"No," Bianca had said, "Never sell that. The picture and the dagger are the only things you have that belonged to your family." Each day she asked to see the dagger, for fear Alondra would sell it without her knowledge.

Bianca had been buried for two weeks and the last morsel of food was gone. Now Alondra must find work. Bianca had never allowed her to go to the rich part of town alone, saying knocking on doors of the wealthy held many dangers, and they had gone together bringing the *ricos'* laundry home. At the river, she and Alondra scrubbed and pounded the clothes on rocks until the whites glistened in the sun and the colors gleamed bright as new. Bianca delivered the clean laundry to her clients and collected the money while Alondra stayed hidden behind flowering bushes. She remembered the large house facing the square, where they were always assured of at least two bundles of laundry. Maybe she could find work there. Bianca had said it was a dance hall.

Bathed and ready to face the unknown dangers, Alondra tucked the dagger in her pocket as protection and, head held high, marched with determined steps until she reached the main plaza. She hesitated at the sight of the square with the green grass, bright flowers, and the well-dressed people promenading under the shade trees.

Huddled on the ground, a woman shrouded in filthy rags begged for coins in a low mumble. She was just one of the many displaced persons who had crowded into the town since war had begun. The beggar sparked new resolve in Alondra; she skirted the square and stared at the large house that sprawled before her. Baskets of red flowers brightened the veranda; flowering trees and shrubs shaded the courtyard and perfumed the air.

She took a deep breath, made her way to the back, and knocked on the kitchen door. A woman with a round face opened it. A white kerchief, tied at the nape, covered her head and a crisp, white apron swathed her ample stomach. The tantalizing aroma of fried peppers and onions made Alondra's mouth water and her head swim.

"What do you want?" the woman asked.

"I'm looking for work."

The woman pursed her lips and arched her eyebrows. "What kind of work do you expect to find here at the Pleasure Garden?"

Intimidated by the woman's manner, Alondra forgot she intended to ask about dancing. At that moment, her stomach growled, a reminder of her hunger. Pushing her shyness to the farthest corner of her mind, she said, "Anything. I've worked as a laundress for many years. Do you have laundry you'd like done?"

"We have a lot of laundry, but you're pale and don't look very strong."

"I'm very strong and a hard worker. I can scrub floors and know how to cook." Once again, Alondra's stomach rumbled.

"I'm the cook." The round woman examined Alondra from head to toe. "I'm sure you can find work here. When did you eat last? I'll fix you some food and while you eat, I'll talk to the *patrona*."

Alondra gratefully accepted the offered plate of peppers and onions with bits of meat mixed in, and nothing in her memory had ever tasted so good.

The most beautiful woman she had ever seen preceded the cook into the kitchen. Alondra jumped up from her chair and curtsied.

The woman wore a gown of purple silk, and a tortoise shell comb held her black hair in place. Her eyes matched the color of her gown. "So, this is the girl you told me about. Yes, with that black hair, she does have possibilities. What is it that you do, girl?"

"I can clean and sew and—"

"I have no need for household help. I'm in the entertainment business."

"I can dance."

"A dancer as well? How would you like to work for me?"

Alondra couldn't believe she had heard right. Saint Louis had answered her prayers. "Dancing? I'd like that."

"Make arrangements with your people. Tell them that from now on you will live here at my house."

"I have no people."

"Then there's no reason why you can't start work now, today. Come, I'll show you the house."

Alondra fingered her patched skirt, faded and worn thin as cheesecloth. "Well, I..."

The beautiful woman cocked her head and looked Alondra up and down. "I have clothes that will fit that slender figure of yours. You can pay me out of your earnings. I think you should wear red, turquoise, any bright color to show off your black hair and creamy complexion."

"Thank you, *Señora*."

"Call me Juanita. How much experience do you have? Have you ever been with a man?"

Alondra blushed and lowered her lashes. "No."

"Very well, that will not be a problem." Her lips set in a

thin smile, Juanita led Alondra through the rambling adobe structure. It had several small bedrooms and a large room with wooden tables and comfortable chairs.

"This is where you will dance," Juanita said. "Your pay for dancing will be what the customers toss to you. Now I will introduce the other girls and show you to your room. Then you will meet *Señor* Rojas, my guitarist. He will judge your dancing and, if you dance well, you will practice together this afternoon. The town is filled with soldiers and their officers, and all are eager for entertainment. I expect that tonight we will be very busy."

The three girls were beautiful. Rosalinda: voluptuous, with soft brown eyes and a mass of auburn hair; Flora: plump with dimpled cheeks, honey-brown hair, and a pink and white complexion; Suelita: blonde, graceful, and slender as a reed. They greeted Alondra with friendly smiles then excused themselves. "To rest," they said because they would probably work all night.

Señor Rojas combed his long, thinning hair to the side, which did nothing to conceal his bald spot. He claimed to have come from Mexico City by way of the palaces of Madrid and knew all the latest dance steps as well as the ancient folk dances. "Let me see you dance," he said, stroking his thin mustache with a delicate finger.

Snapping her fingers, Alondra danced a Gypsy *flamenco*. "You dance with fire and passion," *Señor* Rojas said and handed her *castanets* made of polished hickory wood. "Dance it again using these."

She had sold her own. They were for children, Ignacia had said, but these fit her hands perfectly.

Señor Rojas said, "I have known only one other who dances with such grace, such charm. She was famous and danced on the stage, but you, who are her equal, must dance here at the Pleasure Garden." He shrugged. "Well, we all do what we must to survive. Go now and rest; tonight you will have much work."

True to her word, Juanita had left some dresses on Alondra's bed. Too excited to rest, she tried on the clothes and chose a form-fitting gown, yellow with black lace on the flounces that cascaded from hip to ankle. She peered in the small mirror and imagined herself as the dancing woman in the drawing she'd grown up seeing every day, struck the pose, and smiled.

At a knock, she opened her door to the other girls.

"Has Juanita given you a new name yet?" Flora asked.

"No," Alondra said. "She says my name is just right."

"She probably hasn't thought of the proper one for you," Rosalinda said. "All of us girls are named for flowers."

"Why do you have to change your names to flowers?"

"Because this is the Pleasure Garden. All our bedrooms have a drawing of a different flower painted on the door. Mine is a lily," Suelita explained. "That way, when a man wants to visit me, he'll see the lily and know he's at the right room."

"Maybe Juanita will have a bird painted on your door," Flora said. "After all, birds do live in gardens."

Bianca had once explained that some girls were forced into prostitution to survive. "But not you," she had said. "You must find other ways to earn a living." And Alondra had. She danced. She didn't have to take men to her bed. "Juanita said that all I have to do is dance."

"She's only waiting," Suelita said. "She told us that you are a virgin. She'll get a good price for your first time with a man."

"And since you're new to the business, we were wondering if you'd like some instructions on how to keep from getting with child," Flora said.

"And how to keep yourself clean from diseases," Rosalinda added.

Alondra shuddered and in a weak voice repeated, "Juanita said that all I have to do is dance."

Suelita said, "Maybe for tonight. But we all must do what

Juanita says, or she'll turn us out to the street. And what would we do then?"

"We'd end up working in a *cantina* with a dirt floor and only peons for customers," Rosalinda said. "I don't want that."

"Nor do I," Flora said. "I plan on meeting a rich man and maybe getting married. That's what we all want, isn't that right, girls?"

Rosalinda nodded. "A lot of rich men come in here. Most of them are married though."

"I'm not looking for a man," Alondra said.

In a dreamy voice, Suelita said, "I had a man once. We were together for a long time, but he left me to go to Saint Louis and never returned."

Her heart leaped at the familiar word and Alondra asked, "What is Saint Louis?"

"It's a town, a big city."

"Where? Where is this town?"

"I don't know. Up there somewhere." Suelita flapped her hand northward.

Flora sighed. "Let's not talk about that now." She turned to Alondra. "So then, if you're not in this business, why are you here?"

Obviously, the girls were tired of the Saint Louis story and were eager to hear something new, but Alondra determined that she'd talk to Suelita soon and find out all she could about the mysterious city.

"I need the money I'll get from dancing. When I came here asking for work, I thought the Pleasure Garden was a dance hall."

"Oh, honey," Rosalinda said, "you will dance, but one day you'll end up doing more than that."

Her stomach churning, Alondra brought out her protection—the small dagger.

The girls all exclaimed over the pretty knife with the colored glass stones set in the handle. "What do you use it for?"

"Good luck. I carry it with me for luck."

Flora nodded and said they all had good luck charms they had to keep hidden from Juanita. She looked at the yellow dress that showed every curve of Alondra's slim body. "How will you keep Juanita from seeing it?"

"I have just the thing." Rosalinda ran to her room and returned with a leather sheath. "One of my customers left it. I think he wore it somewhere on his leg. Lift your skirt." She strapped the sheath above the knee on Alondra's right leg and slipped the dagger in it. "No one will ever know it's there. The ruffles hide it. How does it feel?"

"Good." And it did. It made Alondra feel safe, like nothing could harm her.

A bell rang.

"Come on, we'll walk with you downstairs."

CHAPTER 2

Felipe rode back to the square where the soldiers loitered around the water well. "Come with me to the bath house, Lalo. I have the need to wash the dust and stink of Mexico off my body."

"I have no money, *Señor* Felipe. We haven't been paid in over three months. That is why we are like animals, looting the farms for food, stealing from the villages, taking women wherever we find them."

Lalo pointed to the group of women and children huddled around cooking fires alongside the riverbank. "Those *soldadas* have marched across Mexico with food and bedding on their backs, infants in slings at their breasts, young children clinging to their skirts. Many women and children have died from the hardships on the trail, yet Baca won't stop even an hour for a proper burial." Lalo shook his head sadly. "We," he motioned toward the ten soldiers standing around the well, "have no women so we share the little food we have with the family men."

"Where is Captain Baca?"

"Enjoying what the city has to offer." Lalo frowned. "He

17

does not suffer from lack of *pesos*. The government gives him the money to pay us, but we never see it."

Felipe looked at the soldiers, their lean faces, their hungry eyes. He had grown fond of these men. They had ridden together through the lush valleys and dusty plains of the province of Coahuila. They had eaten their meals together, rolled their blankets beside one another at night. "Bring the men, Lalo. We'll find a *cantina*, drink a little beer, tell a few jokes."

"Do you mean it, *Señor* Felipe? The men will be in your debt forever."

"They will owe me nothing. We all deserve a little relaxation after our long ride across Mexico."

They found a *cantina* not far from the square. It was small and dingy, but the soldiers didn't seem to mind, and, as Lalo pointed out, they were still in the poor section of town. "Over on the rich side of town, there is a fine *cantina*," he said. "They don't water the wine and the girls are clean."

Felipe smiled. "Where is this place?"

"It's called the Pleasure Garden. It costs many *pesos* but someday I will go there."

"Why not go now?"

Lalo rolled his eyes. "Ah, *Señor* Felipe, they won't let me in, I'm nothing but a lowly sergeant."

"They'll take your money, Lalo. They won't care who you are so long as you pay their price. Let's get cleaned up and I'll go with you. They will not deny us entry."

"That is true. Your gold will show that you are a *hidalgo.*"

They left the other soldiers drinking beer and pinching the girls and went to the bath house, where they stripped off their clothes and sat in tubs filled with hot water. A boy crept in, snatched up their clothes, and scurried out.

Lalo jumped up, water dripping off his limbs. "Hey, you thief, come back here with my clothes!"

"It's all right, Lalo. They're going to launder them." An old woman carrying towels entered, followed by two girls. Covering himself with his hands, Lalo quickly crouched in the tub. The grandmother sat on a bench and watched every move as the giggling young women lathered and scrubbed the men's backs and washed their hair. The girls poured hot water over the men, rinsing off the suds that smelled of flowers. The old woman left the towels within easy reach and herded the girls out of the room.

Felipe leaned back in the tub and let the hot water seep into his skin.

"When do you leave for your home, *Señor* Felipe?" Lalo asked.

"In the morning. I'm eager to be home. And you, Lalo? What is your next assignment?"

"Captain Baca is going on ahead, taking four Indian scouts with him, but the men and I stay here in San Antonio for a well-earned rest. Those of us without families are to meet Captain Baca in San Vicente in two days. We'll visit villages to replenish our supplies, then return to fight this war with the Texians."

Bathed, barbered, and wearing freshly laundered clothes, the men rode to the Pleasure Garden. To ease Lalo's discomfort, they sat in the shadows at a back table and Felipe ordered wine. "A farewell drink, my friend." He lifted his glass in a toast. "*Salud.* When you are done fighting this war, come visit me in Santa Fe."

"If I still have Baca as my captain, maybe I will. Speaking of *el diablo*, there he is." Lalo pointed his chin to where Baca sat at a front table, talking with a woman in a purple dress.

Candles on a wagon wheel suspended from the ceiling lighted the dance floor, and Alondra stood in the shadows waiting for *Señor* Rojas to strike her entrance music. He sat at the edge of the circle of light, strumming a guitar. He wore an elegant black suit with silver buttons from knee to hem and a black, flat-crowned hat with red tassels dangling from its wide brim. The dance hall, hazy with smoke, looked different in the candlelight and smelled of tobacco and wine. Men sat at tables that ringed the large room, many of them wearing the uniform of the Mexican army. Most of the other men wore black frock coats and fine silk shirts and were smoking fat cigars. The girls wandered from table to table, talking to the men. An officer pulled Flora onto his lap and held a glass to her lips. She giggled, eagerly sipped the wine, and snuggled against his shoulder.

Alondra remembered what Rosalinda had said about doing more than dancing. That wouldn't happen to her; she wouldn't let it happen.

Señor Rojas struck a chord on his guitar, and Alondra brought out her *castanets*. She slipped the leather ties over her thumbs and tightened the knots. With the fingers of her right hand, she beat out the treble. Her left hand answered with the bass. In the circle of candlelight, Alondra forgot everything but the music and the dance. Her body swayed to the rhythm, her feet tapped in cadence with the clicking *castanets*, and her skirt swirled around her knees.

Felipe stared at the dancer who moved to the center of light. The girl from the well. Never would he have dreamed of seeing her at a place such as The Pleasure Garden.

Lalo nudged him. "Isn't that the girl from the well? I can usually tell the difference between a whore and a gentle-woman. I would have staked next month's paycheck that she was of good breeding."

Felipe didn't answer. The girl was no concern of his. Still, he didn't like seeing men ogle her while she danced. He wanted to pick her up and carry her off, as he had that morning. He remembered her soft curves against his body, the touch of her hand, the scent of her hair. He pushed his chair back and stood.

"What is it, *Señor* Felipe?" Lalo whispered.

"I want an early start in the morning. Stay and enjoy yourself." Felipe threw money on the table and hurried out before his urges overtook his good sense.

Captain Baca's eyes glittered as he leered at the dancer. She arched her back, raised her right arm over her head with her left arm behind her back. Her *castanets* clicked, her skirt whirled high around her legs, and Baca caught a glimpse of Alondra's creamy thigh. Without taking his gaze off the dancer, he spoke in Juanita's ear. "She dances with such passion. And you say that she is a virgin?"

"Yes. You know that I always speak the truth."

"Each step she takes sets my blood on fire. How much will it cost for the night?"

With a coy smile, Juanita tapped his arm with her fan. "No, no, Captain, not the entire night, only an hour. There are others who will want their turn with one so young and fresh."

"An hour? No. I will want much more than that."

A sly look in her purple eyes, Juanita said, "Surely a man virile as you won't need even that long."

They negotiated. Money passed hands. And the two turned their attention to the dancer.

James Thornton, an American, sat at a front table watching the dancer with interest. He pulled a picture from his pocket and studied the face he had memorized months before. The dancer twirled toward his table and candlelight caught her features. The resemblance was uncanny. Over the years, he had traveled to New Orleans, Mexico City, and other towns large and small, with no luck. Rumors and gossip had brought him to San Antonio and here the trail disappeared. Discouraged when all leads led only to frustration, he had come to The Pleasure Garden on a whim. He planned to return to Saint Louis in the morning, report to his grandfather, and then go on to Santa Fe. The situation between Mexico and Texas was getting more strained by the day and it was no longer safe for any American to remain in Texas.

*****

The guitarist hit the last note, the crowd cheered and clapped and tossed silver on the dance floor.

"Pick it up, quick," *Señor* Rojas muttered through his teeth and scooped up coins, shoving them into his pocket. Alondra picked up those the guitarist hadn't grabbed and, bowing and smiling, ran from the dance floor.

After the dancer left the floor, James Thornton told Juanita he had to see the girl.

The man spoke flawless Spanish. One could easily mistake him for a Spanish gentleman, a *hidalgo*. "She will be occupied for an hour or more, *Señor*. But you can go to her after. I will let you know."

"I want only to talk with her. I will wait for her in the salon."

Juanita's purple eyes sparkled with greed. "I cannot afford for her to remain idle. It will cost you the same for her time."

Since that was the case, James figured he might as well talk with the girl in the privacy of her own room. Besides, he had no idea how she would react. "Very well, *Señora*, inform me when the girl is free. By the way, what is her name?"

"She calls herself Alondra."

He felt a surge of excitement. Alondra—Spanish, meaning "lark." He had found her at last. But would his grandfather be pleased when he learned of the girl's profession?

CHAPTER 3

In her room, exhausted and exhilarated, Alondra flopped on the bed and counted her coins. Her thoughts went back to the morning and the man with the color-changing eyes. If she had done as he ordered, she'd still be hungry and not have this money. She tied the coins in a kerchief and, weary from the long day, prepared for bed.

Her door creaked open, and a man stuck his head in the room. "You are ready for me, I see." He shut the door.

Startled, she caught her breath when she recognized Captain Baca from the well. He wore his splendid uniform and had a blue silk sash draped across his chest with medals and ribbons pinned over his left breast.

Wearing only her chemise, Alondra drew herself up to her full height. "You are in my bedroom, sir. I must ask you to leave."

His dark, deep-set eyes widened in recognition. His thin lips turned down in an arrogant sneer. "Ah, *Señor* Felipe's doxy. Does Juanita know? She's passing you off as a virgin."

Panic and anger knotted inside her. "You have made a mistake, sir. You are in the wrong room."

He laughed. "Juanita said you were of good breeding, but even so you are nothing but a *puta*, so don't put on airs with me."

Alondra stood still, her mind whirling. Maybe she could talk reason to him. She spoke with desperate firmness, "Please leave my room. I am not one of the girls, I only dance."

"Is that what you tell Felipe? And does the fool believe you? I don't, and I will get what I paid for."

He reached for her. She stepped back. Her legs hit the cot and she fell backward. He lunged at her, put a knee on her stomach, and pinned her to the bed. She squirmed, beat on his back with her fists, pulled his hair.

"Don't fight unless you like it rough," he growled.

He fumbled with his pants, lay on top of her, and shoved a knee between her legs. He ripped the chemise off her shoulders, grabbed her left breast, and pinched her nipple, all the while tearing at his clothes. She pushed at his shoulders to get him off her. He pinched harder, thrust his knee deeper, trying to spread her thighs.

Wave after wave of revulsion washed over her, and Alondra lifted her right leg and pulled out her dagger. She jabbed it at his stomach and slashed upward.

He jumped up. "What the ...?" His silk sash hung in tatters, his wool jacket was ripped, candlelight reflected off two brass buttons that lay on the floor. He glared at her. "You little bitch! Look what you've done to my uniform. Do you know who I am?"

Fear and disgust turned into rage. Kneeling on her bed, Alondra clutched her knife in both hands to keep them from shaking. "I told you to get out of my bedroom."

"You haven't heard the end of this." Mustering what little dignity he had left, he straightened his uniform and slammed out the door.

Alondra stared after him, wishing her knife were bigger or his clothes not so thick. She hadn't drawn one drop of blood.

She couldn't stop trembling. She wrapped a blanket around her shoulders and huddled on the bed, shivering under the warm cover.

A few minutes later, Juanita swept into the room. "I'm disappointed in you, Alondra. Do you realize that was Captain Edmundo Baca, an aide to General Santa Ana himself? I went to a great deal of trouble to introduce you to him, to give you this wonderful opportunity."

"I am not a prostitute, Juanita."

"You stupid girl. What did you think we do here at the Pleasure Garden?"

"I thought all I had to do was dance."

"I can't afford for you to be so selective. I lost a lot of money because of you. I'm sure, now that you understand your position here at the Pleasure Garden, you will be more accommodating."

"No. I am not a prostitute."

Juanita narrowed her eyes and tightened her lips. She slapped Alondra. "You owe me and will do as I say. Tonight, you will entertain a gentleman who has asked for you. You will do whatever he wants with no more dramatic behavior on your part. You look a disgrace. Get yourself cleaned up and straighten this room. I will send him to you in fifteen minutes." Her skirts swishing around her ankles, Juanita stalked out the door.

Alondra stroked her stinging cheek. Fifteen minutes. She couldn't go through that again. She would not go through it again. Her heart hammering in her chest, Alondra dressed quickly in a red calf-length skirt and a white blouse, considered a moment, picked out another dress, and she would need her dancing shoes and *castanets* for her next job. Even though these things belonged to Juanita, Alondra felt that she had earned them. Besides, *Señor* Rojas had said, "We all do what we must to survive."

A sudden thought entered Alondra's head and she

trembled. What if Juanita was a shape-changing witch? Bianca had told her tales of witches who could change their shape into that of a beautiful woman or sometimes into the form of bats that flew only at dark, and they would entangle themselves in her hair and suck out her soul.

Alondra needed prayers, candles, and holy water for protection.

Thankful that she had some money, Alondra wrapped a shawl over her head and a *serape* around her shoulders. Clutching her small bundle, she crept out the back patio door and into the night. Her pulse racing, she ran to the mission church, glancing over her shoulder every few minutes. No one followed her. No bats flew overhead.

She slipped into the empty church, dark but for the eternal light on the altar and a few flickering votive candles glimmering on a picture of the Blessed Mother. Alondra breathed in the holy scent of oil, incense, and candle wax. Here, she was safe from witches and ghosts and all unholy things. She placed a coin in a clay pot that sat on a table and lit a candle. For five minutes, she prayed to the Blessed Virgin and then sprinkled holy water on her head, her face, and on her clothes. Protected from witches, she once more braved the night.

With nowhere to go but her old home, Alondra walked through the dark to the poor section of town. The moon was high when she arrived at the small adobe hut and pushed the door open. She reeled at the stench of unwashed bodies, human waste, and stale urine. The moon's dim light showed dark shapes scattered throughout the hut. A bony hand clutched at her ankle. A woman's thick voice spoke. "It costs one *centavo* for the night. Pay me two and I'll find a place for you near the door."

Only one day, and the homeless poor who had been pouring into San Antonio over the past months had taken over her house. "No," Alondra said, "I'm not staying." She turned and ran from the hut. With her strict rules of cleanliness, Bianca would be horrified if she knew what had happened to her home.

Alondra rested a moment at the well, took a deep breath, shouldered her bundle, and started walking.

"The girl is not in her room, *Señora*," James Thornton said. Surprise replaced greed in Juanita's purple eyes. "That is not possible. I left her there myself, not more than ten minutes ago."

"Perhaps you could find her for me."

A half-hour later, Juanita returned. "We have searched everywhere, *Señor*, and cannot find her. Perhaps one of the other girls would suit?"

"No, only Alondra." James cursed himself for letting the girl slip away. He should have talked to her immediately after her performance. In the morning, he'd start searching again. San Antonio was a small town. The search would be easier now that he had a name. Santa Fe would have to wait.

*****

At sunrise, Alondra was so far from town that not even the church steeple was in sight. She faced the west and didn't know what lay ahead, but she trudged alongside the wagon ruts that stretched into the horizon because logic told her that they led to a place where she could start a new life.

She rested on a rock by the side of the road and wished she'd thought to bring food and water with her. She dozed for an hour or so and woke to the sound of creaking cartwheels.

The cart, loaded with household goods and a family of four, was pulled by a lethargic donkey. She waved and the man jumped from the cart. The donkey plodded on.

The man walked beside the cart. "How can I help you, *Señorita*?"

Alondra adjusted her stride to his. "I must leave San Antonio. Where are you going?"

"San Vicente. My old parents live there and need our help. Are you in trouble with the authorities?

"No. Some people have taken my house and are living there. I don't know how to get them to leave, and now I have no home. But I have money. I'll pay if I can join you and share your food and water."

The man glanced at his wife, who nodded. "Hop on," he said.

Alondra settled herself in the cart and wondered about the distance to San Vicente and what lay before her in that unknown town. Hopefully someone there would know about Saint Louis. She would go there and find her family, and she would finally have a last name.

*****

Buzzards wheeled in the shimmering Texas sky and peered at Felipe Montez lying propped against his saddle. One, less patient than the others, swooped down. Its large wings fanned a breeze against his face and jolted him to consciousness.

Felipe opened his eyes to the white light of the glaring sun. He squinted into the brightness at the blurred image of the buzzard settling on the ground. *Madre de Dios*, the Angel of Death had come for him. He blinked, and his eyelids scraped sand across his burning eyeballs. He tried to raise his hand to shield his face but couldn't move his arms.

The buzzard hopped away. Three others joined it. They carried the stink of blood and death. With open yellow beaks and fiery red eyes, they watched Felipe in eager anticipation. He was not yet ready for the dark angels to take him—let them wait. "Go away!" he shouted, but with his throat dry as a desert *arroyo* he could only croak. He struggled to sit up. Impossible. His hands and feet were tied behind his back to a dried cottonwood branch.

A hundred galloping mustangs pounded in his head. The hot wind seared his skin and the relentless sun sucked moisture from his body. Perspiration stung his eyes and dripped down his back. The nearby creek murmured, and his tongue swelled from thirst.

He dropped his head and gazed dully at his blood-soaked shirtfront. They had attacked while he slept. He'd fought them, even used his knife, but there were too many of them. He remembered the moonlight glinting off brass buttons of a blue uniform, the flash of a saber as it thumped across the soldiers' backs, a rough voice saying, "That's enough, you fools. We are not thieves and murderers. We want only the black horse."

El Moro. Felipe lifted his head and whistled for his horse, but no sound came from his parched lips. Hard hooves thudded in his brain. He groaned and closed his eyes. A noise jerked him awake.

A hazy white object shouted and flapped its wings at the dark angels, and they flew away. *Gracias a Dios.* Thank God, the Angel of Mercy. "*Socorro, por favor.* Please, help me." Even to his ears, his voice sounded weak and cracked.

The angel bent over him. He felt the soft touch of her hand on his cheek. "He's badly hurt," the angel said, "he needs water.

Felipe blinked, the better to see his savior. In his wildest dreams, he'd never thought the Angel of Mercy would have the face of the girl from the well, the girl who danced with such abandon at the Pleasure Garden.

Someone put a cup to his lips. Water dribbled down his throat and over his chin, wetting his shirt to a blessed coolness.

"Can you stand, *Señor?*" a man asked.

"I think so." And surprisingly he could. They had cut his bindings and Felipe stood on wobbly legs. He looked around and saw a cart loaded with household goods. He saw a woman and two children. And he saw the girl. These were not angels, only simple travelers. He wanted to ask the girl what she was doing on this road, but his mouth wouldn't form the words, and the next thing he knew he was lying on his saddle and staring at the cloudless sky.

"He's too weak to travel," the man said.

"We can't leave him here," the girl said. "He's been beaten and stabbed and has a bad head wound." She continued speaking, but Felipe heard only the music of her voice.

When next he opened his eyes, Felipe was lying on the floor in the dim interior of an adobe hut. Sunlight pouring through the single window gave the only light. A niche in the mud wall held a crudely carved wooden *Santo* decorated with dry flowers and faded ribbons. A tallow candle flickered at its feet. Two sticks tied with grass in the form of a cross hung over the doorway. A red and black-striped *serape* lay in the middle of the dirt floor.

Felipe's stomach growled at the smell of cooking. He sat up and winced.

With the gentlest of hands, a woman touched his arm. "Let me help you, *Señor*." She helped him stand and handed him his washed and mended shirt.

"Thank you." Felipe pulled the cotton shirt over his head. "Where am I?" he asked. "How did I get here?"

A man walked in the door, milk jug in his hand. "Some travelers brought you to us," he said. "My name is Bernado and this is my wife, Inés. She is a healer."

"*Mucho gusto, Señora*." Felipe bowed his head. "How long have I been sleeping?"

"For two days," Inés said. "I put medicine on your knife wound and the gash on your head. You woke up yesterday and I gave you water, then you went back to sleep. Now you must eat. There is water for washing on the bench outside."

Felipe stooped through the low doorway. He washed in

cool water with soap made from a yucca root and dried his hands and face on a spotless square of cloth that smelled of sunshine and pine trees. He looked around for a slop jar but a little girl with tightly braided hair said, "It's our turn, *Señor*." The three children, two boys and the girl, scrubbed in the same water, dried on the same cloth.

Inés called from the doorway, "Come, it is time to eat."

The family sat on the ground around a clay pot of beans that was placed in the center of the red-and-black *serape*. Inés set a stack of *tortillas* next to the beans, she arranged herself on the floor, and Bernado said a prayer of thanks for the food and for the health of the stranger. The family blessed themselves with the sign of the cross, and Inés passed the *tortillas*.

The family had no eating utensils. They piled the *frijoles* on their clay plates and folded *tortillas* to form a spoon. Although accustomed to eating with pewter or tin utensils, Felipe said nothing and scooped his beans with a *tortilla*. The children drank their milk, warm from the goat, and giggled at their foam mustaches.

After the meal, Bernado said, "Let us sit outside, *Señor*. We will smoke and talk."

Felipe ducked his head as he walked out the low doorway. They sat on the wooden wash-bench, and Bernado rolled a corn-husk *cigarrito*. Felipe refused the offer of a cigarette. He had no taste for *punche*, the plant widely used throughout the province as a substitute for royally priced tobacco.

"You are a rebel then, *Señor*?"

"No, Bernado, I have no interest in your Mexican politics. My country also has its unscrupulous leaders."

"You are American?"

"No, I am Spanish. My name is Felipe Montez, and my father owns a *hacienda* in New Mexico. I have been living in Mexico City for the past three years, and I am on my way home."

"It is dangerous to travel such long distances alone, *Señor.*"

"I was traveling with the soldiers."

Bernado's family gathered around to hear the story. Inés sat on the bench next to Bernado, and their children sat cross-legged on the sun-hardened ground. They all listened in wide-eyed silence as Felipe told his tale.

"In Mexico City," Felipe said, "I lived with my father's cousin. He raises horses, as does my family, and I bought a black stallion from him as stud for our mares. I named my horse El Moro and I have trained him well.

"You are correct, it is not safe to travel alone, but my cousin has a friend who is a colonel, and he made arrangements for me to travel with the Mexican Army. I joined Captain Edmundo Baca's troop about six hundred leagues south of here. They were on their way north to help with the trouble here in Texas."

Felipe paused and gazed into the distance at the sere winter grass, the dry corn shocks in the small field, the withered bean vines that curled around stakes pounded into the ground.

"I traveled with Baca's troop for two months," Felipe said. "And every day, he'd ask for my black horse, saying that a civilian didn't need such a fine animal. When I wouldn't give him up, Baca threatened to confiscate him. I left Baca in San Antonio and thought I was through with the army. Then, the other night, they attacked me while I slept and left me trussed like a lamb for slaughter. The captain said he only wanted the black horse, but..." He stood and looked around. "El Moro. Did you see my horse?"

"He is here." Bernado pointed to a gray nag. Its hipbones jutted out at an angle and ribs showed through its mangy coat. Felipe mumbled a curse.

"Did they steal other things as well?" Inés asked.

"I don't know." Felipe patted his pockets.

Bernado said, "My sons found this dagger. Is it yours? It is covered with blood."

"Yes." Felipe grinned and his hazel eyes turned a brilliant green. "That's my knife, but the blood is that of a soldier." He took the dagger, rubbed it clean in the dirt, and shoved it in his boot sheath. "And my saddle?"

Bernado pointed, and Felipe rummaged through the saddlebags. His money pouch, pistol, and ammunition were there. His sword was in its scabbard. Nothing was missing.

Felipe took money from the wallet and offered it to Bernado. "Thanks, my good friend, I can never repay you for what you've done to help me."

"No, no, *Señor* Montez. The girl who brought you here has already paid me."

Taken aback for a moment, Felipe could not fathom why the girl would pay for his care; she had not been friendly to him. Still, these people had done him a great service. They deserved payment for their kindness. "Take this for the children, then." He handed the money to Inés. She gasped and her eyes widened at the amount. She smiled her thanks and quickly tucked the *pesos* in her pocket.

"What will you do now, *Señor*?" Bernado asked.

"Follow the soldiers and find El Moro. Then I will take him home to Santa Fe."

Bernado puffed on his cigarette for a moment, narrowed his eyes against the smoke, and said, "I have heard that the soldiers are headed for San Vicente."

*****

Ten leagues to the north and west in the small village of San Vicente, Armando's *Cantina* drowsed in the noonday sun. Alondra sprinkled water on the *cantina*'s dirt floor, worn hard and smooth as baked clay from the years of countless sweepings, scuffles, and dancing. She swept the litter out the door and into the dusty street. She smelled the bartender's oily sweat, felt his hot gaze on her back, and whirled with the broom across her body. "What do you want, Armando?"

His brown eyes, sunk in the folds of his pudgy cheeks, held the look of the village dogs: hungry, pleading, rejected. "I want only to speak with both you and Dolores. Come closer so we can talk."

"I can hear from where I stand."

Dolores plopped her voluptuous body on a low wooden stool and leaned back, elbows on the table, legs sprawled. "What do you have to say, Armando?"

"I have word that the soldiers are camped two or three leagues from the village. They will be here tomorrow, and if you, my little doves, treat them with kindness, maybe they will stay here in San Vicente for a few days and spend their money in my *cantina*."

"When the soldiers are in town, I can be with no man other than Captain Baca," Dolores said. "He expects me to save myself for him."

Anxiety stabbed Alondra at the mention of Captain Baca. She'd never forget the horror of the night he'd forced himself into her room. She could feel his rough hands on her body as though it had been only yesterday, and her skin prickled at the memory. She glanced wildly around the *cantina* looking for a place to hide, because if Baca recognized her ... She breathed deep, pushed her panic aside, and listened.

"Yes, yes, we cannot afford to anger him," Armando said. "But you, Alondra, you give yourself to no man. You could charge a good price, yet you refuse them all. I've had offers for you, and—"

"I clean the *cantina*, I serve the beer, and I dance, nothing else."

"You are making a mistake, little skylark. Soldiers need a woman after a battle. For a small fee, I'd allow you the use of my bed in the back room."

Alondra shuddered. She'd seen that bed in the airless room. The soiled blanket, the stained mattress that probably held bedbugs and who knew what other vermin crawling around in the corn-husk stuffing. "No! Not for any amount of money."

Armando edged toward her. "A young girl like you needs a protector. I could be that man." He reached out and stroked her hair. His hand slid down to her shoulder.

Alondra jerked away, pulled the knife she wore strapped above her knee, and pointed it at his belly. "Take your hands off me, Armando. Don't ever come near me, and don't you ever touch me."

Armando held his hands up. "All right, all right, put your knife away, but remember I'm always here and someday you'll come begging for my protection." He backed away from her and stepped behind the plank set on two kegs that served as the bar.

"He's right, you know," Dolores said. "That's why God made women. To pleasure men and bear their children."

"The very thought of a man touching me in that way makes me sick to my stomach."

"Someday you'll meet a man whose slightest touch will make you tremble with desire. You won't shiver with disgust then but will do whatever you can to please him."

Alondra narrowed her eyes and waved the knife. "Bah! No man will ever have that kind of power over me." And Dolores laughed.

Chin in her hands, Alondra sat at a scarred wooden table, her brain working on ways to escape from the *cantina* before Baca arrived in San Vicente. If he recognized her, no doubt he'd mention that he'd seen her at the Pleasure Garden. She trembled at the thought of what Armando would do to her then.

She could neither read nor write, had no family or money and only limited choices. But someday, somehow, she would escape from the *cantina* life.

CHAPTER 4

James Thornton led his horse through the dark and empty alleyways of San Antonio. Distant gunshots disturbed the night and the air smelled of gunpowder. He'd lingered too long, chasing rumors with no results, the girl had vanished without a trace. He needed to get out of Texas before he got caught up in the war.

After days of fighting in the streets, a group of 182 Texians had barricaded themselves in an old mission they called the Alamo. Although no longer used and in disrepair, it served well as a fort. He sympathized with the cause and had considered joining them, but they didn't need him. Already, Colonel Travis had sent a rider with a message requesting reinforcements, and they thought the United States Cavalry should arrive within a few days. Meanwhile, the brave men at the Alamo could hold out. The Mexican Army was no match for the courageous Texians—sharpshooters, every one of them.

At the edge of town, he gazed at the hundreds of campfires that dotted the countryside. Their muskets stacked beside them, Mexican soldiers lounged in the glow of the fires.

Somehow, he had to get through the maze of fires and soldiers without getting shot.

A cannon boom split the air, answered by a rifle blast, followed by a human cry from the Mexican ranks. Thornton didn't try to suppress a small grin of satisfaction. He climbed on his horse, wrapped his cloak close around his body, and boldly rode into the Mexican camp.

A soldier stepped in front of him, rifle at the ready. "*Quien es?* Who goes there?"

Remembering the name of the officer at the Pleasure Garden, Thornton said, "Captain Baca," and touched his hat brim in a two-fingered salute. "As you were, soldier."

The soldier clicked his heels and returned the salute. "Sorry, Captain. I didn't recognize you in the dark. Please pass."

Shoulders straight and head held high, keeping to the dark outer edge as much as possible, Thornton rode through the Mexican ranks undisturbed. What at first had appeared as only hundreds were thousands, and the Mexican soldiers had the Alamo surrounded. For the first time, Thornton felt a twinge of fear for the Texians. He pushed it aside. Surely, help would come soon, and he couldn't wait.

Finally, he was past the encampment. He dug his heels in the horse's flanks and galloped into the dark. A musket ball whined over his head, another thumped in the dirt behind him. He didn't slow down.

He galloped northwest on the trail forged by a Spanish explorer over 30 years before, which was the shortest distance between San Antonio and Santa Fe. Thornton reached the high plains by sunrise and slowed his horse to a walk. He removed the bridle bit and allowed the horse to leisurely graze, all the while moving northwest. He made dry camp on the caprock and, the next morning, started the journey across the rolling prairies of central Texas. At Blanco Canyon, he turned east, skirting the dusty plains of the *Llano Estacado*—the staked plains—stronghold of the Comanche Indians.

Four days after leaving San Antonio, he arrived in Saint Louis and left his horse at a livery stable, instructing the stable hand to rub the horse down and give it an extra measure of grain.

Thornton went to the hotel for a hot bath, a thick steak, and a night's rest in a soft bed. Next morning, he dressed in his town clothes and walked the short distance to his grandfather's house, a large brick building surrounded by a wrought iron fence.

Surprised that the gate hung open, he walked up the pebble path and stared at the black ribbon wreath tacked on the front door. True, his grandfather Maurice was more than eighty years old, but he'd been in good health, last Thornton saw him. He hesitated a long moment before he lifted the heavy brass door knocker.

A servant wearing a starched white apron over her black dress opened the door. Her face, brown and smooth as a hickory nut, wrinkled in distress when she saw him. "You is too late, Mr. Thornton. They done buried the master two days gone."

"What happened, Lilah?"

"I don't rightly know, they never did say. He took sick with the croup or something that the doctor couldn't cure. Cook even tried sneaking some of her own herbs and medicines to him, but that didn't help none. Now we don't any of us know what's going to happen to us. That lawyer feller is here now, going through the master's papers. It don't seem right somehow, but I didn't know what to do."

Thornton patted her shoulder. "Don't you fret, Lilah. Everything is going to be all right. I'm sure the master has made plans for all of you. I'll go in now and talk to the lawyer and let you know what I find out."

Lilah's face brightened as she led him to the den. The heavy drapes had been pulled back, allowing the morning sun to filter through the window. Dust motes danced in the sunbeams, a small fire burned in the fireplace, and the room smelled of pipe tobacco and wood smoke. Sitting behind the large mahogany desk, the lawyer, Adolphus Petty, rummaged through papers. His white hair curled around his ears, meshing with the white mutton-chop whiskers on his ruddy face.

The lawyer glanced up. "Ah, you're back, good." He stretched out his plump hand for Thornton to shake. "Sit, sit. We have a lot to discuss. Bring us coffee, Lilah. And maybe some cake?"

Thornton sat in a chair near the fire and Petty joined him in anticipation of the cake and coffee. He sat on the edge of the chair, but his short legs barely touched the floor.

"The servants are worried," Thornton said. "What provisions have been made for them?"

"As executor, I will see to their needs. They are all to remain here and keep the house open. All, that is, except for Joseph. The horses will be sold, so there will be no need for a stable hand. Your grandfather has bequeathed Joseph to you."

"No. I don't believe in slavery. That is the one thing the Texians were fighting against that I approved of."

"You can free him if you like. The papers are already made out to you. But forget about the servants," Petty said as Lilah set a tray with coffee and slices of gingerbread on the tea table. "Did you find the girl?" He tucked a napkin under his chin.

"Yes." James Thornton told the lawyer about finding Alondra dancing at the Pleasure Garden and that she had disappeared. "With the war going on down there, the entire territory is in an uproar. There is no telling where she is by this time. The one thing I'm certain of is that she is no longer in San Antonio."

Around a mouthful of gingerbread, Petty said, "Your grandfather, her grandfather, left this house to her. And there's money, a great deal of it. You must find her and soon."

"I fear there's not much I can do until the war is ended," James said. "Hopefully, it will be over by the time my business in Santa Fe is completed. I'll continue my search then."

"Your grandfather was a very proud man. I'm not sure how he would feel about leaving all his money to a girl who works in a bordello. His fortune came from generations before him, and he intended it for future generations. From my experience, that type of girl isn't interested in family but is interested in money."

"Grandfather Maurice was also a fair man. If he were alive, he'd listen to Alondra's side. The madam told me the girl is a virgin and that she only danced. Which is understandable, since her mother was a famous *flamenco* dancer."

Petty set his coffee cup on the tray. "Well, if you don't find the girl, or if she doesn't want to come back here, you will inherit all the money and this house as well."

James winced. "Even her mother's money?"

"Yes, everything except, of course, for the small stipend I am due for handling your grandfather's affairs."

With a wry smile, James said, "I am sure that amount will be fair. I'll find Alondra, no matter what it takes."

CHAPTER 5

On the trail to San Vicente, Felipe stopped often to rest the trail-weary nag the soldiers had left him, and he had plenty of time to think. He had enjoyed his three years in Mexico City but had yearned for the open plains and red *mesas* of home. He practiced every day with his dagger and grinned as he remembered his cousin's shocked face when, with the speed of a rattlesnake tongue, Felipe had pinned a toad to the ground with his knife.

In Mexico City, gentlemen used the sword and Felipe perfected the art of fencing. In the city, they no longer used the bow, and he hoped he'd not lost his skill with that weapon. Although his cousin despaired of making Felipe a gentleman in the Spanish tradition, the man gave him a new-styled pistol, one with six chambers, each loaded separately with powder and ball, an improvement over the old flintlock.

After three days of slow travel through stands of sycamore and rolling hills sprinkled with bluebonnets just beginning to bloom, Felipe arrived at the small village of San Vicente. The village sat on the shore of the San Antonio River, where it made a wide bend on its course south.

A crumbling rock-and-adobe wall encircled the scattered group of mud huts. A church with an empty bell tower sat at the far end of the square. Prayer book in hand, a black-robed priest strolled among the wooden crosses in the cemetery. A woman, large with child, herded two urchins down the dusty street. A pack of dogs snuffled at their heels. Candlelight twinkled in several windows.

Guitar music and laughter sounded from an adobe building that bore a crudely lettered sign, "Armando's *Cantina—Vino y Cerveza.*" Several army horses were tied to the hitching rail. El Moro was not among the tethered horses.

Felipe unsaddled the poor nag, left it in a corral at the rear of the *cantina*, and made his way to the front entrance.

Inside the *cantina*, soldiers sat at the wooden tables drinking beer and watching a dark-haired girl dance. The girl from the well. And the Pleasure Garden. And, he owed her his life.

The dance ended and the girl stood with her hands on her hips, waiting. The soldiers turned their attention to their beer and jokes. Felipe tossed her a handful of coins. Wide-eyed, the girl nodded her thanks and ran from the dance floor.

Lalo beckoned. "*Señor* Felipe. It's our turn to buy you a beer."

Felipe grinned and sat next to him. "It's good to see you, Lalo."

"The paymaster paid us a month's back wages. What would you like? Wine? Beer?"

"A little wine would taste good, and maybe something to eat."

"Alondra, bring wine and food for my friend," Lalo shouted.

Felipe stared at the dark-haired girl who grinned and nodded. "What is she doing here?"

"She ran away from the Pleasure Garden and is hiding from Baca."

Felipe raised an eyebrow in question.

"She's a good girl. She didn't know about the Pleasure Garden; she thought it was just a dance hall."

Felipe snorted in disbelief.

"You can ask her yourself, *Señor* Felipe. I talked with her, and you and I both know a trollop when we meet one." Lalo winked.

Felipe didn't want to discuss this girl with the flashing brown eyes and independent nature, but he did need to find a way to repay her. A handful of coins was not enough.

Alondra had glanced up when Felipe tossed her the coins. She had thought about him often, after they found him bound and beaten with blood trickling down his face and crusted on his shirt. The healer had charged a great deal of money, but Alondra couldn't leave anyone, not even a stranger, to die alone in the desert. She dashed to the kitchen to serve him the choicest food the *cantina* had to offer. She decided against the two-day-old rice, and the sausage smelled bad. In the end, only the *chili con carne* appeared edible and the *tortillas* were fresh.

He was traveling and would probably leave San Vicente soon. She'd talk with him, find out when he planned to leave, and go with him. She lit a candle on the knife-scarred table and set a bowl of *chili* in front of Felipe. "The wine is sour, *Señor,* so I brought beer instead."

He nodded without looking at her and continued talking with Lalo. She moved behind him and listened to his tale of the stolen horse. He said he wouldn't leave until he got his horse back. Maybe she could help him, and he'd be so grateful that he'd take her with him.

"You are looking for Captain Baca, *Señor?*" she asked.

"What do you know of him?"

She paused a moment, then said, "You do not live in Texas, *Señor?*"

"No, my home is north of here, over there across the river, in New Mexico. My father has a ranch about ten leagues from a town called Santa Fe."

"I do not know where that is, *Señor*, but it must be a long way from here. Do you wish to return?"

"Yes. As soon as I get my horse back, I'll be on my way."

"Tonight? This very evening?"

"Yes."

Her heart beat faster. There was much to do before she could leave this place forever. Food to pack, gather her few belongings. She would leave nothing behind.

Four Indians entered the *cantina* and sat quietly at a table. "Baca's scouts," Lalo murmured. "He'll be here soon."

A woman, heavy-hipped and large of bosom and with a cigarette dangling from her lips, entered the *cantina*. The soldiers greeted her with shouts of welcome. She wandered about the room, stopped at table after table to tease a man or to laugh at another's crude joke. She draped her shawl on the edge of the bar and spoke to the dancer. Heads together, the women talked until the bartender shouted at them.

Carrying two beers, Alondra walked to Felipe's table.

"I talked with Dolores," she said. "Captain Baca just arrived in town. He will be here at Armando's soon."

Felipe stood and threw some money on the table. "Thanks. I'll meet him outside."

"What are you going to do?" Lalo asked.

"This is between me and Baca," Felipe said. "No need for the soldiers to get involved."

Alondra snatched the coins from the table and pocketed them. "Come with me, I'll take you out the back through the kitchen." With a dancer's grace, she walked around tables, stepped over outstretched boots, warded off reaching hands, and led him out the back door.

Felipe crossed to the hitching post where a black horse stood, twitching its tail. "*Hola*, El Moro, are they treating you right?" With experienced hands, he went over the animal's body. Its coat was damp with sweat. "I don't like the bit on this bridle. Does your mouth hurt, my friend?" He loosened the bridle and removed the spade bit from between the horse's teeth.

"What are you doing, *Señor*? I asked Dolores and she told me that the captain bought that horse."

"No, Alondra, he did not buy him. He stole him." Felipe removed his shirt. "El Moro was taken from me and now I'm taking him back." He unsaddled the horse and dried its pelt with his shirt. "The captain can use this *caballejo* they left with me." Felipe went to the corral, brought out the poor nag, and exchanged the army saddle for his own.

"Are you really taking the horse? What are you going to do? Are you leaving here now?" Alondra asked, her voice vibrating with excitement.

"Yes, now that I have my horse, there is no reason for me to stay in Texas."

"Wait then, I'll bring you some food. Don't go until I get back. I won't be but a minute."

Felipe filled his water flask at the well, pulled on his buckskin coat, and stuffed his cotton shirt in the saddlebag. Alondra stepped into the moonlight with a bundle of food clutched in her hands.

"I am going with you *Señor*."

"No, I can't take you with me. I am grateful for what you did for me back there on the plains, but ..." he reached in his pocket. "Here, take this money."

Alondra shook her head. "I don't want money. I am going with you."

"It's too dangerous, Alondra, and I do not have time to worry about your safety."

"And you do not have time to argue, *Señor*. The soldiers are making ready to leave. I can show you a place to hide so they don't find you."

Felipe peered through the *cantina*'s dimly lit windows. Already, men stood at the tables, taking one last swallow of beer. With good-natured humor, they cursed the bartender for his weak *cerveza* and assured him they'd return on the morrow. Armando laughed and told them they were always welcome.

"Hurry, *Señor*, we must leave now before the captain finds out you have the horse."

Felipe considered. He had his horse now and he had no quarrel with the soldiers. They outnumbered him and they had no choice but to obey the captain. Besides, El Moro would benefit from a few hours' rest before their long trip. "All right then, where is this hiding place?"

"I will ride behind and show you. It is not far where we are going."

"Hurry then, we don't have much time and I have no intention of getting caught."

She placed a light foot on the toe of his boot, took Felipe's hand and he swung her up behind him.

Felipe turned El Moro toward the river. "No, no, *Señor*. Not that way! Go to the village." Alondra reached around him, yanked on the reins, jabbed her heels in the horse's flanks, and slapped it on the rump. El Moro galloped down the dirt street, dodging the yapping dogs that nipped at his heels.

"Where are we going?"

"Don't stop. See that stand of trees? Turn that way. Hurry, before they see that you have the black horse."

El Moro galloped past the village of adobe huts and down a dusty *arroyo*. The dogs stopped at the *arroyo*, whined, turned tail, and ran back to the village.

"Slow down," Alondra said. "See that shed? This is where you will hide until the soldiers leave." She slipped off the horse. Felipe dismounted, and together they pulled dry brush and tumbleweeds from the entrance to the shed.

A flock of bats swarmed out, and Alondra gave a startled

cry, threw her arms around Felipe's waist, and buried her head in his chest. He held her tight.

She lifted her head and looked up at him. "I'm sorry, *Señor*, but they frightened me." She placed her hands on his arms and pushed away.

"They're only bats."

She nodded. "But I forgot my shawl. Bring the horse in here."

Felipe blinked. "What does a shawl have to do with bats?" She didn't answer and he asked, "What is this place? Doesn't anyone use it?"

"No, not for a long time. Get in and I'll put the brush back. You'll be safe here; no one ever comes to this shed."

The brush once again covering the entrance, Alondra said, "I will return now to the *cantina*, and when the soldiers are gone from the village I'll come and let you know. I might not get back until morning, so don't leave. Wait for me." She turned and ran toward the village.

"Well, El Moro," Felipe said, "I can think of worse places to spend the night, so I might as well make you comfortable." He unsaddled the horse and El Moro rolled in the dirt. Felipe laughed. "That feels good, eh?" He sat on the ground and removed his boots. "This is a good place. I feel that the angels are watching over us."

El Moro stood, shook his coat, and nosed the brush. "Looking for food, old friend? In the morning, I'll find you a nice grassy pasture." Felipe removed his hat and relaxed against his saddle. Through holes in the roof, he could see the twinkling stars. He wondered about Alondra and why she was so determined to help him.

He listened for sounds from the village and heard nothing but a coyote yipping in the distance.

*****

Alondra ran from the shed and down the *arroyo*. She ran fast and didn't look back. An owl hooted, a sure sign that witches were about, and the hair on her arms prickled. Even if the soldiers left town, she wouldn't return to the shed tonight. She'd never felt so safe as when riding behind Felipe, as though nothing could harm or frighten her, but it was different alone in the dark.

She hadn't told him that no one ever went to the shed because the villagers believed it was haunted. Many years ago, there in that very spot, soldiers gunned down a young man falsely accused of horse theft. Since that time, many people had seen his spirit running from the *arroyo* to the shed. The old ones said he was seen more often when the soldiers were in the village, and a shiver ran down her spine.

At the edge of the village, Alondra stopped to quiet her pounding heart and thought about the young Spaniard with eyes that changed color. When the bats frightened her and he'd held her close, the words that came to mind were "strong," "safe," "gentle." His scent and his touch lingered, and she brushed her hands down her arms to feel the sensation once again. Her instincts told her he was a man she could trust. With his good manners and fine features, anyone could see he was a *hidalgo*. Even the rough soldiers left him alone, but if they found him with the black horse they would shoot him on sight.

But she, Alondra, would care for him and hide him from the soldiers. When it was safe, she would ride with him to his father's ranch. Even though his buckskin clothes were dark from long use, she was certain his people were *ricos,* and, grateful for what she'd done to help their son, they would allow her to work at their *hacienda*. Never again would the shadow of the *cantina* hang over her.

A small twinge of conscience rippled through her when she thought of Felipe alone in the shed. The old people said the spirit was harmless, but it couldn't rest until its name was cleared of thievery. She hoped the ghost would not walk tonight.

She heard shouts and glided into the shadows between houses. Two men ran down the street, and she crouched behind the broken adobe wall. At the *cantina*, men and horses stirred up dust. In the confusion, Alondra slipped through the back door and into the room emptied of customers.

"Ah, there you are, little one. I wondered where you went." The bartender beamed at her, showing his yellow teeth. "It is not safe for you to be out alone when the soldiers are in town. You must allow me to protect you." He reached out to stroke her arm.

Alondra hid her revulsion and pulled away. Every day, she had to contend with his advances and threats. And every day, it became more difficult to keep him and *los borrachos* from fondling her, but by this time tomorrow she'd be far from the *cantina*, on her way to a new life, and would never have to worry about the drunkards again. "I had to go outside for a few minutes, Armando."

"Were you alone, my little dove? What of the *hidalgo*? Did he pay you well for a dance?"

"Of course, I was alone. What do you think? There is no one in this place I'd walk out with, not even a *hidalgo*." Alondra turned to the buxom woman sitting on a table with her knees drawn up and her red-and-yellow skirt wrapped around her legs. "What's all the commotion, Dolores?"

"The soldiers say that a witch is flying tonight."

"Why, what happened?"

"They say that the *bruja* changed the captain's fine black horse into a worthless sack of bones."

"What does the captain say?"

"He says it is the work of a thief, but the men are

frightened and won't go hunting a thief. Some have already run away." Dolores laughed. "They're cowards, all of them. Only my captain, Edmundo Baca, is not a coward. He will find the thief."

"But, Dolores, I heard an owl just now. What if it really is a witch? And don't forget the spirit that walks the *arroyo*."

"Bah," Dolores said, "Edmundo is not afraid." But she shivered and drew her skirt tighter around her legs.

CHAPTER 6

Felipe awoke with a start. He lay still, listening. From the village, he heard shouts and pounding hoofs. He sat up, pulled on his boots, and peered through a chink between the logs. A man dressed in white stood by the shed. Suddenly, he broke into a run. "It must be a villager," Felipe muttered to himself. "I wonder if he plans to report me." He watched the man run across the *arroyo* and fade into a cloud of low-lying fog.

Felipe picked up his saddle. "We'd better get out of here, El Moro, before we have the army and entire village on our heels."

He looked out to check on the villager. The man in white stood in shadows, not ten paces from the shed. He stood without moving, as though watching or waiting. Felipe wondered if he should speak to the man, but the villager held up his hand, shook his head, then turned, broke into a run, and disappeared.

A sense of peace and security settled over Felipe. "Alondra must have sent the man to warn me." He leaned against the wall and thought about the girl. She was pretty, rather than beautiful: her dark, almond-shaped eyes were too large for her small oval face. He liked her mouth, with the white, straight teeth and red lips that curved in a ready smile. But he didn't like the way his heart thumped or how his breathing quickened and his blood ran hot when he thought about her.

He kept close watch on the village but could see little of interest. A few horses galloped off into the night, nothing else. The man in white was nowhere to be seen. Felipe retained his sense of wellbeing.

"Alondra wants to go with us, El Moro. I understand that I owe her. She saved my life and is helping me now, but we must leave her. I'll tell her in the morning."

The horse shook his head and snorted.

Felipe sat on the ground, crossed his ankles, and in his mind mapped the road home. He'd turn west to the *Rio Grande* and follow that river as much as he could, but the trail held many perils. First was the Mexican Army. Felipe held no illusions about Captain Baca with his dark rattlesnake eyes. Even though Felipe was not a Mexican, the Texians would consider him their enemy. Then there was the constant threat of the Comanche and Apache Indians who believed all white men their enemy. Felipe shook his head. No, he couldn't take Alondra on such a dangerous trip; he'd have to leave her in San Vicente.

Dolores and Alondra finished cleaning the *cantina* and draped brightly colored shawls around their shoulders. "Walk with me to my house, Dolores?"

Dolores laughed. "Did all the talk of spooks frighten you, child? All right then, I'll walk with you."

"Where is your captain tonight, Dolores?"

"He is out chasing the horse thief. Edmundo said he knows who it is and when the thief is caught ..." Dolores sucked breath between her teeth and slashed a finger across her throat. "Edmundo says that a thief needs harsh treatment as an example to the people."

"Who is the thief?"

"That good-looking young man with the light-colored hair, the one they tell me sat drinking beer with the soldiers. Edmundo says that *hombre* is too proud of his pure Spanish blood and needs a lesson."

"But isn't Captain Baca a Spaniard?"

Dolores laughed." No, he's *mestizo*, same as you and me. His father was a Spanish soldier, but his mother was Indian."

"I'm not *mestizo*," Alondra said. "My father came from Saint Louis. He was a Frenchman."

"But what of your mother?"

Alondra could not say. She knew nothing about her mother but had dreamlike memories of a laughing woman, hair piled high on her head and dancing with a man Alondra assumed was her father.

"It doesn't matter," Dolores said. "Edmundo says that one day all people in Mexico will be of mixed blood and the Spaniards need to understand that."

Alondra wanted to get back to the matter of the young man. "Do you suppose they'll kill the Spaniard?"

Dolores shrugged. "Probably. I don't know, but before they kill him, Edmundo will find ways to make him sorry he took the black horse. I thought I saw you talking to *el guapo*. Did the handsome one say anything to you about running away?"

"No, he didn't talk much. He looked lonely, so I asked him to dance with me, but he said 'no' and walked out the door. He didn't even finish his beer."

Dolores clicked her tongue and shook her head. "Well, here's your house. Sleep well and don't worry about the ghost."

Alondra was not concerned with ghosts. She was planning her escape from the *cantina* and all it stood for.

She paused at the door of the adobe hut that smelled of *frijoles* and tobacco. The moon poured a faint light through the barred window. Dark forms, sprawled on the floor, breathed with gentle snores. A child murmured in her sleep. Alondra silently crept to her corner, gathered her scant belongings, and tied them in her *serape*.

She took the few coins from her pocket. Pickings had been meager tonight. The Spaniard was the only one who paid her. She had done the best she could, but the soldiers were poor too and didn't like to pay for only a dance. She fingered the *centavos* for a moment then placed them on the fireplace. These people had been good to her, they could use the money and she'd be with a *rico*.

She didn't want to wake them so early in the morning, so she'd go without saying goodbye. Alondra lay on her sleeping mat for a few hours' sleep before she left her old life behind her forever.

Morning was but a gray streak on the eastern horizon when Alondra made her way down the street to the *cantina*. She ignored the village dogs that sniffed at her ankles and followed her in hopes of a scrap of food.

Alondra gently pushed on the back door of the *cantina*. The door had no lock, only rawhide straps for handles, and it swung open on its leather hinges without a sound. Grateful that Armando hadn't bothered to place the stone against the door, she stepped into the *cantina*. In his cubicle off the kitchen, the bartender snored with loud gasps and snorts.

She wrapped a stack of *tortillas* in a cotton cloth, hesitated, shrugged, and put the sack of corn meal in her *serape*. Armando could hire one of the village women to grind more corn for his flour. A large, curved knife with a bone handle stood upright, piercing the battered table. She pulled out the knife and cut off a chunk from the slab of salt pork that hung tied to a smoke-blackened rafter. She stowed the knife and the meat into her pack and tiptoed out the door.

Alondra turned the corner of the *cantina* and couldn't believe her luck. Tethered to the hitching post was a horse, no doubt abandoned by a soldier frightened of witches. She packed her stores of food into the saddlebags and led the horse at a walk through the sleeping village. The soft yellow dirt muffled the sound of its hoof beats. The mongrels followed until they reached the *arroyo*. At the edge, they turned tail, yelping and nipping one another with playful bites.

Felipe shoved the brush away from the shed entrance and, with a rope halter, led El Moro into the cool morning. He stiffened at the sound of creaking saddle leather and the soft thud of horse hoofs. He relaxed at the sight of Alondra. "What are you doing with that horse, Alondra? It belongs to the army."

"It was abandoned by the soldiers, *Señor*. Now I have my own horse and we can go faster." Alondra climbed into the saddle. "Come, we must hurry. Captain Baca knows you have the black horse, and he will have the men searching for you before sunrise."

"It is too dangerous, Alondra. I must leave you here. The soldiers will treat you badly if you are caught with me."

"Then we won't get caught. Come, *Señor*, let's go. Why must you always argue?"

"What of your people? Do they know you are leaving home?"

"I have no people, *Señor*. My father is with the angels, and my mother disappeared so long ago I can no longer see her face in my mind."

"Even so, Alondra, you shouldn't go away with me. You don't know me, and your home is here. What of your work?"

"I have no home and don't want to work at the *cantina* any longer. I don't want to be like Dolores." Her voice quavered and her lips trembled.

Concerned that she might weep, Felipe asked, "Where are you going, Alondra?"

"I would like to go to Saint Louis, *Señor*. But, if not there, then as far from here as I can get."

"What's in Saint Louis for you?"

"I don't know, maybe nothing. But I must find out, and anyway I can't stay at Armando's any longer."

Apparently, Alondra was alone with no one to care for her. He was deeply indebted to her, and his sense of honor wouldn't allow him to ride away and leave her without protection. He would take her to the next town, find a good family where she could live and work safely. He mounted his horse and turned toward the river. "I'm not going to Saint Louis, but I'll take you as far as I can. If we are to ride together, you should call me by my name."

Her eyes sparkled. "But I do not know your name, *Señor*."

"It's Felipe. Felipe Montez." He set El Moro to a fast trot.

She grinned, jabbed her heels in her horse's flanks, and hurried after him. "Thanks, *Señor*. You won't be sorry, I promise."

Felipe cast a glance over his shoulder at Alondra bouncing in the saddle. The stirrups flapped with each stride, she held the saddle horn with clenched fists, and her wide-brimmed *sombrero* hung down her back. He changed the gait to an easy lope and rode upstream until he found a ford. He took the reins of Alondra's horse and led it into the water. "Hang on tight, the horses may have to swim."

Alondra clung to the silvery mane of her grey gelding. The dark-green water eddied around the horses' knees. Gradually the river deepened, and a wave slapped at her feet. She drew her legs up. The water shallowed until it reached the horses' hocks, but Felipe continued wading upstream in the shoals. Sun topped the trees with gold before he guided the horses toward the bank. On dry land, he returned the reins to Alondra.

"We'll rest in that oak grove," he said and loped away.

Alondra followed at a canter, her mind filled with thoughts of the salt pork she would fry for breakfast.

Felipe waited for her beside a large oak tree. "One

moment," he said before she could slip off the horse. "I need to shorten your stirrups." He measured the length with a string of rawhide. "You can get off now."

"I'll gather wood for a fire and cook breakfast."

"No fire. We are too close to the village."

"We've been riding for hours."

"Only two hours." With his dagger, Felipe slashed the rawhide bindings on the stirrup leathers. "I still have the boiled eggs you gave me last night. We'll eat those."

Alondra gazed at Felipe for a moment. This was not how she'd imagined it. She had meant to cook for him, care for him, but already he had reversed the roles.

"What is it?" he asked.

She shrugged. "Nothing. Thank you for helping me. I'll look for some wild onions."

"No, don't disturb the earth. We don't want to leave tracks and I'll be done in a few minutes."

She understood his reasoning, still ... never mind. They would stop for a proper meal sometime, and when he tasted her cooking he'd realize how much he needed her.

Felipe finished with the stirrups. "This is a nice horse; what is his name?"

Alondra laughed. "He is only a horse. Animals are the servants of humans and don't have names."

"I think he should have a proper one."

"What do you think I should call him?"

"He's your horse, you should be the one to name him."

Alondra stroked the gelding as she'd seen Felipe stroke El Moro. She compared the two animals. "I will call him Segundo. He is a fine horse, but second to El Moro."

Felipe chuckled. "All right, Segundo, are you ready for your new mistress? Come, Alondra, I'll help you mount."

"Aren't we to have breakfast this morning, *Señor*?"

"I thought I told you to call me Felipe. We'll eat as we ride. Let's see how the stirrups fit." He placed his hands around her waist and lifted her into the saddle.

Her body tingled where he touched. She enjoyed the sensation, wanted him to touch her again, hold her as he had when the bats frightened her.

"*Dios mio!* You weigh no more than a spring lamb." Felipe adjusted her feet into the wooden stirrups. "Perfect. Did you ever ride with a saddle before? No? Well, you'll find the stirrups a great help. Let's go. We have to keep moving."

They walked their mounts while they peeled eggs for breakfast. "I've been meaning to thank you, Alondra," Felipe said, "for sending that man to me last night. I confess I was ready to run when I heard all the shouting. I thought the soldiers would find me, but your friend made me understand I'd be safer in that shed."

"I sent no one to you last night."

"Then who was the man dressed in white who told me to wait at the shed?" Felipe turned to Alondra. All color had drained from her face and her hands trembled.

"Who was it?" Felipe demanded in a voice that Alondra instinctively obeyed.

"It was the ghost." Alondra crossed herself and told him about the restless spirit of the young man who walked the *arroyo*.

Felipe laughed. "That was no ghost I saw. If he was the spirit, then he is now an angel, for never have I felt such peace as when he watched over me."

"Even so, it is true that the spirit walks the *arroyo*. And last night the soldiers were frightened by a witch." Alondra told Felipe how the captain's horse was transformed from a fine black steed into a worthless nag.

"You don't believe any of that, do you, Alondra? You know it was I who changed horses."

"Yes, and Dolores told me Captain Baca also knows it was you. He says you are a thief and has plans for exquisite torture when he captures you."

"Then we won't let him catch us." Felipe winked and glanced at Alondra with a smile that sent her pulses racing and unfamiliar warmth deep in her belly.

CHAPTER 7

"Fools," Captain Edmundo Baca fumed. "Use your eyes and find the trail." These blockheads couldn't find the trail even if the Spaniard had staked it with yellow flags.

The captain watched the scattered soldiers search the west bank of the river. Earlier they'd found the ford where Felipe entered the stream, and now they searched for the spot he'd climbed out. Baca was certain Montez had not waded the river for very long.

Baca's troop was sadly depleted. First, some had run because of a *bruja*. Then an enlisted man claimed that a spirit haunted the *arroyo* and others had disappeared. *Borricos*, every last man of them. He cursed the only good trackers in his troop, the Indian scouts, who had fled at the first mention of witches and ghosts. Now he, Captain Baca, had to spend precious time searching for a trail that was hours old.

The sun was high, and perspiration stained his wool uniform under the armpits and down his spine. He pulled out a dingy kerchief and mopped his wet brow, grateful for the breeze that swirled the sand and fanned the river into white wavelets.

Lalo saluted. "We have found tracks, Captain, but they are of two horses."

"Simpleton." Baca lashed the soldier across the shoulders with his riding crop. "There is only one horse thief."

Then the captain remembered Dolores had told him that the new dancer at Armando's had disappeared and was suspected of running off with Montez. She had recently come from San Antonio, Dolores had said, and Baca remembered the dancer from the Pleasure Garden. It couldn't be the same girl. Yet Juanita had said the girl had run away, which had given him a small measure of satisfaction.

He tried to recall what the dancer looked like. Small, he thought, scrawny, with not much meat on her bones. He preferred his women round and full like Dolores. A hot fist of desire punched him in the gut when he thought of her cushiony bosom. Baca clenched his teeth.

So, the Spaniard had a woman with him. *Bien.* It would make it easier to catch him. If it was the girl from the Pleasure Garden who had ruined his uniform ... Baca spat. He had buried that unfortunate incident deep in his mind and now the shame flooded back. His thin lips quivered, and his face twisted with rage.

Los mojones de perros would pay for the trouble they caused him. They had doubly insulted him, and he would not tolerate it.

"Show me the trail then." The captain glared at the brawny soldier.

"This way, sir." Lalo set his jaw and trotted off.

Baca followed, his mind filled with the joy he would feel when he had Montez trussed like a pig. First, he'd torture the girl and force the Spaniard to watch the executioner pull her fingernails off one by one. Her cries of pain would mean nothing to Baca, but Felipe would suffer.

Baca's black eyes glittered. His greatest satisfaction would come when Felipe begged for death. His wish would be granted, but oh, so slowly. One hundred lashes with a lead-tipped whip caused many a strong man to scream in agony. The captain squeezed the riding crop until his hands cramped.

"Here are the tracks, sir." The soldiers stood a respectful distance from the riverbank.

Captain Baca jumped from his horse, squatted, and examined the hoof prints in the mud. The riverbank had a slight slope, and the tracks were plain, even to the globules of mud drying in the grass. "He follows the river, no?"

Lalo shuffled his feet. "The wind has swept the tracks away."

Baca stood and surveyed the terrain. An oak grove lay to the northeast, but he'd bet a month's pay that Montez would turn northwest toward New Mexico. The Spaniards were sentimental about the old road leading to Santa Fe.

Still, he couldn't take any chances. General Santa Ana's orders to march to San Antonio could not be ignored for long. The thought of facing Santa Ana with so few of his original troops turned Baca's mouth dry. He swallowed hard and sipped from his water canteen.

"Take five men and scout the trees for tracks," he told the sergeant. "I will take the others and follow the river. And hurry, we must catch the thief today."

The captain rode behind his depleted group of soldiers. They led their horses while they searched the ground for hoof prints. The sun shimmered in the sky and the going was slow. Baca wiped his forehead with his damp kerchief and cursed that he was forced to chase a thief in the sweltering heat. He added one more item to his list of crimes against Felipe Montez.

He turned to the sound of galloping hoofs and a soldier reined in. "We found some evidence in the forest, Captain." He opened his hand. In the palm lay bits of tan eggshell.

The sight heartened Baca. "*Vamonos!*" He waved to his men. "Lead the way," he said to the soldier, and the troop of ten men galloped to the grove of trees.

Tracks showed that the fugitives traveled in a northeast direction. Baca chortled. "We have him now. He's headed for Austin."

He sent his five best men ahead as scouts. But the trail puzzled Baca. Felipe crossed the river and rode east. This was not the direction to New Mexico—it led deeper into Texas. That suited Baca, however, as the matter of San Antonio weighed heavy on his mind.

"Do you know the language of the Americans, Alondra?" Felipe kept the horses at a brisk walk. He wanted to conserve their energy as he planned to ride long past dark.

"No, but Armando said an American gave him this *cuchillo*." Alondra held up the Bowie knife.

Felipe admired the innovative design of the blade, with a cutting edge on both sides of the curved tip that could easily hook the jugular vein of a quarry and a groove to carry the blood away. He handed Alondra her knife. "I will teach you the language while we ride. You will have a better chance of getting work here in Texas if you can speak American."

"But I'm not staying in Texas. I'm going to Saint Louis."

"Then you should definitely learn to speak American. That," he pointed, "is a knife."

Alondra laughed. "What a funny language is this American."

"From now on," Felipe said, "I will speak to you in American, and in a few days you will not think it is such a strange language."

She grinned and cast a sidelong glance at him through her eyelashes. "How is it you know how to speak American so well?"

He smiled back at her. "I've known the language all my life. My father taught me. He learned it first from the men who trapped beaver in the mountains during the summer and spent their winters in Taos." Felipe chuckled. "Some of their words are not so nice. We won't learn those."

"I heard plenty of bad words at the *cantina*."

"Ladies do not hear or speak bad words." At the stricken look on her face, he said, "I'm sorry, Alondra, you couldn't help what you heard at the *cantina*."

"I don't want to hear any more bad words or think about the *cantina*."

"All right then, let's continue with the lessons."

Felipe taught her that *caballo* was horse, *huevo* was egg, *hombre* was man, *mujer* was woman. He pointed out objects as they rode east and gave her the word in the American tongue. He taught her to say "thank you" and "pleased to make your acquaintance" and was amazed that, by the time the sun was low, she had grasped the rudiments of the new language and used some of the simpler words in sentences.

El Moro pricked his ears and Felipe reined to a stop.

"What is it?" Alondra asked.

Felipe shook his head, pressed his finger to his lips, and listened. He heard nothing but looked around for a hiding place. He took them to a thick stand of brush and slid off the horse. "Stay here," he whispered. "Be very quiet and don't move from this spot. I'll be back in a minute."

Felipe slipped through the brush, careful not to step on fallen branches. He stopped to listen but heard only the buzzing insects, the chirping birds, and in the distance the low rumble of thunder. He dropped to his stomach and slithered behind trees and rocks until he came to a rise. He lifted his head and looked around. A whitetail deer stood in a clearing, not fifteen paces distant. From the size of its antlers, it was young, not yet two years old. It flicked its ears and stared at Felipe with curiosity.

Felipe pulled out his pistol, loaded and primed it, took careful aim, and shot the deer. With his knife, he field-dressed it, and then draped the deer across his shoulders.

A smile lit her face as soon as Alondra saw him emerge from the brush and his world tilted. How could this girl, this woman he had known for only a few hours, suddenly cause his emotions to bubble in turmoil? He promised himself he'd not let that happen again.

He threw the deer carcass across El Moro's rump and tied it down. "We'll have meat for supper tonight. Let's keep moving." Dark clouds heavy with rain gathered in the south. With luck, they'd find shelter before night.

Their trail led north and east through the forest. There were few villages west of the Pecos—the Americans had not yet ventured that far. Their settlements were to the east, beyond the *Rio Brazos*, but Felipe hoped to find a village before they reached that river. After he found a good family where Alondra could work, he'd return to the Pecos and angle westward toward New Mexico. Perhaps taking this route would throw the soldiers off his track. He knew Captain Baca was anxious to get to San Antonio.

Lightning streaked across the southern sky and the sun had set with purple and red streaks on the rain-laden clouds when they entered the plains. They came to a centuries-old buffalo wallow with a pool of rainwater in the center. Through the years, the wind and weather had eroded the sides until the wallow was a deep gully. Felipe led the horses down the slope to the water. "We'll camp here, it should be safe for the night. It looks like we missed the rain, it's blowing southwest," he said and picketed the horses.

He built a fire and skinned the deer. Coyotes barked, in the distance a wolf howled, and Alondra's stomach quaked. "Will they come near us?" she asked. "I don't like wolves."

"The fire will keep them away. They're only hungry and smell the fresh meat. Cook all that we can carry, and we'll leave the rest for them." As if in answer, the wolf howled a second time. Felipe unsaddled the horses and led them to graze on the rim of the wallow.

While Felipe buried the deer head and pelt, Alondra speared venison slices on sharpened sticks tamped into the ground and slanted toward the fire. The howling, yowling wolves sounded closer. In her mind, she saw their sharp teeth, their slavering mouths, their cruel yellow eyes. Her chest constricted in fear. The wolves could tear her and Felipe apart in moments. Panic clouded reason and she grabbed a flaming stick from the fire.

From the corner of his eye, Felipe saw Alondra run up the slope carrying a torch. On the edge of the wallow, she set a pile of sticks and dry grass ablaze.

A fire on the ridge could be seen for miles and Felipe had no doubt that the soldiers were trailing them. He ran up the bank and clasped her arm. "What are you doing?"

"Building fires to keep the wolves away."

Felipe grabbed her by the shoulders and glared at her. "And making a signal fire for the soldiers?"

Alondra struggled in his grasp. "No. I swear by the Virgin. It's to keep the wolves away."

His grip tightened. "Were you sent by Captain Baca to lead him to me?"

"No! I swear by all that's holy. I thought only to frighten the wolves."

Alondra squirmed and fought to free herself and Felipe loosened his hold. Her foot slipped on the rim of the wallow, dirt clods and rocks rolled down the hill. She swayed on the edge. Felipe reached for her arm. She pulled back and fell. He grabbed her around the waist and together they rolled down the slope and landed on the bottom against a clump of weeds.

Alondra lay underneath Felipe without moving. "It's the truth. I'm sorry. I didn't think about anyone seeing the fires," she whispered, her breath warm and moist against his cheek.

He felt her heart thudding against his own, and a wanting such as he'd never known surged through him. Felipe turned his head and his lips brushed hers. Her mouth trembled under his, her scent intoxicated him into oblivion.

A harsh voice jolted Felipe to awareness. "Well, boys, look what we have here." Rough hands pulled them apart.

Felipe glared at Alondra. How could he have trusted this woman? He had believed all that she'd told him. Lies, all lies. And to think he had kissed her.

Rocking on her knees, Alondra pressed her hands to her face.

Felipe averted his eyes. "What do you want, Baca?"

"My property, of course. Only my property."

Felipe stood and longed for his knife lying where he had butchered the deer. "I have nothing that belongs to you. Unless ..." He shot a glance at Alondra.

Baca laughed in apparent high humor. "Oh, no, not that little piece of baggage. As you can see, she only causes trouble, and I don't need that. No, I want my horse. My black horse." He swaggered to the fire and spread his hands to its warmth. "Bind his wrists."

Felipe made no protest when Lalo stepped forward and tied Felipe's hands behind his back. The other soldiers drifted to the fire, lured by the scent of cooked venison.

"Serve the men," the captain ordered Alondra.

"What shall I do with this one?" Lalo asked.

"Tie him to a tree so he can't get away."

"There are no trees down here in the wallow."

"Take him up on top then," Baca thundered. "Must I do your thinking for you?" He turned to Alondra. "Bring me some food."

Lalo and Felipe trudged up the slope. "I thought we were friends, Lalo."

"We are, but I am a soldier and must obey my captain."

"You know I could overpower you in an instant."

Lalo flicked a glance over the slighter man and grinned. "Maybe you could, but I don't think so, and anyway you won't because you're smart. There are too many of us and you would be killed. Give Captain Baca the horse, *Señor* Felipe. Then he will let you go."

"I can't do that."

They crouched on their heels and, from the ridge, watched the scene below. Horses milled, cropping the short grass, the soldiers squatted around the fire eating, and Alondra moved about serving the men. It appeared to Felipe that she spent more time than necessary with Baca.

Felipe wanted to believe that she hadn't set the fires as a signal, but his eyes told him differently. What were they talking about? Had Baca paid Alondra for information? Were they lovers? Felipe didn't want to believe that about her. She was too innocent, too ... He shook his head to rid the image of her lying on the ground beneath him.

He turned his gaze to the fire she had set. The embers glowed and a sudden gust fanned puffs of blue smoke across the prairie. Her fragrance lingered in his mind and his flesh burned where her fingers had touched. "Have you ever been betrayed by a woman you trusted, Lalo?"

"The girl didn't betray you. We trailed you all day, not stopping for food or rest." Lalo chuckled. "But we got here in time to watch the two of you roll down the hill. No, she didn't betray you."

Felipe sat quietly for a moment. "*Verdad?*"

"Yes. That is the truth."

Lalo told the truth as he saw it, but either way it didn't matter. Felipe had promised to take Alondra to a safe place, and his code of honor wouldn't allow him to do anything less. "Cut me loose, Lalo. I have to get her away from Baca."

"Are your bindings so tight that you can't loosen them yourself? Or are you so besotted by love that you can't think? My mouth waters at the smell and my stomach demands some of that venison. I'm going now."

"Come with us, Lalo. You'll find plenty of work in New

Mexico."

"No, I am a soldier and that is the only life for me."

"New Mexico has a militia and can use some good men."

"I'll think about it. Now I will go have a word with your little skylark." Lalo slipped and slid down the bank.

Felipe freed his hands, ran along the ridge, down to where his horses grazed, and whistled. El Moro lifted his head, trotted toward him and Segundo followed. Felipe glanced up at the pale quarter moon and prayed Alondra would understand when he spoke to her in the newly learned American language. He planned that they would slip away in the dark while the soldiers occupied themselves with eating.

CHAPTER 8

Alondra cooked venison steak and served the hungry men. For every piece of venison she served the soldiers, she placed one in her shawl. Felipe hadn't eaten and she determined that somehow she'd sneak food to him.

She glanced at the ridge where her fire blazed red and orange against the purple sky. The flames leaped with every gust of wind and glittering sparks brightened the heavens. Felipe was up there on the hill somewhere, tied and helpless. It was her fault. She had wanted him to kiss her, and if she hadn't enjoyed his kiss so much, never would the soldiers have overpowered him. She hefted the Bowie knife. Felipe was strong and would know what to do with it. She would give him the knife and maybe he'd think of her each time he used it.

He hated her now. She could tell from the way he had looked at her, his eyes green and hard. But she would cut him loose, give him the venison, and help him escape. Baca was a cruel and ruthless man. She had to save Felipe from him. Alondra wished she had some of Armando's sour wine. She would serve it to the captain until he fell over drunk and senseless on the ground.

Alondra could think of only one way to stop Baca and she quacked at the thought. She would offer herself to the captain, and, when he had his clothes off and least expected it, she'd take her small knife and rip his belly open. This time, she'd make sure her knife struck deep enough. It was a sin, a mortal sin, but she would do it. It didn't matter what she did; she'd never see Felipe again anyway. Tears welled in her eyes.

"Could I have some of that delicious-smelling venison, please?"

Alondra turned to Lalo. He was one of the good ones.

"Are those tears I see, Alondra?"

"No. It's the smoke. It makes my eyes water."

"Well, I think that soon you will be smiling again."

"What do you mean?"

At that moment, Felipe whistled. Alondra looked at Lalo, her eyes wide in question.

Lalo nodded. "Be ready. I don't know his plans."

Her shoulders sagged. "It doesn't matter, Lalo. He won't take me with him. He hates me."

"That's not what he told me."

Her heart leaped. "Why? What did he say?"

Lalo laughed. "Never mind, just be ready when he makes his move."

"I'll be ready." Alondra wrapped the cooked venison in her shawl and bundled it in her *serape* that lay beside the campfire. She picked up Felipe's knife and shoved it in her sash.

"Get over here where I can see you," Captain Baca said. "I don't trust you. What are you doing?"

"I'm cleaning up. If I'm to spend the night here, I want the campsite neat." Alondra put more venison on the fire to cook. Maybe the soldier pigs would eat themselves into a stupor.

"And shake out your blanket," Baca said. "We will share it tonight and this time you will not argue."

Alondra tensed. He had recognized her after all. Beyond

the firelight, she saw a vague shape moving in the shadows and knew it was Felipe saddling their horses. She slung her *serape* over her shoulder and sauntered into the dark.

Where are you going?" the captain yelled.

"I need privacy."

Out of the darkness, Felipe whispered. "Alondra?"

"I'm ready."

He helped her into the saddle and led the horses up the slope.

"*Dios mio*," Felipe muttered. "Look at that."

On the rim of the wallow, small fires burned. The wind moaned and the fires leaped. Orange and yellow tongues licked the dry grass and red flames danced. Higher and higher, the flames twisted until they reached the treetops. The wind howled, fanning the fires to an intense heat, and the prairie blazed, lighting the sky. Dry tree branches popped and crackled, black and gray acrid smoke blanketed the plains.

From the center of the wallow, someone shouted, "Prairie fire!" The soldiers panicked and the camp exploded into turmoil.

Felipe jumped into the saddle and grabbed Segundo's lead rope. "Hang on tight, *querida*. This time we're truly running for our lives."

Alondra clutched the gelding's mane and resolved that, no matter what happened, she would not fall off. *Querida*. He didn't hate her; he'd called her his beloved. She felt as light as the smoke darkening the sky, and strong enough to fight off the entire Mexican army single-handed.

She looked over her shoulder at the fire that burned her former life to cinders. The flames lit Felipe's face with a rosy glow—her future.

Felipe wished he could swallow his words. He hadn't meant to call her *querida*. It had slipped out. He didn't want her to get the wrong idea about him. Maybe she hadn't noticed. He nudged the horses, and they stretched their legs into a full, hard, gallop.

The wind pushed the fire south, so he rode north, into the shrieking wind that stung their faces and tore at their clothes. He glanced at the blackening sky and prayed the promised rain would extinguish the raging fire. He turned his head to look at the burning grassland. Horses whinnied and bucked, men shouted and cursed, frantic black shapes outlined against a red and yellow curtain.

A rider hurtled toward them. Felipe recognized Lalo and slowed the pace.

"I decided to join you after all," Lalo said when he caught up to them.

"Good," Felipe said. Lalo was too good a man to be wasted in the Mexican Army. "Let's ride!"

They bent low over their horses' necks and raced into the wind. Small animals ran with them: rabbits, squirrels, polecats, badgers. Birds swooped overhead and a trio of deer burst from a thicket.

They galloped until Segundo stumbled, caught himself, and ran on. Felipe glanced over his shoulder. The fire was but a glow in the sky and Lalo's horse was faltering. Since before daylight, all three horses had worked hard with little rest. Felipe slowed to a walk.

"We'll rest the night over there in that clump of trees," he said when Lalo caught up.

"Good. My horse is fatigued. I don't know how much farther he can go."

The men dismounted and led the horses. "You don't have to walk," Felipe said when Alondra slid off her horse.

"But I want to."

"Take my hand then. Smoke and rain clouds have covered the moon and it is dark."

She tucked her hand in his. His heart skipped a beat at the firm clasp, the fragile-as-a-lark's-wing bone structure, and a wave of protectiveness swept through him.

They stopped at the first large tree and unsaddled. They wiped the foam off the sweating horses and lay the saddles upside down to dry.

"El Moro does not need a tether," Felipe said, "but what of the others?"

"They're too tired to go far, but we shouldn't take chances," Lalo answered.

They tied the horses together with a length of rope between each and fastened the rope to a tree.

Alondra sat beneath the tree on her *serape*. "Tired?" Felipe asked.

"A little."

Felipe dropped beside her and put his arm around her. "Rest against me."

She laid her head on his knee and threw her arm across his leg. He brushed hair from her face and covered her with his *serape*. Alondra gave a small sigh of contentment and soon fell asleep.

"Where do you think Captain Baca and the regiment are?" Felipe asked Lalo.

"I don't know. But they think you got burned in the fire. I got away from there before the captain learned different."

"They'll be on our trail in the morning then."

"I don't think so. The men were going all directions, trying to save themselves, and who knows how many stayed with Baca. Not many, I'll wager. He is not popular with the troops. Also, he has orders to go to San Antonio. He needs to be there next week. No, I don't think he'll take the time to hunt you down."

"I hope you're right. The horses need a good long rest, and so do we." Felipe moved Alondra's head from his knee and stretched out beside her. She snuggled against him in her sleep. He smiled and arranged the *serape* over them both. "Good night, Lalo." But Lalo was already snoring.

*****

The earth trembled and shook them awake. The clamor of a thousand hooves pounding the ground rumbled across the plain.

"What is it?" Alondra clutched Felipe's arm.

"Stampede! Come, quickly." He lifted her up into a tree. "Stay here. Hang on tight to the tree. Lalo! The horses!" Felipe whistled. Over the din, he heard the horses whinny.

Tied together, the horses tossed their heads, rolled their eyes, pawed the air, strained against their tethers, tried to escape the deafening noise. The men ran to their mounts, caught them, and leaped onto their backs.

Wild cattle, lean and swift as deer, thundered toward them in a cloud of dust. Their white-tipped tails waved like flags bobbing on a black, surging sea. Flashing white in the moonlight, long horns clashed and rattled. Bulls snorted; cows bawled.

The cattle raced with mindless purpose and flattened anything in their path. They crashed into trees, uprooted bushes, and trampled one another. Minutes later, the last cow limped past. Dark shapes lay hammered into the dirt. A black haze of dust hovered and then sank across the prairie.

Their faces coated with dirt, the men calmed the trembling horses with soft voices and gentle strokes and led them back to camp. Alondra sat in the tree branches, tears glistening on her grimy face.

Felipe lifted her down and held her in his arms. "It's all over, Alondra. It's all right."

She buried her face in his shoulder and sobbed. "I've never been so frightened in my life."

"You were safe in the tree."

"Not for myself. I was terrified you'd be trampled to death."

Speechless, Felipe rolled his eyes and spread his palms in a helpless gesture.

Lalo laughed. "You're in trouble, my friend."

Felipe reddened and turned away. "We'd better get what rest we can. The fire probably frightened the cattle and other animals may also be running away. I'll stand guard. You two get some sleep."

"I'll sit up with you." Alondra shook the dust from her *serape*.

"Sleep," Felipe said. "Tomorrow will come soon enough."

Alondra didn't argue. She lay curled on her *serape*. Lalo chuckled and wrapped his blanket around his shoulders. With a soldier's practiced ease, he soon fell asleep.

Felipe paced. Alondra had embarrassed him with her concern, but also he was strangely pleased. It had been a long time since anyone had worried about him, not since he'd left home. Images of home and what awaited him there flickered through his mind. He tried to picture Maria, but her face was in shadows, faint and indistinct.

Nearby, a coyote yowled, and a chorus answered.

"Felipe?" Alondra whispered.

"What?"

"Will the wolves come?"

Felipe knelt beside her on one knee and took her hand. "It's only coyotes. They were running from the fire and scented the remains of the stampede." He stroked the back of her hand with his thumb.

"Wolves attack people and steal babies."

"No, Alondra, wolves are wary of humans, they won't come near us."

"But, Felipe, I heard that some years ago there was an American couple who settled not far from my old village. The parents died from the plague or something and the wolves came. They left bloody footprints all around the dead parents and took the baby. Some say the child still lives with the wolves." Her lips quivered, her eyes shone large and luminous in the pale moonlight. "I don't like wolves."

"I know, *querida*. I know." He slipped his arm around her and held her close. He'd heard the story of the wolf-girl long ago and had dismissed it as just that—a story to frighten children from straying too far from their homes. But many people believed the story and men always took careful aim before shooting a wolf so as not to kill the wolf-girl by mistake. Felipe lay down beside Alondra and pulled his blanket over them both.

Lalo woke to the sound of barking, snarling coyotes. Dark shapes slinked by, snuffling noses to the ground. Intent on their share of the slaughter, yelping and growling, the pack fought over tidbits and bones.

Lalo glanced at the peaceful faces of the two young people asleep in each other's arms. Felipe stirred. "Coyotes?"

"Yes, they are feasting."

"There's enough to keep them occupied until morning," Felipe murmured, more asleep than awake.

Lalo smiled. Love was never easy, but those two young people seemed to have enough to sustain them through all of life's trials. He prayed the angels would spread their wings over the lovers and shield them from harm.

CHAPTER 9

Buzzards came in the morning. The three fugitives mounted their horses, turned their backs on the carnage, and left nature's clean-up crew to its grisly work.

The morning sun was high when Alondra called a halt for breakfast. She served cold venison steak wrapped in a corn *tortilla*. They stopped next when she spotted soap plant and, with her Bowie knife, dug out the roots.

In the heat of the day, they reached the west bank of a stream, where they made camp at a rock outcropping near a bend in the river. To the relief of the weary travelers, Felipe announced they would rest for a day or two.

Alondra declared she would bathe and do laundry while the men tended the horses and set up camp. She took the shirt Felipe had used as a towel for the horses and asked Lalo if he had anything he wanted washed.

"I have only the one shirt," he said.

"All the more reason to launder it, give it here. And it wouldn't hurt either of you to take a bath." She handed each of them a piece of soap plant.

Alondra walked upstream until she found a secluded spot.

She spread her extra clothing on bushes to air, undressed, and put the soiled laundry in the river to soak, weighted with rocks to prevent it drifting downstream.

She glided into the cold water and gasped. Goose bumps spread over her skin and her teeth chattered. Even thoughts of Felipe didn't warm her. She recalled her conversation with Dolores and chuckled to herself. That day seemed so long ago. She didn't believe it at the time, but it turned out Dolores knew about men and women, because Alondra wanted Felipe to touch her, to kiss her. Just being near him made her senses spin and, suddenly, getting to Saint Louis was no longer important.

She scrubbed quickly with the soap plant, took a deep breath, and, before she lost her nerve, ducked under the water to rinse her hair. Shivering, she climbed out of the river. A light breeze fanned her body, and she hastily wrung out her long, black curls and dressed in her dry clothes.

She pulled the soaking garments from the water and beat them against rocks, praying her woolen *serape* would dry before night. Alondra gathered the laundry in a bundle and carried it back to camp. She draped the clothes on bushes and cast a worried glance at the sky. Heavy rain clouds had gathered in the south. She hoped her laundry would dry before the rain came.

The men had stacked rocks as a windbreak and built a fire in the three-sided shelter. They had gone hunting, and two fat rabbits hung from a tree limb.

Alondra spread her hands to the small fire, grateful for the heat. "I see you haven't bathed yet," she said.

"We haven't had time," Felipe said.

"It would probably be a good idea to do it while the sun is high and before the wind comes up and it rains. The water is cold."

"Ah, that is why you are so pink," Lalo said.

Felipe had no desire to discuss the state of Alondra's skin.

He picked up the soap. "Come on, Lalo. Surely we can bathe in cold water if a woman can."

Lalo rose to his feet. "But I am a weak man."

"All men are weak," Felipe muttered and with a sidelong glance at Alondra said, "and no man is weaker than I."

After the men went to the river, Alondra sat on a stone and with her small knife dressed the rabbits. She wondered about the date. If it was Saint Agnes' feast day, she was in luck. Everyone knew that on the eve of Saint Agnes a girl would dream of her husband-to-be, and last night she had dreamed of Felipe. Marriage to a *hidalgo* was beyond her wildest imagination, but if she dreamed it on Saint Agnes Eve, then it would happen.

She sharpened a stick, skewered the rabbits, and placed them over the fire.

But was she worthy of Felipe? And what of his parents? She had heard about the proud and rigid Spanish *Dons*. Would they accept her, and would she know how to act in that rich society? Felipe didn't speak of his parents, but she was sure he thought about them often.

Absorbed in her thoughts, it was minutes before Alondra became aware of the methodical thump of hoof beats. Without lifting her head, she replaced her knife in its sheath on her leg. Her hand stole to the Bowie knife.

In a slow drawl, a man said, "Hey there, gal, you all alone here?"

Alondra stood and looked up at the speaker. He was a big man with light blue eyes. His straggly, wheat-colored hair poked out from a black slouch hat. In his right hand, he held a pistol, had another strapped to his waist, and he wore a bandolier filled with cartridges buckled across his chest. His companion could have been his twin, except for a scar that reached from the corner of his left eye to his chin and both his guns were in their holsters. Both men wore stubby beards. They were Americans, but even with Felipe's coaching she hardly understood this man with the strange accent. She said nothing and clutched her knife tighter.

"Maybe she don't understand you, Sam. Maybe she's deef, or maybe a Mexican."

Alondra understood the word Mexican. "No, Texian."

"Well, she don't seem to be deef." The man named Sam dismounted and advanced toward Alondra.

She didn't move, ready for anything the man might do. She had a sharp knife and would make him bleed before he touched her. She narrowed her eyes and concentrated on his breastbone. He was tall, not fat, but still the belly was softer and easier to reach. She searched her mind for the American words but couldn't find them, so in Spanish she said, "If you come any closer, I will kill you."

"Hey, Sam, she's got a knife."

"I seen it. Where'd you get that Bowie knife, gal?"

Yancy laughed. "She aims to use it on you, boy."

"Well, hell, I ain't never had a knife fight with a li'l ol' gal before."

"You can bet she ain't alone. A purty little thing like her has got a man around here some place. Ever been in a knife fight with a Mex, Sam? See this scar? Did I tell you about the time I—"

"You done told me a dozen times and I don't want to hear it again. Where's your men folk, gal?"

Alondra wished she could understand more of what these men said. At the cantina, when men talked in a light tone like this, they were only teasing and not dangerous, but she kept a tight hold on the knife and a wary eye on both men.

"What y'all aiming to do, Sam?" Yancy dismounted, strolled to the campfire, hunkered on his heels, and rolled a cigarette.

"I got a idee but ain't decided for sure yet."

Alondra caught the change in tone and tensed. She glanced from Sam to Yancy and took one step back. She recognized the look in Sam's eyes but could not read Yancy. If Sam attacked her, she would kill him and before Yancy could act she'd shout for Felipe and run to the river.

Yancy lit his cigarette with a flaming stick from the campfire. "Hell, Sam, this here's a poor camp. Ain't nothing much here worth stealing."

"That rabbit smells larruping good, and there's this li'l ol' gal here. We ain't had us a woman in a long time, Yancy, and I got a powerful itch." Sam crouched and reached a hand toward Alondra.

She stepped back, brought her knife shoulder-high, and, with her hand steady, pointed it at him.

He grinned and swayed on the balls of his feet with his hands outstretched. His pale eyes gleamed with a strange light. "I ain't going to hurt you, gal. Just want to show you a good time."

She narrowed her eyes, took another step back, and thrust her knife forward.

Yancy howled with laughter and rolled on the ground. "If she don't cut your balls off first."

"Well, damn, it sure don't look like she wants to cooperate. I ain't never had to force a woman before." Sam took a step toward her.

She felt Felipe's presence behind her, and Alondra moved to the side.

Felipe hurled his dagger. It pierced Sam's right shoulder. He yelped and dropped his gun.

"Now would not be a good time to start." Felipe stepped forward and yanked his knife from Sam's shoulder. Blood splattered down Sam's shirt and onto the ground.

Yancy giggled. "What did I tell you? Now damn if you ain't bleeding like a stuck hog." He stopped laughing when he saw the gun barrel Lalo pointed at his chest. "We ain't done nothing wrong," Yancy said. "We was only funning."

"Take his guns, Lalo." Felipe removed the pistol from

Sam's holster and picked up the other from the ground.

Sam clutched at his shoulder. "Hey, you're with the Mexican army and she ain't nothing but a camp follower. I don't see why you got so het up just because I—"

Felipe struck him across the mouth with the butt of the gun. Sam screeched. He spit blood and teeth.

"Get their ammunition belts too, Lalo, and check if they have any other weapons in their saddle bags." Felipe turned to Alondra. "Are you all right?"

"Yes." She set the knife down. "Thank you, but I would have killed him before I let him touch me."

Felipe laughed, but there was no humor in his green eyes. "I know you would have."

Yancy gathered his feet under him to stand. Lalo shoved him down. "Good gawdamighty," Yancy shouted. "You people are savages, no better than the Comanche. My brother is over there bleeding, and you laugh. Let me up so I can help him."

Lalo grinned. "I don't think so. It does my heart good to see a man like him suffer."

"What are you going to do with us? Torture us? Kill us? Whatever it is, get it over with."

Lalo scratched his chin with the gun barrel. "What do you say, *amigo*? I say death is too good for men like these."

Felipe took a rope from Sam's saddle. "We'll tie them up until we decide. Right now, I'm hungry. Is the food ready, Alondra?"

She wiggled a rear leg. "Yes. I'd planned to make some fresh *tortillas*, but ..." She shrugged.

They tied Sam and Yancy to a tree, and Felipe and Lalo sat by the campfire. Alondra served them the food, and the three began to eat.

"We're hungry too," shouted Yancy. "Ain't you going to feed us?"

The trio ignored him and talked among themselves. The meal finished, Alondra tidied the camp and gathered the dry laundry. She gave Lalo his shirt.

He took off his uniform jacket and pulled the clean shirt over his head. "Thank you, Alondra, it is good to wear clean clothes again."

With his dagger, Felipe pointed to Yancy and spoke in Spanish, "That one has a buckskin jacket. It does not yet have blood on it and perhaps you should exchange it for your uniform. The Mexican army is not popular here in Texas."

"Good idea," Lalo said, also in Spanish. "I'm through with the army anyway." He strolled toward Yancy.

"Hey," Yancy yelled. "What are y'all talking about? I can't understand your damn lingo." He paled when Lalo loosened the bindings. "What are y'all going to do to me?"

Lalo grinned. "Not so tough now eh, *cabrón?*" He pulled the buckskin off Yancy and retied the man's wrists. Lalo donned the coat. "What should I do with my uniform jacket?"

"Give it to me," Alondra said. "It's a good wool fabric. I'll remake it." She stuffed it in her saddlebag.

"I like his hat too," Lalo said. He examined first Yancy's hat, then Sam's. "This one is cleaner." Lalo jammed the hat on his head and threw his military cap into the fire. "What do you think?"

"You look like an American," Felipe said. "I'm thinking we need to get out of here."

"What will we do with those two?" Lalo jerked his thumb at the prisoners.

"Untie them. We'll drive their horses about three leagues up the trail and turn them loose. Maybe they'll catch up to their horses, or maybe not."

"And their saddles?"

"Leave them. Except for their pistols, we don't want anything that belongs to those two *renegados.*"

Felipe and Lalo examined the brothers' guns. "This is a good idea, Lalo. Two guns, keep them both loaded, and we'll have two shots to an enemy's one."

"Three," Lalo said. "We have our own guns as well." The men strapped the holsters around their hips and the bandoliers over their shoulders.

Alondra looked around the camp. "I'm sorry we have to leave; I was becoming fond of this place."

Felipe caressed her shoulder. "We'll stop before dark, and I'll make you a soft bed of ferns so you can rest."

His touch ignited a glow in her shoulder, spread through her arms, and settled warm and snug in her heart. She would never have believed that a man could be so gentle, so caring, so thoughtful. She recalled her dream and prayed that today was Saint Agnes' feast day.

Alondra packed the camp and was ready by the time the men came back with the horses.

"You ain't leaving us here like this, are you?" Yancy shouted. He turned to his brother. Sam sat slumped against the tree trunk, chin on his chest. "Looks like they're fixing to leave, Sam."

When Sam didn't answer, Yancy poked him with his foot. "You ain't dead, are you, Sam? That little ol' tap didn't kill you, did it?"

Sam mumbled and Yancy shouted. "My brother needs a drink of water." They ignored him.

Felipe held his hand up. "Listen," he said. "Horses."

CHAPTER 10

Five horsemen rode into view: two Americans, Captain Baca, and two other soldiers. The Army men's hands were tied to their saddle horns.

"Stay behind me," Felipe said to Alondra. He and Lalo stood side by side and watched the riders approach.

Fifty feet from camp, the tallest rider raised his arm. "Hello, the camp."

Felipe lifted his hand. "What can we do for you?"

Baca had lost his plumed hat; his uniform was smudged with charcoal and smoke. He shouted, "That's him! That's the thief! Arrest him. He's the one who stole my horse. I demand that you arrest him now!"

"My name is Taylor," the tall American said. "This is Ramsey, we're Texas Rangers." The Rangers dismounted.

"I'm Felipe Montez and these are my friends."

Yancy shouted, "Hey, Ranger, make him cut us loose."

Taylor strode to the tree, peered down at the brothers, and laughed. "I'll be damned if you ain't captured the Gorley boys. We've been trailing them for days. They're a couple of mean *hombres*. What do you have against them?"

Felipe shrugged. "They are ill-mannered."

The Rangers chuckled.

"Where do you hail from, Montez?" asked Taylor.

"New Mexico. We're on our way home."

"Where in New Mexico?"

"Up near Santa Fe."

"Any truth in what this soldier claims?"

"About the horse? No. That black is mine. I bought him in Mexico. I'm taking him home to my father's *hacienda*."

"Well," Taylor said, "that makes sense now. I was kind of curious as to why you were wandering around this part of Texas. So, you're a *norteno*, eh? Mind if we share your fire? We're kind of damp from the rain."

"Yes, of course. Please. Make yourselves comfortable. Is it a heavy rain? It looked like the wind was blowing it south."

"Yes, it rained pretty hard there for a while. It put the prairie fire out."

"We were getting ready to start on the trail, so you can have our campfire."

"Why would you leave so late in the day? This is a nice camp you have here."

Felipe flicked a cold, hard glance at the Gorley brothers.

Taylor nodded. "I see. Well, they're not going anywhere. They came into the territory a couple of years back and haven't done an honest day's work since. They've murdered and robbed and are horse thieves besides."

"What are you going to do with them?" Lalo asked.

"Take them to Austin, have a necktie party, and see that justice is done. Want to come with us and watch?"

Felipe shook his head. "No thanks. We have no time for a hanging."

"Speak for yourself," Lalo said. "It would give me great pleasure to see those two dangling from the end of a rope."

"Why would you want to go all the way back to Austin just to see a hanging? You have a good job waiting back home."

Felipe said.

"You're right," Lalo said. "Still, the sight would do my heart good."

The Rangers squatted at the fire and lit cigarettes. Ramsey had been eyeing Alondra. "And who is the young lady?" he asked.

Lalo put his arm around her shoulders. "She is my sister."

"That's a lie," shouted Baca. "She's nothing but a bar girl."

"Careful what you say about that gal," Yancy said. "Them fellers is mighty particular about her. Look at what that young one did to Sam, and he didn't hardly say nothing."

Taylor sighed. "I guess we'd better do something about the prisoners. It would be easier if we just hanged them now."

"Sure would be a lot less trouble," Ramsey agreed. "But there's a lady present."

"She's no lady," Baca said, his voice hoarse. "And that man is one of my soldiers. Arrest him. He's a deserter."

"You and your sister are going on up to Santa Fe?" Taylor asked.

Lalo nodded. "We have a good job waiting for us there."

"Well, you don't look like a soldier to me." Taylor tossed his brown cigarette into the fire. "A cup of coffee would sure taste good right about now."

"I'm sorry, but we don't have any coffee," Felipe said.

"We do. Would you share a cup with us?" Ramsey got to his feet and from his saddle took a narrow tin pail, blackened from the smoke of a hundred campfires. "I'll get the water."

"Thank you, it would be our pleasure," Felipe said. "Alondra, do we have any more rabbit?"

Lalo whispered in her ear and Alondra spread the leftover rabbit and *tortillas* on a cloth before the fire. She set out their tin cups and plates.

"I demand that you let me off this horse," Baca said.

"Won't do you no good to scream and shout," Yancy told him. "They won't pay you no never mind. They're worse'n them Indian savages."

"I'm an officer of the Mexican army and demand to be treated with respect."

"They don't care. Look at poor ol' Sam here," Yancy said. "They won't even give him a drink of water."

Ramsey heaved a weary sigh. "What are we going to do with those men?"

"We'll take them back to San Vicente. We'll have to ride all night and most of tomorrow, but that's the closest village and I don't know if they even have a jail house." Taylor blew on his coffee, took a sip, and sighed. "Ah, that is good. I've been needing it. Did you all get caught in the fire, Montez?"

"Yes. That's why we're here on this stream. It was the closest water."

"They started the fire," Baca shouted. "They're the ones responsible for all this trouble."

As though Baca hadn't spoken, Taylor said, "We found the soldiers running from the fire. The captain says there are other soldiers somewhere."

"If you don't mind my asking, why are they under arrest?" Felipe asked.

"Because they are Mexican soldiers. Don't you know what's going on here in Texas?"

"I know there is some sort of trouble."

"Trouble? Say, man, Texas is getting ready to secede from Mexico. We Texians are tired of their laws and taxation. We're going to be a free nation, separate from any country, and make our own laws." Taylor finished his coffee and threw the dregs into the fire.

"I wish you good luck," Felipe said. "But what of New Mexico? We too are heavily taxed for every head of sheep and ear of corn we grow. When Texas secedes, will we be a part of Texas, or still under Mexican rule? I've been away from home so long I haven't heard any news."

Taylor gave him a quizzical look. "Actually, Santa Fe and

even farther north is a part of Texas and has been for around fifteen years."

Felipe drew himself up, squared his shoulders, and lifted his chin. "I am not a Texian. I am a Spaniard from New Mexico. My people have lived and worked the same *hacienda* for over a hundred and fifty years."

"It has something to do with politics and when the United States bought Louisiana from France. That's when they decided where Texas was and it's all under the Mexican government. They gave me a map so I would know my boundaries. I'll show you." From his saddlebag, Taylor brought out a folded paper, creased and faded from use, and spread it on the ground in front of the fire.

He pointed to a spot on the map. "See, this is about where we are now. All this land on the east, from here to here is in land grants given by the Mexican government to Americans." Conical shapes in the form of trees and wiggly lines representing rivers covered this part of the map. He pointed to a portion in the northwest section that showed neither trees nor rivers. "This here is Comanche country. Stay away from there. This black line is the border. Over here on the west is California and the ocean; we don't ride that far. This river, here, is the *Rio Grande* and up here in the mountains, see, there's Santa Fe and the Texas border is north of there."

Taylor folded the map and replaced it in the saddlebag. "So, when the fighting starts, Montez, whose side will you fight for, Mexico or Texas?"

"Neither. I am not Mexican nor am I Texian. My people and I will do as we always have. We will protect our families and our land from all marauders, be they Texian, Mexican, or Indian. We Spaniards in New Mexico have been fighting for our land for over three hundred years. We will continue to do so."

Taylor gave him a measuring look. "Yes, I guess you will. I understand that you *nortenos* have prosperous ranches and farms despite the weather and the Indians." He rolled a cigarette and lit it from the campfire.

Felipe shrugged. "My grandfather says that we were better off under the protection of the Spanish crown. He says that the only good the Mexican government has done for us is to allow trading with the United States. And my father wrote me a letter and said that now we no longer have our own governor. The Mexicans sent a soldier to rule us, and he calls himself the *comandante*. He set up a tax base such as we've never had before, and my father says the price for goods is high because the *comandante* takes such a great share of the profits that we lose money on a trade. Some of the ranchers take their mules, hides, and wool over the Santa Fe Trail and sell them in Saint Louis. They make a good profit and the *comandante* doesn't have to know about it."

Taylor stood and stretched his shoulders. "Yeah, it seems there are rascals in every government. But let me give you some advice, Montez. Get out of this part of Texas soon as you can. Lots of folks carry hard feelings against Mexicans, and there's some who shoot first and ask questions later."

"But I am not Mexican and neither are my friends."

Taylor shook his head. "Like I said, some folks don't know the difference and don't take the time to ask."

The sun glowed red in the darkening sky. "We'd best get on our way it'll be dark soon. Ramsey, get the prisoners ready." Taylor emptied the coffee grounds on the fire. He took the pail down to the river and rinsed it.

Ramsey stood and winked at Felipe. "I doubt the Gorley boys will make it all the way to San Vicente. I'm not so sure about the soldiers either."

"Can you do that without a trial?" Felipe asked.

"Out here on the range, we are the judge and the jury. The Rangers were formed a few years back to fight off the Indian attacks. Now, we are the only law in all of Texas. If it weren't for us, there would be a lot more of that kind of no-good trash running around." Ramsey pointed to the Gorley brothers.

Felipe shrugged. "Good luck."

The Rangers secured the prisoners and tied the brothers' horses to Baca's. "Thanks for the hospitality," Taylor said.

Felipe and Lalo wished them goodbye and good luck. Alondra waved her hand. They watched until the Rangers disappeared into the dusk.

"I want to learn the American language. I want to speak it as well as you and Lalo do," Alondra said. "I understood most of the words, but those two brothers ... I couldn't understand anything they said."

"The only way to learn is to hear it and speak it, so from now on that is the only language we'll use. Agreed?" Felipe looked from one to the other. They nodded. "All right. If one of us forgets, the others will remind them."

"There is no reason to leave this camp now, is there?" Alondra asked.

Lalo grinned. "I'll unsaddle the horses."

Felipe threw a log on the fire and the three settled in for the night. Coyotes sang their nightly serenade.

"Felipe?"

"What is it, Alondra?"

"I don't think I'm afraid of wolves anymore. No wild animal could be worse than those two men."

"But the Rangers were good men, don't you think?" Felipe rolled himself in his *serape*.

"Before you fall asleep," Lalo said. "I want to thank you for offering me a job at the end of this trip. Good night."

Silence descended on the camp. Alondra looked up at the darkening sky and counted stars so near she could almost touch them. One shot across the inky sky and she smiled. A shooting star was supposed to be good luck.

*****

Captain Edmundo Baca trailed behind Taylor, his brain seething and his limbs trembling with anger. How dare these Texians treat him, a captain in the Mexican Army, like a common criminal?

The night deepened and he turned his thoughts to escape. In hopes of weakening it, he sawed the rope between his bound wrists against the saddle horn.

A Ranger muttered something, and he strained to hear their low voices. That they would hang the two thieves seemed certain, but what they'd do with the soldiers was another question.

Baca sent a silent prayer to the heavens that the Rangers would withhold their decision until San Vicente as he had many friends in that village. He twisted his wrists. The rope held. He stretched his hands as far apart as possible and rubbed harder.

The moon waned and only a few stars still twinkled when the Rangers spotted an oak grove. "We should find a good, stout tree here," Taylor said and angled toward the trees. They stopped underneath a large oak, its branches outstretched in invitation.

Ramsey threw a rope over a sturdy limb. "Who goes first?"

"The Gorleys." Taylor led the thieves' horses to the tree, leaving Baca's horse loose. "Don't worry, Captain, we'll be right with you." He dropped a loop around Sam and then Yancy.

Baca watched, his eyes cold with disdain. The Anglos knew nothing about killing a prisoner. So much quicker to simply shoot a man in the head and leave him to the buzzards. Slowly, Baca backed his horse into the shadows, deep into the thickets. Their attention fixed on tying a proper noose, the Rangers took no notice of him. The two soldiers stared dumbly at the hanging. Baca wasted no thought on them.

He heard the slap of a whip on a horse's rump, the snap of the rope, and Baca stabbed the large rowels of his spurs into his mount's flanks. The beast jumped forward and crashed through brush and rounded trees, leaped over downed logs. A single gunshot resounded in the night, and he heard the bullet whine past his ear. Baca bent low, clutched the saddle horn with both hands, and gave the horse its head. With luck, he'd be far away before the Rangers completed their task.

Using knee pressure, he turned the horse south, toward the river and away from the trees. Somehow, he'd have to hide his tracks before full daylight.

At the river, he guided his mount into the water. It ran swift and deep and the horse had to swim.

The Rangers would know he'd ride in the river, but perhaps he could fool them. He forced the horse to climb the bank, then down into the water, up the opposite bank, back into the water, three times, mixing the tracks. Far downstream, he turned the horse out of the river and into a brushy thicket.

Baca recognized the area—he was only a few leagues from San Vicente. He questioned his mount's ability to continue the pace and stopped for rest. He noticed blood on the rope, his wrists were chafed and raw. Still, better his wrists than his neck.

He glanced toward the east, the sun glowed pink on the horizon, and he spoke to his horse. "Those Rangers are in league with the devil and are on our heels. Hold out for only another hour or two and you can rest and eat. Let's go."

Edmundo Baca cantered into San Vicente and past Armando's *Cantina*. At last, he could breathe easy. He rode up to Dolores' house and called through the window, "Wake up, lazy woman. Quick!"

Rubbing sleep from her eyes, Dolores peeked out the window. "Edmundo! What—?"

"Bring a knife, and hurry. I'll tell you everything later."

With a shawl draped over her nightdress, Dolores stepped out into the quiet street. "What is going on?"

"Cut the rope on my wrists and hurry."

She slashed the rope and Baca jumped off the horse and unsaddled him. "Hide him some place, quick. There's not much time."

"Your wrists, Edmundo, they're bleeding."

"We'll take care of that later. The Rangers are right behind me. Hide the horse and hurry back here."

Dolores led the horse down the street. He did not ask where she took him. Baca dragged his saddle into the house and shoved it under the bed. He removed his uniform jacket and bathed his sore wrists.

Dolores returned and, while Baca told his story, she applied a healing salve on his wounds. She pulled peasant clothing from a chest. "Put these on. The Rangers don't know me. I'll say you're my husband if they ask. Keep your *sombrero* low to hide your face." She stashed his uniform under the bed with the saddle.

The Rangers arrived in San Vicente midmorning. The villagers bustled about, concerned with their own affairs. Captain Edmundo Baca sat on a bench, barefoot, repairing sandals.

Taylor rode up to him. "Have you seen a soldier?"

Baca kept his face in the shadows and shrugged. Dolores came to the door. "Do you speak American?" Ramsey asked.

Dolores answered in Spanish, "I do not understand, *Señor*."

"How about this fellow here?" Taylor pointed to Baca.

Dolores stared at him, round-eyed.

"Do you speak any Spanish at all?" Taylor asked Ramsey.

"A little. Not enough to make these people understand what we want."

"*Señor*." Dolores tugged at Taylor's sleeve and pointed to the church.

"I think she's telling us someone over there can understand us. Let's go."

The priest knew nothing of the captain, unaware that, in the mission barn, a strange horse munched hay alongside his burro. "But," the priest said, "when the soldiers are in the village, they spend a lot of time and money at Armando's *Cantina*. Perhaps he knows something."

Armando had not seen the captain. "Oh yes, I know him well. He left the village two or three days ago."

"His tracks led us here," Taylor said and enlisted Armando as interpreter. No one in the village had seen Captain Baca.

When the Rangers and Armando reached Dolores' house, she was sweeping the front yard, the man nowhere in sight. "No," she said, "I haven't seen him for several days."

Next morning, the Rangers were gone from San Vicente.

*****

A week later, his splendid uniform washed and mended, Captain Edmundo Baca arrived in San Antonio. He reported for duty with lies on his tongue about his lost troops and found the colonel, his commanding officer, in high good humor due to the successful battle at the Alamo. The man didn't even question Baca's late arrival without his squad.

"The Texians are becoming very aggressive," his colonel said. "We must protect our northern borders. Since your godfather is the *comandante* of the New Mexican province, we are sending you and a company of men to Santa Fe."

Within the week, Baca and a small company of ten men headed north with orders to command the New Mexican militia and protect Santa Fe at any cost.

CHAPTER 11

In Saint Louis, James Thornton made ready for his trip to Santa Fe.

"Take me with you, Master James," Joseph said.

"You're a free man, Joseph," James said. "You can do anything you want, go anywhere you want."

"I got nowhere to go. Please, Master James, take me with you."

On his search for Alondra, James had traveled long distances and knew the dangers of an unsettled country. Joseph had been born and reared on Grandfather Maurice's estate and knew nothing but city life.

"It's a long and dangerous trail, Joseph. There are no people, only Indians."

"I ain't afeared, Master James. I know how to shoot a gun. And the horses, they know me. I can help you with them."

He knew that Joseph was apprehensive about his new status as a free man, and it was Thornton's responsibility to teach the former slave how to live independently. Thornton had a pack mule loaded with food and essentials needed on the trail, as well as schoolbooks, slates, paper, lead pencils, ink, and the new-style wooden pens with metal nibs that were rapidly replacing the old-style quill pens. Although he was not a teacher, James planned on teaching his friends in Santa Fe to read and write. Joseph could be his first student.

"All right, then," Thornton said, "you can come with me. Pick out a good sturdy horse for yourself and ask Lilah to give you some warm blankets because we'll have to sleep out in the open."

Joseph rolled his eyes but hurried off and soon returned with a bedroll and a small bundle of his belongings.

They rode down to the docks on the Missouri River, and James Thornton purchased passage on the next steamship heading north.

The ship was crowded with men hoping to make their fortune trading with the New Mexicans. Some men had traveled on the Santa Fe Trail several times and told their tales to the eager greenhorns.

One old-time trader said, "Back in '28, I was with a caravan retuning home after a successful trip to Santa Fe. Two young men, names of McNees and Munroe, was in the party. Down near the Cimarron, these two young fellows somehow got separated from us and stopped to rest beside a small creek. Comanche sneaked up, shot the men with their own guns, and then run off.

We heard the shots and came a-running, but McNees was already dead, so we buried him by the stream and named it McNees Creek. We carried Munroe with us for forty mile or more, then he died, and we buried him alongside the Trail.

"Just as the funeral ceremonies came to an end, six or seven Indians appeared on the opposite bank. Kiowa or maybe Pawnee, they'd had nothing to do with the killings, but the boy's pa was hot for revenge and fired a shot, wounding a horse. The Indian rider fell to the ground and was instantly riddled with balls. The rest of our party discharged their guns, and all the Indians were either killed or wounded, except for one who hightailed it back to his tribe with the news.

"We were well on our way when an enraged band of Indians attacked us down on the Arkansas River. We were only twenty men strong and no match for the savages, they killed one of our men and stole every dang head of our horses and mules.

"Left afoot, each of us carried over a thousand dollars in silver on down the Arkansas until we found a safe spot to cache it. We weren't able to get back to it until the next spring."

Another old trader said, "Injuns ain't the only thing you got to worry about. Back when the Trail first opened, it wasn't as well marked as it is now. A bunch of us, heading for Santa Fe, was about to die from thirst and couldn't find water. Finally, we come upon a lone buffalo, shot him, and found his stomach filled with water. We drank it, and I tell you boys, no water ever tasted sweeter. That little dab got us through until we found a river and filled our canteens."

"Hell, that ain't nothing," another man said. "One time on the Trail, we were so starved for water, we cut off our mules' ears and drank the blood."

"Is what those men say true, Master James?" Joseph asked.

"Maybe, but it all happened a long time ago," Thornton said. "The Santa Fe Trail is a lot safer now. But if you decide not to go on, remember, you are free to do anything you want."

"No," Joseph said, "I want to go on to Santa Fe with you."

*****

The steamship discharged its passengers at Westport Landing, and James found a caravan of traders to travel with. "It'll take forty-five days to get to Santa Fe," the wagon master said, "maybe more, depending on the weather and the Indians."

"You're still bothered by Indians?" James asked. "I thought

the Army protected the caravans."

"There's an Army troop stationed up at Fort Leavenworth, but they don't figure the Indians will attack us on the American side and the Army is not allowed on the Mexican side of the Arkansas. Anyway, my guards are seasoned Indian fighters, so it's safe enough. You and your man know how to shoot?"

"Yes," Thornton answered, "we can take care of ourselves."

"Good. On my wagon train, every man pulls his own weight." The wagon master strode off, shouting orders, cracking his long bullwhip, and leaving no doubt that he was the man in charge.

At daybreak, the wagon train started its long trek west. Men shouted, mules and donkeys brayed, and dogs barked. Dark clouds of dust billowed behind as the caravan lumbered down the Trail. It stretched out for over a mile: wagons loaded with trade goods, fully armed guards riding beside them, men herding livestock.

Three days later, they camped the night at 110 Mile Creek and the wagon master said, "We're making good time."

But Thornton was restless. "Joseph," he said, "I can make better time alone, so I'm riding ahead of the wagon train. I'll take only what I'll need on the Trail and leave the pack horse with you. I'll meet up with you in Santa Fe."

Joseph didn't hesitate. "No sir, I'm sticking with you."

"You'll be safer with the wagon train, Joseph."

"Didn't you say I was free to do what I want? Well, I done made up my mind—I'm going with you."

Thornton saw that Joseph was serious and, truthfully, he'd be grateful for the companionship. "All right, but we're going to ride hard. I'm already a month later than I'd promised, so I plan on getting to Santa Fe in about ten days. Are you up to riding seventy to a hundred miles a day?"

Joseph grinned. "Yes, sir, and so are the horses."

"You won't have any trouble finding your way," the wagon master told them. "Just follow the wagon ruts, but once you get past the Arkansas River keep your eyes skinned. That's the most dangerous stretch—two or three hundred miles of Indian country—until you get past the Little Colorado River."

After three days of hard riding, the two men were at the ford of the Arkansas River. Joseph stared at the lazy river. "I ain't never learned to swim," he said.

"You won't have to," Thornton said. "See the tracks? Loaded wagons cross here. I'll ride beside you."

Side by side, the packhorse trailing behind, the men crossed the river. "That weren't so bad," Joseph said, "didn't even get my feet wet."

They followed the Arkansas for another fifty miles to where Sand Creek flowed into the Cimarron River, and they camped for the night.

Thornton figured they had traveled close to five hundred miles. Three hundred more miles, and they would be in Santa Fe.

"We'll be seeing Indians now, won't we, Master James?" Joseph asked.

"The wagon master told me the Indians don't often bother just two travelers," James said. "They attack large parties because they are afraid so many people will kill all the game."

They met no war parties, but Joseph filled their water bags at every stream and pond they passed. "I ain't going to drink no horse's blood," he said.

Four days later, they arrived in Santa Fe. Joseph rode with his eyes lowered. "Look around you, Joseph," Thornton said, "you're in a new country."

"I can't look at the young ladies, Master James. They wear their dresses so short I can see their ankles."

Thornton laughed. "They wear them short because it's more practical. If their skirts were long as the ladies back home wear them, the hems would get all dusty and worn out."

James asked around and found a house where they could live, an adobe structure with two rooms.

"You can't live in this house, Master James, it has a dirt floor."

"Yes, we can," James said. "Here's some money. Go to the plaza and buy us some food to cook and rugs for the floors. I'll be back in an hour or so."

Eager to see Maria, James Thornton changed from his traveling clothes and went into the village to find the Fuentes' house.

CHAPTER 12

Felipe awoke in the gray dawn to a robin announcing morning. From a low bush, a mockingbird answered, and for a moment Felipe lay listening to the birds duel with their sweet songs. He threw back his blanket and built up the campfire. He glanced at his sleeping companions. Alondra lay curled on her side, cheek resting on her hand. He wanted to lie beside her, take her in his arms and lose himself in her warmth. As though she could hear his thoughts, she stirred, and her tempting lips spread in a slow smile.

Bastante, Felipe, enough of that kind of thinking. The scolding voice in his head sounded like that of his old grandmother. *You have been raised to respect women,* continued the relentless voice. *Go to the river and wash, maybe the cold water will calm your mind.* Felipe sighed and stood. It was not his head that was giving him trouble. He carried water from the river, put some of the chicory coffee the Rangers had given them in the pail, and set it on the fire to boil.

The Americans drank their coffee "any way I can get it," Taylor had said. Spaniards liked their coffee sweet and with milk. Felipe recalled that his grandfather used honey or molasses to sweeten his coffee when they had no sugar.

Felipe wondered why his grandparents came to mind this morning. In the past weeks, his thoughts had often turned to his family. He had been away from the *hacienda* far too long. Lambing season would start in a few weeks, and he should be home to help. But Maria's presence lurked in the shadows of his mind, and that brought up the question of Alondra.

He had first thought to take her to the nearest town or village and leave her, but after their scuffle in the buffalo wallow, his feelings for her changed. She was more than just another woman; she'd become important to him. He had never known such rage as when he saw Sam dancing around her with a leer on his face. Felipe hadn't trusted himself and decided to break camp before he killed the man. He was grateful that the Rangers had taken Sam and his brother with them.

He curled his fingers around the tin cup of hot coffee, warming his hands. The mornings were chilly and would get colder the farther north they traveled. He decided to take the Ranger's advice and head for New Mexico and home. Maybe one of his relatives in Santa Fe would give Alondra a job.

He prodded Lalo with the toe of his boot. "Wake up, comrade. The sun is already topping the horizon. We have a long trip ahead of us."

Lalo squinted with one eye open. "We're not resting here one more day then?" He stretched and yawned. "Is that coffee I smell?"

Alondra awoke and sat up. "It's morning already? I'll get us some breakfast." She looked up at Felipe, her brown eyes sparkling with a light that set his blood afire.

He thrust his half-filled cup at Lalo. "Take my coffee. I'll see to the horses," he said, his voice thick and unsteady.

Alondra watched him walk away. "Is he angry with me, Lalo?"

Lalo winked and sipped his coffee. "No, Alondra. I do not think he is angry at all."

She folded her blanket. "I'll go talk with him."

She saw Felipe at the river, hunkered on his heels and tossing pebbles in the water. Without looking up, he said, "See how the water spreads in widening circles when I toss a stone in the river? Then it connects with another circle. Our lives are like that, Alondra. Every action we take reaches out and affects everyone and everything around us. Sometimes, the result is not what we'd like, but by then it's too late to change."

"You are educated, Felipe, and I am not, so I do not understand when you talk like this."

He stood, dropped the pebbles, and dusted his hands on his trousers. "Never mind, it doesn't mean anything. I'm in a thinking mood." He placed an arm around her shoulders. "Are you ready to ride, *querida*? We have to start on the trail, I am eager to get home."

"Do you want some breakfast?"

"Yes, we should eat, so that we won't have to stop at midday." He dropped his arm and led the horses to camp.

Alondra followed with her brow bunched, trying to comprehend what Felipe had said. By the time they reached camp, she had given up trying to work it out. He was a difficult man to understand in any case. He called her *querida*, yet not once had he sought her bed. She had expected it. It was, after all, the way of men, but it seemed he didn't want her. Even though other men had admired her, maybe in his eyes she was ugly.

Alondra ran back to the river and peered into the still water of a small pool. She examined her reflection, touched her cheeks, her lips, and ran her fingers through her hair. She looked no different than when she had lived in San Antonio. Alondra walked back to camp, thinking. Although she had never used wiles to attract men, she set her mind working on ways to entice Felipe.

*****

They traveled northwesterly at a swift walk to conserve their mounts. The trees thinned and grasslands lay before them. Prairie chickens whirred into the air, disturbing the short winter grass, and making the horses shy away.

As the trio rode, they conversed in English, the language coming more easily to Alondra as they talked. From her subconscious, she dredged long-forgotten words, quickly learned new ones, and formed them all into sentences.

The red sun was low in the west by the time Felipe called a halt at the top of a grassy knoll. Below them, bunched around a spring-fed pool, longhorn cattle grazed and lowed for their calves. A hand-hewn log cabin with smoke coiling from a stone chimney squatted in a bushy grove.

"We'll stop and ask permission to water the horses and camp for the night," Felipe said. He stopped fifty paces from the cabin and raised an arm. "Hello, the house."

A ruddy-faced man carrying a Kentucky long rifle stepped out the door. "State your business."

"We'd like to water our horses, and then we'll be on our way. We're passing through on our way to New Mexico."

The man shaded his eyes with a work-roughened hand. "Is that a woman?"

Felipe moved his black horse in front of Alondra. Lalo guided his horse to stand beside El Moro.

"I'd surely appreciate if you folks would step down and come on in the house," the man said. "My woman would welcome some female company. She's kind of poorly right now."

"What's her trouble?"

"She's about to have a baby, and I don't know what to do."

Alondra jumped from her horse. "Where is she?"

"Right in here. Come on in," the man said with evident relief.

"Take care of the horses, Lalo." Reluctant to leave Alondra alone with a stranger, Felipe followed them into the one-room cabin.

A fire blazed in the fireplace and the house smelled of wood smoke and charred beef. A woman lay on a bed made of pine logs with a cowhide stretched between poles as a mattress. She clutched the pine poles above her head, sweat poured down her face.

"Put a bucket of water on to heat," Alondra told the men.

"Why?" Felipe asked.

"To wash and, anyway, that's what the midwife always said to do," Alondra answered.

"Do you know anything about birthing a baby?" he asked.

"I helped the midwife when my neighbor in San Antonio had her last two." Alondra grabbed a towel and turned to the woman on the bed. "What do they call you?" She wiped perspiration from the woman's face.

"Millie. That helpless ox over there is my husband Zeke." She grimaced and with a soft moan said, "The pain is getting mighty heavy." She grasped the bed poles, groaned, and lay back, panting.

"Bring the water, Zeke," Alondra said, "then go outside and help Lalo with the horses." After the man left the house, she turned to Felipe. "Do you know anything about birthing?"

"Not babies. I've helped a lot during lambing. I've had to pull lambs from the ewe when she had trouble, but not babies. Never a baby. I thought you said you'd helped the midwife."

Alondra flushed. "The only thing I ever did was wipe the mother's face, and after the baby was born, I bathed it. That's all. I don't know anything about this part."

Millie clenched her teeth and moaned.

"Please, Felipe," Alondra said. "You've got to help; I don't know what to do."

Millie let out a short scream. "I think the baby's coming."

"All right, Alondra. It can't be much different from a

lamb." Felipe pushed up his jacket sleeves. "It's going to be all right, ma'am. We'll help you."

Her blue eyes dark with fright, Millie cried out, "It's coming. I can feel it! Oh, mercy, Lord, have mercy, it's coming out." She screamed at the searing pain.

"Take care of the baby, Alondra, I'll hold Millie." Felipe unconsciously lapsed into Spanish and talked to Millie in the soft soothing voice he used with frightened animals.

Although Millie didn't appear to understand a word he said, she grew calmer, and at the next pain, with groans and pants, she pushed.

Alondra worked with confidence, surprised she knew what to do, but then, with Felipe beside her, she had discovered she could do anything. "Push hard, Millie. Scream if you want to. I can see the head. Bear down now, it's almost over." A few more pushes and the baby slid into her hands. "It's a boy. You have a son." Alondra wiped mucus from the baby's face and laid the infant on Millie's stomach.

"Is he all right? I didn't hear him cry." Millie stroked the baby. Her face radiated with awe and her eyes glowed with rapture. The baby curled his tiny fist around her finger.

"He's a man," Felipe said with a broad grin. "He won't cry. I'll go outside and tell Zeke he has a son."

"Don't let him in yet," Alondra said. "I still have work to do. Find me some string."

"Why?"

"Don't ask questions. Just find it."

"There's some thread in that basket by the fireplace," Millie said.

"Go outside with the men, Felipe, I'll call when we're ready." Not remembering what the midwife had done, Alondra tied the umbilical cord in two places with the thread, dipped her knife in the hot water, and slashed between the ties. She handed Millie a square of flannel that lay nearby.

Millie wrapped her child in the blanket and flicked the sole of his foot.

The baby howled and neither woman noticed when Felipe walked out the door. With gladness and wonder, they murmured and cooed at the bit of humanity lying in Millie's arms.Outside, Zeke slouched against the rough-hewn logs of the cabin, worry etched around his eyes. "Everything all right? I heard screaming."

"You have a son."

Zeke let out a whoop. "I'll go right in."

Felipe caught his arm. "You can't. They'll call us when it's time to go in."

"Why? It's my woman. My son."

Felipe spread his hands and shrugged. "It's all very mysterious. I do not understand women. First, they wanted me in there with them, and then they said we have to stay out here until they call us."

"I've got a jug of corn liquor, squeezed from last fall's crop," Zeke said, "Get Lalo, and we'll celebrate my new son."

The three men sat on their heels and passed the jug around, Zeke taking the first drink. Felipe's first sip of the clear liquid seared his throat, the hot flame reached his stomach, the fire blazed and spread through his body, warm and soothing.

Lalo and Felipe congratulated Zeke, slapped him on the back, and listened while he talked about how the boy would grow big and strong and help build his ranch.

Felipe's second taste of liquor burned but was pleasant. He laughed at the sensation and took another sip. The third pass of the jug turned into a long gulp for Felipe. His feet slipped out from under him, and he sat in the dirt. The other two men didn't appear affected by the liquor.

Zeke said, "I surely do appreciate you and your wife for helping Millie."

Felipe reached for the jug. "We're not married."

"Hell, man, neither are Millie and me. At least, not by any

preacher. The priest is due to come around here sometime. When he does get here, he'll marry us in the Catholic faith and baptize the baby. If he waits too long, no doubt he'll have another baby to baptize." Zeke laughed and Lalo joined him.

Felipe set the jug on the ground. "You are living together as man and wife but not married?"

"You see it's this way. I came out to Texas to settle on some free land. Either of you could get land the same way. The Mexican government allows each settler four thousand acres of pastureland and two hundred for farming. Only requirement is that everyone who settles here in the Texas territory must become a Mexican citizen and a Roman Catholic. The government sends priests to the settlements to perform marriages, baptizing, that sort of thing."

Felipe stood, his feet were uncertain, his vision blurred, but never had he understood the truth with such clarity. He paced to hold on to his thoughts. "Then why didn't you and Millie get married?"

"I've been here on this ranch for over five years and haven't seen a priest in all that time. There was a man come by one day, riding a mule and carrying a Bible, said he was a preacher." Zeke chuckled then sipped from the jug. "Millie and me, well, we just couldn't wait, so we let him say the words over us, and he said we was married. It don't matter, everyone does the same. The priest will be along some day."

"You say anyone can have that much land?" Lalo asked and took his turn with the jug.

"Sure," Zeke answered and explained the legal procedures of applying for a land grant.

Felipe didn't listen to their talk. Millie was a nice girl and watching the birth of her baby was an experience he would never forget. It was nothing like ewes lambing. It gave him strange thoughts about a family of his own.

When he was sixteen years old, his father had taken Felipe to Santa Fe. There at *Doña* Elena's gambling house, while his father played *monte*, one of the girls took Felipe to a back room. Although he visited her several times after that, she was not the type a man like him could marry. In Mexico City, he had met other girls at dance halls and at friends' houses, none, however, that he'd consider marrying. Alondra, though, was the kind of girl he could ... He stopped pacing and cursed. He kicked at the dirt and cursed in English. He cursed in Spanish and cursed in the French words he'd learned as a boy from the fur trappers.

Lalo waved the whiskey jug at him. "Come have a drink."

"This is a time for celebration," Zeke said. "What's got you so riled?"

Felipe grabbed the jug and guzzled the whiskey. Lalo took the jug from him. "Go easy, corn whiskey is nothing like the wine you usually drink."

Felipe sat on the ground. "I don't know what to do, Lalo."

"Do you want to talk about it?"

Felipe sat silent, head in his hands. Finally, he said, "I'm betrothed."

"Does Alondra know?"

"No."

"Why haven't you told her?" Lalo sounded only curious.

"I didn't think it was important."

Zeke gaped. "You're engaged to be married and you don't think it's important?"

"Our parents arranged it years ago. I was only eight years old, and I haven't seen her for almost four years. I don't want to marry her and I try not to think about it."

"Can't you tell your folks you don't want to marry that girl?" Zeke asked.

Felipe shook his head. "It wouldn't be honorable."

"Hell, man, there ain't nobody who'd tell me who I could marry."

Felipe stood. He swayed slightly and spread his arms to steady himself. "It's complicated. I'm going to sit under that tree over there and think about it." He picked up the whiskey. Lalo took the jug from him. "Leave that here, you'll drink it all and leave none for us."

With careful steps, Felipe walked to the tree, sat, and leaned against the trunk. He pondered his dilemma. His brain whirled, but he held one thought in his mind, clear and steady as the north star, and knew without a doubt that it was the truth ... he wanted Alondra by his side, now and for all time. He twisted the silver bracelet on his wrist, the item the men of his family traditionally gave their intended bride.

Alondra called from the door of the cabin. "Your wife is ready, Zeke. You can come in now and see her and the baby." She had helped Millie dress in a clean nightgown, sponged the baby, set a pot of stew bubbling on the fire, and tidied the cabin.

"Whoopee! Come on, Lalo, you want to see the baby?"

Lalo smiled and shook his head. "You go on, Zeke. I'll meet your wife and see the baby later."

Without a backward glance, Zeke ran to the cabin. "I'm coming, Millie honey."

"You've been working hard, Alondra?"

"Oh, no, Lalo, no. It was so wonderful helping Millie bring her baby into the world. Millie is such a sweet person, and the baby is so precious." Alondra glanced at Felipe. "What's he doing over there?"

"He's thinking."

Alondra sighed in exasperation. He was always thinking. She marched to the tree. "Felipe."

He looked up at her with a crooked smile, his eyes large and dark. "Alondra, my little skylark. Do you know that you are my very life? Without you, I am nothing." He slurred his words. "Come sit beside me." He tugged her hand and she sat.

He brushed her unruly hair from her face. "Since the first time I saw you, you've been on my mind. I think of nothing but you." He put his arm around her and held her close. She smelled the whiskey on his breath. He muttered words of love and endearment in a vague and blurred voice. "I need you beside me now and always. Come, my love, and lie down with me."

Madre de Dios, he was drunk. "Yes," she said. "I'll get a blanket."

He clutched her hand and kissed her palm. "Wait. Don't leave me." He pressed his lips to her wrist and up her inner arm.

Why did he have to be drunk? She had longed to hear him say those words of love, but not when he didn't realize what he was saying. She pulled her arm free and wadded her shawl into a ball. "Here, lay your head on this for a pillow." She gently shoved him in the chest, and he lay down. "I'll be right back with your blanket."

She stood and looked down at him. His eyes were closed, and his chest moved with deep and even breaths.

Alondra went to the three-sided shed that served as barn and stable and got a blanket from his saddle. "He's drunk, Lalo. Why?"

Lalo shrugged. "Sometimes a man has a problem and drink is the only solution."

If Felipe had a problem, maybe she could help him with it in the morning. Now, he needed sleep. Alondra tucked the blanket around Felipe, laid his hat on the ground beside him, and stroked his hair. She leaned over and kissed him on the lips. He murmured and reached for her. She patted his shoulder. "Sleep. Sleep well, *querido.*"

Alondra hurried to the cabin. Later, she would spend the night beside Felipe and keep him warm, but right now the stew needed tending.

CHAPTER 13

A mockingbird's squawk exploded in Felipe's brain and shattered his sleep. His head throbbed. He swallowed and licked his lips. The inside of his mouth tasted worse than a hog pen smelled. He felt the warm presence of Alondra and slowly opened one eye. She lay with her head snuggled against his shoulder and an arm draped across his chest.

Felipe groaned. He had little memory of the previous night, only a shadowy impression of holding Alondra and talking with her and a dreamlike sensation of kissing her. What had he told her? Had he made promises he couldn't keep? Had he made love to her? He lifted the blanket. He was dressed, he wore his boots, and he uttered a small prayer of thanksgiving. He would rather rip his heart out than hurt Alondra.

Gently he moved her arm and stood. His head whirled. On shaky legs, he made his way to the spring. He dunked his head and sipped on the cool water. He picked mint leaves that were growing around the pond, chewed them, spit them out, scrubbed his teeth with mint leaves, and drank more water.

His mouth no longer tasted as foul. He stood on steady legs

and his head didn't spin. Felipe vowed he would never drink corn liquor again. He didn't like the memory loss, the not knowing what he'd said and done.

Zeke came out of the cabin carrying an axe, his yellow hair tousled from sleep. "I'll chop the wood," Felipe said.

Zeke handed him the axe. "I'd appreciate it. I've got chores stacked up. I didn't get much done yesterday."

"I'll help with those too if I can." Felipe swung the axe high over his shoulder, brought it down with a resounding thud, and split a chunk of wood in two. He welcomed the work, the rhythm of the swinging axe released tension. Sweat trickled down his spine, but he thought only of the cottonwood log at his feet.

He chopped wood until Zeke called to him. "Felipe, you know horses. Lalo told me you trained that black of yours."

Felipe leaned on the axe handle. "Yes."

"The dang Comanche ran off with my horses a few days ago, and, what with Millie and the baby, I haven't had a chance to get them back."

"You are planning to steal your horses back from the Indians?"

"Well, I can't very well run this ranch without my horses. The McFarlanes over to the east will help."

"What of the women? It is dangerous to leave them with no protection."

"I was thinking Lalo could stay and protect them while we hunted the horses."

"Lalo is a soldier. He knows the way of the Comanche. He'd be more valuable fighting the Indians. Millie is your wife; you should be the one to protect her and your baby."

Zeke sat on the log. "It don't seem right, Felipe, for me to stay on the ranch all safe while you fellows risk your lives for my horses."

"I have a better idea. There must be some wild mustangs close by. We'll capture a few to replace your lost ones and I'll help you train them."

Zeke scratched the stubble on his chin. "You'd do that? There's a herd of mustangs that range about twenty-five miles north of here."

"We still need protection for the women. How many men can we count on from the McFarlanes?"

"Three. The old man and his two sons."

"Do they have women?"

"Yes, but we don't need to worry about them. The McFarlanes have been in the territory since the twenties. The old lady has seen her share of Indian fighting, and the daughter handles a rifle as easily as I do."

"Maybe they could come here and stay with Millie and the baby. There's safety in numbers."

Alondra called them to breakfast and the three men discussed the wild mustang hunt while they ate.

"Did you tell him what we named the baby?" From her bed, Millie gestured to Felipe.

Zeke blushed. "No. You tell him."

Millie grinned at her husband with affection and turned to Felipe. "We named him Flip. After you."

"Flip." Felipe nodded. "I see. I am greatly honored. Thank you." He bowed and brought her hand to his lips.

Millie reddened and ducked her head. "Get along with you. Finish your breakfast, you men."

After breakfast, Zeke saddled Segundo and made ready to ride with Lalo the twenty miles to the McFarlane ranch. "We'll be home early tomorrow, honey," Zeke said to Millie as he walked out the door.

*****

"I need to teach you to handle a pistol, Alondra," Felipe said. "We'll go out behind the corral away from the house, so the gunfire doesn't disturb the animals."

"What about you, Millie?" Alondra asked. "Do you know how to shoot?"

Millie nodded. "I've had to learn. Don't worry about me. No Injun will take either me or my baby alive. I keep a pistol here, under my pillow. But I've laid abed long enough and I'm getting up. I've chores to attend."

"It's too soon. I'll do your chores, you rest." Alondra followed Felipe out the door.

Behind the corral, in a clearing inside a thick stand of brush, Felipe handed Alondra one of the pistols he had taken from Sam. "Feel the heft, Alondra. It's heavy. Use both hands. Get comfortable handling it, and then I'll show you how to load the ammunition."

The pistol smelled of oil and gunpowder, the wooden grip was scarred and warm, the iron barrel smooth and cold.

Felipe stood next to her, explaining the workings of the gun, how to load and prime it. "This is where the powder goes, and here is where you put the ball. We won't do that yet."

The hairs on his wrists glinted gold in the sunlight. Alondra heard his voice as from a distance, aware only of the touch of his hands, the closeness of his body. She remembered the words of love he'd spoken the night before. Had he meant what he said, or was it the liquor talking? She stroked the back of his hand with her fingertips.

"Now, I will show you how to shoot." Felipe backed her against him to show her how to aim and pull the trigger. His hands moved over hers, and she pressed closer to him, delighting in his nearness, his scent. She leaned her head back against his chest, heard the quickening beat of his heart, the sharp intake of his breath. He lifted her hair, nuzzled her neck below her ear. With a soft cry of delight, she loosened her grip on the pistol and it fell to the ground.

She'd been thinking only of Felipe, the feel of his body next to hers. Had she broken the gun? She leaned to pick up the fallen pistol.

He took her hand, pulled her to him, bent his head, and kissed her with a consuming hunger. Maybe he had meant those words of love. She returned his kiss to show how much she loved him. His mouth never left hers as his hands caressed her shoulders, her back, every touch new and thrilling. She pressed close to him, molded her soft curves to his lean body, eagerly returned his touches, his kisses. Heat waves flooded through her veins. Consciousness ebbed. There was only Felipe and the exciting sensations surging through her body.

Felipe cradled her face in his hands, kissed her tenderly on the lips, his breathing ragged, and gently stepped back. With a light finger, he traced her lips, her brow. His touch, and the love that spilled from his eyes, was almost more than Alondra could bear.

Her hand unsteady, she reached up and smoothed his hair.

He smiled, but the change in his soft hazel eyes brought a lump to her throat and fear to her heart. "What is it, Felipe?"

He led her by the hand to a large rock. "Now, sit and listen. Don't say anything until I am finished." He took both her hands in his. "Alondra, I love you. I didn't want to, I fought against it. But there it is. I love you."

His words warmed her heart and her world turned bright and beautiful. The wind sang a happy tune in the trees. "I love you too, Felipe."

His lips twisted in a wistful smile. "There is a problem. I'm betrothed."

Her world turned bleak and barren. In the distance, a mourning dove called, lonesome and sad. An icicle pierced her heart and she shivered. She pulled her hands from his.

"Our parents arranged it long ago."

Alondra stared at her hands folded in her lap. She noticed a broken thumbnail. "Is she beautiful?"

"I don't know. I suppose so. It's not important."

"She's a lady then, and a dowry has been paid?" Alondra concentrated on keeping her voice steady.

"Yes."

"You must marry her, Felipe. It is the honorable thing to do."

"Yes, but I don't want to. How can I marry her when I love you?"

"You are a man of honor, Felipe, and will do the right thing. The marriage will bring your two families together and I know that is important to the *hidalgo*."

"Not to me, but I don't want to bring shame to my parents."

Alondra fluffed her hair, smoothed her skirt.

"Please understand, Alondra, I don't want to hurt you either."

"No matter what you do, Felipe, you won't hurt me. I love you. I always knew we could never marry, but I will be proud to be your mistress."

"No, Alondra. You don't know what that kind of life is like—always taking second place to a wife. You deserve better than that. I will never dishonor you in that way."

She stood. "If we're not going to finish my lesson, I'm going back to the cabin and help Millie with the baby." Without a backward glance, head held high, she walked away before he saw the tears she could no longer hold back.

Felipe sat on the rock, head in his hands. The conversation had gotten away from him. He had wanted to make pretty speeches, make her see how much she meant to him. He had wanted to explain again the analogy of pebbles and rings in the water and how his actions affected others and there was no going back. But Alondra had walked away from him, leaving him empty, bereft, and loving her more than ever. She was the greatest lady he had ever met, gentle, generous, brave, and completely honest. As soon as he was home, he would find a way for them to be together. His parents would love Alondra once they met her, and they wouldn't expect him to honor the betrothal.

Having made that decision, he went to the shed and stretched and coiled rope. He braided halters and hobbles, with an eye out for Indians and his mind focused on the mustang hunt.

When Alondra was sure Felipe could no longer see her, she broke into a run. The wind tugged at her hair and dried the tears on her face. She entered the cabin, bedraggled and pale.

"What is it, Alondra honey? You look right frazzled," Millie said.

With her shoulders slumped and her brown eyes dark hollows, Alondra choked back a sob. "He's betrothed, Millie. I can never marry him."

"Ah, honey. Let's fix us a cup of tea and we'll talk about this."

Weary of discussing weather, crops, and livestock with Zeke, Millie had hungered for women talk, and in the way of women, Alondra had spoken of her dreams and longings to Millie, and they had discussed Felipe, his finer points, and his faults. Both women agreed that the good outweighed the bad and Alondra should do her best to marry the handsome Spaniard.

Over their mint tea, sweetened with clover honey, Alondra explained the betrothal. As a married woman, both girls considered Millie the expert on men.

"What you must do," she said, "is make him want you so bad he'll forget all about that highborn lady."

"He will never do it. It wouldn't be honorable." Alondra paused for a moment before she said, "How would I go about doing that?"

"Let's study on it a bit." Millie stirred her tea, her brow furrowed in thought.

Alondra leaned her elbows on the table, cupped her chin in her palms, and, with hope in her eyes, stared at Millie.

Finally, Millie spoke. "Zeke will be back tomorrow sometime and the McFarlanes will be with him. We'll have a party. We'll say it's for the baby's christening. You will be the godmother, and I'll ask Felipe to be the godfather."

"Won't we need a priest for the baptism?"

"They gave us a book when we got our land grant because the priest might not get this far into the territory. It has prayers for baptizing and even for the dead in case someone dies without a priest. They even gave us a jar of holy water. So, don't worry about it. We'll go ahead with our party. Old Mr. McFarlane plays the mouth harp, and the missus does pretty good with a homemade guitar and fiddle."

"And I'll dance," Alondra said.

"Sure, dance with Felipe. Take him outside afterward, with a glass of buttermilk or something to cool off, but don't let him kiss you or anything."

Alondra was doubtful. "I asked him to dance with me one other time and he refused."

"I'll shame him into it," Millie said. "And besides, there's them two McFarlane boys. They're kind of young but are sure to ask you to dance. You can dance with them all you want, and it will make Felipe jealous."

"But that's not honest, Millie. I don't feel right flirting with men I care nothing about."

"Oh honey, it's harmless fun. All us women do things like that to catch our man. Let's get cracking, we have a cake and pies to bake. I'll ask Felipe to go hunting and bring home some prairie chickens or a deer." Millie left the cabin with purposeful steps, excited about the prospect of a party.

CHAPTER 14

Relieved that Millie had asked him to go hunting, Felipe rode El Moro around the homestead in ever-widening circles, alert for any sign of Indians or game. He needed distance between himself and Alondra to think things over. He knew he'd hurt her, the one thing he hadn't wanted to do. Would she treat him any differently now? He'd become accustomed to her warm presence next to him at night. He could no longer permit that. With Alondra sleeping beside him, he was not sure he could control his feelings.

She had offered to be his mistress, why had he refused? Many men, especially in towns such as Mexico City, kept mistresses. Even his cousin had one. And the wife, happy with her silk dresses, jewels, and social position, didn't appear to mind.

But that was not the type of life Felipe wanted for Alondra or himself. He wanted them to walk through life side by side, grow old together, with pride and respect for one another.

From the corner of his eye, Felipe caught movement and turned his head. The rear end of a horse disappeared behind some bushes. He guided El Moro downwind into the brush. He stopped and heard the soft thud of hooves, branches crackled, and dried leaves crushed. Apparently, the horse had no fear that he might be seen. Felipe moved closer until he saw the wild chestnut stallion. The horse seemed to know where he was going, and Felipe followed him.

The chestnut turned his head, stomped his forefoot, and snorted. Felipe stayed downwind behind a bush. The sleek and well-muscled horse had no brand or white saddle marks on his glistening hide. Felipe estimated that the horse was around five years of age and wondered if he should try and lasso him, it would be one fewer mustang they would have to capture.

The stallion stopped, lifted his head, pointed his ears, and blew softly through his nose. They were on the crest of a hill, overlooking a valley that was dotted with shade trees and had a creek running through it. A small band of mustangs grazed. A dark bay stallion sniffed around a roan mare.

The chestnut reared, pawed the air with his front hooves, whistled a challenge, and galloped down the hill. He crashed through the brush, whinnying and braying, fire in his eyes. At the bottom of the hill, he challenged once again, and the bay rushed to meet him with neck outstretched, ears flat, teeth bared, screaming in outrage.

Neighing and snorting, the two stallions met each other on their hind legs, front hooves hitting with crushing blows.

The bay stallion's muzzle was sprinkled with white, his hide marked with battle scars. But what the bay lacked in strength and agility, he had experience and cunning. He dodged the greater number of the more violent blows and then swiftly whirled and kicked out at his opponent with a stunning force that would have finished the chestnut had he not wheeled out of range. Biting, kicking, and squealing, the horses battled. Sharp hooves pounded on solid muscle, teeth nipped on flesh.

The mares grazed, unconcerned of the outcome, but the young males in the herd watched the struggle with interest.

One day, they too would battle for their right to a harem.

The chestnut gave two well-aimed kicks to the ribs, one after the other, and the fight was over. The old stallion stood, legs splayed, head down, defeated. A gouged piece of hide hung from his flank. The younger horse reared, whinnied, and with bared teeth rushed at him. The bay stallion ran to the safety of the trees—an old warrior whose days were numbered. He would stay on the edges of the herd for a day or two, and when they moved on, he'd drop farther and farther behind, easy prey for pumas and wolves.

Felipe determined to bring the old horse in with the rest of the mustangs. Too old for heavy work, the bay stallion could be used as a mount for women and children, or even for an occasional ride to round up cattle on short drives.

The chestnut neighed and pranced in victory. He arched his neck and snuffling each horse, acquainted himself with the herd. Sniffing and nipping, he claimed his prize and mounted the roan mare.

Felipe recalled the time he sat with his grandfather on the top rung of the corral. Grandfather had selected two of their horses for breeding—a white mare and a mouse-colored stallion. Grandfather watched to ensure that the animals did indeed mate so that he could predict an accurate birth date for the foal.

"That mare will throw a fine foal," Grandfather had said. "I judge its coat will be deep silver." The old man sat quietly awhile as though thinking. After a moment, he said, "Remember this, Felipe, when a man and woman walk in the moonlight and end up in the barn, when the loving is done, all a man needs to do is shake the hay out of his coat, but a woman has to wait for a month to know the result of that moment of pleasure."

Felipe had been stunned and embarrassed that his grandfather had talked of such things to him and wondered how the old man could know about women and the desires of young men.

But that was what Felipe had wanted to talk about with Alondra, that was what he tried to explain with the stones thrown in the water, but somehow, he couldn't put it into words. His grandfather was much more eloquent. He wondered if he should use the old man's words but didn't want to embarrass her. He'd just not say anything to her. He would never let her know how he yearned to hold her, how complete he felt with her beside him. It would be better that way until he could talk to his parents and cancel the betrothal that hung over his head with the weight of a millstone.

He stood and brushed his hands on his trousers. The mustangs were close to the ranch, and they could capture them in one day. He felt better now, as though a burden had been lifted. Horses affected him in that way, just looking at a horse eased his mind. He was eager to begin the training.

The sun was low in the west. He'd wasted time with the horses and had not yet gone hunting. The prairie chickens should be coming to roost about now, back there in that stand of trees. He tracked the chickens, shot three, and hurried home.

*****

Felipe reined in El Moro at the top of the hill and looked down at Zeke's ranch. Lalo's horse and Segundo were in the corral along with two mules. An empty wagon sat in the cleared space in front of the cabin. Felipe galloped down the grade. With every stride, the three chickens tied to his saddle flapped against the horse.

Four women sat on the stoop. An old woman, wearing a bonnet and with a pipe clenched between her teeth, held the baby. A young woman with hair the red-gold of a cloud at sunset sat next to her. Millie's hair shone as yellow as ripe wheat stalks in sunlight. Alondra sat beside her, her hair, black as a moonless night, curled around her face. Felipe's heart turned over when she looked up, met his eyes, and smiled.

Zeke stepped out of the cabin. "I'll take those." He untied the chickens and handed them to Millie. "Here you go, honey. Looks like we'll have a feast after all. Come on in," Zeke said to Felipe. "I want you to meet the McFarlanes. I've told them all about you."

Felipe dismounted. "I'll need to unsaddle first."

"This here is Ma McFarlane," Zeke said. Felipe bowed and tipped his hat. "And this is Clory McFarlane."

Felipe flicked the brim of his hat. Clory blushed and ducked her head.

"Hey, you, Robbie, Davie, get yourselves on out here," Ma McFarlane shouted.

Two teenage boys rushed from the cabin door. Fiery red hair stuck out from under their misshapen slouch hats. "Yeah, Ma?"

"Take care of this gentleman's horse for him."

Both boys looked at El Moro with round-eyed wonder. "Honest, mister, can we?" asked one of the boys.

"Of course," Felipe said. "Which are you, Davie or Robbie?"

"I'm Robbie and two years older than Davie. I'll be sixteen next month. I ain't never seen a finer looking horse than this'n."

"This is El Moro, Robbie. Let him get to know you and he'll be your friend. After you unsaddle him, he likes a good rub down and brushing. He'll probably want a drink of water too."

"He won't bite, will he?" asked Davie. "Old Jack, our mule, bites and kicks us sometimes."

"No, he won't bite, and he won't kick. He's gentle."

Felipe smiled as he watched the boys lead El Moro to the corral, arguing which would rub him down and which would brush him.

Zeke took Felipe by the arm. "Come on in and meet Pa

McFarlane."

Felipe glanced at the women and with a special smile for Alondra, bowed. "Ladies." He turned to Zeke. "I saw a herd of mustangs about a two-hour ride from here. If we leave before daylight, we can have them corralled before noon."

The two men entered the cabin talking about the horses. "Are there enough horses for the McFarlanes? The Comanche hit their place too, and Ma got worried about Millie. We met them halfway. They were on their way here."

With her elbow, Millie poked Alondra in the ribs. "I thought you was going to play hard to get."

"From the look that passed between them two, it appears to me he's already hooked," Ma said.

Millie held a plucked hen up by the legs, scanned it for any feathers she'd missed. "But she ain't landed him yet." She told the McFarlane women about the betrothal.

Clory asked, "What're y'all aiming to do?"

Millie told them about the planned party, and Clory said, "I sure don't see as how that's going to do any good. There are no men here for her to flirt with unless she flirts with Lalo." And her cheeks flamed.

"It ain't my fault," Millie said. "How was I to know your brothers were so danged young? I never did see them before. All I ever heard was Zeke talking about the McFarlane boys. I thought they was men grown."

"They're fine boys," Ma said. "Already they're durn near as tall as their pa."

"I don't want to flirt with anyone. Come on, Clory, let's put these birds on to cook." Alondra held up a pole sharpened on one end. Together, the girls threaded the chickens on the pole and carried them to the fire.

"Lalo is a good man, Clory. He is honest and brave, but I don't love him, and I like him too well to use him to get the man I do love."

Clory adjusted the spit, her twinkling blue eyes held a dreamy expression. "I like his eyes; they are brown and soft as a deer's. And he is strong, but his hands were gentle when he helped me in the wagon, even though I didn't need no help."

Alondra put her arm around the other girl's waist. "You could do a lot worse than him, Clory."

*****

In the cabin, Zeke said, "This here's Felipe, Pa. He was telling me he found a mustang herd a few miles east, easy to get. How many did you say there were, Felipe?"

"It's a herd of around twenty-five, but there are only twenty we can use, the others are too young. There are two stallions, several mares with foals, and some three- and four-year-old fillies and horses."

The men talked over their plans for the mustang drive. "We have five mounts if you count the mules," Felipe said. "That leaves one man to protect the women. Do you want that job, Pa? The boys can ride the mules, and I'd feel better with a man in charge here."

"I reckon I could do that. Them boys of mine are mighty handy, and they'll pull their weight all right. I ain't worried about that."

"What are you worried about, Pa?" Zeke asked.

"Supposing the Comanche attack while y'all are bringing in the horses?"

"We'll let them have the mustangs. We won't lose a man over a bunch of wild horses," Felipe said. "Does everyone have plenty of ammunition?"

Each man checked his weapons, oiled his rifle and pistol, and sharpened his knife blade. Felipe outlined his plans for corralling the mustangs, and, with the topic of horses finally exhausted, Lalo picked up a crude guitar that was leaning against the wall. "Whose is this?" he asked, "It's been a long time since I've held a guitar in my hands. Do you mind if I strum it?"

Pa shook his head. "Heck no, son. That's Ma's, she'd be plumb tickled if you played it."

Lalo picked a few tentative chords. As he became accustomed to the instrument, he strummed louder and began to sing:

Suspiros que de aqui salen,
Y otros que de allá vendrán,
Si en el camino se encuentran,
Que de cosas no se dirán.

Outside on the front stoop, the women stopped talking and listened to the music.

"That's Lalo," Clory said. "I'd know his voice anywhere. What's the song say, Alondra?"

"I sometimes get the American words mixed up and I might not say them right, but it goes something like this:

My sighs, that go and leave me here,
And yours from yonder stealing out—
If on the road they chance to meet,
How many things they'll talk about!

"It's a *dicho*, a little made-up song. It doesn't mean anything."

"But his voice is so beautiful." Clory sighed.

"I do believe that gal of mine is smitten," Ma said. She saw the boys coming from the corral. "Hey, you young'uns, bring me my new guitar." She handed the baby to Millie.

Davie scrambled up in the wagon and brought out a homemade guitar.

"This one is brand-spanking new," Ma said. "I ain't even

broke it in good yet." She tested the strings, made adjustments, and then strummed lightly.

Lalo came to the door, grinned, and nodded at Ma, and they plucked their guitars in unison. The other men joined the group and Pa pulled out his harmonica. Soon, the three were playing a lively tune and the others tapped their feet and swayed to the rhythm.

"Come on, Alondra, dance," Lalo said.

Alondra looked around at the smiling group and grinned. "All right."

Arms folded across his chest, Felipe stood on the fringe and watched her dance. He recalled the time he saw her at the *cantina* and smiled at the remembrance of her skirt swirling above her knees and the knife strapped to her thigh. But the strange sensation that crawled up his spine had nothing to do with Alondra.

She finished her dance and dropped to the ground. Ma struck a slower beat, and the McFarlanes sang about a woman named Barbara Allen. The song was a gentle ballad but did nothing to ease the tension that prickled the back of Felipe's neck. He stepped back into the shadows of the cook fire and listened. The horses were restless, they snorted, and El Moro neighed. Horses generally enjoyed music; they should not be nervous.

Felipe slipped through the dark to the stable. The horses and mules were milling in a circle around the corral and El Moro was snorting and trotting back and forth through the other horses as though he were being stalked.

Felipe whistled. El Moro whinnied, kicked with both hind legs, and ran to him. The other animals bunched together in a corner, snorting and blowing. The quarter moon and the few stars shone with a feeble light, but Felipe thought he saw a dark shape huddled on the ground. He shouted, "Lalo, Zeke, bring torches!"

Carrying torches and rifles, the men sped to the corral in

time to see a form scale the corral. They searched the stable and the grounds but found nothing.

"Comanche?" Lalo asked.

"Probably. I don't know, they didn't take anything, but they did leave something." Felipe held up a set of rawhide hobbles. "Now I understand why El Moro was nervous. He doesn't like hobbles. We'll sleep out here tonight, Lalo, and take turns guarding the horses."

"I'll take my turn at guard," Zeke said.

"You and Pa take turns guarding the house," Felipe said. "All the women will sleep in the house tonight. We'll take what precautions we can, and in the morning we'll search for tracks."

"The Comanche don't like to attack at night unless there's a full moon to see by," Pa said. "If they want these horses, they'll come towards daylight, so we best be prepared."

"I'll take my turn at guard," Robbie said.

"Yes, Robbie," Felipe said. "Both you and Davie will guard inside the house. Keep your guns loaded and take turns sleeping across the doorway, so no Indian can enter."

Millie clutched her baby to her breast and dashed into the cabin.

Ma leaned her guitar against the door. "Seems as though the party is over, folks. But you still have to eat. Come on, you men, get some vittles inside yer gut. It could be a long night."

With her large knife, Alondra cut up the chickens and placed slices on tin plates. Clory dished up stew, and Ma sliced cornbread. After everyone had eaten, the women crowded into the one-room cabin and the men took up their guard posts for the night.

CHAPTER 15

Felipe pulled his hat low against the northeasterly wind and glanced up at the gray dawn. "Looks like it's blowing up a big storm."

Lalo pointed to the ground. "Two horses stood here for maybe an hour."

"Those Indians were watching us for that long?"

Lalo nodded. "They were maybe lured by the music and then, in the way of the Comanche, decided to steal a horse to make it worth their time."

"Which direction did they go?"

Lalo pointed northwest. "But there's no point in following them, we'd never catch them. We could find a group of them maybe, but never one or two. They'd hide their tracks and blend with the earth, and, after all, they didn't steal anything."

Pa McFarlane and Zeke joined them. Pa agreed with Lalo. "Them Injuns won't come back. They was probably two young bucks on some kind of scouting trip. You fellers might as well go on and get them mustangs before the storm blows in."

"They'll weather the storm just fine there in the valley," Felipe said.

"Or," Pa said, "They might move on south away from the storm. But you never know about storms that come this late in the season. It might turn into a nasty norther or blow right past and it'll be hot and dusty by noon."

"Pa's right," Zeke put in. "I don't want to miss out on the chance to get some horses. I'm hogtied without them, can't do a thing."

Robbie ran out from the cabin. The wind caught his hat, and it somersaulted toward the corral. Robbie chased it and jammed it on his head. He ran to the men, holding his hat on with one hand. "Ma says to come in for breakfast."

The men trooped into the cabin. "I don't like the idea of leaving the ranch with Indians so close," Felipe said.

Pa helped himself to a biscuit and poured gravy over it. "With that storm blowing in, them Injuns are hightailing it to their camp. They're nowhere near here, and, if they do come, Clory and me will send them to their happy hunting grounds in no time flat." He patted his musket.

Zeke said, "There won't be any horses here for them to steal, so there'll be no need for them to come back."

"I suppose you're right. Let's get moving. The sooner we leave, the sooner we'll get back." Felipe gave one of his pistols to Alondra. "Do you remember how this works?" He covered her hand with both of his.

She nodded. He brought her hand to his lips and gazed into her eyes. "Take care, Alondra, *mi amor.*"

He squeezed her hand, turned, and with the other men walked from the cabin without looking back.

"*Vaya con Dios,*" she whispered and pressed the back of her hand against her lips. With tears in her eyes, she watched the men ride from the corral.

"Don't worry, honey," Millie said. "They'll be fine. Our men are strong and brave. There ain't no Indian that can stand up to them."

"That's right, and if any of them come around here, I'll spit in their eye." Ma took the pipe from her mouth, cleared her throat, and spat into the fireplace. The embers sizzled and sparks flew up the chimney.

Alondra laughed. "You're right. I won't worry anymore. Come on, Clory, let's get the cabin straightened out."

Pa grabbed his musket and went out the door. "Now, I don't want none of you women going outdoors alone. If you need to come outside, holler and I'll come running. I'll be close by. I'm going to scout around some."

*****

The bitter wind stung their faces and snatched the words from their mouths as the men rode east toward the mustang herd in silence. They reined in at the crest of the valley. The wild horses huddled under trees, backs to the wind.

"The wind is in our favor," Felipe said. "It carries away our scent and will be at our backs on the way home. I'll wait down in that draw. The rest of you go behind and start them toward me. The palomino under that pine is the lead mare. Get her pointed my direction, and the others will follow. Zeke, you and the boys keep them bunched together, Lalo will take drag, and I'll take point."

He turned El Moro down the hill then stopped. "Make sure the old stallion stays with the herd, Lalo. I don't see him; he must be hiding somewhere in the brush."

Lalo grinned and saluted. "*Si, Señor.*" He went with the others to round up the mustangs. Felipe waited at the small ravine listening for the horses. When the palomino mare ran toward him, he guided El Moro beside her and they galloped down the draw, the herd thundered behind. Freezing rain pelted them as the wind whipped them westward.

Pa McFarlane stomped his feet on the doorsill. "That wind's colder than a witch's tit, and the rain is freezing my balls off. This storm is turning into a blue norther all right. I best bring in some more firewood."

"I'll go with you," Alondra said, "and fetch some water." She wrapped her *serape* around her shoulders and over her head and shoved the Bowie knife in her sash.

Pa moved to the woodpile. "Make it snappy, gal. I got my eye on you."

Alondra hurried to the spring and dipped the pail. She heard Pa's voice. "Hey, gal ..." She turned and saw an Indian running toward her, saw Pa lying face down across a log, a tomahawk buried in his back, his rifle on the ground beside him. She dropped the bucket, pulled out her big knife, and ran toward the cabin, screaming.

A musket boomed.

An Indian rapped Alondra across her shoulders and knocked her down, the Indian on top of her. She smelled him. The musky scent of a wild thing, an odor she would never forget. Adrenaline surged through her. She shoved him off and scrambled to her feet. The Indian grunted and grabbed her ankle. She kicked him in the jaw. He loosened his grip. She shook him off.

From the corner of her eye, Alondra saw another Indian. She pulled air into her lungs and whirled, with her knife raised. Strong arms grabbed her from behind, and she dropped the knife. She kicked and screamed. The Indian wrapped her, from head to foot, in an animal hide that had the odor of wood smoke and rancid grease.

The musket boomed again. Alondra squirmed and screamed. A swift blow to her head sent her into blackness.

Felipe led the mustangs to the ranch at a trot. The men herded the animals into the corral and shut the gate. The horses milled, snorting and blowing. The chestnut stallion reared and whinnied. His eyes rolled white, he lashed out with his front feet.

"We better hobble him," Felipe said. "Or he's likely to jump the corral." He shook out his *reata*, made a loop, twirled it over his head, and lassoed the stallion by its hind feet. He jerked the rope and the horse crashed to the ground, landing on its side. He held the rope taut while Lalo twisted the animal's head back so it wouldn't hurt itself by thrashing around. With a length of cotton rope, Zeke fashioned hobbles and fastened them around the mustang's forefeet.

With a swiftness born of practice, Felipe loosened the ropes from the mustang's feet and yelled, "Turn him loose." Lalo jumped away from the horse and all three men climbed the corral rungs before the stallion got to his feet.

"We'll wait until morning to work with the horses," Felipe said. "That will give them time to settle down and maybe the weather will clear by then."

Already, the mustangs crowded into the shed to escape the wind and freezing rain.

The men walked to the cabin, laughing and talking, satisfied with the day's work. Clory met them at the door, musket in her hands, her face a distorted mask of anger and sorrow.

Felipe glanced around the cabin and dread filled his soul. Pa lay on the table, hands folded across his stomach and coppers covering his eyes. Ma sat beside the fireplace, gray head bent, tears streaming down her withered cheeks. Millie sat rocking on the bed, eyes wide, her baby pressed to her breast.

"What happened here, Clory?" Felipe asked. "Where's Alondra?" Clory explained why Pa and Alondra went outdoors. "I shot at them Indians, Felipe. I'm sure I didn't miss, but they took Alondra with them."

Felipe grabbed her arm. She shrank back. "How many were there?"

"I saw only two. I shot twice before they galloped off. And

I hit at least one of them, there's blood on the ground."

His mouth a grim line, Lalo said. "Probably the same two who stood in the bushes watching us."

Felipe touched Ma on the shoulder. "I'm so sorry. Pa was a good man and I feel responsible for all this. We never should have gone after those mustangs."

Ma patted his hand. "You forget. He is the one who insisted there would be no trouble. And he scouted the place all morning and never did see any Injun sign. It weren't no one's fault. Is the ground too froze for the buryin'?"

Robbie and Davie rushed to her side. She gathered them in her arms and the three wept together.

"Don't worry, Ma, me and Robbie will take care of you," Davie said.

"Bless you, child. I know you will."

Felipe spoke in Lalo's ear. "I'm going after her, Lalo. I'm leaving now."

"Wait until we bury the old man, and I will accompany you."

"Thank you, but these people need you here."

"Ah, but the little skylark is my friend too. Besides, you need me to track."

"What of Clory? I've seen how you two look at each other."

Lalo stroked his mustache. "Ah, yes, Clory. But I shall return and claim her. Wait, my friend. We will need supplies to cross the plains. I promise we will leave before nightfall."

Felipe reluctantly agreed to wait. He was impatient to trail Alondra, but his heart went out to the McFarlanes in their grief. No matter what Ma said, he felt responsible. He walked out the door.

Lalo followed him. "Where are you going?"

"To dig a grave. Where does Zeke keep his shovel?"

"Over here," Zeke said. "I'll help." He grabbed a pickaxe and handed the other two men shovels.

"Do you have wood I can use to make a coffin?" Lalo asked.

Zeke shook his head. "No. They are more than welcome to wrap him in one of our blankets." He led them to a rise overlooking the valley. "This is where I'd planned the cemetery. Pa is the first."

The wind howled and swirled sleet but sweat beaded their brows as the men dug into the earth's hard crust. The deeper they dug, the easier the digging. Lalo climbed out of the pit, walked down the hill to the corral, and hitched the mules to the wagon. Behind the barn, he found fragments of boards and fashioned a cross, then went to the cabin for the women.

They had wrapped Pa in a quilt, so new the colors had not yet faded, and Lalo helped Clory and the boys carry the body to the wagon. He lifted Ma onto the seat. He glanced at Millie, her baby bundled in blankets, and remembered she had only recently given birth. "You better ride too, Millie." He helped her onto the wagon seat and climbed up beside her. He slapped the reins across the mules' backs and started the wagon up the hill. Clory and the boys trudged behind, Robbie playing the Barbara Allen tune on Pa's mouth harp.

At the gravesite, the wind moaned, whipped the women's skirts, bent the men's hat brims. Lalo and Zeke lowered Pa into the grave. "Does someone want to say a few words?" Zeke asked.

Millie held out her prayer book. "The prayers are in here." She reddened. "Can someone read them?" She investigated each face, and each in turn shook their head.

Felipe took the book and flipped the pages to the prayers for the dead. The men removed their hats and held them tight to their chests against the wind. Felipe read the prayers in a solemn voice, made the sign of the cross over the body, picked up a handful of dirt, and sprinkled it into the open grave, intoning, "... dust thou art and to dust thou shalt return ..." The others did the same, and Zeke and Lalo shoveled dirt into the grave. Clods thudded on the quilt-wrapped corpse, and Ma crumpled into Clory's arms.

In a shaky voice, Millie started singing ... "Shall we gather at the river ..." and Clory joined her, "the beautiful, the beautiful river ..." Ma straightened and sang with them, their voices faint against the howling wind.

Lalo pounded the cross into the ground and led Ma to the wagon. Felipe, the boys, and Zeke piled rocks on the mound of earth.

At the cabin, Felipe took Ma's hands in his. "I'm leaving now, Ma. I'm going to find Alondra."

"Yes," Ma said. "You must. Thank you for the beautiful funeral. Pa would have been proud. Will you come back here after you find your girl?"

"If I can. I don't know how long I'll be gone, and Lalo is going with me."

"And so am I, Ma," Clory said.

"No, Clory," Felipe said. "It will be a long, hard trip. Stay here with your family."

"Do you think I can stay here after what the Comanche did to my pa? I can't let you track them down without me."

Ma nodded. "She wants revenge on those savages, and she has that right. Clory is the only one of our family who can avenge her father's death. The boys are both too young. Take her with you, she's a crack shot."

"I don't know when we can get back here," Felipe said.

"She's a woman grown. She will leave here someday anyhow. The boys will help me with the ranch." Ma filled her pipe and lit it with a lighted stick from the fireplace.

"Stay here, Clory," Felipe said. "The weather is bad, we'll be riding hard, and the trail is no place for a woman."

"Hasn't Alondra been on the trail with you for a time?" Clory asked. "I can ride as good as any man and better than some. If you won't take me with you, I'll follow behind. I'm going."

Felipe gazed at her. Strong-minded women were foreign to him, but, since his arrival in Texas, they were the only kind of women he had met. He realized that he respected and admired them. "All right, but we are leaving in ten minutes."

He shook Zeke's hand. "I'm sorry I can't take the time to train those mustangs for you, but the boys can help you and you'll do fine."

Zeke pushed his hat back and scratched his head. "I'm not so sure. How will I get those hobbles off that chestnut stallion?"

"Rope him around the neck, loop the rope tight to the snubbing post until you choke him down. Quickly remove the hobbles and turn him loose." Felipe clapped Zeke on the shoulder. "You'll do fine. Just remember, like a woman, horses respond to a gentle hand and a soft voice. Both react badly to a beating. They always remember and will never forgive you."

"Oh, you," Millie said. "Say goodbye to your godson."

"I'll do what I can to help you and Lalo," Zeke said. "Fill a sack with jerky for them, Millie."

At the corral, Lalo had saddled his gelding and El Moro. "What about Segundo? Do we take him or leave him?"

"Saddle him. Clory is going with us."

Lalo's face wreathed in a smile when he saw Clory striding toward the corral, wearing Robbie's clothes, carrying her Kentucky long rifle and a bag of jerky. "Keep your beautiful hair tucked under that hat, *mi vida*, and maybe a blind man would think you're a boy."

"I don't care what they think so long as I can get that savage in my gun sights." Clory threw a powder horn across her shoulder and tied a bag of shot to her waist. "I'm ready."

"Let's ride then." Felipe raised his hand. "Goodbye, Zeke, thanks for your hospitality."

Zeke gave him a tanned cowhide. "This will help keep the wind and sleet off you at night. Good luck."

"Thanks. Which direction, Lalo?"

"Northwest." Lalo nudged his horse and led the way toward the rolling plains of central Texas.

Felipe remembered the map the Ranger had shown him and saw it again in his mind. Northwest. Comanche country.

CHAPTER 16

Even before she opened her eyes, Alondra heard the sleet pelting the rawhide-covered lodge. The wind shrieked and shook the teepee. What happened? Where was she? She muffled a groan and peeked through her eyelashes. She was lying on the ground, wrapped in a dirty buckskin blanket. She took in her surroundings. The flickering flames of a fire gave the only light. Yellow moons and red stars decorated the wall. On the other side of the fire pit, an Indian lay sprawled on a buffalo hide. He was asleep. She gulped and lay still, hardly daring to breathe. She remembered the terror, the struggle, the blackness. She had to escape.

The Indian stirred, rolled over on his side, and pulled the buffalo robe closer around him. Maybe she could slip away without waking him. She looked for a door but saw no opening. She tried to sit up. They had tied the blanket around her like a cocoon.

She relaxed and wriggled to loosen the blanket, but the bindings were tight. She felt for her big knife. It was gone. Alondra touched her leg. She still had her small knife. Maybe she could cut her way out.

The Indian sat up and shook the sleep from his eyes. Naked to the waist, he wore a buckskin loincloth, leggings, and moccasins. Thick, black hair hung loosely around his shoulders, a long thin plait tied with rawhide dangled over his right ear. He threw a stick on the fire and the flames leaped. He prodded Alondra with his foot and in flawless Spanish said, "Wake up."

"What do you want of me?" she asked. "Why did you bring me here?"

"To do as I ask. You are my slave."

A cold hard lump landed in her stomach. She would not show fear. "I already belong to another man. He will track you down and take me back." But would he? Alondra wasn't sure. Then she remembered his parting kiss on her hand. Warmth settled around her heart giving her courage. Felipe would come.

"I am not worried," The Indian said. "The rain has washed away our tracks. Already the sun is trying to break through the clouds and your man is not here."

Morning. What happened to the night? Maybe the Indian was right, and Felipe couldn't track her. She would have to escape and make her way back alone. There wasn't much time though, as all her life she'd heard stories of what the Comanche did to captured women. Alondra vowed that she'd think of some way to trick the Indian and never let him discover her small knife.

He stood and limped toward a fur hide hanging on the wall. She remembered the musket blast and wished that Clory's aim had been more accurate. And Pa. What of him? Had the Indian killed him?

The Indian lifted the fur that hung over a round opening and stepped out. She saw only a gray bit of sky before the flap fell to shut her inside. He shouted something and returned in a few minutes with a wooden bowl of food. "Now, we eat," he said. "But after this, you will cook my food."

"Who cooked this?"

He only grunted. "Eat."

"I can't, I am tied in this blanket."

He cut the ropes with a large knife. Her knife. She would steal it back from him while he slept. The Comanche plunged his fingers in the bowl and, after he had eaten his fill, shoved the bowl to her. There was no spoon. Alondra dipped her index finger in the stew and tasted it. Some kind of meat. She had heard that Indians ate dog. Bile rose in her throat at the thought, but she fought it down. She would need her strength to escape.

"Why did you tie me up like that?" she asked.

"To bring you here. That is the way we carry wild animals. You fought, you kicked, and you bit. My friend Bent Nose wanted to call you She-Cat, but you are my slave, and you will be known as Bird Who Dances. You will dance for me whenever I tell you.

"Two Elk," he pointed to his chest, "is a great hunter. You will have much meat to cook and many hides to tan."

After she had eaten, Alondra stood and said, "I have to relieve myself."

"Go to the trees, but do not try and escape. You will be watched. Everyone knows that Bird Who Dances belongs to Two Elk."

Alondra wrapped her *serape* tightly around her and stepped out of the teepee. A weak sun attempted to break through the heavy clouds. She glanced around the camp and her terror returned. There were several lodges scattered about. A few women tended the fires, cooking food and feeding children.

She made her way toward the trees, and a woman followed ten paces behind. Alondra walked faster; the woman stayed with her. Tied in the trees, horses stood with their backs to the wind, heads down, tails tucked between their legs.

In the tree windbreak, Alondra whirled and stared at the

woman. She was wrapped head to foot in a buffalo robe. Tendrils of yellow hair curled around her face. In the American language, Alondra said, "You are not Comanche."

"These are my people now."

"Don't you ever want to leave and go back to your own home?"

"Why would I want to leave my husband and child? I am happy, and the white people would shun me now that I'm married to a Comanche."

"But doesn't your husband beat you? I've always heard that Indians are cruel to their women."

The woman laughed. "A Comanche warrior is fierce in battle. He is stronger than a woman, so he has no need to prove it by beating her."

"What's your name?"

The lines around the woman's mouth softened. "Yellow Flower. My husband tells me I've captured the summer sky in my eyes and that I'm more beautiful than the spring flowers that bloom on the plains. But I am not beautiful. Look." She pushed the buffalo robe off her head. A red birthmark covered her right cheek and down her neck.

Alondra could think of nothing to say.

"He loves me," Yellow Flower said. "He doesn't see this ugly mark but as I really am. Some day he might take another wife, but I will never leave him."

Alondra had always thought of Indians as savages, incapable of love or other human feelings, but that didn't seem to be the case. Maybe this woman would help her escape. "Why were you sent to spy on me?" she asked.

"Two Elk does not trust you. But you do not seem foolish to me. I don't think you will try to run away. If you do, he'll bring you back and then have every right to beat you. If you do as he says, he won't harm you, he'll give you a buffalo robe to keep you warm and buy glass beads for you to wear." She turned her back. "I'm going to my lodge now. Listen to what I say. Do not try and run away." She disappeared into the trees. Alondra thought about what the woman said, but if she did not escape she might never see Felipe again. Now that she knew where they tied the horses, she would sneak out at night and steal away in the darkness.

As she walked back to the teepee, Alondra realized that she had no idea where she was, how far they'd traveled, or in which direction. She thought they were north of Zeke's ranch, but the sun hid behind heavy gray clouds. She stood in the clearing to get a sense of direction. A strong breeze blew her hair across her face. At the ranch, the storm had blown in from the northeast. Alondra turned her back to the wind and assumed she faced the southwest. She looked for a landmark but saw only stunted bushes and cholla cactus. No matter, she would walk facing the wind.

Alondra shivered against the cold. She was not accustomed to the biting north wind. For a moment, a longing for the warm wind and sunny skies of San Antonio washed over her, but she shook it off. She would never return to the life of the *cantina*, dancing for *centavos* and fighting off *borrachos*.

She stepped into the lodge, thankful for the shelter. A woman sitting beside Two Elk glared at Alondra.

"Sit," Two Elk said, and Alondra sat.

The woman snatched the *serape* off Alondra and grasped her wrist. She pinched Alondra's forearm and squeezed her breasts. The woman turned to Two Elk and said something in her native tongue.

Two Elk nodded and answered in the same language and used a word Alondra understood—*Comancheros*.

Terror swept everything else from her mind. *Comancheros*. White men who traded whiskey and guns to the Comanche in exchange for slaves and gold and who rivaled the Comanche in the monstrous atrocities they inflicted on captives. Her stomach quaked, and her heart pounded so hard it filled her chest and interfered with her breathing.

Two Elk stared at her for several moments before he spoke. "My wife, Willow," he pointed to the Indian woman, "tells me you are well named. Your bones are frail as sparrow legs and of no use for hard work. Your breasts are small as bat tits and of no use for suckling babies. Willow is my sits-beside wife, and she does not want Bird Who Dances as a sister wife."

Alondra heaved a sigh and some of the tension eased. "You will take me home then?"

"No. You belong to me. You are too weak to work as a slave. I will sell you to a white-eye who sells whiskey to the Indian and the white men. Bird Who Dances will dance for those men and inflame their loins so that my friend will sell more whiskey for the yellow and silver metal he craves."

"I do not wish to do that."

Without rising or change in expression, Two Elk reached out and backhanded her across the face. She fell back on her blanket. Willow smiled and nodded.

In an even, impassive tone, Two Elk said, "You are my slave. You will do as I tell you. We leave for the *Comancheros* at the next sunrise."

Alondra picked herself up. Her insides quivered and her limbs trembled, but she would not show fear. She clenched her fists at her sides to prevent her hands from shaking. "What will your friend pay you? How much am I worth?"

"You're not worth so very much, no flesh on your bones. Maybe one pony and two buffalo robes."

That surprised Alondra. She had heard that, even though it was against the law, those men sold guns to the Indians. "Not even one rifle?"

Two Elk sneered. "A Comanche has no need for the fire stick. See my wound." He pointed to his leg. "It is nothing. An arrow would do much more damage."

"I won't dance unless he pays you at least two ponies, three buffalo robes, and an iron pot."

Two Elk guffawed and spoke to his wife. Willow smiled

and gazed at Alondra with a hint of respect in her eyes.

Alondra thought she might have a chance to escape, but she would have to control her terror and stay alert for every opportunity. It seemed to her she'd lived her life in that manner, hiding her fear until it became a cold, hard ball that she juggled from one corner in her mind to another to keep it from rolling over her. This time, though, she had Felipe to give her strength. He was coming. She could feel his nearness, could almost smell his scent. Alondra wrapped her *serape* around her shoulders. She would be ready when he came. Her mind busy on escape plans, she waited for Two Elk to issue his next order.

CHAPTER 17

Felipe, Lalo, and Clory spent the night wrapped in blankets. They huddled together under the cowhide that did little to protect them from the storm. The wind flapped the hide, whipped the rain sideways, and nipped their faces. Felipe had built a fire, but fuel was scarce, and the wild gusts overpowered the meager flame. They were grateful when, toward morning, the wind carried the freezing rain south.

At the first streak of dawn, they rose from their cramped positions, stomped their feet, and blew on their fingers. The horses hadn't fared any better and were eager to move but balked when forced to face the wind.

"This danged horse is stubborn as my pa's mules," Clory shouted. Lalo grabbed the reins and led the reluctant horse.

Felipe rode stiff and silent, his face like carved marble, his eyes as hard as green malachite. Neither Lalo nor Clory spoke to him, and he was free to focus on Alondra. Without her, he felt aimless as the tumbleweed, wandering where the wind blew. An invisible thread joined them, and the bond between them was strong, so powerful he was certain that he could find her even without Lalo's expert tracking ability. The wind wailed, and, to Felipe's mind, it was her voice calling him, begging him to hurry. He sent her thoughts of love and encouragement and prayed he would reach her in time.

On the third day, Lalo caught sight of horse tracks. He reined his horse, dismounted, scanned the ground, and touched the earth. The trail was maybe a day old, but they were on the track. He walked around a few paces, found further evidence of horses, and mounted his gelding. He raised his arm in a forward motion. Clory jabbed Segundo with her spurs. The horse leaped forward and followed Lalo.

Felipe sat on El Moro and listened. He heard the wind, the soft crunch of horse hooves, his own breathing, but he did not hear Alondra, nor did he sense her. It was as though the cruel wind had blown her fragile essence into a dark place where he could not follow, and dread struck him to the core. He nudged El Moro and followed Lalo.

They rode without stopping until the sun passed the midday mark. Lalo raised his hand, and Felipe and Clory rode even with him.

Felipe sniffed the air. The wind had eased but it carried the faint scent of burning mesquite wood. They rode until they reached a clump of brush. Spirals of campfire smoke blew southward.

"The camp is near. I smell the smoke of their fires," he said. He dismounted and tied El Moro to a bush. "You two stay here while I scout the camp. I'll return shortly."

"I want my chance at those savages," Clory said. "I'm going with you."

"Keep her here, Lalo. When you hear this," he gave the four-toned call of the mourning dove, "you'll know I'm coming in."

"I should go with you. I know what those Indians look like."

"You'll get your chance soon enough, Clory. I want to see where they are keeping Alondra." Felipe disappeared in the brush.

He slipped through the bushes without making a sound, sometimes on hands and knees, sometimes on his belly, sometimes upright, until he came to a clearing. The camp was situated on the east side of a stream and near a stand of trees. He counted fifteen rawhide lodges, all facing east. He saw no men, only women working around their teepees and a few children playing. He knew, without knowing how he knew, that Alondra was no longer in the camp.

In the time when his grandfather was young, the New Mexicans had formed an alliance with the Comanche. Together, they had fought the Apache, ancient enemies of both peoples. The Apache were forced west and south over the mountains and to the deserts. The nomad Comanche moved southward, so Felipe learned little of their ways. What he knew was stories told around campfires, of Comanche raids across Texas and deep into Mexico, of how they stole women and children for slaves, of horses stolen at night under a full moon, what the storytellers called the Comanche moon.

Felipe knew the Apache though. His ancestors had fought them for centuries, and he had grown to adulthood hearing tales of massacres and plunder. The Apache still made an occasional raid on the ranches for horses and for the mules that they considered an especially tasty delicacy. If the Comanche were like the Apache, they had a guard posted.

Felipe slipped through the trees, dropped to the ground, and listened. From the camp, a man's voice shouted, a nearby voice answered. Felipe lifted his head. A fully armed warrior stood ankle-deep in the river. He wore owl feathers plaited into his scalp lock, and in one hand he held a tether line. Horses milled about him, drinking, pawing the water.

Silent as a snake, Felipe slithered through the tall grass to the river's edge. He drew his pistol, leaped over the bank, and waded into the water, skirting the milling horses. Before the man was aware of him, Felipe struck the Indian on the head with the butt of his gun. The Comanche fell into the river. Felipe bound him hand and foot with the tether line, cut off a length of the rope, and gagged him.

Felipe caught the nearest pony and threw the unconscious warrior across its back. The other horses scattered, and he led the pony up the bank and through the meadow, unconcerned that he left a track of flattened grass.

He whistled the dove's call before he reached the brush where Lalo and Clory waited.

"What do you have there?" Clory asked.

"An informer."

"What has he told you?" Lalo asked.

"Nothing yet." Felipe dumped the Indian on the ground and stroked the pony. "This is a good horse. We'll need him for when we get Alondra back."

Lalo glanced from the warrior to his friend. He could not think of the American word, but he had never seen Felipe act so *despiadado*, although handling the mustang seemed to relax him. "I think it would be a good idea to get this man far away from camp before he wakes up. He'll make noise when you remove the gag to question him." He helped Felipe load the warrior on the horse, and, with the Indian pony between them, they rode downwind from the camp several miles until they reached a dry riverbed. The horses scrambled down the steep sides, and Felipe shoved the warrior off the pony and into the dirt and pebbles.

The Indian was awake and glared at them, his eyes flashing threats of sharp knives and poisoned arrows.

"Watch the horses, Clory." With his dagger, Felipe cut the gag from the Comanche. "Do you understand what I say?" The warrior stared at him, face blank, muscles taut.

"You have gotten in the habit of speaking American," Lalo said. "Try Spanish. Many Comanche speak our language."

Felipe repeated his question in Spanish. The Indian's eyelids flickered. "I think Owl Feather understands." Felipe hauled the warrior upright and held him against the dirt bank.

The Indian squirmed and twisted.

Felipe ignored his gyrations. "What do you know of the captive woman brought to your camp two suns ago?"

The man didn't reply; his body quivered with hate and resentment.

In English Lalo said, "He's embarrassed, Felipe, ashamed that he was captured. He won't answer, there's no way we can make him talk. He'll die first. He pretty much figures he's a dead man anyway."

"We have to make him talk, Lalo. Alondra isn't in the camp. They've taken her someplace and we have to find where."

"I'll go scout around for tracks. Was it a large party of them, do you think?"

Felipe released the Indian and he fell to the ground. "Besides Owl Feather and one other warrior, I saw only women and children in the—"

"Look out," Clory shouted, and her rifle boomed.

Felipe turned, the Indian lay at his feet, blood gushed from his shoulder. Lalo pulled out his pistol and scanned the *arroyo* crest.

"I was watching him," Clory said. "I had to shoot him before he got loose."

"He was tied up, Clory. I think I could have handled him."

"I don't know. Indians are mighty tricky. My pa always says that the only good Indian is a dead Indian. Look out! He's still alive." She trained her gun sights on Owl Feather.

"Don't shoot him again, Clory," Felipe said. "We need him to tell us where they took Alondra." He bent over Owl Feather. "Can you hear me?"

"He won't talk. He already knows he will die, and of course we can't let him live." Lalo scratched his chin with his pistol barrel. "But we can let him choose the way he dies."

"What do you mean?" Felipe asked.

"Like a warrior, with honor, free and with a weapon in his hand, and before nightfall."

"Why wait until nightfall?" Clory asked.

"Because the Comanche do not want to die at night. They believe their spirit can't find its way to the Shadow Land in the dark," Lalo said.

"Don't wait," Clory said. "Shoot him now. Them Indians are worse than coyotes, you can't trust them."

"If he gives us his word we can trust him," Lalo said. "It's a matter of honor with the Comanche, and for some reason they think it is for us too."

"I always keep my word," Felipe said. "He will die with honor."

Lalo nodded. "I will talk to him. I think he respects you, thinks of you as a chief. After I talk to him, you can give him your word. Then maybe he will believe us."

"You're wasting your time," Clory said. "I still think you should shoot him and get it done with."

Lalo went to her, held both her arms, and smiled down at her. "Put your gun away, *mi vida*, first we have to get information from him."

Clory leaned her head on his shoulder. "You don't understand, Lalo. They killed my pa."

He held her in his arms and gently rocked her. "I do understand, *querida*. But let me take care of this. You've already done more than a woman should."

She backed away and glared at him. "What do you mean, more than a woman should?"

Lalo laughed and kissed the tip of her nose. "Even when you're angry, those beautiful blue eyes sparkle with laughter."

"You can't sweet-talk me, Lalo Chaves, let me tell you that I—"

He stopped her words by pressing his lips to hers. He gazed into her eyes. "Put your gun away, mi *vida*," he said, his voice low and tender.

Clory turned from him and leaned her forehead against her horse.

Lalo placed a gentle hand on her shoulder. "We won't let your father's death go unavenged. I promise."

"On your honor?"

"On my honor." Lalo flashed his white teeth in a wide grin. "If that's not good enough, then on Felipe's honor."

Clory chuckled and picked up her rifle. "All right, but I'm holding you to it."

Smiling, Lalo sauntered toward Felipe and the Indian they called Owl Feather. "It's good to hold a woman again," Lalo said to Felipe. "Even if she is dressed in boy's clothes and has the temper of a caged wildcat."

They sat on their heels beside Owl Feather. "What have your people done with the woman captive?" Lalo asked.

Owl Feather said nothing, his eyes flat, his expression immobile. Blood from his wound trickled on his bare chest.

"You know that we cannot allow you to live, so you might as well tell us." Lalo picked up a pebble and tossed it from hand to hand. "Because if you don't tell us, we will wait until it is dark, when there is no moon, and then kill you."

Owl Feather blinked.

Lalo threw the pebble into the dirt bank. "But if you do tell us, we will allow you to die with honor." Owl Feather tried to sit up. "You have my word on it and that of the chief here." Lalo jerked his thumb to Felipe.

Owl Feather turned his gaze to Felipe. "Does he speak the truth? I will be allowed to die with honor?"

"Yes," Felipe said. "If you tell us what we want to know, I will set you free and give you a weapon."

With a sly look, Owl Feather asked, "And will I die with a horse between my legs?"

"No, no horse." Felipe glanced toward the sky. "The sun is low in the heavens. You better make your mind up soon. After sundown, we will tie you to a stake, and when it is full dark, we will kill you."

Owl Feather turned his face skyward and with a worried frown said, "I will tell you what I know. They took the woman to the *Comancheros*."

Felipe kept his features a mask, but his eyes flashed green. "Why?"

"To sell her, of course. She is a slave."

Felipe stood. He clenched his hands. Alondra would have little chance with the *Comancheros*, renegades afoul of the law, men with no respect for women and with no regard for human life. His insides roiled at the thought of what the *Comancheros* would do to a woman like Alondra, and Felipe vowed that he would see the man dead who so much as touched her.

"Where is the *Comancheros*' camp?" Lalo asked.

Owl Feather jerked his head and, with his chin, pointed to the south. "Their cabin is down that way, a half day's ride."

Lalo turned to Felipe. "Do you believe him?"

"Yes. Cut him loose so we can be on our way."

"With that many horses, the trail should be easy to follow even though it will be dark soon. Do you really want me to turn him free?"

"Yes, we gave him our word," Felipe said.

Lalo shrugged. "With that gunshot wound, he won't live long anyway. What weapon?"

"A knife. But be careful, step back, and then throw it at his feet." Felipe drew his own dagger, held it ready.

Lalo cut the bindings, stepped back ten paces, and tossed his knife. Swift as a lizard, Owl Feather grabbed the knife. With a wild yell that split the air, he leaped at Lalo and with the speed of a rattlesnake struck at him with the knife. Lalo sidestepped, swung his arm, and knocked Owl Feather to the ground. Clory's musket roared and the Indian lay curled in a pool of blood.

They turned at the sound of galloping hoofbeats. Another Comanche, in full war paint, whooping, brandishing a war club, and riding a mustang smeared with red and yellow paint, thundered toward them. The Indian kicked his pony's flanks. It jumped the bank and, without breaking stride, sped toward Felipe.

With only a split second to act, Felipe threw his dagger, dropped to the ground, and rolled in a ball to escape the horse's hooves. The Indian clawed at his neck, blood gurgled from his throat. He fell to the ground, twitched, and lay still. The mustang galloped down the draw.

Felipe picked up the fallen weapons: the war club, bow and attached quiver of arrows, and a leather sling. He pulled his knife from the dead Indian and wiped the blade on his leg. "Pack up. Let's go before the entire village comes down on us." He tied the Comanche pony's reins to his saddle horn.

CHAPTER 18

Alondra rode behind Two Elk with her wrists tied together and a rope around her waist that the Indian held in his hand. Seven Comanche warriors rode bunched around them. She believed that Felipe would search for her, but he wouldn't know the *Comancheros* had her. Her breath caught in her throat when Alondra thought of those ruthless men.

After several long hours of nonstop riding, doubts that Felipe could find her crowded her mind. Maybe the rain had washed away the tracks. Maybe the Indians had killed everyone at Zeke's house. She remembered seeing Pa with a tomahawk in his back. Alondra shook her head, she couldn't think about that now, but so many things could keep Felipe from finding her right away, she would have to escape on her own.

She noted landmarks of every large rock and grove of trees. The sun slipped past the midday mark and shone on her left shoulder. They were headed south, so when she escaped, she'd travel to the north, and hide in the trees and rocks from the Indians until Felipe found her.

She would wait two days, then if Felipe didn't find her,

she'd continue north until she reached Saint Louis. He knew she wanted to go there, and he'd follow her to that city. She hadn't thought about Saint Louis for days, but now the old dream came back, blotting out the fear of the *Comancheros*.

The *Comanchero* camp, a cabin built of natural sandstone blocks, smelled like a *cantina*, of stale sweat, tobacco, and whiskey. A bulky Mexican they called Tito, who apparently was in charge, greeted Two Elk and his warriors. They called the other man Julio. He was old and didn't talk much.

Several tables and benches were placed in a circle around the large room. Buffalo robes, wooden crates, bolts of cloth, and tin and iron goods were stacked in the corners and along the walls.

Two Elk shoved Alondra into a dark room at the rear of the cabin and shut the door. Someone struck a light and lit a tallow candle. It glowed on a small table and showed two cots with rawhide mattresses shoved against one wall. There was a slit of a window near the ceiling and a stinking chamber pot in a corner. Two women sat on one cot, and Alondra was heartened. Maybe they would want to come with her when she escaped.

"Are you captives too?" she asked. They ignored her and whispered together about the new woman.

Alondra studied the women: their stringy and unwashed hair, their soiled and stained clothes, their faces as pale as balls of *tortilla* dough. They aroused her pity. "Is there no escape from here, then?" she asked.

As one, they rose from the cot, and, with curled lips and slitted eyes, they cast dark glances at her. They walked out, leaving the door ajar.

In some ways, they were more frightening than any of the men Alondra had seen. Never would she be like those women. She touched her leg where her little knife rested on her thigh. It comforted her.

She peeked through the open door. The Indians drank

whiskey and Two Elk argued with Tito. Alondra blew out the candle and sat on a cot. She heard rustling noises in the corner and pulled her feet up on the bed and wrapped her arms around her knees. For what seemed like hours, she stared at the *cantina* through the square of dim candlelight.

No one went to bed. They slept curled on the floor or with their heads on tables. They awoke and poured more whiskey, argued, and fell asleep again. Two Elk wanted to complete the sale. Tito insisted that he couldn't do business without his other partners, and until they arrived he wouldn't even watch Alondra dance.

Alondra sat on the cot and plotted her escape. Eventually, these *borrachos* would drink themselves into a stupor, and then she'd sneak out and head toward the Comanche camp. But Tito and Julio took turns sleeping. They warily watched the Indians and sent an occasional speculative glance her way. She was grateful no one had touched her or even spoken to her. Toward dawn, she rested her head on her knees and fell into a light doze.

*****

Felipe, Lalo, and Clory rode until full dark, with only a sliver of moon to light their way.

Lalo pointed to the black shapes of trees. "We better stop there for the night. We're not sure how much farther the *Comancheros'* cabin is, and there may be a lookout or a trap that we'd never see in the dark."

They angled toward the trees and stopped at the edge of the dark shadows. They dismounted and approached the grove, alert for any danger sign. In the distance, a coyote yelped. Deep in the trees, an owl hooted. A small animal rustled in the bushes.

"It's safe, I think," Lalo whispered.

They wound their way around trees and bushes, toward

the sound of a river, until they came to a place where the undergrowth thinned.

"We'll camp here," Felipe said. "There's grass for the horses. It will be a cold camp; we can't risk a fire." They unsaddled the horses and spread their blankets under trees.

With only the stars to see by, Felipe led the horses to the river. He filled the leather water flasks and, after the horses all drank their fill, returned to camp.

He spent a restless night listening to the night sounds and praying he would reach Alondra before she was harmed. In the hour of the false dawn, he saddled the horses. He made a saddle for the Comanche pony from the cowhide and lengths of rawhide rope. He cached the Indian weapons under a bushy tree and covered them with dry leaves and twigs. The others awoke, and all three chewed on jerky and sipped from the water bags.

"What are your plans, my friend?" Lalo asked.

Felipe shrugged. "Enter the *Comanchero* camp, bring Alondra out, and head for New Mexico."

"Yes, but we should have a plan. It won't be easy getting into their camp."

"It will be easier for one man. You and Clory stay here."

Lalo snorted. "I don't think so. I can't let you have all the fun. Besides, I gave Clory my word, remember?" He turned to her. "You will see that I, too, am a man of honor."

Clory looked up into his face. "I don't want you to do this for me, Lalo. I got my revenge. I'll stay here with you."

Lalo shook his head. "You tempt me greatly, *mi vida*, but two men with guns have a better chance against the *Comancheros*. I will go with Felipe."

In Spanish, Felipe said, "Now it is you who are in trouble, my friend."

Lalo grinned. "All she needs is a strong hand and a tight rein. I could soon tame her, but then it would not be so exciting."

Clory glared at them, hands fisted on her hips. "Y'all are talking about me, ain't you? I'll take it kindly if from now on when you talk about me, you'll say it in American, or else teach me Spanish."

Lalo chuckled and put an arm around her shoulders. He hugged her tight. "Ah, my little spitfire, I can teach you many things. After this is over, we will spend many hours in the moonlight learning from each other."

Trying not to laugh, her lips twitched. "And don't think I'll let you forget that promise, neither."

Felipe clapped Lalo on the shoulder. "I'll dance at your wedding, *amigo*, but for now, let's get moving."

The sun was but a golden glow on the eastern horizon, and they were on the trail. With the Comanche pony tied to his saddle horn, Lalo rode ahead scanning for tracks. The trail led away from the river, through a rocky valley and up a gradual slope.

Lalo raised his hand. Felipe and Clory reined in beside him. A thin plume of smoke rose from an unseen chimney. "I've been thinking, Felipe. We'll tell them that we're *banditos*, running from the soldiers in Mexico and we want to join the *Comancheros*. We'll strap on two of our pistols, walk into their camp with one in our hand, a rifle in the other, and dare them to doubt us." Lalo grinned. "Make sure all the guns are loaded, Felipe, and that you speak only Spanish."

"That's a good idea, but you don't have to come with me, Lalo. I'll go alone."

"No, it would work much better if there are two of us and we can watch each other's backs. It will be like a rattlesnake pit in there, they'll come at us from all sides if we're not careful."

They rode to the crest of the hill and surveyed the valley. Nestled among pines was a rock cabin built against a high sandstone bluff. The roof was made of sod, the door of hand-hewn planks. They saw no windows. A corral built of upright pine poles held horses and mules. Eight Comanche ponies stood tied to the corral posts.

A horse nickered. To the east, a cloud of dust rose in the clear morning air. "Dismount," Lalo murmured. They led their horses into a stand of brush.

Two men rode into the corral and turned their mounts loose. The animals crowded around a hollowed-out log, snorting and stomping their hooves. In a loud voice, one of the men said, "Tell Julio to water the horses. They're as thirsty as I am." The two men strode toward the cabin.

Felipe, Lalo, and Clory crouched behind the bushes. "We'll wait half an hour and then go in," Felipe said.

"I know I can't talk any sense into you two, so what will I do while y'all are getting yourselves killed?" Clory asked.

"We'll find a good lookout point with protection, and you can watch the door," Felipe said. "Give us a warning if anyone else shows up. Keep our horses near you and be ready to ride when you see us come out."

"Their horses are thirsty," Lalo said. "I think we should open the gate and allow them to find water."

Felipe nodded. "And cut the tethers of the Indian ponies and urge them on their way with a slap or two on the rump."

"How're y'all going to do all that without them *Comancheros* seeing you?" Clory asked. "While you two are in the cabin, I'll sneak down and turn the horses loose."

"I haven't seen any sign of a lookout and that bothers me," Felipe said.

"They probably don't have one," Lalo said. "The Rangers don't come this far north, and the Mexican and American soldiers are all fighting a war."

Felipe pointed to a pile of boulders surrounded by bushes about a hundred yards from the cabin door. "Wait until we are in the cabin before you set the horses free, Clory. Wait for us there in the rocks and be ready to ride."

*****

Pots and pans banged on a table and jarred Alondra awake. Julio had prepared a meal and shouted that food was ready. She rose from the cot and peered into the *cantina*. The two women sat at a table, sloe-eyed and slack mouthed. Several Indians slept with their heads on a table. One lay sleeping on the dirt floor, unaware of the red ants crawling up his arm. Two Elk was awake, still arguing with Tito, who sat at a corner table, shoveling down his food.

Julio glanced up and noticed Alondra standing in the doorway. Without saying a word, he offered her a filled plate.

The smell of cooked bacon and the sight of a biscuit drenched in sorghum molasses made her stomach grumble from hunger. Alondra took the plate, sat on the cot, and wolfed down the food.

Outdoors, spurs clanked, and a gruff voice shouted, "Hey, in there. Are you awake?"

Tito answered with a babble of loud talk. A tall, blond man they called Mac and a swarthy, shorter man they called Pepé entered the cabin. "We've been riding all night," Mac said, "with no rest and nothing to show for it."

Pepé laughed. "He's in a temper now, but all he needs is something to eat."

"Julio," Tito shouted, "Bring food. The boss is here." The two new men sat at a table and the women climbed on their laps.

Mac asked, "What did the Comanche bring for trade?"

Alondra held her breath while Tito answered. "A woman. Two Elk claims she is worth two ponies and three buffalo robes."

"What makes her so valuable?" Pepé asked.

"The way she dances. Two Elk tells me that he stood in the bushes until after dark, watching her dance. He wanted to keep her for himself, but his wife wouldn't allow it. He claims her dance will inflame the loins of any man and cause him to spend gold just to watch her."

Pepé snorted. "A woman is a woman. They are all alike."

Tito shrugged palms up. "I do not know. I haven't seen her dance, we waited until you arrived."

Mac shoved his woman away and cleared the table with one swipe of his massive hand. Tin plates clattered to the ground and the column of red ants marched to a shiny glob of molasses on the dirt floor. "Tell Two Elk to show us what his woman can do."

"You will see what happens when she dances." Two Elk rubbed his crotch.

Alondra shrank back into the dark room and slipped her small knife into her pocket. Two Elk burst into her hiding place and dragged her out by the arm. He pulled her to the center of the floor. She stood with shoulders hunched and head down. Maybe if she didn't dance, they wouldn't want her.

"She doesn't look like much," Mac said, and his woman smirked.

Two Elk poked Alondra in the ribs. "Dance."

With one arm around his woman's waist, Pepé pounded the tabletop with his other palm. "Up here where we can see."

Alondra stood very still. Her brain whirled. She had spent the night thinking only of escape, somehow this moment hadn't crossed her mind.

Two Elk squeezed her arm and spoke in her ear. "Dance or I will sell you for their woman. You'll be no better than those *brujas*."

Terror swept through her. For years, Alondra had used wit and bravado to pull herself from tight places, and now she prayed that something would occur to her so she wouldn't have to dance. She pushed her fear away, breathed deeply, and, when she could speak, said, "I can't dance without music."

Mac picked her up as though she were nothing but a rag

doll and stood her on the table. "Julio," he shouted, "bring your guitar. Tito, pour us some whiskey, and let's see what this woman can do."

Tito held up his hand. "Wait, someone is coming." He stepped out the door, his frame filled the opening.

Felipe and Lalo rode side by side down the hill, singing, laughing, and talking loudly.

"Who are you? What do you want?" Tito asked.

"Whiskey," shouted Felipe. "We want whiskey."

A wave of relief swept through Alondra when she heard his voice. Felipe was here. Her fears evaporated and her inner strength returned.

"Where do you come from?" Tito asked.

Lalo waved his pistol. "Mexico, and we've had no rest. The soldiers chased us for many leagues."

"Did you lead the soldiers here?" Tito asked.

"No." Felipe blew imaginary smoke from his pistol barrel. "Those soldiers will never chase anyone again."

Tito laughed. "Come in. If you have gold, we have whiskey, and today we have entertainment. They call me Tito. Who are you?"

"They call me Felipe, this is Lalo. We've not been idle; we have plenty of gold."

"These two *hombres* come from Mexico and want a taste of our whiskey," Tito said.

"Come in," Mac shouted. "We can always use some of that Mexican silver."

Felipe entered the cabin, Lalo at his back. Standing on the table, Alondra noticed Felipe's slight wink. He and Lalo took seats on benches nearest the open door. She had no idea what plans they had, or how they could overpower twelve men, but she would be ready.

"Dance," Two Elk demanded, and Julio plucked the guitar.

"Wait," Felipe shouted. "We came here for whiskey. Where is it?"

"Give them their whiskey, Tito," Mac said. "I want to watch the dancer."

Tito plunked a bottle on the table. "All right, Julio, music."

Julio strummed a lively tune. Alondra glanced at Felipe. With the barest tilt of his head, he nodded. He wanted her to dance. She twirled, rolled her shoulders and hips, and her skirt swirled high.

"Oh, ho," Pepé shouted. "That's more like it." He stood, and his woman fell to the floor with an angry thump. He leaped on the table and danced.

Once again, Alondra glanced at Felipe. He rose from his seat and leaned against the doorjamb. Not a muscle twitched in his face, but his eyes had turned the dangerous shade of green. Alondra knew that whatever he planned, it would happen soon.

Felipe clapped his hands, stomped his feet, and shouted "*Olé!*"

Alondra whirled faster. The men stared at her, mesmerized by her grace, her agility.

Julio slowed the tempo, pulling notes out of the guitar until they throbbed with passion, and Alondra danced with the music. Pepé drew her to him and ,with one hand on the small of her back, leaned over her. His other hand crept under her skirt and up her leg. Alondra twisted away from him, jumped off the table, and twirled in the direction of the open door. He laughed and hopped down, circled his hands over his head, and danced toward her with short, tapping steps.

From the corner of her eye, Alondra saw Felipe's knife flash. Pepé stopped dancing. Eyes wide, he gaped at the dagger protruding from his belly.

Alondra danced and twirled until she stood directly in front of Pepé. She gripped the handle, twisted the dagger, and with an upward stroke pulled out the blade. She whirled to the door.

"Go," Felipe mouthed and filled the doorway with a

commanding stance.

She ran out the door, the bloodstained knife clutched in her hand. Outside, she paused, dazed by the bright sun.

Clory waved to her from behind the boulders. "Over here, hurry."

Alondra ran to Clory and sank to the ground gasping for breath.

In the *cantina*, Julio plucked the guitar, his eyes half-lidded. Pepé grabbed at his stomach. Blood oozed through his fingers and puddled on the dirt floor. He sank to his knees in a pool of blood. For a moment, everyone watched the scene in stunned silence.

Julio stopped strumming and Mac came to his senses. "What the hell? That little bitch stabbed him!" He made for the door. Lalo stretched out his foot and tripped him.

"Sorry," Lalo said and helped Mac to his feet.

"Get the hell out of my way." Mac shoved Lalo aside and ran out the door.

Clory's musket boomed, and Mac lay sprawled across the entrance.

Women screamed, men shouted and rushed to the door. Felipe broke the bottle of whiskey on Tito's head. Lalo kicked a table over and threw a bench into the crowd of men.

With their guns drawn, they backed out the door and stepped over the fallen *Comanchero*.

Two Elk pushed his way through the knot of men and out the door. The only horses in sight were El Moro and Lalo's gray gelding. "The woman took my horse!" He reached for El Moro.

Felipe grabbed the bridle. El Moro snorted and tossed his head.

The Comanche brandished his knife. Felipe shoved his gun into the Indian's chest and pulled the trigger, and Two Elk lay crumpled in the dust.

"Let's ride," Felipe shouted and vaulted onto El Moro's

back.

Lalo jumped on his horse, and they followed Alondra and Clory, who were already mounted and galloping up the hill. Arrows whined over their heads. A lone pistol shot sounded. The bullet thudded in the dirt behind them.

CHAPTER 19

They galloped until they reached the juniper grove where Felipe had stashed the bow and arrows. He dismounted and picked up the weapons. He turned to Alondra. "Did they hurt you?"

"No."

Felipe nodded, face grim. "Let's keep moving. We're not far from the Comanche camp, we can't take the chance they won't come looking for those two back in the *arroyo*."

He heard a soft sound and glanced up. Lalo's face was gray and lined with pain, an arrow protruded from his side. "*Dios mio*! You've been hit!"

Clory jumped from her horse. "The arrow has to come out. I'll help you down."

Lalo shook his head. "I can ride farther."

"Don't be stubborn, Lalo. We can stop for a few minutes."

"Get on your horse, Clory," Lalo said in a voice that left no room for argument. "Felipe is right. Let's ride on."

"I'll scout ahead for a safe place to camp for the night," Felipe said. "The rest of you follow at a slower pace."

Alondra reached her hand toward him. "Felipe—"

"Later, *querida*, we'll talk later." With a pang, Felipe realized she had lost her *serape*. She would be cold, but he could do nothing about that now.

Clory climbed onto the Comanche pony and held her rifle across her lap. Without a word, she primed the musket and poured powder in the pan. He had no need to remind her to watch their back trail.

Felipe mounted his horse and loped north, following the river, careful to stay among the trees.

He was in unfamiliar territory, and again visualized the map the Ranger had shown him. The prairie fire had pushed them far to the east but since then, they'd continually traveled in a northwesterly direction. Zeke's ranch was situated on the westerly edge of the grasslands, and the Comanche camp on the southerly end of the *Llano Estacado*. There was little water on the staked plains, but to the west of the *llano* lay the Pecos River and, beyond that, the Guadalupe Mountains. Felipe realized he was on the Pecos River.

The meandering stream with its headwaters in the *Sangre de Cristo* Mountain range in New Mexico would lead them home. He thanked the saints that they had not, after all, wandered too far off course.

The mountains were still gripped in winter, but with the spring thaw the river would swell from snowmelt. The Comanche camp was situated on the east bank so they would have to cross the river.

He'd find a safe crossing and they'd travel home on the west bank of the Pecos.

A flock of geese winging north veered west, following the river. Felipe reined in El Moro and scanned the horizon. Nothing moved, but they were near the Comanche camp. At the next bend of the river, he found a gravel bar for a safe crossing. He turned and loped back to his companions.

Alondra had donned Lalo's old uniform jacket and led his horse. Lalo sat hunched in the saddle, chin on his chest. Clory brought up the rear, turning in the saddle every few yards, a watchful eye on the back trail. Felipe's heart soared at the sight of the valiant women. He vowed that, when they were home, he would send to Santa Fe for new weapons: for Alondra, a new knife made of the finest Toledo steel, and for Clory, a modern, shorter-barreled rifle.

"We'll follow the river," Felipe said. "The Comanche camp is upstream, but we'll cross below them and find a campsite on the other side."

"Lalo can't ride much farther, he needs rest," Clory said.

"We'll stay in the camp until he's well enough to travel. It's not far to the crossing. I'll ride beside him, so that he doesn't fall. Let's go." Felipe took the gelding's reins from Alondra, and knee to knee with Lalo, set the pace at a canter.

The sun was sinking by the time they reached the shallow crossing. Felipe led Lalo's horse across, the women followed. Fifty yards from the riverbank, Felipe stopped in a bower of cottonwood and low-growing pine with grass and bushes for the horses. He helped Lalo dismount.

"Tend to him, Clory," Felipe said.

Clory rummaged in the saddlebags for her healing herbs and rushed to Lalo. With his knife, Felipe cut pine boughs, and Alondra made a bed of the boughs and spread Lalo's saddle blanket over them. She and Clory helped him lie down.

"The arrow needs to come out, Felipe," Clory said. "I'll need hot water. Is it safe to have a fire?"

Felipe built a fire under the green limbs of a pine, where the branches diffused the smoke, and the wind would blow it away before anyone could detect it. He warned of the need for caution because they were only about a league from the Comanche camp. The women nodded.

Felipe took his cotton shirt from the saddlebag, knelt beside Lalo, and prodded for the arrowhead. Lalo grunted.

Felipe said, "I don't think it's too deep, but it will hurt if I pull it out. Some people leave the arrowhead in, and sometimes it does work its way out."

Lalo shook his head. "Take it out. It can't hurt much worse than it does now."

"I'll try to get it out in one pull. Do you think you can stand it, *amigo*?"

Lalo gritted his teeth. "I wish I had some of that whiskey you emptied on the *Comanchero*, but find me a stick, just in case."

Felipe whittled a piece of pinewood smooth, and Lalo placed the stick between his teeth and clenched his hands.

"Hold his shoulders, Clory," Felipe said. "Sit on his legs, Alondra, and hold him down." He braced his foot on Lalo's back, bent, grasped the arrow shaft, took a deep breath, and pulled. Flesh tore and blood flowed as the arrowhead came out. Lalo groaned and spat out the stick.

Felipe handed his cotton shirt to Clory, tears streaming down her cheeks. "Use this to bind the wound," he said.

Clory wiped her eyes with her fist and poured water from her flask into her tin cup. "Heat this," she said to Alondra, "until the powder dissolves."

Alondra took the cup. "What is it?" Tears stood in her eyes.

"Comfrey root powder. Ma insisted I bring it, she thought we might need it." Clory tore Felipe's shirt into strips. She removed Lalo's shirt and, from her water flask, moistened a cloth and dabbed at his wound. He gasped, moaned, and twitched.

Clory leaned down and kissed Lalo on the forehead. "It's not just a little scratch, how do you call me? *Mi vida*? It's a deep wound. Lie still, it's going to hurt powerful bad."

Lalo tried to smile, but it turned into a grimace. He clutched her hand. "Don't leave me."

Clory sat on the ground, stretched out her legs, and put his head on her lap. "I won't. Not ever, you can't get rid of me."

Felipe handed her the tin cup. "What are you going to do with this?"

"It's a healing herb," she said and with a piece of the shirt, smeared the jelly-like substance on the wound. "It's good for cuts and such, he'll be better in the morning, as long as he doesn't move around too much." She wound cloth around Lalo's middle.

Felipe cut two stakes from some dry wood and pounded them in the ground on either side of Lalo. He draped the cowhide over the stakes and anchored the lean-to with rocks. "Stay with him, Clory, and keep him warm." He handed her one of the water bags. "Have him drink plenty of water."

He cut more pine boughs. "Make our bed, Alondra, I'm going hunting." He picked up the bow and arrows and slipped into the woods.

Alondra stared at Felipe's retreating back. She couldn't believe her ears. "Our bed," he'd said. She wanted to talk to someone about it, but Clory had crawled under the lean-to and lay snuggled next to Lalo.

Alondra chose a secluded spot under a low-growing pine and spread the boughs. She gathered ferns that were growing by the river and carried an armful to her bed. She tested the softness and covered the greenery with a saddle blanket. Wedged in the bottom of her saddlebag, she found a piece of yucca root and her extra clothes.

At the river, she used her dirty blouse and scrubbed herself to remove the stench of the past four days. She wanted a full bath, but the water was too cold, so she dunked her head in the river and washed her hair. She put on her clean clothes and laundered her soiled clothing.

She remembered what the blonde woman at the Comanche camp had said about not ever going back to her home after being with the Indians. What did Felipe think of her now that the Indians and the *Comancheros* had held her captive? He had said little.

Alondra draped her laundry on bushes deep in the woods, combed her hair, filled the coffee pot with water, and set it on a flat rock next to the fire. With her small knife, she sharpened green sticks and made a spit for whatever game Felipe would bring home.

Home. It didn't matter where they were, if she was with Felipe, it was home. She hoped Felipe hadn't changed his mind about her since her capture. She wondered how far they had traveled and when they would reach his ranch. A cold knot twisted in her stomach when she thought about what would happen when they reached his *hacienda*. Did he still intend on marrying that highborn lady? Alondra wouldn't ask him, she wanted nothing to ruin this time with him, even if it didn't last. If only he'd talk to her.

She sensed his presence long before he walked into camp with a goose dangling from his hand. He glanced at her, smiled into her eyes, handed over the wild game, and, without a word, walked away.

Alondra plucked and cleaned the goose, put the liver and heart in the pot of water, cut off the wings, and added them. This would make a good broth for Lalo. She worried about him. She placed the goose on the fire to cook, buried the feathers and innards, and waited for Felipe's return.

Grease sizzled and sputtered into the fire. "That smells good," Felipe said.

She glanced up. He'd been to the river. His face shone, water glistening in his hair. "Dinner's not ready yet. I'm making broth for Lalo and saved the goose fat in case we need it for his wound. I wish we had an onion, it would make the goose taste better and it would be good for the broth. I guess we lost the corn flour because I couldn't find it, so we won't have any *tortillas*, and—"

Felipe laughed and placed a gentle finger on her lips. "Shh, *querida*." He put his arm around her and held her close. "Are you really all right?"

She relaxed against him. "Yes, I wasn't harmed in any way, but I was frightened, not so much with the Indians, but those

Comancheros made me feel, I don't know, dirty somehow."

He tightened his arm. "It's over now." He chuckled softly and kissed the top of her head. "I'm not going to let you out of my sight ever again."

She put both arms around his waist and leaned her head in the hollow of his shoulder. She stared into the flickering flames, heard the fat sizzle, and smelled the cooking meat, content in his embrace.

They talked then. He spoke of his family and shared tales of growing up on the ranch, but not once did he mention his betrothal. "I want to know all about you," he said and listened with interest to the story of her life. But Alondra wanted to hear more about his family and asked questions until he stopped her with a kiss.

Clory crawled out of the lean-to and spread her hands to the fire. "That bird sure does smell good, is it about ready? Lalo is bellering for food."

Alondra reluctantly moved from Felipe's embrace. "I made him some broth." She poured the soup into a cup, tested the goose. "It's ready. We can eat now."

After they'd eaten, Alondra tidied the camp and Felipe banked the fire. He held out his hand. "Come. It's time for bed."

She took his hand and led him to the bed. He shucked off his boots and removed his buckskin shirt. He had a scar on his shoulder above his heart.

He patted the blanket and a flicker of apprehension swept through her. She had slept next to him almost every night on the trip north, but this time was different, they were alone, together in the same bed, sharing the same blanket. This is what she wanted, what she had dreamed of, what she had prayed for. Her heart thudded; her stomach churned. Did he think differently of her now that she'd been with the *Comancheros*?

His arms encircled her. He pulled her close, his touch a

soothing balm on her trembling limbs, his voice a low, husky murmur. "It's all right, *mi amor*. I want you beside me, now and forever."

His gentle touch sent shivers of desire coursing through her. She forgot her doubts and returned his kisses with raw passion. "Slowly, *querida*, tonight we go slowly," he said softly against her lips.

Carefully, as though she were a precious piece of porcelain, he removed her blouse, her skirt. His hands skimmed her breasts, her thighs, her stomach, inflaming a hot pulling sensation deep in her belly. She needed more than just a touch and instinctively arched toward him.

His fingers gently explored the secret places of her body and she gasped softly, calling his name. As he tenderly guided her through the depths and heights of passion, her love for him grew and she opened herself to him body and soul. When at last she felt the sting of him in her deepest core, the world whirled and the stars exploded in thousands of colors. Felipe sank against her, spent, and she knew that he too had felt the wonder.

Alondra listened to Felipe breathe, soft and slow. She placed her hand on his breast and lightly traced the scar with her fingertips. She thanked the saints that Captain Baca and his cruelty were far behind them in southern Texas.

Felipe's chest moved gently with each breath she felt the rhythm of his heart. She covered her own heart with her other hand. It beat in cadence with his and it was then that Alondra knew that she and Felipe were forever linked.

She understood him now, knew him as she'd never known anyone else. It no longer mattered that she had no second name, she belonged to Felipe, and nothing could ever change that. She was his and he belonged to her, this night proved that. His betrothal faded from her mind, and the heavy mantle of fears and uncertainties slipped away into the darkness. She closed her eyes, a faint smile on her lips.

The coyotes yelped their nightly serenade, but neither Alondra nor Felipe heard them.

They stayed in the camp for two idyllic days, emerging from the trees only at full dark. Alondra and Felipe spent their time together under the pines with no thought but to dispel the hunger that had consumed them for much of their time on the trail. They took this time to explore, to arouse, to give each other pleasure, and they made love with delightful abandon and with heartbreaking tenderness, never losing the passion and love they held for one another.

Constantly aware they were only three miles from the Comanche encampment, the four friends spoke little and then in soft murmurs. They built no fires at night, concerned that the flicker of the flame would alert the Indians to their whereabouts.

By the third day, Lalo became restless. "How much longer are we staying? I'm able to ride, no need to stay here on my account."

"Wait," Felipe said. "Wait until your wound is healed. We're in no hurry."

"I'm getting fat and lazy. Clory won't even allow me to undress myself."

Felipe winked and grinned. "Enjoy it while you can, *amigo*."

On the morning of the fifth day, when the sun had risen fully, Felipe lay on his stomach under a bush on the riverbank, checking the fish seine he'd made from river reeds and grasses. A cloud of dust on the other side of the river caught his attention. He backed deeper under the bush and peered through the tall grass.

A party of fifteen Apache warriors rode through the dust, headed for the river. They were outfitted for war: naked but for breechcloths, knee-high buckskin moccasins, and the leather bands that kept their long flowing hair out of their eyes. They wore simple necklaces made of beads and magic berries, and copper or silver bracelets and earrings. Each had a bow and quiver of arrows strapped to his back and held a flint-tipped lance in one hand, and they all carried rawhide shields painted with sacred symbols.

Their horses, too, were stripped for battle. They had no bridle or reins, only a *reata* looped around the lower jaw. The saddle was a sheepskin pad strapped on with rawhide stirrups. A leather loop was woven into the horses' manes for the rider to hook his foot when shooting arrows from underneath the pony's neck or belly. The Apache did not often wear war paint, nor did they paint their ponies, the better to blend with the rocks and earth.

Felipe wormed his way back to camp. "Break camp, hurry. Douse the fire, scatter the ashes, and toss the rocks into the bushes. Quick."

Lalo crawled from the lean-to. "What is it?"

"An Apache war party is headed this way. Can you ride? We don't have much time. I'll saddle the horses." Felipe snatched the cowhide shelter, folding it while he ran to the horses.

Alondra and Clory broke camp. They packed every morsel of food, buried bones under dry leaves, mixed the ashes with dirt, and scattered them into footprints and body depressions.

Lalo used the pine boughs from their beds as a broom and swept the campsite, scattered dried leaves, pebbles, and broken tree limbs on the swept earth. He saved several of the larger branches and hid the others under bushes and trees.

Felipe led the horses into camp and nodded approval. "The Apache don't miss much, but we've done the best we can."

He packed their supplies into saddlebags and fastened their blankets onto the cantles. Lalo tied a pine bough on each horse's tail. "To erase our tracks while we ride," he explained.

"Won't they see that something is being dragged?"

"Yes, but the wind is blowing sand, and it will make it more difficult to tell how old the tracks are. I suggest we leave the trees and ride on the river edge where the ground is covered with rocks. I suppose we are going north?"

"Yes," Felipe said, "north. You lead, Lalo. I'll take flank. We'll ride single file and no talking. Let's go."

They rode at a swift walk—Lalo, Clory, Alondra, and Felipe—the only sound the soft clop of horse hoofs, the swish of the trailing pine boughs, the wind blowing through the trees, until they were directly across the river from the Comanche camp.

Lalo reined his gelding and raised his hand. They heard faint yells and war whoops from across the river. "Sounds like the Apache have attacked the Comanche. We'll take advantage of that," Lalo said. "They are busy and not likely to hear us." He jabbed his horse in the flanks and the others galloped after him.

The horses were fresh, and they ran until Lalo judged they were several miles from the Comanche camp. He pulled his horse to a stop and raised his hand. "We'll stop here, let the horses blow, and rest for a few minutes."

He and Felipe cut the pine branches from the horses' tails and tossed the sticks under bushes. They loosened the saddle cinches and found shade beside a juniper.

"So, why is it, Felipe, that we camped within spitting distance of the Comanche, but sight of the Apache sends us running like scared jackrabbits?" Lalo asked.

"I don't underestimate the Comanche, Lalo, but the Apache are ruthless. They are ferocious and cruel, have you ever seen one of their victims?"

"No." Lalo sipped from his water flask, replaced the wooden stopper. "But I expect they scalp them, same as other Indians do."

"The Apache don't often take scalps, but war and plunder is their way of life. They swoop down on some unsuspecting farmer or another Indian tribe, steal livestock and sometimes women and children. Most often, they merely kill those who get in their way, but, if they are carrying an old grudge against their foe, the torture they inflict makes their victims pray for death. I'd rather fight ten Comanche than one Apache."

"Then we'd better get as far from here as we can," Lalo said.

"Are we headed back home?" Clory asked, "I'd like to see my ma, tell her all that we did."

"We'll write to her, Clory," Felipe said. "We'll find a village and you can write a letter and send it to her by the next mule train going south."

"That would be nice. I don't recall her ever getting a letter, but I don't know how to write, and she don't read too good."

"You tell me what to say, and I'll write the letter for you," Felipe said.

"I'd like that. How far to the next village? Let's get moving." Clory tightened the cinch on her pony.

"Can you write a letter for me too, Felipe?" Alondra asked. "I'd like to write to Millie."

"Yes, of course," Felipe said and wondered how long they'd have to wait before he could keep his promise.

They rode through the heat of the day, not stopping for food or rest. The sun was on its downward swing when they topped a rocky hill. In the valley, a cluster of adobe huts sat in the red dirt. Toward the river was a freshly plowed patch of earth. In the empty street, a yellow chicken fluttered its feathers in a dust bath. A black and white goat ambled to a watering trough; a kid gamboled beside it. There was no other movement.

"*Siesta* time?" Lalo asked.

Felipe shrugged. "Maybe there's a *cantina* where we can get some food."

"And a beer," Lalo said, "but it is a very small village."

Alondra and Clory chatted, excited at the prospect of writing a letter.

"I don't know if we can send a letter from here," Felipe

said as they neared the houses. "It looks more like a family farm or ranch than a village."

A sudden gust carried the unmistakable odor of death. Felipe and Lalo exchanged glances, neither spoke. Lalo pointed to the sky. Buzzards wheeled in lowering circles.

"You women stay here," Felipe said and nudged El Moro to a gallop.

Lalo rode beside him. "What do you suppose ...?"

A man lay spread-eagle beside the well. Wooden stakes were pounded in the palms of each hand and through each foot, his ears were pinned to his face with cactus thorns. Deep slashes on his naked body had brought a slow and painful death. Flies, ants, and beetles crawled in and around the yawning mouth, the staring eyes, the blood-soaked earth.

Speechless, Felipe and Lalo stared in horror. The buzzing flies sounded loud in the stillness.

"*Dios mio.*" Lalo removed his hat and crossed himself.

"Apache," Felipe said. "I doubt there's anyone alive, but we better check the houses."

In one house, a woman sat slumped sideways in a chair, an arrow in her chest, her gray hair hanging over her face. Felipe picked up a *serape* and covered the body in the yard. "So that the women won't have to see it," he said.

They found the decapitated body of a man sprawled on the threshold of a hut, his head impaled on a stake driven into the dirt floor. Next to him, a woman, burned and beaten, lay with a bloody club in her lifeless hand.

Lalo wiped his face with his kerchief. "I've seen a lot of death in my years as a soldier, but never anything the likes of this."

Felipe shook his head, his mouth a hard, thin line. "We have a lot of tidying up before the women see this. Listen. Even the wind is crying."

"I heard it before. It sounds like a child and makes my skin crawl."

"We haven't seen any children," Felipe said. "Mostly men and the only women are either old or the ones who fought back. The Apache probably took the others for slaves and the younger children will be raised as Apache."

One house was untouched and free of death. Bundles of dried tobacco leaves and ears of corn hung from its turquoise door, yellow cornmeal and pottery shards lay scattered in the dirt. "Looks as though the people who lived in this house ran out to fight the Apache," Felipe said. "And the Indians didn't bother to ransack this place."

They opened the door of the last house and gaped in horror at the baby pulling on the breast of his dead mother.

"*Dios mio*," both men said in unison, and the baby wailed. Fat tears rolled down his cheeks, he waved his fists in frustration. Blood and dirt streaked his hands and face.

Eyes wet with tears, Lalo stepped into the house and picked up the grimy child. "What are we going to do with it?"

"Alondra will know," Felipe said and signaled to the waiting women.

Alondra and Clory trotted their horses down the dusty road. "What is it? What's happened?" Alondra asked.

"Apache," Felipe said. "They butchered every soul except for this baby."

"Oh, the poor little thing." Clory took the child from Lalo. She patted and crooned to him until his sobs turned to hiccups.

"Did they kill even the children?" Alondra asked.

"No, we found no other children," Felipe said. "They must have taken the others with them but somehow missed this one. Maybe he was asleep when the Indians attacked, and his mother covered him with a blanket to hide him. I don't know, and I don't know what we'll do with him."

"Well, one thing I do know," Clory said, "is that the poor little guy is dirty and hungry. How do we feed him?"

"There's a goat, she has a kid, we could milk her," Alondra said.

"That house over there." Felipe pointed. "The one with the open door is empty. Use it to care for the baby and don't come out until we say. Lalo and I have work to do out here."

"Will the Apache return?" Clory asked, her voice small.

"No," Felipe said. "They're a long way from here, fighting the Comanche. We're safe for now, but even so, I'd like to leave here first thing in the morning."

The men went to a lean-to shed in search of digging tools. "I'll use the pickaxe, Lalo," Felipe said. "Shoveling will be easier on your wound."

"Don't worry about that, Clory has me bound so tight I can scarcely breathe. *Dios mio,* but this is a bad business. How many dead?"

"Six. If we can dig deep enough, we'll put them all in one grave."

They exchanged no further words, saving their energy for the grueling task, each locked in his own dark thoughts. Felipe swung the pickaxe, digging up rocks and hard-packed clods of red earth. Lalo threw out the larger rocks by hand and shoveled out the dirt. They removed their shirts. The sun beat on their backs. Sweat dripped between their shoulder blades and down their faces. Dust clogged their nostrils. They stopped only for a drink of tepid water or to wipe an arm across their eyes.

The only sounds were the droning insects, the clang of iron against rock, the thud of steel on dirt, the moaning wind.

CHAPTER 20

In the cool interior of the adobe hut, Alondra took a clay jug from a shelf. "I'll milk the goat, Clory, if you want to bathe the baby."

Clory shifted the baby on her hip. "I can do that, but how will we get the milk down him?"

"He looks old enough to drink from a cup. I hope the goat is close by, I know Felipe doesn't want us to see what they're doing."

Clory stripped the baby and sat him on the dirt floor that had been swept, sprinkled with water, and swept again so many times it was hard and smooth as sandstone. "I wonder if there's a bathtub."

"Any large bowl or pan will do," Alondra said.

The baby whimpered.

Clory soothed the baby. "I swear, Alondra, I feel like whimpering right along with him. I've never seen anything like this."

"I know," Alondra murmured and slipped out the door. Her heart ached for the victims, for the baby, for Felipe. One look at his face and she'd shared his sorrow. Nothing in her sometimes-hard life had prepared her for a tragedy like this.

She found the nanny goat lying in the shade behind one of the houses, the kid beside it. Alondra prodded and pushed until the goat stood. She squatted behind the nanny, set the jug on the ground, and squeezed the goat's teats, praying the animal was gentle and wouldn't kick the milk jug over.

The goat cooperated and Alondra soon filled the jug and hurried to the house. A tin chest, its lid open, stood in the middle of the room. Clory had bathed the baby and wrapped him in a white cotton cloth. He sat on her lap, gnawing on his fist. "He's just the sweetest little thing," Clory said. "We'll have to take him with us."

Alondra said nothing, she hadn't thought that far ahead about the baby. She poured milk into a cup and held it to the baby's lips. He slurped, milk dribbled down his chin, he drained the cup, and Alondra added more. Finally, he pushed the cup away, rested his head on Clory's arm, and fell asleep.

Clory laid him on the floor in a bed she'd made of sheepskin and a *serape*. "I've been thinking of a name for him," she said. "I kind of like the name Heath. What do you think?"

"I don't know, Clory. I've never heard the name before."

"I like the sound of it: Heath McFarlane. A good name for a Scotsman."

"I know Felipe won't want to stay here long, how will we feed the baby while we're on the trail?" Alondra asked.

"We'll just have to take the goat with us. I'll put a rope around her neck, and she can follow my horse."

Alondra said no more. She knew they wouldn't abandon the baby, but Felipe would probably want to leave poor little Heath at the next village, just like he said he'd leave her. She suddenly realized this was the first settlement they'd seen since leaving Zeke's ranch, and these adobe huts weren't even a village. Texas was vast, wild, and unsettled, filled with menacing Indians and dangerous white men.

"Do you think we'll ever get to a village, Clory?"

"I never cottoned to big towns much. I spent all my life back in the piney woods on our ranch. Never saw too many other folks. Once in a while, a Mexican *vaquero* wandered by. Ma would feed him, and Pa would work him, then, in a few days, the *vaquero* would disappear.

"I've been studying on it some, and I think Ma wanted me to see how other folks lived. That's why she didn't make a fuss when I said I wanted to hook up with Lalo and Felipe to track the Comanche. When we said goodbye, Ma told me we might never see each other again, but not to worry because that's the way life is. I would like to send her a letter though, so I hope we do get to a village soon."

While Clory talked, Alondra investigated the clay jars and bowls on the shelves. "Look, here's some corn flour, we can make *tortillas*. Let's see what else we can find. Maybe they have some coffee or even chocolate."

"It don't seem right, going through other people's belongings."

"They won't mind. They'd want us to help ourselves. I saw a hen. I'm going to look for eggs. While I see what I can find for a meal, why don't you look for something to dress Baby Heath in?"

"I guess you're right, it's not like they'll be coming back or anything." Clory knelt beside the chest of hammered tin. "This is where I found the towel. There are some nice things in here."

Alondra slipped out the door, a basket in her hands. Twenty minutes later, she returned with the eggs and blinked. "Is that you, Clory?"

Except for her moccasin boots, Clory had removed her brother's clothes. She stood in the middle of the hut, wearing a yellow skirt and white blouse that molded to her lush figure. Her freshly washed hair curled in damp ringlets around her face. She twirled, held her skirt out. "Do you think Lalo will like me in a dress?"

"You look beautiful, he'll love it."

"I won't wear it on the trail, but I thought the men would like to see something pretty after what all they're doing. There's another dress in the chest if you want to try it on."

Alondra grinned and ran to the well for a bucket of water, averting her eyes from the *serape*-covered body. Back in the house, she bathed and washed her hair and searched through the tin chest.

"These are some woman's best clothes, Clory, they've never been worn. She was probably saving them for something special, and now she will never wear them." Tears ran down her cheeks.

"I know, but don't you suppose she'd want us to get some use from them? Try not to think about it."

"You're right, Clory, but it is so sad." Alondra wiped her tears and dressed herself in a red skirt with a matching blouse. She held up a white *mantilla*. "You could use this as a veil when you and Lalo get married."

Clory fingered the bit of lace. "It's right pretty, but I don't know as how I'll ever use it. Lalo ain't never said nothing about getting married. You keep it. Felipe will marry you once we get to his ranch. You'll see."

"I'm not sure about that, Clory. He's never mentioned marriage."

"After all you've been through together, he wouldn't dare to marry that highborn lady."

"I don't know. He won't talk about it." Alondra folded the *mantilla* and replaced it in the chest. "I'll cook some food if you clean the house." The girls worked until they heard laughter and shouting.

They looked out the doorway and saw Felipe and Lalo cavorting about the well, naked, throwing buckets of water on one another.

Clory and Alondra exchanged glances and smiled. "They're

like little boys," Clory said. "They remind me of my brothers."

"They need to play, after the work they've just done." Alondra shut the door and the girls returned to their tasks.

*****

Felipe and Lalo entered the hut. Their dripping hair hung loose, their scrubbed hands and faces shone, their clothes damp but clean. Neither man said a word. They stared open-mouthed at the women.

To Felipe, Alondra, in her simple cotton dress, looked more beautiful than any *señorita* in Mexico City dressed in silks and laces. Her eyes glowed with a welcoming light, and his heart lifted in response.

Lalo held his arms wide. "Surely we've been forgiven all our sins, Felipe, and are now in heaven with the angels."

Clory stepped into his waiting arms and leaned her head on his shoulder.

"I have been praying for the souls of those poor murdered people," Alondra said.

Felipe took her hand and pulled her to him. "Thank you," he murmured. He kissed her on the forehead and held her close, needing the comfort of her body next to his.

Alondra lifted her head. "I made coffee and milked the goat. There's some honey if you'd like coffee before we eat."

"You are an angel," Felipe said. "Lalo, our angels made us coffee."

Alondra served the chicory coffee on the only furniture in the hut, a low table, and the men sat on the ground.

Heath cried.

"I'd almost forgotten about the baby," Lalo said.

Clory picked up the infant and brought him to the table. "You better not forget about him. He's mine and he's going with us, and nobody better say different." She poured milk into a cup and held it to the baby's lips.

"Of course he's going with us," Felipe said. "There's never been any question about that."

Clory beamed. "His name is Heath. Heath McFarlane."

"Heath Chaves y McFarlane," Lalo said. "Now that we're parents, we should get married."

Clory blushed and bent her head. She kissed the baby's black silky hair.

Felipe clapped Lalo on the shoulder. "Well, *amigo*, that calls for another cup of coffee, you can even have the last of the milk in celebration."

"No," Lalo said, "I will save the milk for my son."

Felipe envied his friend's simple acceptance of fatherhood. If the roles were reversed, could he have so easily said the same to Alondra? At the most inconvenient times, he heard those nagging voices in the back of his head, reminding him of duty, family, and honor. Still, he did not intend to give Alondra up, no matter the cost. Often, he thought about all of them riding west to California. He had heard that the California ranches spanned thousands of acres, that the Indians were no threat, and the weather so mild that cattle never needed winter pasture in deep canyons.

Blankly, he watched Lalo and Clory play with the baby on the dirt floor. Clory held the baby between her knees, Lalo lay on his stomach, murmuring to Heath, and the baby gurgled and cooed, obviously enjoying the attention. "How would you like to go to California with me, Lalo?" Felipe asked.

"California?" Lalo rolled to his back. Heath crawled on Lalo's chest, tugged on his mustache. "I don't know. Mexico has sent troops there and I'm through with the military. I'm a family man now." He held Heath high, the baby squirmed and squealed with laughter. "Why do you want to go to California?"

"It was just a thought."

Lalo sat up and handed the baby to Clory. "You know you wouldn't be happy in California, Felipe. You'd no sooner get there than want to turn around and come back home to New

Mexico. Everything will work out for you, you'll see."

"You're right, of course, Lalo. I have to go home."

He pictured his family seated at the dinner table: mother, father, grandparents. An only child, they doted on him, but more than that, they depended on him. He twisted the silver bracelet on his wrist. If he were forced to marry that girl they had chosen for him, he would never love her. He wondered if he could lie next to her at night, if he could give her the children his family thought so important. The thought turned him cold.

Three years had passed since he'd been home. Still, his father had given his word and it would bring dishonor on the family if Felipe refused to marry that girl. Her name was Maria, he knew that, but she was a wisp of wind in his thoughts and he couldn't bring her face to mind. He was twenty-one when he left for Mexico City, his pockets lined with enough silver to buy the stallion and plenty left over to live comfortably for three years.

"Enjoy yourself," his father had said, "Mexico City will teach you many things you could never experience here in the province."

His father had been right, but Felipe had the chilling thought that perhaps the dowry money had been used for his big-city education. If he didn't marry Maria, the dowry money would have to be paid back. He shook his head. Knowledge was useful, but instead of enjoying himself spending the dowry money, he should have been working to make money, maybe by mining for gold or silver. Silver ...

"There's a legend in my family of a silver mine that one of my ancestors discovered over one hundred and fifty years ago. There is a bowl at my house that holds two pieces of silver ore that are said to have come from that mine." Felipe had everyone's attention.

Immediately interested, Lalo asked, "No one knows where the mine is?"

"Yes, we know where the mine is, but we aren't allowed near it because it's on what we've always called the Blue *Mesa*. It's a sacred mountain that belongs to the Pueblo Indians."

"Then how'd you get a hold of those two pieces of ore?" Clory asked.

"My ancestor brought them down, but it was very dangerous. The story is that he was chased and almost killed by a whirlwind that lives in the mine."

"And no one has been back since then?" Lalo asked.

"Yes, but no one ever met with any success. The Indians don't go up there, only their medicine men, and they don't go often. My people claim the mine is haunted."

"Then the silver is still there," Lalo said, his brown eyes dreamy.

Alondra frowned. "Are you planning on mining that silver?"

Felipe smiled at her. "It would solve my problem."

"And mine," Lalo said.

Alondra shook her head. "It's not worth it. Not if there are ghosts."

"That was almost two hundred years ago," Felipe said. "People were superstitious back then. They believed all those old myths and legends."

"And you don't?" Alondra asked.

"No, not entirely. There may be a bit of truth in some of them, but for the most part, I don't believe in them."

"What about *La Llorona*? The woman who walks the riverbanks, weeping for her drowned children. People have seen and heard her."

"Probably only fog and wind."

"And the Blue Lady, who causes blue flowers to bloom where she steps. What of her?"

"Maybe. But how do you know all these legends, Alondra?"

"I like to listen to stories. What happened to those who tried to mine the silver?"

"Yes," Lalo said. "I want to hear more about that silver mine. How far from here is it?"

"A long way, if we follow the Pecos as I'd planned, but the *mesa* is only half a day ride from the *hacienda*. We could cut the distance if we travel northwest over the mountains and then cross the *Jornada del Muerto*."

"What's that?" Clory asked.

"They call it the Journey of Death because it is a desert with no water for many leagues. People have lost their way and died of thirst before they could reach the *Rio Grande*."

"We should have no problem if we carry water with us," Lalo said. "We've been traveling a long time, and if it would cut the distance then let's take that road. I'd like to find a place to settle down and raise my family."

"It won't be easy, especially with a baby."

"I've been thinking on it," Clory said. "I'll make me a cradleboard like the Indians, and strap Heath on my back."

"What will he eat?" Felipe asked.

"We'll take the goat with us." Clory laid the baby on his bed. "I'm going to sleep now. I have a lot to do in the morning."

"You haven't told us what happened to those who tried to mine the silver," Alondra said.

"I don't really know," Felipe said. "I've only heard stories. They say that some never returned, and others would never speak of it. It all happened long ago, and no one has been there in over fifty years. We all better get some sleep. I'd like to get an early start in the morning."

Before Felipe joined Alondra in their bed, he stepped out the door and gazed at the North Star, shining bright and steady in the purple sky. A baby and a goat on the *Jornada del Muerto*. Impossible. It was the quickest path home, but he wished he'd never mentioned the silver mine, it had never brought anything but bad luck to those foolish enough to mine it.

A bat swooped, chasing an insect. The half-moon cast the shadow of the crude cross, long and dark, across the mound of earth and rock. In the distance, a lone coyote wailed a mournful song.

CHAPTER 21

A rooster crowed. Felipe opened his eyes and gazed at the whitewashed ceiling. It had been weeks since he'd slept under a roof and, for a moment, didn't remember where he was. The rooster crowed once again, and Felipe awoke fully. He glanced at Alondra lying next to him, curled on her side, eyelashes sweeping her cheeks, and resisted the impulse to waken her. It had been three days since they had made love, and each day it became more difficult to control his desire, but he would not dishonor her by getting her with child before marriage.

He wanted to make a child with Alondra, but not yet. Their time would come. He fingered a strand of her black hair that lay spread on the pillow and smiled as he pictured their child. A little girl, perhaps, with black curls and a mischievous smile, or maybe a boy with Alondra's honesty and courage.

He pulled on his boots and stepped out the door, the urge to leave this village of death strong. He strode to the corrals, his brain working on the problem of travel with a baby and a goat and a kid.

Alondra heard the rooster crow and felt Felipe's hot gaze. She didn't flutter an eyelash and breathed a small sigh when he walked out the door.

Something had changed between them since those nights under the pines when they'd pledged themselves to each other in soul-binding oneness. She had no other words to explain the wondrous feeling.

Now, though Felipe was gentle and loving, he held himself back. No matter what she did, she couldn't capture that same unity and it saddened her. "We love each other. Is that not enough, *querida*?" he said when she questioned him. And worried he would think her brazen, she hadn't the courage to press him further.

Heath whimpered. Alondra heard Clory's soothing murmur, Lalo's soft whisper, and although she couldn't help but feel a prick of envy she was happy Clory and Lalo would marry. She loved them both and wanted the very best in life for them.

Alondra sat up, combed her fingers through her long, dark curls, and made a decision. She loved Felipe with all her being, but if he couldn't love her in the same way, then she would harden her heart, distance herself from him so that when he left her, and she had no doubt that he would, she could find the strength to sew the tattered pieces of her soul together.

Felipe stood in the morning sunshine and considered his problem. The Apache had left no livestock, but he was only mildly surprised that the goat and kid had survived. The animals had probably been lying in the shade and frightened by the noise, remained hidden. As for the chickens, Felipe pictured them running from a warrior, squawking, wings flapping, scuttling under a mesquite or juniper, until the Indian lost patience and rode away in disgust.

Felipe figured they'd need a brace of mules and a wagon for their journey, as the goats would not be able to keep pace with the horses. There were no mules, and behind the shed lay a wagon chopped beyond use. But sitting drunkenly on two mismatched wheels made of solid rounds of cottonwood was a *carreta*. The cart, built of *piñon* poles held together with dried rawhide thongs and used to haul corn or wheat from the fields, was meant to be pulled by a yoke of oxen. Maybe, by using pieces of the wagon, he could fix the cart so the horses could pull it.

He removed the traces from the wagon and affixed them to the cart. Inside the shed, he pieced together a harness to fit Segundo and Comanche Pony. Felipe didn't worry about using a pair of saddle horses as draft animals, he had confidence in his ability as a horse trainer to have them working as a team before they reached the mountains.

He hitched the sturdy mustang and the army horse to the heavy cart, climbed in, and slapped the reins across their rumps. The horses whinnied and snorted, pitched and bucked, kicked and ran. The cart lurched and bounced behind them, the wheels wobbled and squealed. Balanced on the rounded floor-poles, Felipe clutched the reins in one hand, held on to the careening cart with the other. His hat blew off, the cart rolled over it. The wind picked up the flattened hat and sailed it into a tangle of tumbleweeds.

The nervous horses galloped down the road, stirred up dust, kicked at the traces. The crude cart reeled from side to side. "Whoa," Felipe shouted and sawed on the reins. He lost his balance and sat with a thump. The horses ran onto the rocky plain. Felipe grabbed hold of the side-poles, got to his knees. The cart hit a bump and slammed him against the side. He gained his footing, swayed, hit the other side, braced his legs, pulled hard on the reins, and brought the team under control. He leaped from the cart and held the horses' heads, spoke to them in soothing tones. The animals were skittish but no longer fought the cart as Felipe led them back to the farm.

His friends stood gathered around the well, laughing. He grinned and waved and continued to the shed. He found his hat, slapped it against his leg to shake off the dust, rubbed his sleeve across the brim to remove the sticky tumbleweed seeds, and jammed the hat on his head.

After his wild ride onto the plain, he realized the women would be uncomfortable in the cart, so he placed boards from the wagon bed crossways on the pole floor of the cart.

Lalo ambled to the shed, chuckling, and carrying a pot. "Those wheels screech louder than a wounded bear. I found some tallow. We better grease the axle or the whole territory will hear us coming."

"A layer of straw will ease the bounces and jolts for the women." Felipe picked up a pitchfork and tossed in piles of straw. "We'll tie the goat behind; the kid will follow, and when he gets tired he can ride in the cart with the baby and women." He placed Alondra's saddle in the cart.

"I found some goatskin *botas* I'll fill with water," Lalo said. "With those and our own water flasks, we should have enough water to cross the desert. How big is the desert?"

"Not so large. On horseback, a two-day's ride to the *Rio Grande*, but with this cart, I'd say it will take us over four days. First, though, we must cross through the mountains, and that will take another two days or more. I don't know."

Lalo placed an iron pry bar in the cart. "In case we get stuck in the rocks," he said.

Clory insisted on taking the tin chest with them. "As long as we have the cart," she said, and laid a *serape* over the straw and fastened another over the top of the cart for shade. Heath sat on the blanket, chewing on a wooden pistol Lalo had carved for him.

Alondra packed an iron pot, a tin bucket, clay pots, and bowls filled with salt, *chilis*, and various foodstuffs. By its rope handle, she hung a large clay pot that held dry beans and corn soaking in water. She had gleaned winter squash and onions from the field, and they lay in a heap in the cart.

Felipe sighed and shook his head. They'd traveled across

half of Texas with only what they carried in saddlebags. "Let's get started. It's a long trip."

"Wait," Alondra said. "We have to take the chickens too."

Felipe exploded. "*Dios mio*! We already look like homeless peons. We can't be bothered with chickens!"

"I'm not leaving them for the coyotes." Alondra ran behind the shed to hunt the hens, the straw *sombrero* she'd found in the hut flopped around her shoulders.

"How are you going to carry them?" Felipe shouted.

"I saw some reed cages that will hold a couple of hens," Lalo said. His eyes danced and his lips twitched. "They were probably used to carry fighting roosters."

Felipe cursed and kicked the dirt. He stalked to a low hill behind the houses and stood, hands on hips, head thrown back, breathed deep, and wondered why the matter of the chickens should make him angry. He gazed at the white moon riding across the blue sky, at the distant peak, rising above the low-lying mountain range. Spring was in the air and in the earth. Shoots of green peeked through the sere winter grass.

He turned and looked at the *carreta* laden with goods and animals and tasted the bitter gall of shame. He'd done his best, and it embarrassed him that they were forced to travel like peasants.

He sighed, removed his hat, and ran his fingers through his hair. He punched a fist in the crown and reshaped his hat. An old saddle sat unused in the shed. He might as well take it with them for Clory. At the first opportunity, he'd exchange the cart for a carriage drawn by mules, hire a driver, buy new clothes for everyone, and they could all ride to the *hacienda* in style.

He marched to the shed, slung the saddle over his shoulder, and, without a word, deposited it in the cart. He swung onto his waiting horse and glanced at his companions, who all seemed to find something vastly amusing.

"I'm sorry you ladies have to ride in this cart," he said. "But

I could not repair the wagon. I'll lead the horses until they become accustomed to pulling the cart." His mind filled with misgivings about taking the desert route, he turned El Moro northwest, away from the river, toward the mountains.

Lalo led the way. The cart lurched and creaked with each turn of its uneven wheels.

CHAPTER 22

With the high peak on his left and the sun burning his back, Lalo searched for a pathway on the rocky plain. He found wagon tracks leading to the mountains and into the pine forest. They rode at a brisk pace until the sun set and Felipe called a halt at a sparkling creek. He figured that game would be plentiful here, so he left the others to set up camp and went hunting.

By the time he returned with a mule deer draped across El Moro's rump, Lalo had built a campfire, Alondra had prepared a meal, and Clory had milked the goat and fed the baby. The chickens clucked sleepily in their pen, the goat and her kid lay chewing cud, and the horses were staked in a patch of new grass.

Felipe relaxed at the sight of the peaceful campsite.

Lalo sat near the fire whittling a piece of pine into a toy horse for Heath. "How far to the silver mine?"

"About a day's ride from the *hacienda*. But first, we need to find a pass through these mountains, then cross the desert. Another week of travel if we find the pass tomorrow." Felipe tacked the deer hide to a tree and cut the rawhide into narrow strips. "That awkward cart …" He shook his head.

"It will get us through, I greased the axle again. The hubs are sturdy chunks of wood, the wheels won't come off. Do you expect more Indian attacks?" Lalo asked.

"Unless we run into Apache here in the mountains or on the desert, the only Indians we'll see from now on are the Pueblos, and they are friendly."

"I'll tell Clory she can put her musket away."

Felipe chuckled. "She'll not do that easily. Her rifle is as much a part of her as Alondra's dagger is a part of her. Our women are brave, Lalo. They don't cling to us or faint at the sight of blood. Yet they are ladies, gentle, generous, and kind."

Lalo nodded, smoothed the toy horse with a piece of sandstone. "Have you decided what you're going to do about your betrothal?"

Felipe's hands went still, his body tensed. "No." He sheathed his knife and strode to the creek. The waves swirled around boulders, danced in the moonlight, and seemed to sing "family, duty, family, duty." He tossed a pebble in the water and returned to camp. It would be another week at least before he had to deal with duty. Although he hadn't told her, he'd already pledged his love and honor to Alondra.

They were on the trail by sunrise. The horses fidgeted. Segundo fought the traces, and Felipe had to hold the horse by the halter. The she-goat bleated whenever the kid scampered from her side. The animals became more nervous the farther into the mountains they traveled.

"Something is bothering the animals, Lalo," Felipe said. "I'm going to scout around, you keep moving."

"Indians?" Lalo asked.

"I don't think so. The animals wouldn't act like this at a human scent. A puma, a bear maybe, or a wolf. Although the cartwheels are making so much noise, I don't think any wild animal would get near enough to attack us." Felipe said. "But maybe you better tell Clory to keep her musket handy just in case." He turned into the forest. Even the thick greenery didn't muffle the sound of the screeching wheels.

Felipe rode through trees shiny with morning dew. He searched for tracks, a freshly broken twig, an overturned pebble, a bent blade of grass, anything to show an animal had passed. He found nothing. A bear fresh from hibernation had a strong odor, so Felipe turned to the wind and sniffed the air, smelled nothing but the musty green of the forest. Not a bear then. He reined in El Moro and listened. In the distance, the cartwheels protested; overhead, tree branches rustled. He scanned the forest top. Nothing.

He sat still, waited for the rustling sound. Silence. No birds chirping, no squeaking wheels. Felipe nudged El Moro to a gallop, ducked under tree limbs, crashed through bushes, rounded boulders.

He reached the cart, heart pounding. "What's the matter?"

Lalo was retying the goat. "The kid won't stay with its mother. The nanny goat is fighting the rope and choking herself. I had to hogtie the kid and he doesn't like it. The horses haven't calmed down yet. What did you find?"

"Nothing," Felipe said. "I found nothing, not a track of any kind. I followed a game trail for a short way, but all I saw were deer tracks and they were several days old."

Lalo stroked his mustache. "Maybe the animals smell old spoor, or maybe they just don't like the mountains."

Felipe shrugged. "Is there enough space in the cart for both goats, Alondra? I want to get through the mountains quickly and the nanny might lose her milk if she gets too nervous or tired."

"We'll make room." Alondra pulled on the goat's lead and Felipe heaved the nanny into the cart. "I'll hold her rope," Alondra said, "so she won't jump out."

Felipe started the horses at a trot. The team strained against the yoke and broke into a lope. The cart rumbled behind, bounced, and lurched. Clory cradled Heath against her breast. Alondra clutched the rope and put her arms around the nanny's neck to steady her.

The horses ran until sweat lathered their sides. Felipe reined them to a stop in a small clearing. The team stood, tails tucked, heads down, legs shaking, while Felipe and Lalo unharnessed them and wiped foam off their heaving sides.

"We'll have to camp here. The horses are too tired to go farther," Felipe said.

Lalo built a fire, Alondra and Clory set up camp. "Stay close to the fire," Felipe said, "and we'll picket the horses near us. Lalo and I will take turns at guard."

"Do you suppose it's a *difunto,* Felipe?" Alondra asked, "a restless spirit that walks these hills? Maybe it's even *La Llorona* who is walking the creek bank."

"No, it is not a spirit, and I heard nothing, no wailing, not even a whisper. It's an animal that has frightened the horses. I think it's a puma stalking us, waiting for night and a chance to snatch one of the goats."

Clory jumped up and dragged the she-goat to the circle of fire. "We can't let it get the nanny. She'll sleep next to me, and, if that cat comes near, I'll blast it to kingdom come."

"You won't get the chance, *mi vida,* I'll shoot it before even the goats know it's nearby. I'll take the first watch, Felipe." Lalo picked up his rifle and disappeared into the trees.

"We all better get what rest we can." Felipe lay down, wrapped in his blanket, feet toward the fire, hat covering his face.

A horse snorted and stomped its foot. The nanny bleated softly, the kid curled beside her, rested his chin on his hind legs, and fell asleep. The night was quiet but for the wind murmuring in the trees.

"Alondra," Clory whispered, "are you asleep?"

"No. I'm wide awake."

"Me too. I've been thinking about the crying woman. Tell me her story. How did her children drown?"

Alondra scooted nearer Clory and whispered, "It's a tragic story and they say *La Llorona* is the bearer of sorrow, and, where she walks, trouble is sure to follow.

"It is said that she was born a peasant, blessed with a natural beauty, tall and slender with flowing black hair. She had two young sons, and by day lived among the poor, but by night she dressed herself in a long white gown and attended the *fandangos* of the richer class, where the men toasted her beauty and she was admired by all who saw her.

"It is said this attention became important to her, and her children soon became a burden. One night, while she was at a dance, the children drowned. Some say it was an accident, others say it was not, but, from the time of their deaths, the beautiful *La Llorona* mourned her sons night and day. She walked the riverbank in her white gown, weeping and calling their names, hoping they'd come back to her.

"She wailed constantly, her white gown became soiled and torn. She neither rested nor took nourishment, until her body, but a mere skeleton, crumpled in death beside the river. But her spirit could not rest, and, when darkness fell, she was often seen walking the banks of the river, and her wailing soon became a curse of the night.

"No one knows where or when she might appear, she's been seen along many rivers. Mothers keep their children in, for it is said that *La Llorona* will take them. Some have already been taken, lost in the rivers and creeks and never seen again."

Clory shivered and glanced at Heath sleeping beside her. Firelight played on his face, his lips turned up in an angelic smile. "Do you suppose she's after my baby?"

"It's a puma, not a spirit," Felipe said, his voice muffled by his hat. "And it wants a goat, not the baby."

A yowling, meowing scream rang through the dense forest.

The camp burst into instant chaos.

The nanny leaped to her feet, bleated for her kid that stood trembling beside her. Alondra grabbed the goat's rope and held the kid tight in her arms, smelled its fear, felt the wild flutter of its heart.

Clory clutched Heath to her breast with one hand, her rifle in the other.

The horses whinnied, stomped, and jerked at their tether lines. Felipe gripped the ropes to prevent the horses from running away.

The chickens squawked and beat their wings against the reed bars of their cage.

A rifle shot thundered. The echoes faded into silence, as thick and dark as the surrounding pine forest.

All, man and beast alike, froze, listening, waiting.

Lalo's whistle penetrated the stillness.

Felipe dropped the tether ropes, lit a pine branch from the campfire, and ran into the trees carrying the torch. He met Lalo, whose left arm dripped blood and shirt sleeve hung in tatters, dragging the puma by its tail.

Felipe stabbed the torch into the ground and squatted on his heels to examine the mountain lion. "It's a big one, *amigo*. Tell me about your wound."

Lalo grinned, his teeth white in the torchlight. "I heard rustling in the trees, looked up, and saw yellow eyes glaring at me from the treetop. I stepped back to get my sights on him. He screamed and leaped at me. I shot while he was in the air. His claws scraped my arm when he fell."

"Well," Felipe said, "I don't envy you when Clory sees your arm."

Lalo chuckled. "She likes to fuss over me." He ran his fingers through the yellow fur. "The pelt is in good condition. It will make a good rug or blanket. Help me carry the puma to camp so I can skin it?"

They threaded a long pole through the four feet they had tied together. Each man hefted an end of the pole onto his shoulder, and they carried the puma to camp.

*****

"The horses need rest," Felipe said. "We will camp here a few days. Let's go hunting, Lalo."

From twigs and brush, Alondra made an enclosure for the chickens with a nest of dry leaves and a clay bowl for water. The rooster flapped his wings and strutted. The two hens scratched in the dirt and pecked at insects.

Clory tied the nanny to a tree with a rope long enough for the goat to reach the creek, near bushes just leafing out, and in a patch of new grass. Each day, the nanny denuded the bushes and cropped the grass to its roots, and Clory found a new tree for the goat.

Alondra baked a squash in the campfire coals and put a stew on to simmer. Clory fed smashed squash to Heath. The baby smacked his lips and grabbed at the spoon. "I thought he was too young for squash, but he can't seem to get enough," Clory said. "How long do you suppose we'll stay in this camp? I want to get to a town, so I can write to Ma and tell her about the baby. She'll be right pleased; she has a fondness for young'uns."

"I don't know that I want to get to a town, Clory. I think Felipe will leave me there."

"No, Alondra. He loves you. He won't leave you, ever."

"I'm not so sure. He hasn't been with me in days. That first time was so wonderful, and I thought he loved me, but now ..." Alondra turned to hide her tears and stirred the stew.

Clory put an arm around Alondra. "I know when you love someone hard as all that you want to be with them all the time. But we'll be on the trail at least until we cross the desert. You'll think of something to win him back."

"What, Clory? What can I do?"

"I don't know. I swear I thought he ..." Clory shook her head. "But you'll think of something, I know you will." She laid Heath on the tanned puma hide for his nap and headed to the creek. "I best go down to the creek and do up this dab of laundry, so I'll at least start out with clean clothes for the baby."

Felipe and Lalo entered camp, each with a fat doe across their horses' rumps. They skinned the two deer and butchered them on the spread-out pelts. Felipe gave Alondra a haunch, and she set it on the campfire to cook.

The men cut the rest of the meat into thin slices and hung it to dry in the sunshine on the rawhide lines Felipe had made and strung between bushes.

While Alondra sprinkled salt on the meat to hasten the drying process, she thought about what she'd do if Felipe left her in the next village. Maybe she would find someone who knew the way to Saint Louis. Alondra wished she had brought the picture of the dancing lady with her. Someone in Saint Louis could read the writing on the back and tell her about her family. But what she really wanted was for Felipe to love her as she loved him.

The men set the deer hides in the creek to soak overnight, and the clear bubbling water ran crimson as it washed dirt and blood from the pelts.

In the morning, Felipe and Lalo stretched the hides between trees and, with heavy clubs made from pine branches, beat the pelts until they were soft and pliable.

The next day the little band of travelers resumed their westward trek. Lalo scouted ahead and returned with news that he'd found an easy pass through the mountains. The cart lumbered over the rocky trail, squeaking with each turn of its wheels.

They spent the night at the pass entrance—a wide space between towering sandstone boulders. They'd left the creek far behind and there was little vegetation, only thorny bushes and scrub cedar. They broke camp in the early morning light and continued on their way.

The sun was a red ball sinking behind the distant

mountains by the time they descended the path. They stopped at the edge of the desert and surveyed the expanse of sand, dotted with boulders, saltbush, and cholla cactus.

"We'll keep riding," Felipe said. "We should go as far as we can while we and the animals are rested. Put the kid in the cart, Alondra, so he doesn't wander away."

She picked up the young goat and held it across her lap, petted and stroked it until he relaxed and fell asleep. The nanny bleated, so Alondra pulled her into the cart and the she-goat also fell asleep.

They trudged on past sunset and on through the lavender dusk. The sky deepened to purple, the first stars blinked, and still they plodded across the sand. The three-quarter moon cast a pale light across the white gypsum desert. Clory curled beside Heath and soon fell asleep, not stirring even when the cart jolted over rocks. Alondra leaned her head back against the cart and dozed. Lalo rode behind them with chin on his chest, the horses walked with their heads down. Only Felipe, riding in the lead, was awake.

The breeze carried the scent of hot sand and something only the horses smelled. They lifted their heads, pointed their ears, and whinnied.

Lalo trotted up beside Felipe. "What is it?"

"I think the horses smell water."

Lalo glanced around the black and white landscape. "Water? Here in this desert?"

"I understand that there are springs and pools hidden among the rocks, especially this time of year before the summer heat dries them up. If the water is not alkaline, we'll let the animals drink. It will refresh them and then we can ride past sunrise."

"We'll not stop for the night at the spring then?"

"No, it will be easier on the animals if we travel at night and early morning. We'll look for an *arroyo* or someplace with shade, and we'll rest through the heat of the day."

Felipe slacked the reins and El Moro turned northwest to a black jumble of rocks. The other horses followed.

Grass and bushes grew around a dark stain on the sand. El Moro pawed the dirt. Felipe and Lalo grunted and strained and, with the pry bar, moved a large boulder from the pile of rocks and a small pool sparkled in the moonlight.

"The Apache often conceal springs on the desert. In the summer, the sun dries the sand, and we'd have to dig for the water." Felipe dipped his hand and tasted the water. "It's sweet. Let the horses drink, but only a little at a time."

Alondra led the goats to the pool, the kid leaped on a boulder and danced with hopping steps from rock to rock. Alondra laughed at his antics.

Her gentle laughter stirred him, and Felipe slipped his arm around her waist. "Are you comfortable in the cart, *querida*? Or would you like to ride with me?"

He sensed her surprise at his question. "It wouldn't be too much for El Moro?" She asked.

"No, I'll unsaddle him, and we'll ride bareback. We're traveling slowly and we'll stop an hour or two after sunrise." He looked up at the stars. "It's after midnight now."

"All right then, I'd like that." She smiled up at him, and he thought his heart would burst with love for her.

Alondra fought back a gasp of joy. Maybe he did love her. The moonlight brightened and the stars sang. "It will be like riding to a *fandango* with a suitor," she said.

Felipe clicked his heels and bowed from the waist. "May I have this dance, *Señorita*?" His eyes locked on hers, he brought her hand to his lips.

And they danced. They danced on the white sands of the desert to the music in their hearts. They twirled and they swayed and held each other close, matching step for step. A meteor shower illuminated the sky and sprinkled them with stardust. They held hands and watched the spectacle in awe.

"Surely the angels have bestowed their blessing on us,"

Alondra said.

Felipe kissed her cheek. "Come, the horses have rested long enough. We better get on our way. Everyone ready?" He leaped on El Moro's back.

He was in command again, but he'd shown her his love and Alondra was happy. She placed her foot on his boot and he swung her across his lap. She leaned her head on his shoulder and pressed her face against the hard muscles of his chest, heard the steady beat of his heart, smelled his scent of sun and sweat and salt. He tied the reins around the horse's neck, guided El Moro by knee pressure, and enveloped Alondra in a close embrace.

His tender touch, his breath on her hair, turned her liquid with longing. She turned in the saddle to face him and, with her tongue, tickled the corner of his mouth, traced his firm lips. He groaned softly, held her tighter, parted her lips with his. She drank in the sweetness of his kiss, responded with an urgent hunger, and felt the quickened beat of his heart.

Felipe stroked her cheek with his knuckles. "Easy, *querida*, before I lose control and take you now, here on El Moro's back."

She gazed up at him, breathing softly through parted lips moist from his kisses. "Mm," she said, "I'd like that."

He chuckled low in his throat. "It would be interesting, *querida*. But I promise you, later, when we're home at the *hacienda*." He caressed her trembling limbs with hands that were none too steady, whispered, "Later," and she pressed close against him.

She slid her hands under his shirt and around his waist, nibbled on his bare breast, with her tongue tasted his skin.

"*Dios mio, querida*, I'm only a man."

She grinned, bunched her skirt over her hips, and curled her legs around him.

His wicked smile flashed in the moonlight. "The lady wants to ride, eh, El Moro. Let's see what we can do to accommodate her." The horse only snorted and twitched his tail.

Felipe loosened his buckskin trousers, his hands slipped around her waist, and he pulled Alondra closer. She encircled her arms around his neck, and, with her eyes locked on his, they came together in a burst of shuddering ecstasy. Man against woman, fevered flesh against fevered flesh, they fit. On a fern bed under a pine bough or on horseback riding across the desert, they fit. Together they found the tempo that bound their souls for eternity.

Sometime later, when the moon had waned and the last stars twinkled, Felipe removed the silver bracelet from his wrist and clasped it on her arm. Although he said nothing, Alondra knew this was a declaration of his love. The gesture completed her world and drove all thoughts of Saint Louis from her mind.

CHAPTER 23

Morning dawned, and Felipe turned his attention to the countryside in search of a campsite for the day. The desert stretched before them, stark and empty. Far to the west, a jagged black line marked the mountains of home.

"Put your *sombrero* on, *querida*, the sun will burn your pretty face." Felipe stopped the horse and Alondra slid off. She hopped on the cart and tied her hat strings under her chin.

The heavy cart gouged deep ruts in the soft sand as the travelers trudged on. The sun rose and in two hours its fierce eye siphoned moisture from their bodies. "Take only small sips of water," Felipe said.

He spotted a sand dune and angled toward it. They made camp on the northeast side of the hill, stretching hides and *serapes* over the cart and on dry cactus sticks. They sat under the shade, chewed on salty jerky, and sipped on tepid water from their water bags.

"We'll rest here until sundown. Give the nanny a little water but don't waste any on the kid," Felipe said and laid his head on his saddle, placed his hat over his face and fell asleep.

The horses stood in what shade they could find and dozed,

a hind foot cocked and heads down. The goats lay next to the cart, nipping and chewing on the straw. The chickens sat under the cart, beaks open, wings spread to the still air.

Lalo played with Heath until the baby fell asleep, then he too slept on his stomach, head cradled in his arms. Alondra and Clory wove mats from the straw. "They will keep the sun out and let the air through better than the hides," Alondra said. By midafternoon, the heat drugged them into sleep and the mats lay unfinished on their laps.

The sun set and the wind rose, kicked up swirls of sand, and spurred the travelers to action. While the others broke camp, Felipe soaked his kerchief in water, and with the damp cloth wiped the horses' eyes, noses, and mouths. In fifteen minutes, they were on their way.

Felipe led them south to skirt the Apache camps, then angled northwest across the desert. Day after day they followed the pattern—resting during the day, traveling at night. Twice the cart got stuck in the sand. While the horses pulled, all four of them pushed and, with the help of the pry bar, they were soon on their way. Clory became faint, dizzy, and listless.

"Are you drinking your water, Clory?" Felipe asked.

"No. I'm saving it for Heath in case the nanny goes dry."

"Drink your water, Clory," Felipe said. "You can help Heath only by staying well. We won't run out of water. See that line of trees over there in the distance? That's where we're heading."

"Is that where the silver is?" Lalo asked.

"No, that's the *Rio Grande*. I want to stop in Albuquerque and exchange this cart for a proper wagon and some mules to haul it. We should be there by tomorrow sometime. Already, the sun is not so fierce. We'll be able to travel during the day."

Lalo wiped his brow. "It will be good to see trees again and get out of this heat."

✳✳✳✳✳

They traveled through the night and arrived on the banks of the *Rio Grande* at dawn. Smoke rose in the clear morning air in a thin gray spiral. The men unhitched the horses and pushed the cart into a thick stand of brush. Felipe led the horses to the river and tethered them to cottonwoods. Lalo set out on foot to investigate the smoke.

Three hours later he returned. "It's a troop of Mexican soldiers."

"Can you tell which direction they're traveling? Maybe we can join them."

"I don't think so. Captain Edmundo Baca is with them."

The news stunned Felipe. The last they'd seen Baca he was held prisoner by the Texas Rangers.

"I know," Lalo said, "But he is there."

They speculated as to how Baca escaped the Rangers, but the only thing they knew for certain was that they couldn't allow the captain to see them. Neither man wanted to take the chance of capture.

"How far away are they?" Felipe asked.

"About two leagues upstream."

"Far enough so they won't hear the cartwheels squeaking?"

"Maybe. What are you thinking?"

"I don't want to go back on the desert. If we cross the river we could travel on the opposite bank to the Blue *Mesa*."

Lalo's eyes widened. "The *Rio Grande* is a wide river, *hombre*, and deep. We could never cross it, not with the cart."

"If we go downstream, maybe we can find a shallow crossing."

"You're *loco, hombre*."

"Do you have a better idea?"

Lalo saddled his horse, filled his leather water flask, and stuffed jerky in his pockets. "You wait here, set up camp, and

I'll watch the soldiers. They may be only passing through, and when they leave we can continue north."

"I thought you were eager to find the silver."

Lalo glanced at Heath napping on the puma pelt. "Not if it endangers my family."

"That's why I'm the one who should watch the soldiers. If you are captured, they will be hard on you."

"I know Baca, know how he thinks. I didn't recognize any of the men in his troop, so they won't know I was once a soldier."

"Take care, *amigo*. If you're not back by sunup, I'll come looking for you."

Lalo grinned and waved. He nudged his horse and disappeared in the brush.

"It's already past sunrise, Felipe, and Lalo ain't back," Clory said.

"I'm going after him, Clory. We'll both be back soon."

"And I'm going with you." Clory already had Heath in his cradleboard, strapped to her back. She carried her musket in her right hand.

"Give me one of your guns, Felipe," Alondra said. "I'm coming too."

Felipe glanced at the two women and didn't argue. He knew he would lose the argument, and if they were with him then he could keep an eye on them.

They followed Lalo's trail until it faded under the cottonwoods. They dismounted and led their horses, Felipe in the lead scanning the ground for any sign to tell him Lalo had passed by. He stopped, sniffed the air—smoke. With hand motions and praying Heath would remain quiet, he urged the others forward. They tethered the horses and crept through the brush toward the camp. Six Mexican soldiers lazed around the campfire, smoking and talking.

Lalo was tied spread-eagle between two cottonwood trees. Stripped to the waist, his skin showed stark white against his black beard.

Clory drew in her breath. Felipe clapped his hand over her mouth and spoke in her ear. "Be very quiet. We'll get him out." He made motions for the women to move back.

Far enough from the camp so they wouldn't be heard, Felipe outlined his plan. "They don't know you, Clory, so you'll have to go in the camp. Can you hide Heath somewhere? He may become frightened and cry."

"He stays with me. He don't hinder me none, and once I'm in the camp it won't make no never mind if he does squall."

"All right. Wait for me here. Don't move and do not shoot your musket. I'll be back in a few minutes. Alondra, bring Segundo and follow me. We're going to find Lalo's horse." Felipe took the Indian weapons from his saddle and coiled a rope over his shoulder.

Leading Segundo and Comanche Pony through the thick forest, they skirted the camp without speaking. Suddenly Felipe stopped and dropped to the ground. Alondra hunkered beside him. He pointed to a soldier sitting on a rock, smoking and picking his teeth. "The lookout," Felipe murmured. "He's little more than a boy."

On the other side of the lookout, the horses milled about in a rope corral. Felipe spread his weapons on the ground. His knife was swift, silent, and certain. He didn't want to kill the soldier unless it became necessary; he had no stomach for killing young boys. He replaced the knife in its sheath. His gun was sure but loud, it would alarm the other soldiers. He replaced it in the holster. He could lasso the soldier, but no doubt he'd object and yell. An arrow was quiet but deadly. From the position of the soldier, Felipe didn't think he could get close enough to use the war club without detection. The sling was quick and quiet. Although he hadn't used a sling in years, as a child he'd successfully hunted small game with one.

He searched for the perfect stone—large enough to send the soldier into unconsciousness but not so large as to crush his skull. He twirled the leather sling and tossed the rock. The soldier toppled over with a soft grunt. Felipe ran to him and bound the man's hands and feet. He had a small lump in the center of his forehead. Felipe gagged the soldier with his own kerchief.

Felipe spotted Lalo's gelding in the rope corral with the other horses. He saddled it and handed the reins to Alondra. He left the rope loose so the other horses would wander away quietly. "Mount Segundo and, when I give the signal, bring Lalo his horse. Shoot in the air. You don't want to hit anything." He gave Alondra a quick hug and kiss. "Take care, *querida*." He dashed back to Clory and glanced at Heath. The baby stared back, wide-eyed and solemn. He seemed to understand that his life depended on silence, and a picture of him at the massacre flashed in Felipe's mind.

Silently, they approached the army camp, and he gave Clory his knife. "Circle through the brush behind Lalo and, when I signal, cut the ropes. Alondra will bring your horses. Don't stop, run for our camp, and wait for me. I'll be there shortly."

He watched Clory snake her way through the bushes while he counted to one hundred. When he saw that Clory was in position, he whistled the four-toned lonesome call of the mourning dove. At the sound, Lalo lifted his head and straightened his shoulders.

The next several seconds went by in a blur of activity. Felipe tossed a rock with his sling, then let fly two arrows in rapid succession. Clory slashed the rope and loosened Lalo. "Indians," a soldier shouted, and they scrambled for their weapons. Clory shot her musket. Alondra galloped through camp with the horses, gun pointing in the air and shooting. Felipe fired a pistol, ran to a different side of the camp, and shot an arrow. Lalo and Clory vaulted onto their horses and, with Alondra, streaked out of the army camp.

Concerned for their own safety, the soldiers didn't give them a glance. Felipe shot both his guns at the same time until they were empty. He leaped on El Moro and galloped along the riverbank shooting his rifle. El Moro dashed through the heavy undergrowth, dodging tree limbs and tangled brush, with Felipe praying the soldiers followed him instead of the others.

He stopped and listened to the rustling leaves, the shouting men, the pounding hooves of only one horse. He nudged El Moro and the horse jumped into the swiftly flowing river. Felipe grabbed a loose tree limb, turned El Moro's head downstream, and, keeping the leafy branch between him and shore, the horse swam past the army camp.

Lalo was sitting by the river, legs dangling over the bank, when El Moro climbed out of the water and Felipe dismounted.

"Thank you, my friend, I owe you," Lalo said.

"No," Felipe answered, "We're even now. What happened?"

"I was foolish. I watched and waited until Baca and the troop headed out. Those few soldiers were only a hunting party and planned to follow the others with fresh game meat in the morning. They didn't know me, so I decided to talk with them to find out what Baca is doing in New Mexico." Lalo grinned sheepishly. "They recognized my horse as belonging to the army and accused me of stealing him. They wouldn't listen to any explanations I gave them and figured to gain points when they delivered me to Baca."

Felipe chuckled. "Actually, we have two army horses. We'll have to do something about that when we get to the ranch. Right now, though, we need them both."

"Bah, the army owes me back pay that I'll never get. I'll keep my horse and call it square."

Felipe watched Heath pull up grass with his pudgy fist, gurgling and cooing. "I don't know much about babies, but Heath is special and very brave. He didn't make a sound."

Lalo puffed out his chest. "Of course not, he's my son." And both men laughed.

*****

They decided to camp on the banks of the *Rio Grande* for two more days to make certain the soldiers had gone on. The next afternoon Felipe said, "Come on, Alondra, let's go swimming."

"But I don't know how, I've never tried it."

"I'll teach you," he said.

"Shoot, Alondra, there ain't nothing to it," Clory said. "It's time to teach Heath how to swim anyhow in case the Weeping Woman is walking the *Rio Grande*. Come on, Lalo." She stripped the baby of his clothes, then her own, and, carrying Heath, waded into the river, Lalo right behind her.

Alondra watched the happy family laughing and splashing. "I don't want to intrude on them, Felipe. They're having so much fun."

With the special smile he had that always set her pulses racing, he took her hand. "Come with me, we'll have our own private swimming party." He led her downstream until he found a spot where the river ran slow and large cottonwoods leaned over the water, forming a leafy screen.

Still, Alondra hesitated.

"You trust me, don't you?" he asked. She nodded.

"Take my hand," he said. "I won't let anything happen to you." They removed their clothes and waded into the river until they were chest deep. "Just pretend you're taking a bath."

She sat down. The water covered her head, and she came up sputtering. "It's too deep for a bath."

"That's why you're going to swim. Lay over my arm. I'll hold you up." He held her by the waist. "Now, kick your legs. Good. Now, move your arms. You're swimming. I knew you could do it."

Yes. She could swim. She could do anything with Felipe

beside her. Already she had learned so much: to ride a horse, shoot a gun, speak a new language, now swimming. And there was more to learn and a lifetime with Felipe to learn it. Love for him filled her heart with such intensity that she wrapped her arms around his neck and kissed him. "I love you, Felipe."

He clasped her tightly, his hands cupping her body, and returned her passionate kisses. "I know, *querida*," he said, his mouth hot and sweet against her lips.

They floated, the waves washed over their heads, the river embraced them, held them in a watery bed as their legs intertwined. He gathered her against his warm pulsing body, and she closed around him.

They must have surfaced for breath once or twice, but Alondra had no memory of it. The gently lapping waves, her hair streaming sensuously around them, his silky-smooth skin made her oblivious to all but Felipe and their love.

When at last they did surface, sated and spent, Felipe kissed her tenderly, and they swam to shore. He helped her out of the water and laughed. "You, *querida*, are a lot of woman."

She grinned. "And you, *Señor*, are the man for me."

In the morning, Felipe said it was time to move on. Although he wouldn't admit it, he'd become fond of the unwieldy cart but still wanted to exchange it for a carriage.

"We don't need a fancy wagon to ride in," Alondra said. "We're almost home and this cart has served us well."

Felipe gazed at Alondra his soft hazel eyes filled with love. "Home" his woman had said. He, too, was eager to get home. "All right, we'll bypass the village. It will save us a day or two. We'll go on to the Blue *Mesa*."

Two days later, they reached the foot of the Blue *Mesa* in the late afternoon and set up camp in a clump of juniper near a small spring with forage for the animals.

Next morning before sunup, Felipe and Lalo climbed the rocky path up the *mesa*. "I don't know exactly where the mine is," Felipe said. "I understand it's in a cave somewhere near the top." The wind moaned and swirled sand.

They searched in crevices, behind stunted trees, under rocks, around boulders, but found no cave openings. They climbed higher and searched with no success. A gust tugged at their hats. "Are you sure this is the correct *mesa*?" Lalo asked.

"Yes, our ranch is less than a day's ride from here. I've known about the silver since I was a child and often dreamed of someday riding to this *mesa* and finding it."

The wind howled and snatched at their clothes. They climbed to the highest point of the *mesa*. An Indian sat cross-legged on a flat rock, his back to them. The wind died, and the sudden silence was oppressive.

Before either could speak, the Indian said, "This is a sacred mountain, white men are not allowed here." He didn't turn, nor did he look at them.

"Forgive us," Felipe said. "We mean no harm."

The Indian got to his feet and stared at them, his eyes dark and flat. "You want the silver. You won't find it."

"Do you know where it is?" Lalo asked.

"Yes, but the true treasure of the *mesa* is not the silver."

"Can you show us the cave with the silver?"

"Follow me." The Indian turned down the path.

"Who is he?" Lalo whispered.

Felipe shrugged. "I don't know."

"I am a medicine man of the Tewa. In your language, my name is Cloud Feather."

"My name is Felipe Montez."

"Yes. Many seasons ago, your ancestors came to the *mesa* searching for the silver."

"But they never found it."

"Some did, but it was not theirs and the gods did not allow them to keep it." Cloud Feather stopped before a pile of boulders and rubble. "The cave is behind those rocks."

"What happened?" Lalo asked.

"The elders say that the gods wearied of the Spaniards violating the sacred cavern. One day, they sent a rockslide and sealed the cave opening. Now, no one can enter the holy place. The medicine men come here and pray because the spirits still live here, guarding the silver."

Lalo picked up a rock and shoved it aside. "We could clear these rocks away and find the opening." A low moan from behind the stone made his skin prickle. He jumped back.

"Other men have tried but failed," Cloud Feather said. "The gods crushed some with boulders and sent spirits to frighten others away."

"Was that a spirit I heard?" Lalo asked, an anxious look on his face.

"The spirits guard only the silver."

"What do you mean? What else is there in that cave?" Lalo asked.

"The remains of Spaniards who searched for the silver, and the bones of the Indians who were forced to mine it. There is nothing for you in the cave. Follow your heart and you will find something more precious than the silver in this cave."

"I don't understand what ..."

Felipe took Lalo by the arm. "Come, Lalo. We'll find some other way to make our fortune. Thank you, Cloud Feather. We will not return."

Cloud Feather nodded, turned up the mountain path, and disappeared in a blue mist.

Felipe and Lalo stared at the empty path.

His face ashen, Lalo asked. "Was that Indian real, or was he a dream?"

Felipe, too, was shaken. "I don't know, but I'm not willing to find out by clearing away the rubble to the cave entrance. Are you?"

"No. Even the wind ..." Lalo shook his head.

"Let's go," Felipe said. "There's no treasure for us here."

Lalo leaned against a boulder and folded his arms across

his chest. "Thoughts of that silver kept me going for a long time, Felipe. Now I don't know what I'm going to do."

"Many men have made their fortune hauling wool and hides across the Santa Fe Trail to Saint Louis. We could do that."

"I have no money to buy the goods. There is no way that I can finance such an undertaking."

"There are wagons and mules at the *hacienda*. My father will loan us the money. Come on, we can be at the ranch by this time tomorrow."

"I'm grateful and I will pay you back."

Felipe grinned and slapped Lalo on the back. "Yes, *amigo*, you will pay me back."

CHAPTER 24

SANTA FE, NEW MEXICO

Maria Fuentes—beautiful, pampered, and engaged to be married to Felipe Montez—sat at her table writing. Spread on the desk were a child's primer and a paper with a name written in large block letters—JAMES THORNTON.

Maria dipped a quill in the inkwell and wrote with careful strokes. First, she had to translate a word from Spanish and try to spell it in English. Writing was new to her, and she wrote only in English, a language also new to her. For three weeks, James Thornton had been teaching her both skills. After an hour of hard labor, the ink splotched letter stated:

James, I cannot meet with you tonight. Papa says I must go with him to the Montez hacienda. Yours forever, Maria

She read the note three times, could find nothing wrong with her words, waved it to dry the ink, and folded it carefully. She sprinkled the paper liberally with lilac water, further blotching the ink, and called her maid.

"Luisa, take this to the *Señor* Thornton and be quick about it. If he gets it soon enough, maybe he'll come see me before we have to leave."

As co-conspirator in the romance between Maria and

James, Luisa knew the man well. At every opportunity, while the household rested in the afternoon, she accompanied Maria to the Chapel of Our Lady of Guadalupe. They waited together in the cool interior until Thornton arrived. Luisa would then disappear for an hour while the other two sat, holding hands and murmuring of their love.

Luisa enjoyed those afternoons as they freed her to visit her own lover. Since she had no reason to be as discreet as Maria, she met Juanito in his own home. Before delivering the letter, she decided to stop and tell him that she'd be leaving town for a few days. Maybe they wouldn't be away for too long. She didn't like the idea of Juanito on his own in Santa Fe. Temptation lurked around every corner.

It took longer to say goodbye than she'd planned, and by the time Luisa reached James Thornton's lodging he was not at home. Maybe he'd already gone to the church. And that is where Luisa found him.

In one glance, he read what her mistress had labored over for so long. "When do you leave?" His blue eyes held a look of concern.

Luisa shrugged. "First thing in the morning, I think." She approved of this man. Unlike most Americans, he spoke Spanish. *Señor* Fuentes, though, called him an adventurer, whatever that meant.

"I must see her before she goes, tell your mistress to come to the church."

"She said you might go to her."

"To the house?"

He'd been there only once, and Luisa knew he had not enjoyed the experience. "The *señorita* is occupied with packing, and they are watching her. She cannot leave the house. But, if you come with me, I'll take you around to the back courtyard to her window. You can talk together. No one will see you."

James hesitated but his love was strong, and he led the way

through the dusty streets and twisting alleyways of Santa Fe. Few people were about in this hour before dinner, and they met no one. Luisa trotted to keep pace with the tall man who walked with the easy stride and swagger that matched any *caballero* of the richer class.

James and Maria had met in Saint Louis the previous summer, when *Señor* Fuentes took Maria for a holiday and Luisa went along as chaperone. Maria later confided that when she first saw James, thunder crashed through a clear sky and shook the building. When he took her hand, it was as though he'd touched her with a lightning bolt. "And," Maria whispered, "the best part was that he felt the same." Nine months later, James Thornton arrived in Santa Fe with a box of books and a manservant named Joseph.

But *Señor* Fuentes did not approve of James, and Luisa thought it might be because he did not trust any Anglo. "They will ruin our way of life," he often said. "They brought whiskey and rum into our country, and not many of our people can tolerate the effects. The Anglos don't respect our customs and take advantage of our hospitality. They woo our women with trinkets and promises and then return to their eastern homes, leaving behind a brokenhearted girl and a blue-eyed baby."

At the whitewashed adobe house, James softly called Maria's name. Through the open window, Maria reached out for him with such joy on her face that Luisa was almost sorry she hadn't found him sooner. She left the lovers to themselves and returned to her own neglected work. Anyway, since they spoke in the American language, she couldn't understand their talk.

"Maria, you are going away?" James asked.

"Yes, Papa says it is time. But really, James, I think he just wants to take me away from you."

"Time for what, Maria? Why are you leaving?"

"Let me look at you, I want to carry your image in my heart. If I am fortunate and someday return, will you be here waiting?" She gazed long and lovingly into his blue eyes, ran a palm over his smooth-shaven cheeks, ran her fingers through his brown hair that hung loose to his shoulders.

He took both her hands in his. "Tell me what's going on, Maria."

"Papa tells me I must go to the Montez *hacienda*. There, I will meet my betrothed and then get married."

"Why didn't you tell me of your betrothal before this, Maria?"

"I cannot talk with you like this, James. Wait there, I will come out to the courtyard." She disappeared with a silken flurry of her ankle-length skirt and in a few minutes stood before him in the courtyard. She ran into his arms. "Hold me, my beloved. Hold me."

He held her tight, kissed her hair. "Why haven't you spoken of this before?"

"I don't know. I guess I hoped it would go away if I didn't think about it." Tears pooled in her brown eyes.

"Who is this man?"

"Someone I've known all my life. Our parents arranged our marriage years ago, when I was only eight."

"That's outrageous. We can't let this happen. I'll go now and speak to your father. We'll get married right away."

"That is not possible. What's done is done. Papa will force me to marry that man. I will be devastated and spend the rest of my life remembering you."

"Surely, if you tell him you don't want marriage, he'll—"

She stood on tiptoe and kissed him, stopping his words. "I am doomed, *mi amor*, doomed. There is no way out."

He crushed her to his breast, and she gave herself to the passion of his kiss. "We'll go away, Maria. There is no way I'll let you go into a loveless marriage. I'll take you to my home."

She stepped away from him, her eyes wide. "To Saint Louis?"

"Yes, of course. We'll leave right away. How soon can you

be ready?"

"I can't go away with you."

"It will be a hard trip for you, I know. But I'll buy a wagon and some sturdy mules. We'll travel with a wagon train. Everything will be fine, you'll see."

Maria stared at him in dismay. Did he really think she'd leave her comfortable home and travel for who-knew-how-many months in a bumpy wagon? She'd traveled the Santa Fe Trail once before, borne the rigors of sleeping on the ground, eating out of tin plates, and worrying about hostile Indians. Although worth all the difficulties because she had met James, Maria had no desire to experience those hardships again. "I can't go with you to Saint Louis, James."

His eyes hardened. "Why? Don't you love me? You want to marry that other man?"

She stroked his cheek with light fingertips. "I love you, James. I love you so much that I sometimes hurt. But I can't disgrace my family."

"And this other man, he is willing to marry you?"

"Of course. He has no choice. We, neither one of us, have a choice. We will marry, have children, and—"

"No! I won't let that happen. The thought of you in another man's arms ..." He paced the length of the courtyard.

Maria smiled to herself but kept her face a proper mask of sadness. "I won't enjoy it, James. I will only be doing my duty as the Church dictates."

"I will not allow it to happen. When does the wedding take place?"

Her elation was so great Maria could not keep the smile from her lips. "I do not know, first the banns must be read, a month at the soonest."

"When do you return from this trip?"

"In a few days."

"Good, I will see you then." He took her in his arms and, between each word he spoke, placed a tender kiss on her lips.

"Don't forget ... you belong ... to me." He strode out of the courtyard.

Maria gazed after him, her hands clasped to her breast. *Dios mio*, but she loved that man. A pity they could never spend their lives together. She saw herself in the future, a tragic figure of unrequited love, with all the villagers gazing after her, sorrowing that such a beautiful woman was forced to lead such a sad life. She'd wear only black. No, black tended to make her look old. Maybe a wine-red instead, with bits of creamy lace at her throat and wrists.

"Luisa," she called, "Let's finish packing." But Luisa had already completed that task.

*****

Next morning, Maria dawdled. The morning sun was high by the time the Fuentes party headed south, surrounded by armed *vaqueros*. For centuries, the people of this land had lived by the gun and the sword, the bow, and the lance. Only fools traveled without protection—and Jose Fuentes was not a fool.

"Papa," Maria said, "What would happen if I refused to marry Felipe Montez?"

"I cannot say, because you would not do so, little daughter. You are honorable and would not bring disgrace upon your family."

"But I do not love him, Papa, I love another."

Fuentes tightened his jaw, his eyes glittered. "You are speaking of the Anglo, James Thornton. I will not allow you to marry one such as him."

She pursed her lips in a delightful pout that never failed to move her father into granting her heart's desire. She stroked his rugged hand with her soft palm. "Doesn't love in a marriage count for anything, Papa?"

He glared at her. She flinched and pulled her hand back.

"Love is more than a handsome face and blue eyes, Maria. Love comes with friendship, supporting one another in good times and bad. As the years go by, you will learn to love one another. I arranged marriages for all your sisters. They all accepted the men I chose for them with no argument, and they are all happy. Do you ever hear any of your sisters complain?"

Maria shook her head.

"You will marry Felipe Montez and be a good and dutiful wife. We will not discuss this again. Do you understand what I say?"

He had never spoken to Maria in such a harsh manner. "Yes, Papa."

There was nothing more she could do. Her father's word was law, she had to obey him. When next she saw James Thornton, she'd tell him that no amount of argument could sway her father.

She spent the remainder of the trip thinking of her coming marriage. It had been years since she'd seen Felipe. She could not remember what he looked like or what kind of man he was but had confidence that, in a short time, he too would fall madly in love with her. Perhaps, even now, his heart pined for her.

*****

Felipe, Alondra, Lalo, and Clory reached the *hacienda* in the early afternoon. Felipe stopped at the crest of the valley, and his heart lifted at the sight of the ranch buildings. "There it is, friends, welcome to my home."

Dusty cottonwoods lined the bank of a silver river and new green dotted the cornfields. The house, made of rock and adobe, lay spread out behind an adobe wall, and a rock tower guarded the gate.

The cart's squealing wheels announced their arrival, and they were met at the gate by barking dogs and a man wearing a wide-brimmed hat and a poncho.

"What do you people want here?" the man asked the bedraggled group.

Felipe laughed and removed his hat. "Don't you know me, Tomas?"

Peering at him with narrowed eyes, Tomas shook his head. The dogs crowded around Felipe, sniffing. The old shaggy one licked his hand.

Felipe chuckled and scratched the dog's ears. "It's me, Tomas. Felipe. See, the dogs know me."

Tomas spread his arms in delight, his eyes sparkled, a wide grin spread across his face. "*Señor* Felipe! I didn't recognize you with all that hair on your face. Welcome. It is good to see you. Your parents will be pleased you are safely home. I will send someone to tell them. We have all been waiting anxiously for your arrival. Here, let me take your horse to the stables. Your man can help me with the other animals." Tomas cast a sideways glance at the women. "What do you want me to—?"

"Tomas! These are my friends and guests of the *hacienda*."

Tomas ducked his head. "*Si, Señor.*"

"We all need baths and clean clothes before we meet my parents. Ask Jorge to come to the men's bathhouse. Lalo and I need a shave. Send Vina to the women's bathhouse to assist the ladies." Felipe slapped his hat against his leg. A fog of dust rose in a cloud. "And be quick about it."

Tomas scuttled away, forgetting about the animals.

"I don't need anyone to help me bathe," Alondra said.

"Me neither." Clory picked up Heath and held him against her shoulder. "All we need is the tin chest."

Felipe hauled the chest out of the cart. "What do you want me to do with your chickens, Alondra?"

She grinned. "They're safe now. Turn them out with your own hens."

A stable boy ran up to them. "I'll take care of the animals, *Señor* Felipe." He led the horses to the corrals, the cartwheels groaned, the goats trotted behind.

Felipe heaved the chest on his shoulder. "I'll show you ladies the bathhouse. Take your time and allow Vina to assist you. She's been with my mother for a long time and knows what women like. When you're ready, she'll escort you to the house and you will meet my family." He set the chest outside a log house. Smoke curled from the chimney, marigolds, spearmint, oregano, and other herbs grew around the building. "Good. They're already heating the water. Let's go get our baths, Lalo." He strode off and Lalo followed.

Clory glanced at Alondra. "I ain't never seen anything like this."

"Me either." Alondra took a deep breath. "Come on, Clory, I really do need a bath." She pushed the door open.

A pleasant-looking woman pouring hot water into a wooden tub said, "Hello. My name is Vina." She noticed Heath. "A baby! They didn't tell me about a baby. Wait right here, I'll get Rosa. She'll take care of the baby for you." Vina dashed out the door.

Clory sat on a wooden bench. "Do they do everything for you around here? Won't we be allowed to do anything for ourselves? I don't know that I'm going to like this fancy living."

"Give it a chance, Clory, it might not be so bad. And anyway, it will be better than bathing in a cold river."

Vina entered the room with a short, round woman in tow. Rosa bent toward Heath. "*Qué lindo el bebé, y tan bueno.*" Heath gurgled and held out his arms. Rosa picked him up. "*Le voy a bañar y alimentar.*"

Clory jumped up. "Wait. Where is she taking him? He needs a bath, and his milk, and then a nap."

Rosa looked puzzled and turned to Alondra for translation.

"It's all right, Clory. They don't understand. They speak

only Spanish. She's going to bathe and feed him."

"Tell them I'm sorry my Spanish is sketchy, but I'm trying to learn."

Alondra spoke with the women, they laughed, and Rosa left the bathhouse, taking Heath with her.

"She will set up a cradle for him in your room, Clory," Alondra said.

"Will Lalo be there too?" Clory sounded anxious.

Alondra grinned. "I told them you two were married."

"Did you tell them you and Felipe were married?"

Her smile faded and Alondra shook her head. "I didn't dare."

Vina motioned to them. "Remove your clothes, please."

The girls shucked off their garments, glad to be rid of their dusty trail clothes.

"Leave them on the floor," Vina said.

Alondra stacked her clothes in a pile. "You're right, Clory. Someone will launder these for us."

Vina poured a bucket of warm water over each of them. Water and desert dirt flowed over the floor and dripped through cracks between the planks.

"That ain't so bad," Clory said, "If that's all there is to it."

But Vina wasn't through with them. She had each step into a wooden tub filled with steaming water and gave them both bars of perfumed soap and cloths to scrub with. She washed their hair, poured more water over them, asked them to step out of the tubs, and swaddled them in cotton sheets.

Vina told them to sit on the bench, and she brushed Alondra's long black curls. She lifted Alondra's chin and studied her face. Vina pulled a tortoiseshell comb from her pocket, brushed Alondra's hair back, and held it in place with the comb. She looked at Alondra's hands and clicked her tongue. She took a pot from a shelf, dipped her fingers, and rubbed a yellowish balm on Alondra's work-hardened palms. The ointment smelled of wool and honey. "Use this two or three times a day, and your hands will soon be soft and smooth again," Vina said.

She turned her attention to Clory. She brushed and combed Clory's shorter hair and said something to Alondra.

"She said your hair is the color of a cloud at sunset," Alondra told Clory. "She says your eyes are blue as a summer sky, sparkle like the stars, and that you are very pretty."

"Aw, shoot," Clory said and blushed.

Vina had a different concoction for Clory's sun-reddened skin. "She says to rub this on your face and arms every day, and, when you go out in the sun, spread a flour paste on your face and you won't sunburn."

"I ain't got time for all this foofaraw," Clory said, but when Vina held up a mirror, both girls gasped in surprise.

"I won't mind going through all this if it makes me look better for Felipe's family," Alondra said. The girls dressed themselves in the clothes from the tin chest, and Vina gave them cowhide slippers and toeless cotton stockings.

Head cocked to the side, Vina surveyed her handiwork. Pleased, she smiled. "Come. You are ready to meet *Señor* and *Señora* Montez." She led them across the courtyard to the house, opened the door, and ushered them into a large dim room.

The glow of a single beeswax candle on a small table lit one corner of the room. Next to the candle lay a thin leather box with a clay bowl perched on top. A *retablo* of the Blessed Mother hung on the wall. The holy picture, painted on leather, was faded, the paint chipped and cracked. Heavy, dark, furniture filled the room, crimson worsted curtains covered the window.

Alondra caught her breath at the sight of Felipe leaning against the fireplace mantel. Bathed and barbered, he was heart-stopping handsome. Elegant and at ease in the luxurious surroundings, he wore the clothes of a *caballero*—close-fitting woolen trousers with silver buttons from thigh to hem, unbuttoned and flared at the knee. Blue and gold braid decorated his waist-length buckskin jacket.

Doubt flickered in her mind. How could she hope to fit in his world?

Also dressed as a gentleman, Lalo tugged at his cuffs, an anxious furrow between his eyes.

An elderly couple sat in wooden chairs near the window, a small table between them. Candlelight played on the handsome features of a middle-aged couple seated on a dark-red settee. All four stared at the girls with undisguised interest.

Felipe smiled. "Good, the ladies are here." He crossed the room and took each girl by their elbow. "Come, I want to introduce you to my family. This is Clory."

He spoke in Spanish, and Alondra worried that Clory wouldn't understand, but she ducked her head and said, "Howdy." Then she hurried to Lalo and tucked a hand in the crook of his arm.

Felipe led Alondra forward. "And this is Alondra. My parents, Enrique and Seraphina Montez, and my grandparents, *Señor* and *Señora* Montez."

Alondra bowed her head. "*Señoras, Señors*. It is a pleasure to meet you." They all fixed their gazes on her. No one spoke.

The silence and intensity of their stares unnerved her. The flicker of doubt flamed higher, and Alondra stepped back. Her cotton dress suddenly seemed inappropriate. She rubbed a pinch of the red cloth between her thumb and forefinger.

Finally, Seraphina spoke. "Alondra is a very pretty name. Who are your parents, my dear? Who are your people?"

Alondra froze. The one question she had been dreading, the question to which she had no answer. She couldn't find her tongue. Her mind wouldn't work. She twisted the silver bracelet on her arm.

Felipe came to her rescue. "Alondra was orphaned at an early age. She has no parents."

Seraphina clicked her tongue. "Oh, you poor dear."

"You are a very brave young lady," Enrique said.

Lalo cleared his throat. "Pardon me, Felipe. But Clory and I are concerned about Heath. If you would excuse us, please, we will go now and see to his needs."

"Of course, Lalo," Felipe said. "We will see you both later for dinner then."

Lalo bowed from the waist. "With your permission, *Señoras, Señors*." Clory beamed with pride at his courtly manners.

The grandparents' bird-like eyes never wavered from Alondra. Enrique lifted a limp hand as Lalo and Clory hurried from the room.

Seraphina didn't glance at them. She tapped her fan on her palm. "It is very unusual for a young woman to travel long distances with no chaperone. Tell me, my dear, why did you perform such a ... such a courageous act?"

Alondra hesitated. Courageous? They wouldn't think her brave if they knew she trembled to her very soul. She had to answer but didn't want to lie to Felipe's parents. Yet how could she tell them the truth? She couldn't tell them she'd first tricked Felipe, so he'd take her away from poverty and prostitution, but that now she wanted their son for her husband. The silver bracelet felt tight, and she moved it lower on her wrist.

Again, Felipe stepped in. "Alondra helped me escape from the Mexican Army. She was forced to leave San Vicente; her life was in danger there. Besides, Lalo and Clory traveled with us the entire way." He didn't seem to have a problem with stretching the truth.

"You are a heroine, young lady. You must tell us the story of how you accomplished such a dangerous feat," Enrique said.

Felipe took Alondra's arm. "Not now, Father. Alondra is fatigued. It was an exhausting trip. She needs a few hours rest before dinner."

"She does look ill," Seraphina said. "She is pale and trembling. Rest well, my dear."

CHAPTER 25

Outside, Felipe put his arm around Alondra and pressed her close to his side. "I'm sorry, *querida*, they mean well and didn't intend to frighten you. It's just their way. I understand that it can be a little overwhelming with all those questions, but they are kind, and once you get to know them you'll learn to love them."

Alondra had no desire to discuss Felipe's family with him. She had a sudden urge to see her possessions, although meager, they were all she had. "Where's Segundo, Felipe?"

"At the stables. The *vaqueros* are washing and brushing him."

"And my saddle? Where is it?"

"At the stables, they are cleaning it too. Why?"

"I left some things in the saddlebags that I might need."

"They are in my room. I'll have them brought to you." He stopped outside a plank door. "This is your room. Get some rest."

"Which room is Lalo and Clory's?"

"That one." He pointed across the courtyard. "Two doors down from the room we came from."

"Felipe, I—"He placed a gentle finger on her lips. "Shh, *querida*, it will be all right. You'll see. Take a nap, things will look better when you're rested." He opened the door and ushered her inside, turned, and crossed the courtyard.

Alondra sat on the bed. She wasn't tired; she needed to gather her resources, both physical and mental. Nothing in her past had prepared her for the polite hostility she'd experienced with Felipe's family. The words they used were courteous. It was their hawk-like scrutiny that made her feel like a rabbit caught in a snare.

She wanted to believe Felipe but was sure that, although his family might accept her as his friend, never would they accept her as his wife. No one mentioned his betrothal, and Felipe hadn't spoken of it in a long time. She shivered, hugged her arms across her stomach, and rubbed the bracelet.

She removed the comb and shook her hair loose. She needed friendship and warmth. She'd go talk with Clory and Lalo.

Alondra stepped out into the courtyard. The house was built in a horseshoe shape, with rooms added as needed, each with its own outside door and a window with no panes. A covered veranda extended across the center section, apparently the oldest part of the house. Her room was at the end, directly across the courtyard from the kitchens.

She crossed the courtyard and took the one step up on to the veranda. Felipe's voice sounded from the open window. " ... forcing me to choose between my family and friends." Alondra stopped and held her breath.

"How is that?" Seraphina's gentle voice.

"These are my friends. We have traveled together for weeks."

"They are welcome here. We have extended every hospitality." Enrique's deeper voice.

"You gave that girl the silver bracelet." An old woman's accusing voice, the first Alondra heard the grandmother speak.

"It is mine to give," Felipe said.

"But only to your betrothed." The grandmother said.

"I know the meaning of the bracelet," Felipe said, his voice tight. "And I have the right to give it to the woman of my choice."

Alondra slid down the adobe wall to the floor.

An old man coughed. The grandfather. "Perhaps we erred in sending the young scamp to Mexico City, Enrique. He has come home with his head so full of modern notions, all teachings of family honor and duty have been erased."

"The dowry has been paid, Felipe," Enrique said.

"I will repay the dowry, Father, but I don't even know how much or who—"

"How could you forget about Jose Fuentes, who owns more sheep than he can count?" Seraphina asked.

"He chooses to forget," the grandfather said. "Listen to me, Felipe. The amount of the dowry means nothing. The marriage between you and the Fuentes girl was arranged to assure that the veins of the two oldest families in the province remain untainted by Indian blood. The Montez family has followed that custom for over a century. My father's marriage, my marriage, your father's marriage, all arranged by parents who know better than a young man who does not think with his head."

"Alondra is not an Indian. Her father was a Frenchman from Louisiana."

"What kind of a Frenchman was he, this father of Alondra?" Enrique asked. "A pirate who sank Spanish ships and stole the king's gold? A trapper who took beaver pelts from the rivers until there are few remaining? A *Comanchero* who sold guns and whiskey to the Indians and made it easier for them to steal and murder? I've not known many Frenchmen who show good breeding."

Alondra clutched her stomach. Why hadn't Felipe chosen

an American or even an Englishman as her father? Enrique did not like Frenchmen. Bile rose in her throat, and tears stung her eyes.

The grandfather's milder voice said, "It is a matter of honor, Felipe. We cannot bring disgrace on the good name of Montez."

Felipe muttered something, but Enrique's words degrading her supposed heritage pounded in her ears, and Alondra didn't hear.

She did hear the grandmother's voice clear and soft with concern. "Is the girl with child, Felipe?"

She couldn't listen to any more. On her knees, Alondra crawled to Lalo's door and scratched on the heavy planks.

The door creaked open. "*Alondrita*! What's the matter?

Lalo pulled her up and held her in his arms. Between sobs, she told them what she'd heard. For fifteen minutes, they spoke words of comfort and compassion, but nothing either Clory or Lalo could say eased her tormented mind.

The sound of running footsteps pounded on the veranda's wood floor. Clory peeked out the window. "It's Felipe. He's going to your room, Alondra."

"Please, let me stay with you. I don't want to see him."

"Why not? It sounded like he was siding with you."

Alondra wiped her eyes with the hem of her skirt. "That's just it. I don't want to come between him and his family. If we marry and stay here, they will be polite but will never accept me. If we go away and live someplace else, Felipe will come to resent me. I love him too much. I don't think I could bear that."

"What're you aiming to do?" Clory asked.

Alondra fondled the bracelet. "I'm going to Santa Fe. I'll find work there."

"Will you tell Felipe?" Clory asked.

"No. If I did, he wouldn't let me go, or else he'd want to come with me. His place is here with his family, and I won't force him to choose. Please, don't you tell him either."

Clory and Lalo exchanged glances. "When are you leaving?" Lalo asked.

"Tonight, after dark. I don't want to see or talk to anyone."

"We'll go with you," Lalo said. "Clory and I have been talking about going on to Santa Fe."

"I thought Felipe gave you a job here at the *hacienda*."

"He did. But like you, I value Felipe's friendship, and I don't think I can work here and still be his friend. I have two hands and a strong back. I can find work in Santa Fe."

"It's a sorry thing what's happened," Clory said. "I feel bad for Felipe. He was so sure his family would welcome us."

Alondra wiped her cheeks with the back of her hand. She was through with tears. "They are polite, but even the servants think we are low class. I can't face eating with his family. If anyone asks, say that I'm tired and want to take dinner in my room."

"I think we should tell Felipe we're leaving here," Lalo said. "It's not right that we sneak away like thieves. It is not honorable."

"Tell him that you're going if you like, but don't say anything about me."

"You should tell him, Alondra," Clory said. "Honor is important to Felipe. You don't want him to think bad things about you."

"I know, but I don't dare see him. All he'd have to do is touch me and I'd change my mind."

"You could write him a letter, Lalo," Clory said. "You know how to write."

"Only my name, *mi vida*. Anyway, we have no paper, no ink, and no quill."

"Please don't tell him." Alondra shut her eyes and took a deep breath. "I'll never love anyone else, and I'm sure he loves me, but ..."

"Don't throw it all away, *Alondrita*, love is precious and hard to find." Lalo put his arm around Clory and squeezed her shoulder. "Felipe loves you and deserves the chance to defend himself."

"He has no choice, Lalo. He can't turn his back on family honor and tradition. You don't have to come with me; I'll go to Santa Fe alone."

"I can't allow you to travel that distance alone. Since we can't change your mind, we'll go with you. My friend will thank me, and besides I've been longing to see a big town." Lalo grinned and winked.

Alondra hugged him. "Thanks, Lalo." She ran across the courtyard to her room. Her saddlebags lay on the bed. She pushed a chair against the door, huddled on the bed, and pulled a blanket over her head. She would never forget Felipe and the time they'd spent together, but she was doing the right thing. She fell asleep recounting the tender moments, the bracelet clutched in her hand and a tear on her cheek.

CHAPTER 26

Felipe went to the corner table and picked up the clay bowl and spoke to his family. "I want to remind you of something." He ran his finger over the design—a white wolf.

"Be careful of that bowl, son, it is very old," Seraphina said.

"I know how old it is, Mother, it was made over a hundred and fifty years ago by one of our ancestors. She made this design to venerate her husband, White Wolf, a Tewa Indian. We have many Montez cousins with Indian blood."

"That was many years ago, Felipe, things are different now," Grandfather said.

"We are still the same people." Felipe pointed to the small leather box. "The old journals tell how when the Pueblo Indians rebelled in 1680, White Wolf saved the *hacienda* for our family."

"Some of his descendants live here on the ranch," Enrique said.

Felipe set the bowl down. "As servants."

"You are right, my husband," the grandmother said. "The young man has come home with new and strange ideas. He has forgotten his family and our traditions."

Felipe knelt beside her on one knee and took her thin, wrinkled hands in his. "No, Grandmother, I never forgot my family. I bathed in icy creeks because I remembered you telling me that cleanliness was next to godliness. Each time I slept on the hard ground, I thanked Mother for her excellent weaving and my warm woolen blankets. I trained El Moro using the methods Grandfather taught me. Father was with me when I hunted, and he led me home by teaching me to read the stars."

Grandmother pressed her dry lips on his cheek. "Bless you, child."

Seraphina dabbed a handkerchief at her eyes. Grandfather cleared his throat and sucked on his pipe. Enrique shifted in his chair.

Felipe stood before them, hands on hips. "But my friends were with me on the trail. They were loyal when the Mexican Army tried to capture me. They stood beside me when the bullets and the arrows flew. I will not forget them either."

He gestured to the leather box. "The journals tell us that it was White Wolf who began the tradition of giving a silver bracelet to his intended bride. I've had mine since my eighteenth birthday, and not until Alondra have I met anyone I wanted to give the bracelet to."

"Marriage is a sacred sacrament and not to be taken lightly, Felipe. That's why parents are the best judges in choosing mates for their children." Enrique sat forward, elbows on knees. "We can trace our family bloodlines back five hundred years to Spain, to the *conquistadors*, and to the first colonists who settled here along the *Rio Grande*.

"For the past fifteen years, since Mexico broke away from Spain's rule, people from the east have been coming to our land. They bring with them new ideas, new ways of doing things, and they threaten our way of life. It is our duty to protect our family customs, so the next generation will know their roots. And now you, our son, bring home a woman with no past. A woman who doesn't even know who her parents were."

"What does it matter who her parents were? It's Alondra I love."

"It is clear that you do not understand the importance of a suitable marriage. This, all this," Enrique waved his arms around the room, "is yours. With the proper wife, you—"

"Alondra is the proper wife for me."

"Eight generations, Felipe," Enrique said his voice soft, compelling. "Eight generations of your ancestors soaked the earth with their blood and sweat to make this *hacienda* what it is today. Go up on the hill, walk among the white crosses, and tell the decaying bones of your forefathers that their work, their sacrifices, mean nothing to you."

"I understand all that, Father, but without Alondra beside me I don't think I can carry out my duties with honor and pride." Felipe turned and stomped from the room. He had a need to see Alondra, talk with her, hold her in his arms, feel the beat of her heart on his breast.

But Alondra wasn't in her room. He remembered she'd asked about Segundo; maybe she was at the stables brushing her horse.

He crossed the courtyard, passed the kitchen ovens, and caught sight of an ancient *horno*. They no longer used that crumbling clay oven for baking, but hens often nested in its smooth and smoke-blackened mouth.

At the corrals, he ran his hands over the upright *piñon* poles, weathered to a gray satin finish and strung together with old and stiffened rawhide. The corrals carried the dry, dusty odor of generation upon generation of livestock.

He turned, walked to the fields, and stopped at the reed-and-brush lookout. By long tradition, men of the *hacienda*, grown too old for heavy work, sat in similar shelters and, with their slings, protected the crops from rabbits, deer, and other invaders.

He knelt and picked up a handful of dirt. It held the secrets of corn and wheat harvested in years past and of crops not yet planted. This earth, fertile from centuries of silt carried by the *Rio Grande*, was his heritage. Could he give up his birthright? He squeezed the soil into a ball, held it tight for a moment, and let it sift through his fingers.

In the southeast, the sandstone guard tower loomed. Now used for storage, for two hundred years, generations of the family had held off marauders from behind its sturdy walls.

High on the hill, his ancestors lay in eternal rest under the white crosses, now black in the gathering twilight. One of those crosses belonged to Diego, the Montez who wrote the old journals. From him, Felipe inherited his color-changing eyes, hair the color of a bay horse, and, according to the journals, his way with horses, his deep love for the land, and strong commitment to family.

But Cloud Feather, the Indian he met on the *mesa*, said, "He who follows his heart finds the true treasure." Felipe didn't understand what that meant, he knew only that his own heart ached with love for Alondra and his brain reeled with the words—duty and honor.

Dusk settled over the *hacienda*. Here and there, candlelight shone from the workers' homes. A bell clanged in the distance. In his confused state of mind, it tolled his death knell, the death of his happiness. "*Because,*" a voice in his head whispered, "*you can't have it both ways.*"

Felipe returned to the house and faced his family.

Two strangers, an older man and a girl, stopped chatting and looked up as he entered.

For a few moments, no one spoke. Then Seraphina said, "Felipe, you know *Señor* Fuentes, of course, and here is Maria, your betrothed."

Stunned into silence, Felipe only stared.

*****

Jose Fuentes rose to his feet and stepped toward Felipe, hand outstretched. "Felipe, my boy, it is good to see you again." The men shook hands. "You are looking well. Isn't he, Maria?"

Maria fluttered her eyelashes, flicked open her fan, and ducked behind it. "Yes, Papa." She extended her hand.

Felipe bowed and brought her hand to his lips. The older people smiled and nodded to each other.

Maria peeked over her fan at Felipe. He was much more handsome than she remembered. Maybe this arrangement would work out after all. She smiled, taking care to show her dimples.

He didn't appear to notice, but turned away and leaned against the fireplace, arms folded across his chest. Men always noticed her. She would have to do something to get his attention. Most men liked to talk about themselves. "Your parents tell me you've only just returned from Mexico City, Felipe,"

"Yes."

"So, was it wonderful? Did you see all kinds of exciting things?"

"Yes."

Was he some kind of dolt who couldn't even hold a conversation? Papa always said that the union of two people of good blood made for strong families. With Felipe, no doubt her children would be beautiful, but their heads would be empty. "Can you tell us some of your adventures?"

Felipe glanced around the room. "If you'll excuse me, I have some business to attend to."

Enrique cleared his throat. "The dinner bell rang ten minutes ago, Felipe. Call your guests to the table, a feast has been prepared in their honor." He turned to Jose Fuentes. "Felipe brought some friends home with him. They are resting now. It is fortunate you came today; we have much to celebrate."

Maria stood, smoothed down her skirt, and glanced at

Felipe, expecting him to offer his arm, but he turned and walked out of the room. Papa would have a great deal to answer for; she would not enter into this marriage easily. How could anyone expect her to marry that ill-mannered donkey?

Felipe crossed the courtyard to Alondra's room. It lay in shadows, and no candlelight shone through the drawn curtains. He tried the door, but it was blocked. He knocked. "Alondra? It's time for dinner." No answer.

Lalo and Clory came from their room into the courtyard. "She doesn't want dinner," Lalo said.

Felipe stopped his hand in midair. "You've talked to her?"

"Yes," Clory said. "She's all wore out, said she just wants to sleep."

Felipe frowned. "I'll bring food to her later, then." He fell in step with them and lowered his voice. "She's here, Lalo."

"Who?"

"Maria. My betrothed."

Clory clutched his arm. "Oh, lordy. Does Alondra know?"

"What are you going to do?" Lalo asked.

Felipe ran a hand through his hair. "I don't know. My brain is all mixed up. I want to talk with Alondra about this."

Clory shook her head. "Leave her be, Felipe."

"Yes," Lalo said. "Have dinner and talk to her later when you know what you want to do."

At the dinner table, Felipe introduced his friends and extended apologies to his parents and grandparents for Alondra's absence.

"It's been a long trip and she's tired," Seraphina said. "Let her sleep."

"I'm eager to hear of your travels," Enrique said. "And I'm sure our guests are interested as well. Tell us some of your adventures."

Maria clasped her hands together. "Oh, yes. Please do."

Felipe said nothing, so Lalo told them about the puma. In his retelling, the mountain lion was larger, fiercer, and the danger far greater than the reality.

Clory listened intently, trying to pick out a word or two of the conversation. "You do not speak Spanish?" Enrique asked her in English.

"No, sir," she said. "But I'm trying to learn. Our son will grow up knowing both languages."

Enrique nodded. "That is very wise of you. Every day, more and more Americans from the east come to New Mexico. Some learn to speak our language, but most do not, making it very difficult for our people to trade. Many are forced to rely on interpreters, and those men are not always trustworthy."

"That is true," Jose Fuentes said. "The traders come with greed in their hearts and lust in their eyes. Lust, not only for our women but for our land as well."

Worried that the conversation would turn to politics, Seraphina quickly said, "Let us all speak in the American language, then. Tell us about your baby, Clory. How old is he?"

"I don't rightly know." Clory told how they found Heath on the abandoned farm. A much more interesting story than that of the puma, the family and Jose Fuentes shot questions at Clory and Lalo.

Maria didn't listen to their talk; she watched Felipe. He appeared distracted. Perhaps he was thinking of this Alondra they talked about. He excused himself from the table and walked out the door. She murmured an apology to Seraphina and followed him.

From the veranda, she watched Felipe cross the courtyard and knock on a door. The room was dark, and apparently no one answered because he peeked in the window. He stood for a moment, then turned and walked toward the water well, where he stopped and glanced back at the dark room.

Maria stepped off the veranda and went to him, hands outstretched. "Felipe, what is it? Can I help you?"

He stared at her as though she were a stranger. "There is nothing."

She heaved a deep sigh. "If we are to be man and wife, Felipe, we must learn to share our troubles as well as our joys."

"Come, let us sit. I need to talk with you." He led her to the veranda, and they sat side by side on the steps. "Maria, do you really want to marry me?"

That was not a question she'd expected. Confused, she didn't answer.

She couldn't see his face in the dark, but his voice held a smile. "I didn't think so," he said.

"Why? How did you know?"

"A woman like you must have many suitors. I'm surprised you are not already married to some wealthy rancher."

"Papa would not allow me to break our betrothal. He says it would bring disgrace on our family."

Felipe sighed. "I know."

"You mean you don't want to marry me?" That idea was unthinkable of course.

He paused a minute too long. "What I think," he said, "is that two people should love each other if they are to spend a lifetime together."

She let out a happy squeal. "Oh, so do I. And I must tell you, Felipe, that I am in love with another man. But he is an Anglo, and Papa does not approve of him."

"And I admit," Felipe said, "that I have thought and thought but cannot think of an honorable way to break our betrothal."

Maria laughed. "Leave it to me. I will make Papa see things my way, and if I refuse to marry you what can your parents say?"

They rose, and from the shadows of the veranda they walked into the soft moonlight. "They will be disappointed, of course, and never fully approve. They made a pact, the dowry has been paid, and no one in my family has ever gone back on his word, it is not honorable."

"Ah. And that bothers you?" She brushed his hair from his forehead. "Don't worry. It is I who will break my word."

"I can't allow you to take the blame."

"A gentleman to the end, I see." She laughed. A cloud covered the moon. "It is late; I must get to bed. Good night." She ran into the house.

Alondra peeked out the window when she heard Maria greet Felipe. She had heard him tell Lalo that the girl was his betrothed, and although she told herself it didn't matter Alondra strained to see and hear. The couple sat in the shadows, and they were too far away to hear, but still she watched and waited.

After what seemed an eternity, they walked out into the moonlight. She could see their features plainly and her heart sank. The girl was beautiful and when she reached up and touched Felipe's hair, Alondra bit her lip to hold back the tears. The girl's airy laughter floated out into the night.

Alondra felt her knees weaken and she clutched the windowsill. A merciful cloud veiled the moon, and she could no longer see them. She huddled on the bed. What did she expect? A long time ago, he told her of his betrothal, and she never really expected to marry him. Still, he did give her the silver bracelet. She heard his knock and lay still. She no longer had doubts about her decision to go to Santa Fe.

*****

Felipe knocked on the door. Still no answer. He pushed against it. Blocked. He flicked the curtain aside. "Alondra?" No answer. He peered in the window. A still form lay on the bed. Perhaps she was overly tired. He wanted to tell her what he and Maria had talked about, but he'd let her sleep for now and see her in the morning. He went to his own room, shucked off his boots, and lay on his bed. He clasped his hands behind his head and considered what he'd tell his parents. He wanted them to accept Alondra and approve of his marriage, but if they didn't then ...

During his stroll around the *hacienda*, he'd decided to give up all thoughts of personal happiness and marry the Fuentes girl. He could not dishonor his family. But after seeing Maria again, he knew he could never marry her. The girl was conceited and a flirt.

He pictured Alondra, her smiling lips, her trail-worn clothes. He ached with longing and knew he would never give her up, no matter the cost.

Weary, his eyelids drooped closed.

*****

Armor-clad *conquistadors* marched through Felipe's sleep. A young man dressed in buckskin and riding a gray charger burst through the ranks. The horse reared, and the young man brandished his sword and shouted, "Honor and duty!" His eyes flashed a green fire that seared a path to the *hacienda* gate.

An Indian of the Tewa tribe stood in the courtyard, arms folded across his chest. "Trust in your heart," he said.

A woman with cinnamon-colored braids appeared at his side, a silver bracelet on her wrist gleaming with a blinding light. She linked arms with the Indian, smiled, and said, "Follow your heart, Felipe. Therein lies your honor."

"But what of my duty?" Felipe asked.

Cloud Feather stood on the *mesa*. "Follow your heart," he said and disappeared in a blue mist.

The man on the gray horse waved his sword. The *hacienda*, the people, all vanished. Only the land remained: red rocks, *piñons*, and cactus. The words "follow your heart" echoed across the *mesas*.

*****

Felipe woke before the roosters crowed, the dream vivid in his mind. He wadded the pillow under his head, smoothed the blankets, turned on his side. He might as well get up, go to the stables, talk to El Moro, and maybe go for a ride. Somehow, handling horses always soothed his mind. He pulled on his boots and stepped out the door.

The eastern sky was brightening, a band of red stretched across the horizon. He breathed in the clean morning air and admired the pink and gold sunrise. He'd seen the sun rise every day throughout his travels, but only here at the *hacienda* did the sun bless the land in such splendid glory.

At the stables, he whistled for El Moro. The horse trotted up to him, and Felipe stroked its neck, scratched its forehead.

"Grandfather says you'll make a good sire, and he has some fine-looking mares lined up for you. But do we stay, or will we be forced to go?" The horse butted him in the chest.

Felipe opened the gate. "Come, El Moro, let's go for a run and talk about our decision." He leaped on the horse's back, no saddle or bridle, and urged El Moro to a lope. They turned toward the river, jumped an *acequia* in one bound, cantered along the edge of a freshly plowed field, jumped another irrigation ditch, and galloped up the hill.

Felipe stopped and looked down at the ranch buildings. He patted El Moro's neck. "This could be your new home. You'd have good grazing in the pasture over there by the river and fresh corn and apples in summer. The Indian said, 'Trust in your heart,' and we know what our hearts want, but will my parents accept Alondra sincerely and love her for who she is? If not, we will go away from here, maybe to California, maybe south to Texas. If we're together, it doesn't matter. From here, you can see the house; that room on the end is Alondra's. Let's go talk with her, ask her which direction she'd like to go." They galloped down the hill and to the stable.

Felipe slid off El Moro and led him to the stalls. With a shock, he realized the other horses were not there. Segundo, Comanche Pony, Lalo's gelding, all three gone.

He ran to Alondra's room and pushed the door. It swung open with ease. Alondra was not in the room. She had taken all her belongings. On the table lay the silver bracelet.

He picked it up and clutched it in his hand. *Why, Alondra, why? You could have at least talked to me, told me what bothered you.* He stared at the bracelet for a moment and then clasped it around his wrist.

His heart heavy, a hole in his soul, he crossed the courtyard to Lalo's bedroom but knew, without entering, that he would find it empty.

In crude letters, scratched in the courtyard dirt, was the word LALO and three arrows pointing to the north. Felipe sat on the veranda steps and studied the message.

"Follow your heart," the smiling woman had said.

"Follow your heart," Cloud Feather had told him.

Felipe stood, wiped his hands on his trousers, and strode to the kitchen, face taut with determination.

CHAPTER 27

Lalo led Alondra and Clory away from the *hacienda* in a southeasterly direction. "I have it in mind," he said, "to visit the *mesa* with the silver."

"I thought we were going to Santa Fe," Alondra said.

"But we have no money. I'm thinking we can mine enough silver to buy us a wagon and team so we can haul goods over the Santa Fe Trail to Saint Louis."

Alondra rode silently for a few minutes. "But didn't the Indian say that no one had ever successfully mined the silver?"

"Those others were trying to take all the silver. We don't need much, just enough for a small stake."

"Well," Alondra said, "I guess I would like that kind of work better than dancing at a *cantina*. I'm strong. I can help you mine."

"Me too," Clory said. "And Heath is such a good baby, he ain't even woke up since I packed him in the cradleboard."

The sun was high by the time they reached the Blue *Mesa*. They rode single file up the rocky trail, Lalo in the lead. Halfway up the steep path, they dismounted and led the horses to the pile of rubble that marked the entrance to the mine.

Lalo picketed the horses in a patch of winter yellowed grama grass. "We only have to move enough rocks to make a large-enough opening so that I can enter the mine." He tossed a boulder aside.

Clory sat Heath on her *serape* and gave him his wooden toys. She and Alondra stacked the smaller stones in a pile, and Lalo worked with the larger rocks.

Alondra dug at a rock, tugged until it came loose, and pulled it out. With a loud shriek, musty air swooshed out of the hole. It blew Alondra's hair across her face and wrapped her skirt around her ankles. The sudden gust crept along the ground toward Heath, gathering force.

Alondra ran to the baby and covered him with her body. The wind snatched the wooden toy gun and whirled toward the horses. They whinnied and pitched. Their eyes rolled white.

Lalo grabbed the baby. Over the howling wind, he shouted, "Get on your horses and go."

The gale twisted until it formed a funnel, whirling tree branches, dirt, and rocks through the air. Alondra clutched Segundo's mane and sent him racing down the trail. The wind shrieked, tore at her clothes, and stung her face. Clory's *serape* sailed past.

Alondra couldn't see through the swirling sand but felt the other horses galloping behind her.

Segundo ran to the old campsite at the base of the *mesa* and stopped in the shelter of the trees. Alondra wiped the dust from her eyes and waited for the others.

Comanche Pony, with Clory on his back, crashed into the tree windbreak. Lalo rode into the camp holding Heath tight against his chest.

From the protection of the trees, they listened to the wind howl past. "Now I know why no one has ever mined the silver," Lalo said.

"Did I start the windstorm by pulling out that rock?" Alondra asked.

"I don't know," Lalo said. "But the Indian did say that the spirits protect the silver."

Clory shivered. "I don't want nothing more to do with that mine. Anyway, my pa always said that the road to hell was strewed with ill-gotten gold and silver."

"I'm going on to Santa Fe," Alondra said. "Dancing in a *cantina* will be easy, compared to that wind."

Lalo sighed. "Yes, this has been very disappointing. But we'll go on. I know I can find work in the city. I lost my water flask, and Clory lost her *serape*, so we'll not stop but go straight to Santa Fe." He glanced at the sky. "I hope we can get there before nightfall."

*****

Only the family was seated at breakfast when Felipe entered the kitchen. Neither Jose nor Maria Fuentes was there. He poured himself a cup of coffee. Grandfather lifted his cup, Felipe poured the coffee, and Grandfather cut off a chunk of brown sugar, dropped it in his cup, and stirred until the sweet glob dissolved.

"I'm leaving within the hour," Felipe said.

Seraphina dabbed her lips with a napkin. "You're following them to Santa Fe then?"

"What do you know of this, Mother?"

"Only what Rosa told me."

"What did she say?"

Seraphina patted his arm. "No need to get upset, Felipe. Sit down. Rosa didn't understand everything because Lalo and Clory spoke in the American language, but she did understand the words "Santa Fe." And this morning, when she went to care for Heath, they were gone."

"Heath is such a ridiculous name for a child," Grandmother said. "Why didn't they give him a name like Cipriano or Erasmo, something we could all pronounce?"

Felipe sat. "I leave within the hour."

"What of Fuentes? What do I say to him about your bad manners?" Enrique asked.

"Yes," Seraphina said, "It is very rude of you to leave your betrothed when she has only just arrived for a visit."

"We have talked about it, Maria will understand."

"I'm not so sure I do," Enrique said. "This is a disgrace to our family."

"Why? It has nothing to do with you, I've made my decision and Maria agrees."

"Go then, boy," Grandfather said. "It's a long ride to Santa Fe."

He squeezed the old man's shoulder. "Thank you, Grandfather." With a wave of his hand and an "*adios*," Felipe dashed out the door.

Enrique shook his head. "The young people of today. What do I say to Jose?"

"Nothing. If the children came to an agreement, there is nothing we can say or do," Grandfather said.

"In my day," Grandmother said, "we were not allowed to make our own decisions in such matters."

Grandfather patted her hand. "Maybe if we had, old woman, things would have been different between us."

Enrique stared at the two old people; not once in all his fifty years had he considered the relationship between his parents. He opened his mouth to speak, but no words came to him.

At that moment, Fuentes entered the kitchen. "I apologize for my lateness this morning, but my daughter and I had much to discuss."

Seraphina waved her hand in dismissal. "Think nothing of it. The coffee is hot. Let me get you some breakfast."

Jose Fuentes stirred milk and sugar into his coffee. "Thank

you for your hospitality. We have enjoyed our visit, but we are returning to Santa Fe this morning."

"I am sorry to hear that," Seraphina said. "We hoped for a nice long visit."

"What time do you leave?" Enrique asked.

"As soon as Maria is ready." Jose chuckled. "I have never been able to hurry that girl."

"If you don't mind, I will ride with you," Enrique said. "We have some mules to sell and hopefully a wagon train will be in town."

"It will be my pleasure; we shall enjoy your companionship."

"Harness the team to my buggy, Enrique. I shall accompany you." Seraphina set her cup down and stood. "I would like to visit my sister. We haven't seen each other since before Christmas."

"And I, too, am eager to see her. I'll get my shawl." Grandmother hurried from the room.

"I will not be left behind," Grandfather said. "Have the men saddle my horse, Enrique."

Jose glanced around the room, amusement in his eyes and a smile on his lips. "Well, I see that the visit will be extended after all. We shall have a pleasant journey, and I know that Maria will welcome the ladies' company." He did not ask them about Felipe.

✳✳✳✳✳

Felipe reached Santa Fe in midafternoon, his thoughts on Alondra the entire way. Love did strange things to a man. A chunk of meat wrapped in a *tortilla* satisfied the hunger in his stomach, but his heart hungered for her touch. The wind sang in the trees, but his ears were deaf to all but the music of her voice.

A coyote howled in the distance, and Felipe recalled Alondra's fear of wolves and how she gazed at him with trust in her eyes. How had he failed her that she'd left him with no explanation?

But that didn't matter. What mattered was that they would soon be together again. What he'd say to her, he didn't know; he had not thought beyond holding her close to his heart, easing the fever that raged through his brain.

He spent the afternoon and evening searching the town with no luck. He thought he'd find Lalo in a *cantina* or gambling house but saw only strange faces. At last, exhausted and disappointed, he made camp under a juniper on the outskirts of town.

He never considered sleeping at his aunt's house. Uncle Teodoro worked as a government official, something to do with the province's finances, Felipe thought, and his relatives lived in a well-appointed house. Even so, the street noise and dust, the shops and houses jammed together around the square, made Felipe long for the open air. He had no fondness for city living.

*****

The morning sun was high before the little band of travelers started on the road to Santa Fe. It was not Maria, but Grandmother, who caused the late start. She swore Seraphina to secrecy and insisted on packing the white lace *mantilla* and ivory comb that she herself had worn on her wedding day over fifty years before. At the bottom of the chest, she found her white silk dress. She held it up to her body, smoothed out the wrinkles, and turned to Rosa. "I wore this on my wedding day. I would like Felipe's bride to wear it, but I don't think it will fit her."

"You are right, *Señora*, the Fuentes girl would never—"

"Not her; the other one."

Rosa assured Grandmother that Alondra could indeed fit into the fine garment, and Grandmother packed it too. She then informed the group that Rosa would accompany them. In the end, there was no room for Maria in the Montez wagon, so she rode with her father in their own carriage.

Tomas drove the Montez buckboard with Rosa beside him and a rifle propped against the dashboard. Grandmother and Seraphina sat in the back seat, bags and boxes piled around their feet and under the seat. Enrique and Grandfather rode on each side of the wagon, rifles across their laps. Two fully armed *vaqueros* drove the herd of mules.

"Why did you bring your wedding clothes, Mama?" Seraphina pointed to the leather boxes.

"For Felipe's bride, of course."

"And which girl is that?"

"Alondra. She is the one Felipe loves."

"But she did run off, maybe she's not ready for marriage."

Grandmother's eyes widened in shock. "Not willing to marry our Felipe? Of course she is."

"I was not an eager bride," Seraphina said.

"Nor was I. Only after ten years was I comfortable with *el viejo verde*." Grandmother jerked her chin toward Grandfather.

Seraphina laughed. "You're right, Papa still likes to think he's young. He should be riding in the wagon with us. His bones will creak for two weeks after this trip on horseback."

"I don't often agree with him, but this is one time he's right." Grandmother leaned forward, her lips set in determination. "Seraphina, it is time for women to make their own choices in a mate."

"And for men also. Sometimes, I lie awake at night wondering if Enrique would have married me if he'd had his choice."

"We are agreed then. We will ask the young lady if she consents of her own free will to marry our Felipe."

"What of Maria? She has a say in all this."

"Bah! That one is so full of herself that I can understand why Felipe would choose Alondra. And you know, Seraphina, one can always recognize a woman of noble birth by their dainty ankles. Maria Fuentes has broad hips and thick legs. Alondra is small-boned and her ankles are slender as a deer's. She could pass as an aristocrat."

The women relaxed against the seatback, hands folded in their laps, planning the wedding.

Enrique glanced at the chatting women and wondered what they so intently discussed. Ten years his junior, his wife was a beautiful woman, her profile cameo perfect. His thoughts turned to the previous night, where in their bedroom she had loosened the golden braid, and her hair cascaded over her shoulders and down her back like warm honey poured from a jar. He ran his fingers through the silken tresses, and she gazed up at him, her amber eyes soft with promise. Her scent, too, was that of warm honey and even after twenty-five years never failed to arouse him. He kissed the hollow of her throat that was smooth and white as fresh cream, hooked his fingers in her chemise, and slid it off her shoulders.

She helped him take his shirt off, ran her hands over his bare chest, and murmured, "We must talk of our son, *mi amor*." She unwound his sash and opened his trousers.

"Later," he said. "We'll talk later." He kissed her shoulder, neck, ear lobe, jaw.

She leaned against him for a moment. Then, traced his lips with a gentle finger, slipped from his embrace, and went to the wardrobe. She turned, bare to the waist, nightdress in her hand. "No. We'll talk now."

He groaned. "What do you want to say?"

"Felipe is our son, our only child. We must respect his choice or lose him forever."

"He is young. He doesn't understand that love is not

265

necessary for a good marriage." Enrique heard Seraphina gasp but continued. "He has been reared by the Ten Commandments and has always followed the fourth. He will do nothing to dishonor us."

"And he does us credit, my husband. Like you, he is a man of honor and must follow his heart." Her nightgown skimmed over her naked body with a silken whisper.

All thoughts of family honor fled his mind. He took her hand and led her to the bed. "You are right, my wife. Only he knows what his heart wants." He blew out the candle.

But he knew that not all arranged marriages turned out as well as his, and he must remember to one day tell his wife how much he loved her. He wanted no less for his son than what he and Seraphina shared.

As head of the family, Grandfather had the final say in all matters, so it secretly pleased Enrique when the old man gave Felipe his blessing to go to Santa Fe. Enrique wondered what excuse he'd give Fuentes. How he'd explain that Felipe was not agreeable to the arranged marriage and that the Montez family supported him in that decision.

Enrique recalled the day he and Fuentes had arranged to combine their families. The two men had been playing *monte* at *Doña* Elena's gambling house.

"God has not blessed me with sons, my friend. I have five beautiful daughters for whom I must find suitable husbands," Jose Fuentes had said.

"How is your search?" Enrique asked and silently thanked God he did not have that problem. Not that he wouldn't have welcomed a daughter, he hastily told God, but in His wisdom God had seen fit to bless the Montez family with only one child and that one a fine son.

"Not so well. Alas, there are not many families in New Mexico of pure Spanish blood."

Enrique nodded. Fuentes was right, there were few families who did not have Indian blood in their background.

He did not consider the woman who, over a hundred years ago, had married a Pueblo Indian as a part of his family.

By the end of the day, the two Spanish gentlemen had struck a bargain. Felipe was seven years old, and the girl was three.

Enrique never gave it another thought until three years previous when Jose Fuentes delivered two hundred head of sheep to his *hacienda*.

"I have brought the dowry, the bride price agreed upon twelve years ago," Jose said. "Maria is already past fifteen years of age. I will have the priest start reading the banns next month."

Enrique was stunned. "But Felipe is only a little over twenty, much too young to make a good husband. I, myself, was almost thirty before I married."

"I, too, was past thirty when I married, but I am getting old, and the girl is of marriageable age."

"Come into the house," Enrique said. "We will have coffee and discuss the matter."

After they were seated, he said, "Surely the marriage can be put off for a few years. When Felipe was sixteen, I did take him to *Doña* Elena to learn about women, but the boy is still very young."

"How many years are you talking about?" Fuentes asked.

Enrique thought fast. "Only two or three years. I was planning on sending Felipe to Mexico City this summer to visit my cousin. He raises prize Andalusian horses, and we want to buy one of his stallions. When Felipe returns, we will have the wedding."

Jose Fuentes sat in thoughtful silence. After a moment, he said, "Mexico City will teach the boy about life in a big city. That is good. He will return with knowledge he could never receive here in New Mexico and will be a better husband for it. Keep the sheep. Brand them and their offspring with your son's mark." He sipped his coffee. "And anyway, Maria is my last daughter and the joy of my old age. I am not eager to see her married, but I know she is not the type of woman to remain a spinster." He sighed. "Do you think your son would live at my *hacienda* after the marriage?"

"No! He is my only child; his place is here on this ranch." Jose shook his head. "That's what I thought you'd say. Three years then."

The two fathers shook hands and had not spoken of the betrothal since that day. The sheep were healthy and had produced well. Enrique wondered how many he'd be forced to return to Fuentes.

Jose Fuentes snapped the reins across his team's backs. "What are you thinking, daughter?"

Maria scowled; he had interrupted her daydreams of James. "Not much, Papa."

"Are you absolutely certain that you want to break your betrothal to Felipe Montez?"

"We discussed that this morning, Papa. You told me before, that it takes more than a handsome face to make a good marriage. Felipe has a handsome face but can't carry a conversation."

"Why would you need to talk? I'm sure he'd treat you well and will never beat you."

"Only because he'd never know I was around. Papa, we already talked about this. He is so boring, marriage to him would be my death sentence. I can't believe you'd be so cruel as to even consider forcing me to marry him. I would rather spend my days in a nunnery."

Fuentes sighed. "I don't know what I'll tell Montez."

Maria smiled her sweetest and patted his hand. "You'll think of something, Papa. You always do."

*****

Due to the late start, they didn't reach Santa Fe until evening. The walled city slept. A square of light shone from the hotel, a few houses showed candlelight through their barred windows, shops were closed, and the mission church, its twin bell towers reaching for the sky, sat dark and silent. Only *Doña* Elena's gambling house buzzed with activity. Men milled around the doorway, shouting, laughing, talking.

The Fuentes party continued to their home on the west side of town. The Montez family skirted the plaza and corralled the mules at Seraphina's sister's house. Aunt Christina greeted them with enthusiasm and set a late supper for them. Uncle Teodoro plied them with wine.

The ladies spoke of their households, twittering like magpies in a cornfield. The men talked of politics, grumbling and snorting like bulls in a pen.

*****

It was close to midnight before Alondra, Lalo, and Clory entered Santa Fe. They headed straight for the hotel. Lalo did some fast talking, and they were given a room for the night. "It will be all right," he assured the women. "I'll get a job first thing in the morning."

"I saw a couple of *cantinas*. One seemed busy. I could go now and see if I can get work there," Alondra said.

Lalo shook his head. "Get some rest. Tomorrow will be soon enough."

CHAPTER 28

SANTA FE, NEW MEXICO

After a restless night, Felipe awoke to cries of, "*Los Americanos! Los Carros! La entrada el Caravana!*" An American wagon train loaded with trade goods had arrived in town.

The first wagon load of trade goods had entered Santa Fe in 1821, after Mexico won independence from Spain. An enterprising Missourian, planning only to sell trinkets to the Indians, crossed the Rock River. A New Mexican military troop met him with the information that the country was now open to trade. He sold his goods in Santa Fe at a profit and returned to Saint Louis with wool, pottery, bags of gold and silver, and the animal that was to become Missouri's trademark—the mule. From that day on, wagon trains rolled over the Santa Fe Trail each spring. Men mortgaged farms, fought hostile Indians, battled adverse weather conditions, and suffered hunger and thirst to travel the Santa Fe Trail, chasing their dreams of wealth.

Felipe rode into the city and tethered his horse at a hitching rail. The plaza vibrated with noise, caravan bells tinkled and clanged, burros brayed, traders argued, and people shouted in three languages. Children waded in the *acequia* running through the town—the water supply for humans as well as animals.

At the *presidio*, local vendors set up shop under the veranda's roof. They spread fruits, vegetables, jewelry, and clay pots on colorful woolen blankets. The aroma of freshly baked bread, mixed with the odor of animals and unwashed humans, hung in the still air.

With the help of their *vaqueros*, Enrique and Grandfather leashed the mules together and led them to the city square.

"What are you doing in Santa Fe, Father?" Felipe asked when he saw them.

"We brought these mules to sell. Come help us; we should get a good price from the traders."

Felipe shrugged. He could hardly refuse and maybe the excitement of the wagon train would lure Alondra to the plaza.

The moment the men left the house, Seraphina and Grandmother enlisted Seraphina's sister, Christina, in their plans.

"What we must do," Christina said, "is invite the girl for coffee, now, this morning, while the men are out. I have some excellent sweet rolls, still warm from the oven."

Seraphina called Tomas and pressed a coin in his hand. "Go to the plaza, Tomas, and find the *Señorita* Alondra. Do you know her?" Tomas nodded. "Tell her she is invited for coffee and bring her here at once."

Grandmother shook her cane at Tomas. "And don't come back without her."

Tomas scurried to the plaza and lost himself in the array of goods. He fingered the coin in his pocket and considered purchasing a little something for his wife. But a fine clay pipe caught his eye, and after haggling with the vendor for ten minutes he exchanged his coin for the pipe and a twist of real tobacco.

He found Alondra admiring turquoise rings and pendants.

He tugged at her sleeve. "Please, *Señorita*, the *Señoras* asked me to bring you to them for coffee."

"Tomas! The Montez family is in Santa Fe?"

"Yes, and they want you to come with me. They said to hurry."

"Why did they come to Santa Fe, Tomas, and what do they want with me?"

"I do not know, *Señorita*. They only said to bring you to the house for coffee."

He'd come for her! "Is Felipe with them?"

"No, all the men came to the plaza to sell the mules. Only the women are at the house."

So, it was the mother and grandmother who wanted to see her, not Felipe. Well, she didn't want to talk with any of them. "Tell them I'm sorry, Tomas, but I can't come for coffee."

"You must, *Señorita*. If you don't, the old one will beat me about the head with her walking stick."

"I can't believe she'd do that, Tomas." A group of men driving a herd of mules, Felipe at the lead, drew her attention. Her heart pounded, her knees weakened; she couldn't let him see her.

"Come, *Señorita*, they said we must hurry."

Her only thought to escape before Felipe saw her, Alondra followed Tomas out of the plaza. They entered the gate of a large house and crossed the patio before Alondra came to her senses. What was she doing here? She had no desire to see these people.

"Alondra, welcome." Seraphina bustled toward her, hands outstretched. She linked arms with Alondra. "Come in, my dear. I'm so happy to see you."

To ask that she give up Felipe? No problem. She'd already done that and wept herself dry making the decision. "Thank you, *Señora*. It was gracious of you to invite me."

"Here she is, Mama," Seraphina called. "Here's Alondra. You know Grandmother, of course, and this is my sister

Christina."

Amid cries of welcome, Christina offered coffee and rolls to Alondra. She should be out searching for work, instead of eating sweets with these pampered women. She'd planned to refuse any food; one ate only with friends. But breakfast had been only a small chunk of jerky, and her stomach demanded that she eat. She wolfed down a sweet roll and resisted the urge to lick her sticky fingers.

"Alondra ..." Christina said. "One has to wonder why your parents named you the lark."

So, they wanted to hear her story. She'd tell them. She wasn't ashamed and there was nothing they could use against her, Felipe knew everything. "I'm not sure it was my parents who named me Alondra. I think it's a nickname, and it fit well when I danced at the *cantina*."

Grandmother gasped. Seraphina rolled her eyes, and Christina gazed silently at Alondra for a long moment. "You are a dancer, then?"

Alondra hoped Grandmother wouldn't faint. "Yes, but first I was a laundress. I was forced at an early age to earn my living and dancing came easy for me."

Christina arose from the table. "One moment, I'll be right back." With a swish of her skirts, she hurried from the room.

She returned, in her hand a paper with writing and a drawing of a woman. "See this, Seraphina; could this not be a picture of Alondra?" She laid the paper on the table. The women crowded around, peering at the picture. Alondra couldn't control a small gasp as she recognized the drawing of the woman she'd seen every day of her life while living in San Antonio with Bianca.

"Who is it, Christina? Where did you get it?"

"It's a playbill of a performance Teodoro and I saw when we were in New Orleans that time. They called her Gitana. But, oh my, she danced beautifully, graceful as a swallow swooping through the sky. See Alondra? You look enough alike to be sisters."

"There is a likeness," Seraphina said, "But you were in New Orleans over twenty years ago. They couldn't be sisters; Gitana would be too old."

"You said Alondra was orphaned at an early age ... her mother then, or an aunt." Christina pointed to the poster. "I tell you, the likeness is uncanny."

Although she had memorized that face and had often daydreamed about her, Alondra saw no resemblance between herself and the drawing of the woman dressed in a ruffled skirt and posed with *castanets* in her hands. Now though, she wondered. Could it be that there was a connection between her and the dancing woman? She dismissed the possibility. Bianca would have known, and her foster mother could never tell Alondra anything about her parents.

Grandmother clutched at her narrow chest, took a deep breath, and regained her composure. "Enough of this, our Alondra has nothing to do with Gitana." She turned to Alondra. "I brought a dress with me that I'd like you to try on."

"But only if you want to," Seraphina said.

"Why? Why would I—"

Grandmother held up her hand. "Rosa, bring the white silk dress."

White silk? What was going on? Rosa entered carrying a beautiful gown with s wide, full skirt and lace on the bodice and wrists, slightly yellowed with age. "For me? Why?"

"For your wedding, my dear," Grandmother said.

"My wedding? I'm not planning a wedding."

"With Felipe."

"But only if you want to," Seraphina said. "We've been talking and are all in agreement that both men and women should have the right to choose their mates. Times are changing, and we think that the old ways are not always the best."

"What of his betrothal?" Alondra asked.

"Enrique is taking care of that; it will be canceled," Seraphina said.

"You do want to marry Felipe, don't you?" Grandmother's voice sounded anxious, almost pleading.

"Even if I did, I'm not sure he wants to marry me."

"Oh, but he does," Seraphina said. "You should have seen him. He came yesterday to Santa Fe to search for you. But apparently he didn't find you."

"We wanted to talk with you," Grandmother said, "and tell you that we'd be pleased to have you in our family."

Seraphina took Alondra's hand. "I've always wanted a daughter."

Her world was a bright and happy place again. Grandmother was simply a sainted old lady, Seraphina a blessed Madonna, Aunt Christina a beautiful angel. "Thank you," Alondra whispered. "Thank you. I've never had a family."

"You have one now," Aunt Christina said. "Come, try on the dress. Let's see how it fits."

The four women went into the bedroom and Seraphina slipped the dress over Alondra's head. "A perfect fit."

"Humph," Grandmother said, "It's tight in the waist and loose in the bodice. Don't breathe too deeply, girl, or you'll burst the seams."

"Let's see how you look with the *mantilla*," Christina said. She arranged Alondra's hair with the ivory comb and draped the *mantilla* over it. "Gorgeous!"

"You are beautiful, child. Just beautiful. No wonder Felipe loves you," Grandmother said with tears in her eyes.

Seraphina clasped her hands together. "What a lovely bride! Now, what are you going to tell Felipe?"

"That depends on what he says, and he'll have to come to me. I won't go to him."

"You don't have to worry about that," Seraphina said. "He won't leave Santa Fe until he finds you. And when he does, don't tell him we talked. We promised not to meddle."

Alondra laughed. Life was good. "I must go now. I left Clory at the hotel. Thank you for everything. Uh ... do you mind if I take one of those sweet rolls to Heath."

"Of course." Christina filled a basket with the bread.

Alondra ran through the plaza to the La Fonda Hotel, where Clory and Heath waited. She noticed the saloon across the square; she'd go there this afternoon and ask for work. Marriage with Felipe was the future, but today they needed food, and the hotel bill was due.

The wagon master had removed the canvas tops from the wagons, and men were unloading the wares when Felipe and the other men entered the plaza with the mules. He caught the excitement of the town at the sight of the crates of rifles, ammunition, glass windowpanes, bolts of calico and gingham, barrels of nails and knives, adzes and hoes, mirrors and glassware, tin boxes filled with needles, threads, buttons, pins, spoons, and scissors.

Already, people lined up to buy or to trade their clay pots, furs, bales of wool, or woven blankets for commodities that, until the American traders came, were unavailable to them.

In less than an hour, Enrique sold the mules at a good price. The animals, faster than the oxen, tougher and more sure-footed than the horse, were much in demand back in Missouri. The traders would receive double the cost of each mule.

Their business completed, Felipe roamed the square. He caught sight of a familiar figure, surrounded by New Mexicans and Indians, talking to a wagon master. "Lalo! *Qué pasa, hombre?*"

Lalo grinned and waved. "Felipe, I'm glad to see you. I have a job as translator for these people who don't speak the American language, and this wagon master needs help understanding the customs form. Come and explain it to him."

"Where's Alondra, Lalo?"

"Later, Felipe, can't you see I'm working?" Lalo turned back to the wagon master. "This man can help you with these forms." He thrust the papers at Felipe.

Felipe explained the customs and taxes to the wagon master.

"These taxes are outrageous," the man said.

"I know," Lalo said, his voice soft with empathy. "I've heard it said that the *comandante* even taxes a man for cohabiting with his wife."

The wagon master laughed and went on his way. Then others demanded their attention, and Felipe and Lalo kept busy translating, explaining, and bargaining, until the late afternoon meal drove the customers indoors. The clients paid Lalo in coin and goods.

"All right, Lalo, where's Alondra?" Felipe asked.

"At the hotel with Clory. Come with me. I made good money today, Felipe."

"You'd make more if you could read, Lalo. We must see to it that you learn."

Lalo shrugged. "I don't know. I could try, but maybe I'm too old."

"No," Felipe said. "You are not too old. Anyone can learn to read."

Their arms laden with a bolt of checkered calico, two woolen blankets, a tin bucket filled with spoons, a mirror, and glassware, they crossed the plaza to the La Fonda Hotel.

Alondra was not at the hotel. "She went out," Clory said. "She's looking for work and didn't say when she'd get back."

He had waited all day to see her. A dull anger began to gather in the back of his mind. He pushed his irritation aside. Already the sun cast long shadows across the plaza, she would return soon. "I'll wait for her here, then," Felipe said and sat on the veranda floor.

*****

Enrique and Grandfather sauntered by the hotel at dusk and saw Felipe sitting on the veranda.

"We're going to the gambling house," Enrique said. "Fuentes is there, and we must speak with him. You should come with us."

"I'll come too," Lalo said. "I haven't yet seen the famous saloon."

They walked across the plaza where people sat in groups on blankets playing dice or dealing cards, *monte* or faro, the favored game.

The gaming house was filled with smoke, loud talk, and laughter, crowded with traders, mule skinners, *vaqueros*, ranch owners, soldiers, and several women.

The men threaded their way around tables and standing patrons, scanning the room for Jose Fuentes. Enrique spotted him at a corner table, sitting alone, cards spread out, with a pistol lying beside them. On the stroll through the room, Felipe noticed that each dealer had a gun on the table.

"Jose," Enrique said. "It's good to see you again so soon."

Fuentes brightened at the sight of them. "Enrique! Could I interest you in a game of *monte*?"

"Would that I had the time, Jose, but we've come to speak with you."

Jose sighed. "I knew it would eventually come to this. Sit down then." When they were all seated, he said, "Your son is here, I see."

"Yes, that's why we need to talk."

Jose shook his head. "Oh, that I'd been blessed with a son, rather than a houseful of faithless daughters." His eyes glistened with tears.

Enrique touched his arm. "What is it, old friend?"

"It's a bad business and it shames me to speak of it. But it wasn't my fault." Jose thrust out his lower lip like that of a petulant child. "The girl was ripe, and your son was hundreds of leagues away. It was bound to happen."

"Quit stalling, man. Tell us what happened," Grandfather said.

"Last year, I took a wagon load of wool and hides to Saint Louis to sell. Maria begged to go with me. She was bored sitting around the *hacienda* waiting for a husband." Jose glared at Felipe. "She gets bored easily, so I took her with me. I made a good profit on my goods, too."

Impatient, Grandfather shifted in his chair. "Why are you telling us this now? You didn't mention it during your visit at the *hacienda*."

"While in Saint Louis, we were invited to attend a ball. Let me tell you something, *hombres*, it was nothing like our *fandangos*. Oil lamps lighted the room, the ladies all dressed in silks, and the men wore black suits. They had a musical instrument called a piano."

Enrique reached for his tobacco, snatched his hand back. While with his father, Enrique could drink whiskey, curse, gamble, even eye a pretty girl on occasion, but he would never smoke in his father's presence. Respect for Grandfather overcame his urge for a cigarette. "I'm glad you had a good time at the dance, Jose, but what has that to do with us?"

Fuentes reached in his pocket and took out a cigar. He sniffed it, twirled it between his fingers, took his time lighting it. "I learned the pleasure of cigar smoking while in Saint Louis. You should try it sometime; it is very satisfying."

Enrique sighed. "Get on with your story, *hombre*."

Jose puffed on his cigar and blew fat smoke rings. "At the ball, Maria met a young man, an American. Then three weeks ago, he showed up here in Santa Fe. Now Maria refuses marriage to anyone but him—an Anglo. Please forgive me. I have begged her to reconsider, but she threatened to join the church if I forced her to marry your son. I'm sorry, but I couldn't bear the thought of her wasting her life hiding behind a nun's veil, so I gave my consent for her to marry that American. Now I have no daughter to fulfill my obligation to you, and my soul cringes with dishonor."

"Well," Enrique said, "this is a surprise, but as you said, these things do happen, but why didn't you let us know about it? There is the matter of the dowry, after all."

"Oh, yes, the dowry. Well, she and I didn't come to an agreement until we were on the way home from your *hacienda*. And then I was too shamed to come to you about it. I've broken my word to you. The neighbors will gossip." Jose shook his head. "What will the priests think?"

"I have not spoken of the betrothal to anyone. Have you?"

Jose brightened. "No. No one."

"Then there is no harm done," Enrique said. "I shall deliver the sheep to your *hacienda* within the week."

A broad grin wiped the shame from Jose's face. "No, please keep the sheep as my apology. It was only two hundred head, and the Navajos steal more than that from me every year. The sheep are already branded with your son's mark, so let him keep them."

Enrique frowned. "No. I cannot do that. They were meant as your daughter's dowry. Now that our families will not be joined, it is only right that I return the sheep. You will need them for your new son-in-law."

"Please, Enrique, keep the sheep. Do me that honor so that I can sleep at night with a clear conscience."

"And would that not sully my honor, Jose? I shall return the sheep."

"But it was not your fault the marriage contract could not be fulfilled. I do not want the sheep. They are old now anyway and their fleece, not the best."

"You insult me, sir. Those sheep have had the best of care."

"Forgive me, old friend, I did not mean any offense. But if you return those sheep, I must hang my head in shame. Never again could I look you in the eye."

"If it means that much to you," Grandfather said, "We will keep the sheep."

With relieved smiles, the men shook hands all around.

"And anyway," Fuentes said, "The Anglo has agreed to come live at my *hacienda* after the wedding. So, I will not lose my daughter after all." He glanced around the table, beaming. "Now that we have finished with that little bit of business, I invite you to join me in a cup of wine." He signaled the waiter to serve the wine.

Lalo raised his cup to Felipe and in a low voice said, "Congratulations, my friend, now you have no worries."

Felipe leaned toward him and whispered, "You have no idea how relieved I am. Now I must find Alondra. Tell me, why did she leave me?"

Lalo shook his head. "That is for her to say, but she was determined to come to Santa Fe and refused to talk to you about it. I couldn't allow her to ride that distance alone."

"I thank you, my good friend, for escorting her."

Two guitarists strolled around the room, their voices blended in a love song that struck Felipe to the depths of his soul:

'Tis a lie, this love the women all are feigning,
And a lie their beauty and their proud disdain,
And a lie the "I adore thee!" that they murmur,
And their very kisses are a lie as vain.

The musicians moved among the standing patrons until they had cleared the center of the room. Felipe listened, his vision clouded. It was as though the singers could read his heart.

Love! It is the thorn that holds the hidden poison
Wherewithal they wreak their cruel whims and blind;
Wherewithal they slay our trusting hearts forever—
Ah, that wicked, ah, that wicked womankind!

Yes, it was true. Love carried a thorn that pierced the heart and bled the soul. The song ended, and Felipe tossed the singers a gold coin.

The crowd clapped, and after the musicians acknowledged the ovation one of them doffed his *sombrero* and with a clash of chords announced, "Skylark. Dancing!"

Felipe froze.

The guitarists strummed a lively tune and, clicking her *castanets*, Alondra twirled into the clearing. Her red skirt swirled high, and lamplight glinted off the dagger strapped to her thigh. Men clapped and cheered.

Grandfather and Enrique glanced at Felipe, their eyes wide, mouths open in astonishment.

Jose Fuentes clapped his hands and laughed. "Just what we need to cheer us up."

Felipe stood. No, *por Dios*. Enough was enough. No man would ogle his woman as though she were nothing but a dance hall wench. He would not tolerate it. He kicked his chair back. Lalo put a restraining hand on his arm. Felipe shook it off. He stalked to the center of the room and, when Alondra twirled past, caught her around the waist and, without missing a beat, joined her in the dance.

She glanced up in surprise. His eyes flashed a dangerous green.

With a wicked grin, he bent her backward and whispered in her ear, "If you insist on dancing, *querida*, from now on it will be only with me."

She whirled away and he brought her back into the circle of his arms.

"I need to earn a living, Felipe, and this is all I know."

"Then we shall dance together." He spoke to the musicians, and they increased the tempo to a savage beat.

Together, Alondra and Felipe dipped and swayed, leaped, and twirled in an ancient peasant dance of Spain that for centuries told of courtship, love, and passion. The crowd went wild with shouts of *Olé! Andele! Andele! Olé!*

The dance ended, and when she could speak Alondra said, "This is all well and good, Felipe, but men won't pay to see a couple dance."

"Oh, no? Then what is that under our feet?" Gold and silver coins littered the floor.

Alondra gasped. "Never have I been paid so well for a dance." She bent to pick up the money.

Felipe yanked her upright. "Leave it for the *casero* to sweep up."

"But I earned it, Felipe. We earned it."

The crowd clapped, stomped their feet, and shouted, "More, more."

Felipe shook his head at them and pasted a smile on his face. "Bow to the audience, Alondra," he said through gritted teeth. "This is your last performance, and you have been well paid."

She curtsied and smiled with a look of longing at the scattered coins.

Felipe dragged her by the hand to the table and sat her on his knee. "This is Alondra, and she has consented to be my wife." He slipped the silver bracelet on her wrist.

She looked up at him. They smiled into each other's eyes and the people, the noise, the smoke-filled room, all disappeared. For the moment, only the two of them existed.

"Well," Fuentes said, evidently at a loss for words.

Grandfather cleared his throat, opened his mouth to speak, but no words came. He took a sip of wine and it spilled down his tobacco-yellowed beard.

Enrique sat, shoulders slumped, shock and amazement written on his face.

A young boy scooted out from the crowd and filled his *sombrero* with the coins. He came to the table and with a shy grin presented his hat to Alondra. She thanked him and gave him a handful of coins for his trouble. She stacked the money on the table, counting it.

Felipe signaled to the guitarists. "Half for the musicians, Alondra."

"But, Felipe—"

"Half, Alondra!" His lips twitched and he winked at Lalo.

Lalo grinned and jerked his right thumb up.

Grandfather found his voice. "She's a high-spirited filly. Keep a tight rein on her, Felipe, but use control with caution; you don't want to break her spirit."

Felipe laughed. Life was good. "I'll be careful, Grandfather. Now, if you'll excuse us, Alondra and I need to go where it's quiet so we can talk."

"I won't leave the money, Felipe, and I don't have anything to carry it in," Alondra said.

Enrique removed his kerchief. "You can use this." He heaped the coins in the center and tied a knot in the cloth. "This will do until you can get a purse." He patted her hand.

Felipe led Alondra through the throng, nodding and smiling at the crowd's approval. *Doña* Elena stopped them at the door, a cigarette tucked in the corner of her mouth. "You and your partner were very successful tonight, Alondra, but I did not bargain for two dancers." She handed Alondra money and turned her gaze on Felipe. "I will pay double if you dance again tomorrow night. The church banned that dance many years ago as vulgar and lewd, but the crowd enjoyed it and I thought the performance discreet, so the priests should have no objections."

Felipe bowed. "Thank you, madam, but we have retired from the stage. Tonight was our last performance."

"A pity," *Doña* Elena said. "You are a handsome couple and dance well together." She paused. "You remind me of someone." She tilted Alondra's chin and turned her to face the lamplight. "You closely resemble a famous dancer I once saw in Mexico City, and you even dance like her, the same graceful movements. Who was your mother, child?"

Alondra stared at her, speechless.

"Alondra is my wife, madam," Felipe said.

Doña Elena shrugged. "It's not possible anyway. That dancer was married to an American. Well, if you change your mind, let me know." She turned away and blended into the crowd.

Felipe put a comforting arm around Alondra and led her out of the gambling hall and down the street to his tied horse.

"Look at this, Felipe." Alondra shoved the money in her hand at him. "And this." She rattled the coin-filled kerchief. "We could earn a good living dancing. One dance a night— that's all."

"You would dance for that woman?"

"Of course, why not? She pays well."

He embraced her and smiled into her eyes. "I'll tell you why not."

A group of soldiers spilled out of the gambling hall door. "There he is, men," shouted a harsh voice. "Get him!"

*****

Two soldiers seized Felipe's arms. A man shoved Alondra aside and knocked her to the ground. More soldiers crowded around, reaching for Felipe.

He slammed an elbow into a soldier's throat, kicked one in the crotch, butted another in the stomach, punched one in the mouth.

Alondra pulled her dagger. Snarling and spitting like a wild cat, she leaped on a man's back, slashing with her knife. He yelped with pain, reached back, and hit her on the head. Another soldier grabbed her around the waist and dragged her off. She dropped her knife and bit his hand. He backhanded her, slammed her on the ground, and joined the fray against Felipe.

Two soldiers held Felipe down, others glared and shouted

obscenities. Two bled from the nose, another dripped blood from his back, and one lay writhing in the dust.

Felipe glared up at Captain Edmundo Baca. "What do you want?"

"You, of course. Tie him up and take him to the jail, boys."

The noise of the fight brought the patrons crowding out the gambling house door.

Alondra got to her knees and groped in the dirt for her dagger.

Enrique helped Alondra to her feet. "What's going on here?"

Baca pointed to Lalo. "There's his accomplice! Don't let him get away."

Soldiers jumped on Lalo from all sides. He kneed a soldier in the stomach, took two by the hair and knocked their heads together, and smashed one across the face with his forearm. When they finally subdued him, three soldiers lay groaning in the dirt.

"Take care of Alondra, Papa," Enrique said and turned to Captain Baca. "What is the meaning of this outrage? I demand that you turn those men loose at once."

"They are prisoners," Baca said. "I am taking them to the jail."

"On what charges?"

"They are spies. Charged with planning to overthrow the Mexican government."

"That's ridiculous. That man is my son and I know for a fact that he is not a spy. I shall go at once and talk with the *comandante* about this outrage."

Baca smirked. "It is the *comandante* himself who brought the charges against them. Take the prisoners to jail, boys." The soldiers tied Felipe's and Lalo's hands behind their backs, placed ropes around their necks, and marched them to the jail.

His right eye swollen, Lalo grinned when he saw the gash on Felipe's cheek. "Good fight, *amigo*."

Alondra ran to Felipe, held on to his arm, and walked beside him. Warm sticky blood stained her hands. "Get my knife," Felipe whispered in English. "Before the soldiers seize it and I never see it again."

"Your arm is bleeding, Felipe, let me look at it."

"It's nothing. Get my knife. Quick."

She wailed and threw her arms around his waist. She switched to Spanish and said, "Don't take him to jail. You've hurt him; let me take care of him."

"Get away from here." A soldier pushed her back.

Alondra fell to her knees, hugged Felipe around his leg, and wailed. "No. No. Don't take him from me." She slipped his knife from its boot sheath and into her sash.

"Move that woman away from the prisoner," Baca shouted.

"No, no," Alondra sobbed.

"Don't worry, *querida*," Felipe said. "Go now with my father. They won't keep me in jail for long. I'll be with you again very soon."

Baca dragged Alondra to Enrique. "Keep this *cantina* dancer away from my prisoners."

Enrique drew himself up, his eyes flashed. "Take care, sir, what you say about my family. You will soon regret your actions of this evening." He pulled his knife. "I demand you apologize to this young lady."

Baca sneered. "And you, sir, take care what you say, or you will join your son, the spy, in the *presidio*." He turned and followed the soldiers to the jail.

Enrique stepped toward him.

"No, *Señor*, it's all right." Alondra held on to his arm. "What that man says means nothing to me. Besides you can help Felipe better outside the jail." She grinned. "I got his dagger."

Enrique chuckled. "You are a clever young lady. Come, Papa, let's take our daughter home. I want to talk to Teodoro about this insult to our family."

Joy flooded through Alondra. Enrique acted like the father she had always dreamed of. "I can't go with you. Clory is at the hotel alone. I must stay with her. She'll be worried about Lalo."

"We'll take her with us."

"You two get Clory, and I'll take El Moro to the stables." Grandfather led the horse away. Alondra and Enrique went to the La Fonda for Clory and Heath.

CHAPTER 29

At Aunt Christina's house, the family sat at the table and discussed the arrest.

"*Comandante* Salas is not one of us," Uncle Teodoro said. "He is Mexican, sent here to squeeze money out of the province. He has instigated taxes few can pay. Many have protested and, as a result, had their property seized."

"The matter of taxes does not concern me," Seraphina said. "We must get Felipe and Lalo out of jail. I can't bear the thought of them in the *presidio* along with common criminals."

Uncle Teodoro paced, hands clasped behind his back. "The only crime many others locked in the jail have committed is the crime of poverty. Often, I wish the previous governor was still in office. Although a peasant who bragged that he stole the same ewe and sold it back to its owner four times, at least he was a New Mexican."

"I will go to the *comandante* first thing in the morning and demand that he release Felipe and Lalo. He has no proof of the charges against them." Enrique stood. Never had the urge for a cigarette been so strong. "If you will excuse me, I must step outside for a moment."

Grandfather smiled. "Stay here, boy, and smoke your cigarette. I will not watch."

"Are the prisoners treated well?" Seraphina asked.

"The previous jailers were reasonable men," Teodoro said. "I do not know anything about Captain Baca, the new man."

Alondra spoke for the first time. "Captain Baca is a snake, *Señors*. He is cruel and wants revenge." She told them how Baca had stolen El Moro, and when Felipe got the horse back the captain followed them. "The last time I saw Captain Baca, the Texas Rangers held him prisoner; they even talked of hanging him. I don't know how he escaped, but as I said, *Señors*, the man is a snake."

"I will make the *comandante* see reason," Enrique said. "Arrange an audience with him, Teodoro, for first thing in the morning."

"I shall go with you, Enrique. Money is a powerful lever." Grandfather drew a small dagger from his shirt and glanced at Alondra. "I found this in the plaza street."

She reached for it. "It's mine. Thank you for finding it."

Grandfather turned the knife in his hand, examining it. "I noticed that one soldier had knife wounds, and there is blood encrusted among the jewels."

"Jewels!" Christina exclaimed. "Let me see that." She snatched the knife. "These are jewels, Seraphina. Where did you get this, Alondra?"

Alondra shrugged. "I've always had it. My foster mother said it was in a leather bag with some gold coins when she found me."

"You were left on the mission steps as a baby?" Seraphina asked.

"No. My foster mother found me unconscious in the arms of a dead man. I was four or five years old, I think. My foster mother said she thought the man was my father and there was a picture of a dancing woman with writing on the back. But the writing was in the American language and the mission priest could not read it, only the words 'Saint Louis.'"

Christina pointed to the knife handle. "See, the jewels are rubies and emeralds. This is a nobleman's knife. Alondra, you are connected somehow to Gitana. She was married to a very rich man. Maybe she is your mother."

Alondra shrugged. "I used to think it mattered who my parents were. But it doesn't. Not really. It's me and my actions that make me who and what I am." She lifted the hem of her skirt and replaced the dagger in its sheath. "I'm only sorry this knife is so small that I couldn't kill that soldier."

Enrique patted her hand. "Leave that sort of business to us men."

Alondra said nothing, but she would not leave Felipe moldering in prison while the men talked of money and influence. She knew Captain Edmundo Baca. He'd use every means within his power to keep both Felipe and Lalo in jail until he found a reason to execute them.

Later, in their shared bedroom, Alondra and Clory talked deep into the night, forming plans to free their men from jail.

Alondra placed Felipe's pistols and knife on the bed, his sword beside them. She had never seen him use the sword, but he always carried it on his saddle, so it was probably important to him. "Felipe is hurt, Clory. He needs some of your medicine. Let's sneak their weapons to them now, tonight, while the guards are asleep."

"We should wait until morning," Clory said, "after Enrique talks with the comandante. If nothing comes of it, then we'll take our guns and blast them out."

Alondra didn't want to wait, but Clory convinced her that it would be better if the comandante released the men; otherwise, they'd all be fugitives and never safe from arrest. "But," she said, "it's important that Felipe get medicine on his wound right away. We'll take the comfrey root to him tonight."

The girls tiptoed to the kitchen. A pot of water, still warm from dinner, sat on the cookstove, and Clory mixed the powdered herb in a clay bowl. They draped shawls over their heads and around their shoulders and sneaked out into the black night.

Clouds hid the moon, and the girls wound their way through unfamiliar alleyways to the plaza. A single pinpoint of light twinkled; even the gambling hall was dark and still.

"That must be the jail," Alondra whispered.

Their eyes focused on the flickering light as they made their way across the deserted plaza in silence. Clory stumbled against something that clanked hollow and loud. She gasped and held her breath. The girls clutched hands and glanced around. They could see nothing in the darkness.

Alondra tugged at Clory. They moved forward two steps; and both crashed to the ground. Metal rattled and clanged, something rolled with a clatter.

"Buckets," breathed Alondra. The noise echoed in her ears.

The jail door burst open; and the girls flattened against the earth. A bulky form stood outlined in the dim light. "Who goes there?" The man stepped out the door. He waved a gun. "Speak or I shoot."

Alondra pressed her face in the dirt and tried to quiet her pounding heart. Next to her, Clory trembled. Both girls lay still. The guard took a few steps, kicked a pail, and sent it rattling across the plaza. A large furry animal scurried from underneath the buckets. The guard muttered something about cats, went inside the building, and shut the door behind him.

The girls inched backward, careful not to touch the buckets. When they were well away from the *presidio*, they stood and turned back to the house.

Twice they made wrong turns before they found their way home. "I'll find a way to get the medicine to Felipe," Alondra whispered. "Tomorrow, when it's daylight, so I don't stumble into buckets."

*****

Early next morning, dressed in their finest, Enrique and Grandfather rode to the *presidio*. They waited an hour before being called into the *comandante*'s office.

Comandante Salas, short, balding, and going to paunch, sat behind his large wooden desk. Next to him, Captain Baca sprawled in a chair. Sunlight reflected off the toes of his shiny Cordovan leather boots.

"We have come," Enrique said, "To demand the release of Felipe Montez and Lalo Chaves from jail. They've been falsely accused of spying."

"My nephew," the *comandante* waved a hand at Baca, "tells me the charges are not false."

Enrique and Grandfather exchanged glances. Nephew. Family ties ran deep. This would be harder than they had anticipated. "What do the prisoners say?" Enrique asked.

Salas sat, elbow on table, chin on his fist, and thought for a moment. "I am a fair man. Have the prisoners brought to me."

Baca went to the door, barked orders, and sat in his chair, a smirk on his face.

Four soldiers ushered Felipe and Lalo into the room. Their wrists were bound, and each dragged leg irons.

Grandfather gasped and sputtered, as blue veins stood out on his forehead. "What's the meaning of this outrage? How dare you shackle these men as though they are nothing but common criminals?"

The *comandante*'s heavy-lidded eyes were like those of a lizard. "Spying against the Mexican government is a criminal act."

"Not to mention horse theft and military desertion," Baca said, his voice lazy and self-assured.

"Lies," Felipe said. "All lies." His eyes blazed and the *comandante* drew back from the intensity.

"Do you deny that the Texas Ranger showed you a map of the territory?" Baca asked.

"No."

"Or that they enlisted your aid to further their cause?"

"The Rangers asked nothing of me but did give me two pieces of advice."

"And what was that advice?"

"To stay out of Comanche country, to leave that portion of Texas and return home immediately."

"Did you follow that advice?" asked the *comandante*.

"To the best of my ability."

"Ah ha!" shouted Baca. "Then why is it that I, who started a week after you did, arrived in Santa Fe three weeks ahead of you?"

"I was delayed."

Baca snorted. "Delayed, no doubt, by scouting for weaknesses in the Mexican Army."

"Any weakness in the Mexican Army is caused by men like you," Lalo said.

Baca turned to him. "Ah, the deserter. No, Chaves, the weakness is men like you, soldiers who desert their posts in times of trouble."

"How many missions have we been on together?" Lalo asked.

"I do not keep count of my accomplishments."

"And how many times have you ordered retreat?"

"The safety of my men is my primary concern."

"Bah," Lalo said. "Your own safety, maybe. I can recall many times that you sat protected at the rear while brave men lost their lives on the front lines."

Baca shifted in his chair. "I am not the one on trial, godfather."

"No," *Comandante* Salas said, "You are not. Why did you desert your post, soldier?"

"I did not desert. I quit."

The *comandante*'s lizard-like eyelids opened only slightly yet he managed to look surprised. "I did not know a soldier could do that. Why did you, ah, quit?"

"Loss of respect for my commanding officer." Lalo pointed with his bound wrists to Baca. "Not to mention the fact that the Mexican Government owes me six months' wages."

"Other men stayed with me," Baca said.

"The last I saw you, the Texas Rangers had you and two soldiers tied to your saddles. I heard they planned to hang you. What happened to those two soldiers?"

"That is not relevant. Godfather?"

The *comandante* tented his fingers. His eyelids drooped. "I am bored with this bickering. What of the horse theft?"

"I confiscated a civilian's horse for my own use. That man," Baca pointed to Felipe, "stole the horse from me."

"Is that true?" Salas asked Felipe.

"It's my horse. Baca took it without my permission."

"Am I to understand this man stole his own horse?"

"As an officer, it is my right to—"

"It must be a very fine horse." For the first time, Comandante Salas showed an interest in the proceedings. "I will defer my decision on those other charges, but horse theft is a serious matter. I will decide on that immediately."

The *comandante* shifted his gaze between Baca and Felipe. "I am a fair man. You both want the horse. The owner will be decided by a horse race tomorrow morning."

Felipe looked blank.

"If my horse wins, my nephew gets your horse. If your horse wins the race, you keep him, and I will drop all charges. You'll be free to go." The *comandante* cast a sly glance toward Baca.

"How can you say that is a fair decision?" Enrique asked.

"Don't worry, Father," Felipe said. "El Moro will win. Untie me so I can get ready for the race." He held out his wrists.

Salas looked shocked. "Oh, no, I cannot free you until after the race."

"Then how can I ride in it?"

"That is not my concern. I have my own jockey, and I must warn you that he has yet to lose a race."

"And if we refuse to race?" Enrique asked.

"Then the horse belongs to Captain Baca and these men remain prisoners. It is your choice." The *comandante* stood. "Take these men back to jail. You are all dismissed."

"Hold on, there," Grandfather said. "You have yet to tell us the particulars of the race—when, where, and the distance."

"You have decided to race then? Very well. Two hours after sunrise tomorrow morning. There is a half-league racetrack on the north side of the city wall."

"Let's make the race a little more interesting," Grandfather said. "How about a side bet of, say, five hundred silver dollars in addition to the men's freedom?"

The *comandante*'s eyelids popped open. "Five hundred? Done." He scuttled out of the room, a satisfied smile on his face. Baca hurried after him.

"Either of the *vaqueros* that helped herd the mules to Santa Fe can ride El Moro in the race," Felipe said. "Probably Juan would be the best. He is an excellent rider and weighs less than Pedro."

Neither Enrique nor Grandfather had the heart to tell Felipe that they had already sent the two *vaqueros* back to the *hacienda*.

"What did the *comandante* say?" Seraphina asked the moment Enrique and Grandfather stepped inside the house where all the women waited.

"He is a most unreasonable man," Enrique said. He spoke in English for Clory's benefit. "There is to be a horse race."

"But what of Felipe; did they release him?"

"No." And Enrique told the women about the trial. "Our problem now is who will ride El Moro in the race. I am too heavy, and Papa is too old."

"Tomas?" Seraphina asked.

Grandfather shook his head. "Tomas is no horseman."

The group was silent, pondering. Clory spoke. "I'll ride in that race."

"You?" Enrique said, his eyes wide.

"Sure, why not? I can ride well as any man and better than most."

Alondra hugged her. "Oh, Clory, that's perfect."

Enrique shook his head. "I don't think that a woman can compete with a man in a horse race."

"It won't matter who rides," Uncle Teodoro said. "There will be no race. Last winter, the *comandante* challenged the owner of a fine runner that had the reputation of never losing and many *pesos* were wagered. The day of the race, the runner was ahead by two lengths, then without warning fell over, breathing but unable to move. The runner's owner said he had his groom guard the horse all night, but the boy fell asleep. No one knows what happened, but of course the *comandante*'s horse won."

Again, the group fell silent.

Finally, Alondra spoke. "It appears that no matter what we do, we lose El Moro, but maybe there is a way we can win."

"What do you mean?" Clory asked.

"Grandfather," Alondra said, "Could we find another black horse? We'll put him in El Moro's stall and at night they'd look the same. Then we'll find somewhere to hide El Moro until the race tomorrow morning."

Enrique laughed. "I told you our daughter was clever. Teodoro, where can I buy a horse?"

"I know a man ... let's go."

"Clory and I have work to do," Grandfather said. "Come on, girl, I'll give you some instruction on horse racing."

"We'll make Clory a nice jockey suit," Seraphina said. "Green and yellow, don't you think?"

Alondra went to the kitchen and asked the cook for a basket. She put the clay bowl with the powdered comfrey in the bottom of the basket with Felipe's knife beside it. She placed a white cloth over them and filled the basket with bread and cheese. She tucked in a few cinnamon cookies, wrapped the cloth over it all, and went to the *presidio* to visit Felipe and Lalo in jail.

"What are you doing here, *Señorita*?" The prison guard asked. His uniform jacket, missing two buttons, stretched across his belly.

"I brought the prisoners their lunch."

"I must examine it."

Alondra lifted a corner and fanned the napkin. "Bread and cheese and cinnamon cookies."

The jailer inhaled the aroma. "Ah, cinnamon, my favorite."

"I'm not supposed to, but if you don't tell anyone I'll let you have one."

"Oh, no, *Señorita*, I won't tell a soul."

"The bread is fresh too," Alondra said, "But I have to make sure there's enough for the prisoners."

"They won't miss just one little slice. They're prisoners and shouldn't eat so well anyway."

"All right, but you'll get me in trouble if you say anything."

"You have my word." He held out his hand and Alondra gave him a piece of bread and cheese. "And the cookie," he said.

"Where are the prisoners?"

"This way," the jailer said through a mouthful of bread and led her down a dark corridor.

Felipe's face lit up when he saw her, but Alondra put her finger to her lips before either he or Lalo could speak. "I brought your lunch, so be sure you eat it all. I'll return this evening with your supper and pick up the empty basket."

The guard unlocked the cell door and handed the prisoners the food. He locked the door and headed back to his office, munching a cookie.

Alondra surveyed the dim cell, empty except for a bucket in the corner. A few rays of sunshine poured from a small window near the ceiling. When the guard was out of earshot, she whispered, "The bowl holds comfrey root. Put it on your wound, Felipe." She didn't wait for an answer but turned down the corridor.

On the way out, she waved at the guard. "Goodbye, I'll be back this evening with their supper."

"Do you know what it will be?"

"No, but something good, I'm sure." Alondra stopped at the plaza before she returned to the house. At the clothing shop, she picked out two wide-brimmed straw hats. From another vendor, she purchased two *serapes*.

*****

An hour later, Captain Edmundo Baca entered the *presidio*, an old woman at his heels with a clay pot in her hands.

"I've brought the prisoners their rations for the day," he said to the jailer. "They get nothing more until the pot is empty."

The guard gulped. He wiped his hand across his brow.

"What is it, man?" Baca asked.

"They've already had their noon meal," the guard stammered. "A young lady brought a basket with bread and cheese."

Baca stalked to the prison cell, the jailer behind him. Felipe and Lalo sat on the dirt floor, their backs against the adobe wall.

"Unlock the door and search the prisoners," Baca said.

"Yes, my captain. But what am I searching for?"

"Weapons, you fool!" Baca shouted. Why must he always

be cursed with commanding thick-witted men?

The guard picked up the basket, empty but for two cookies. He eyed the cookies and licked his lips.

Baca sighed. "The men. Inspect the men's clothing."

The jailer patted Felipe's jacket, his trousers, found a few coins and pocketed them. He found nothing on Lalo. "They carry no weapons, Captain."

Neither he nor Baca noticed the freshly disturbed earth in the corner of the cell.

"The prisoners are allowed no visitors," Baca said.

"What of the young lady who is to bring them their dinner?"

"Especially not her. Lock the cell door."

Baca visited the *comandante* in his office and spoke of his concerns. "I don't trust the prisoners, Godfather. They are planning something, I am sure."

Salas smirked his lizardry grin. "They are secure for the night in the jail. Tomorrow after the race, you will have a fine black horse to ride. Take a small troop of men and your new horse and march the prisoners to Chihuahua, Mexico. The governor there is fond of firing squads. Let him decide their fate."

With only the moon to light her path, Alondra made her way to the jail cell. Broken bits of a clay bowl lay under the barred window. "Felipe," she whispered, "Felipe."

"Alondra! What are you doing here?"

"I had to see you, talk with you."

"It is dangerous for you here. Go home quickly before someone sees you."

"The fat jailer snores in his chair, he sees nothing. I brought your pistols. Tomas heard in the plaza that after the race, the soldiers will march you to Chihuahua and a firing squad." She told them what Uncle Teodoro said about the race.

"They don't think we can win, but Clory is riding El Moro."

Lalo grinned. "Ah, she will make that horse fly. With her on his back, we have no worries, my friend. El Moro will win the race."

"Give us the pistols, Alondra," Felipe said. "They already searched us and found no weapons. They're not likely to search us again."

She thrust two bundles through the bars, one long and slender the other heavy and bulky.

"Go now, *querida*. Go home and try not to worry." Felipe kissed his fingertips, reached through the window bars, and touched her cheek.

She held his hand against her face for a moment, kissed his palm, and disappeared into the shadows.

"These *sombreros* will hide our faces and the *serapes* will cover our weapons," Felipe said. "I have no desire to face a firing squad down in Mexico, but I do have an urge to observe the race. We leave this cell at daybreak." He dug his knife out from where he had buried it and slipped it in his boot sheath. They strapped their pistols around their hips, and Felipe buckled his sword around his waist.

When the sun's first rays sprinkled the town's adobe buildings with gold, Lalo rattled his tin cup on the iron bars. "Hey, Gordo, wake up and come here. We have something to show you."

The guard shuffled down the corridor. He yawned, spiked his hair with his fingers, reached under his coat, and scratched his armpits. His face wore the rumpled look of disturbed sleep. "What do you want? You make enough noise to wake the dead."

"Come closer," Lalo said. "We want to show you something."

The guard yawned. "You have nothing I want to see. Be quiet and let me go back to sleep." He turned back down the corridor.

"Open the cell door, or I shoot you where you stand," Felipe said.

His mouth agape the guard stared in shock. All thoughts of sleep fled his mind. "Where did you get that gun?"

"Unlock the door." Felipe aimed the pistol at the guard's fleshy head.

The man didn't argue. He took the large iron key attached to his belt and unlocked the door. Felipe and Lalo stepped out to freedom. "Where are you going?" the guard asked.

Neither man answered. Lalo tapped the guard on the head with his own pistol and shoved his unconscious body into the cell. Felipe locked the door behind them.

CHAPTER 30

The morning of the race dawned bright and clear. Enrique and Teodoro had bought a black horse from a farmer on the outskirts of town. The newly purchased horse stood at the watering trough. His belly was distended and sloshed when he walked. His grain had been salted.

Enrique and Grandfather led El Moro out from the goat shed where the horse had spent the night. They brushed his hide until it gleamed like black satin, oiled his hooves with tallow, and polished them with lampblack. They combed his mane, braided a yellow feather into his forelock, and tied his tail with green and yellow ribbons.

Grandfather helped Clory onto the racing saddle. She covered her brilliant hair with a yellow kerchief, but her green and yellow jockey outfit did not hide the fact that she was a well-formed young woman. Enrique and Grandfather rode on either side of Clory. The other women piled into the buggy and, with Tomas driving, followed them to the racetrack. They parked near the end of the course. Enrique reined his horse next to the upright poles that marked the finish line, and Grandfather led El Moro to the starting post.

Spectators lined both sides of the track. Men walked up and down, taking bets. The odds were five to one against El Moro. Most of the women and many of the young men placed their bets on the pretty jockey. Grandfather held El Moro by the halter, spoke in soft tones to calm the eager horse.

The *comandante*'s horse, a well-groomed sorrel, arrived at the starting posts. His muscles rippled in the sunlight. The jockey was a short, thin man dressed in black and red.

"So, today I am forced to compete with a woman. Take care, Chica, that I don't trample you into the dirt." The jockey spoke in Spanish. Clory didn't glance his way.

"Look at me when I speak to you," the jockey said. "I've won many races. Don't think I'll let you win just because you're a woman."

Grandfather shook his finger at him. "Apologize to the lady at once."

The jockey laughed. "I'll apologize after I win the race."

"Don't pay attention to him, Clory," Grandfather said. "You're a good rider, just remember what I told you."

"I ain't worried, Grandpa. I feel good, and El Moro wants to run. We'll do our best."

"I know you will," he said, "and you're prettier than that wrinkled, peanut-faced man, too."

Clory laughed.

Comandante Salas drove up in his black and red carriage, and Captain Baca rode beside him, his sword buckled at his waist. "That's a good-looking horse you have there, *Señor*, but can he run?" *Comandante* Salas asked.

Grandfather heaved a deep sigh. "He's sluggish this morning and cursed with a terrible thirst. Perhaps he'll run only to the watering trough."

Salas pulled his thin lips back in his lizardry smile. "Your horse is poorly and your jockey a girl. I'm a fair man, I'll not disagree if you want to back out of the race and hand your horse over to me now."

"The stakes stand," Grandfather said. "Perhaps the horse will recover in time to run the race. And I have so much faith in my jockey that I'm willing to add another five hundred to our wager."

Salas' heavy eyelids popped open. "Done." They shook hands. Baca smirked, and they galloped to the finish line for a better view of the race.

Grandfather moved away from the horses as the starter stepped to the starting posts and pointed his pistol to the sky. He counted to ten and squeezed the trigger. The shot echoed in the still air.

El Moro shook his head, snorted, and reared. Clory steadied him, patted his neck, and pointed his nose to the finish line. She dug her heels in his sides and El Moro galloped down the track.

The sorrel ran at a steady gait two lengths ahead.

Clory stood in the stirrups, knees on the shoulders, and tapped El Moro with her riding crop. He stretched out his neck and caught up with the sorrel. They ran side by side, stride for stride. The crowd roared.

"Ha!" shouted the other jockey. "See if you can keep up with me now." He whipped his horse a vicious slap on the rump. The sorrel leaped forward. El Moro stayed with him. The crowd bellowed their approval.

The horses pounded down the racetrack, clouds of red dust in their wake. They galloped neck and neck to the three-quarter mark.

Clory didn't hear the crowd shouting, didn't see their upraised fists, their waving hats. She concentrated on El Moro, smelled his sweat, felt his muscles work. He ran with a smooth and steady gait, his ears pricked up and alert. "Keep your hands still and sit balanced in the saddle," Grandfather had said. She didn't need the whip; she had only to lean forward, and El Moro responded.

Next to her, the jockey beat the sorrel about the withers

with a constant rhythm. The horse ran with his head high and ears flicking to the side and back.

The two upright poles that marked the finish loomed ahead. Clory leaned forward. "Now, El Moro, now."

El Moro flattened out and crossed the finish line one length ahead of the sorrel. Clory straightened in the saddle and reined the horse to a trot. A man wearing a big *sombrero* and riding Lalo's gelding grabbed the bridle and led El Moro down the track at a canter. Clory beamed at Lalo. She stood high in the stirrups, tore off her kerchief, and waved it at the clamoring crowd.

Lalo led El Moro back up the racecourse at a walk to the family's buckboard and the crowd cheered. This was a race they would long remember: the shiny black horse decked out in green and yellow, the girl jockey with red-gold hair. Even the losers paid off their bets with good humor.

*****

Grandfather rode up to the *comandante*'s carriage. "A fine race, don't you agree, *comandante*?"

Salas glared. "I understood that your horse was poorly."

"He recovered rapidly," Grandfather said. "Shall we go to the *presidio* now to release the prisoners? And I believe you owe me one thousand dollars."

"Did you do as I ordered?" the *comandante* asked Baca.

"Your instructions were followed, Godfather," Baca answered.

"What, then, went wrong?"

Baca, his mouth a tight thin line, lowered his eyes and shrugged.

"Why do you hesitate?" Grandfather asked. "We agreed to the terms you set. Turn the men free and pay what you owe me." His eyes gleamed with a wicked light. "Or were you so sure I'd lose that you bet money you don't have?"

"Of course, I have the money," the *comandante* said. "I don't carry that much with me. I am a man of honor. I'll pay you tomorrow."

"No. As a man of honor, you will fulfill the terms of the wager now. Set the men free, and if you haven't the money, I'll take the sorrel as part payment. With the proper training, he'll make a good horse."

His eyes pinpoints of hate, *Comandante* Salas glanced around the crowd and saw Uncle Teodoro talking with Enrique and a man wrapped in a brightly colored *serape*. "Teodoro," the *comandante* called, "pay this man one thousand dollars."

Uncle Teodoro strode to the carriage. "What service did this man perform for the province?"

"I owe him a debt of honor."

Teodoro drew himself up and in a loud, clear tone that carried across the crowd, said, "I will not pay your personal debts out of the treasury, money gleaned from the taxpayer's sweat."

The *comandante*'s heavy eyelids fluttered, his skin turned a mottled purple. "You will do as I say or spend a week in the center of the plaza confined in the stocks."

"Do as you will," Teodoro said. "I am an honest man and will not steal from the taxpayers." He returned to the buckboard and his family.

The conversation passed from mouth to mouth through the crowd.

"The *comandante* steals our tax money," a man said. "He imprisons honest men," another shouted. "Send him back to Mexico!" someone yelled. In a few short minutes, the cheerful crowd erupted into a hostile mob. Ranch owners and shepherds, rich men and poor, rushed the *comandante* with flashing knives and machetes.

Baca shouted orders. Mounted soldiers surrounded the *comandante*'s carriage. Horses and the human mass pressed against Grandfather's mount. The animal panicked, snorted, and reared. He pawed the air, his front hooves struck the carriage, smashed the sideboards.

The *comandante* huddled against the seatback. "Get this old fool away from me!"

Baca reached for the bridle. Grandfather's horse tossed his head and whinnied. With his riding whip, Baca beat the animal about the head. The horse snorted, humped its back, crow-hopped, and exploded into a bucking frenzy.

Grandfather bounced in the saddle, hung on with both hands. For over seventy years, horses had been his life and many years had passed since a horse had thrown him. But now, his feeble muscles were no match for a thousand pounds of fury.

Felipe threw off his *serape* and bounded onto El Moro's back. He pushed his way through the milling mob and reached Grandfather too late. The old man lay on the ground, his left leg at an awkward angle. Felipe jumped off the horse, knelt on one knee beside Grandfather, and cradled his head.

Grandfather looked up at Felipe, his eyes bright with pain. "It was a good race, son. Take care of that little filly of yours." His eyelids fluttered shut.

With his kerchief, Felipe gently wiped spittle from the corner of Grandfather's mouth.

Suddenly quiet, the mob stared in shock. Enrique elbowed his way through and picked Grandfather up in his arms. His eyes misted with tears as he carried the frail old man to the buckboard and laid him on the back seat.

Felipe glowered at Baca. "You ignorant fool. You should know better than to beat a frightened horse."

Baca curled his lip. "And you would know better? Grab him, men. This lapdog of a rich Spaniard has escaped from prison."

The mounted soldiers moved away from the *comandante*'s carriage and toward Felipe.

"I don't think so!" Lalo aimed one pistol at Salas and another at Baca. "Make one move, and I shoot them both."

The soldiers reined their mounts. Unsure of orders, they shifted their gaze from the captain to the *comandante*. Lalo held the guns steady.

With his dagger in his left hand, his saber in his right, Felipe said, "Your quarrel is with me, Baca. Fight like a man."

Baca leaped from his horse. "With great pleasure! I will fight you to the death." He slashed at Felipe with his sword, stabbed at him with his dagger.

"Get me away from here, nephew," screamed Salas. "You are paid to protect me, not fight a silly duel."

The crowd shouted him down. "Go back to Mexico where you belong!" "Let them fight with honor!" "The captain is a coward!" "The *comandante* is a thief."

This was indeed a momentous day, one that would be told and retold for generations to come. First, they had seen an exciting horserace and now a duel. Once again, the odds-makers moved through the throng taking bets.

The combatants circled like fighting roosters, measuring each other with a thrust, a feint, waiting for an opening to strike.

Comandante Salas appealed to Lalo. "Stop this senseless duel."

Lalo grinned. "Why? I enjoy a good fight same as anyone. Besides Baca needs killing." He kept a pistol aimed at the *comandante*, holstered the other.

"Save me, nephew," Salas screamed. "Forget the duel."

Not to be denied the prospect of watching a good fight, several men rushed at the *comandante*, pushed against the carriage. It toppled over and Salas tumbled to the ground. The team galloped down the racetrack, kicking and braying. The wagon bounced behind them, lost a wheel, and shattered to pieces.

Salas lay curled in the dirt, knees to his chin, weeping.

"Edmundo, Edmundo, help me."

"The *comandante* is a coward," someone shouted. A group crowded around Salas. A man yanked him to his feet and shoved him. The *comandante* whimpered. "Please don't." Blood lust in their eyes, the mob pushed and yelled. Waving swords, machetes, and guns, the roar "Kill the thieving coward," echoed through the swarming horde. One swipe of a machete and the *comandante*'s head rolled in the dirt. With a triumphant yell, a man kicked the head to another, who passed it on, back and forth from one man to another.

Enemies, but united in the abhorrence of the barbaric spectacle, Felipe and Baca turned to the hot-eyed crowd. Felipe pointed his gun to the sky and pulled the trigger, the shot scarcely heard over the screaming throng. "Stop this outrage at once!" He shouted to the rioting crowd.

Brandishing his sword, Baca shouldered through the mob of yelling men. "Get back. Get back." A gunshot from the mob boomed and Baca crumpled to the ground.

Lalo prodded the stunned soldiers into action. Shooting their pistols in the air, they pushed the mob aside and formed a circle around the fallen victims.

"Go home," Felipe shouted. "It's all over, go home." One by one, the crowd slowly dispersed.

*****

The Montez family carried Grandfather to Aunt Christina's house and sent Tomas for the doctor.

The doctor, an American from one of the southern states, had come to Santa Fe several years before. He came to collect a debt but, intrigued with the sleepy Spanish town, hospitable *hacienda* owners, and beautiful women, the doctor remained. He never did find the man who owed him money and over the years had forgotten the debt. He had few patients. Most people used herbs and prayers to cure illnesses, but only the doctor could set bones straight.

He set Grandfather's leg, clicked his tongue in sympathy, and declared it would be many weeks before the old man would walk.

Grandfather cursed the doctor as a charlatan and begged Grandmother to light candles and pray the rosary three times a day so that he could dance at their grandson's wedding.

*****

The overwrought crowd had no desire to return to their homes. They stood in groups around the plaza, discussing the events of the day. "What New Mexico needs is an honest governor," a *hacienda* owner said.

The word spread throughout the crowd. Soon, a list of *Comandante* Salas' faults and sins circulated, and a man suggested they choose an honest man for governor. One who would return the ill-gotten tax money.

The excited citizens went to the gambling hall and spent the evening playing *monte* and discussing their options.

The next day, Jose Fuentes visited Teodoro. "Since we learned of the corruption of *Comandante* Salas and Captain Baca and the people eliminated them, we have no government. This morning, we held an election and voted you, Teodoro, to be our new governor."

"I'm honored, of course," Teodoro said. "But I don't know what to say."

"Say 'yes.' You are an honest man. If not for you, the *comandante* would have cleaned out the treasury." Fuentes took hold of Teodoro's arm. "Come, the people are waiting to hear your answer."

Without need of further persuasion, Teodoro went with Fuentes to the plaza. Leaving Grandfather and Heath in Rosa's care, the rest of the family followed.

The citizens waited for them in the middle of the square,

and Teodoro climbed onto the bed of an empty wagon and made a fine speech. He promised relief from the burden of heavy taxation, and the crowd cheered. They cheered again when he pledged protection from foreign intrusion.

"And, to do that," he said, "we need a captain for the militia. Please step up here, Captain Lalo Chaves. I would like to introduce you to your troops."

Lalo gulped. "I can't do it, Felipe." His voice shook with emotion. "I have long dreamed of such an honor, but I'm not worthy of the position."

"Of course, you are," Felipe said. "You are brave, and you are a soldier. You'd never be happy as a farmer."

"But I'm not educated. I can't read and can write only my name. How can I be sure each man gets his proper paycheck?"

Felipe pushed Lalo forward. "I'll teach you. Now get up there and face your soldiers. See how eager they are for honest leadership?"

Lalo climbed up onto the wagon bed and Teodoro inducted him into the Santa Fe militia as captain of the guards. A celebration followed with feasting and a *fandango*.

"Now that I have a good job, Felipe," Lalo said. "Clory and I will visit the mission priest tomorrow. Then we can find a house to raise our family."

Felipe shook his hand. "I'm happy for you, my friend." He prayed nothing would happen to mar his friend's happiness. New Mexico needed strong and honest leadership, but he knew this was only the beginning of many new changes for his beloved country. Maybe the Texians were right in their decision to break away from Mexico and govern themselves.

"You must promise to come to the *hacienda* in three weeks for my wedding," Felipe said.

"Three weeks? Why wait so long?"

"Grandmother insists that we have a proper wedding, with the banns read for three Sundays and all the relatives in attendance."

That evening, Felipe wrote a letter for Clory to her mother. From the hollowed-out deer antler he used as an inkhorn, he poured the powdered tannic acid and iron oxide he had brought from Mexico into a glass dish. He moistened the mixture with water until the ink was the proper consistency. Felipe dipped his newly sharpened quill into the ink and said, "All right, Clory, what do you want me to write."

"Tell her that I'm going to have my own house, and I want her to come live with me."

Felipe covered three pages with her words. When done, he taught Clory to write her name and prayed that Ma would someday receive the letter.

CHAPTER 31

The next morning the Montez family had an unexpected visitor. James Thornton rode up to the *hacienda* and asked to speak with Felipe. "Maria Fuentes told me I would find Alondra here," he said.

"What business do you have with her?" Felipe asked.

"I believe that she is my cousin," Thornton said, "and for many years I have searched for her. But I must see her to be absolutely certain."

Felipe invited James into the house and the entire family gathered around the table to hear James' story.

"I understand you carry a small dagger with you," he said to Alondra. "May I see it please?"

She took out her knife and laid it on the table. James picked it up and examined it carefully. "See the marking on the blade? It is our family crest. This knife has been in our family for generations."

He looked up and smiled at her. "Hello, cousin. I have looked everywhere for you. I saw you dancing in San Antonio, but then I lost you. I never thought to find you here in Santa Fe."

"You knew my parents?" Alondra asked.

"I was only a young boy, but I remember them. I remember you, too, when you were a small child."

"Was it in Saint Louis?" Alondra asked.

"Yes," James said, "and you own a house there. I'm only sorry our grandfather didn't live long enough to know you. It was he who sent me searching for you."

"How long ago did he die?"

"Only a few months ago, when I got home from San Antonio."

"I want to go to Saint Louis, Felipe," Alondra said. "I want to meet the rest of my family."

"We'll go there together after we are married," Felipe said. "It will be our honeymoon."

"A good idea. There are not too many of us left," James said.

"I have a last name? Felipe, I have a last name," Alondra said.

Felipe laughed. "When we are married, you will have two last names: Montez-Thornton."

"No, her last name is Raison. Her father and my mother were brother and sister. Alondra, you were named Calandre, which is French for "lark." As a child, you were called Callie."

"You must come to our wedding, James," Felipe said.

"I will be honored if you all will come to my and Maria's wedding."

"You are the American Anglo who is to marry Maria Fuentes?" Enrique asked and laughed.

"And you will stay and manage the Fuentes *hacienda*?" Grandfather asked.

"Yes," James said, "but I must return to Saint Louis and finish some business." He turned to Felipe and Alondra. "We have a lot to discuss. Alondra is heir to a great deal of money and property. A lawyer back in Saint Louis is handling everything for now, but it would be wise for you to go there soon."

"We will be married in three weeks' time," Felipe said.

"Good. I will send a message by way of the wagon train, and let Mr. Petty know to expect you. I will follow shortly after."

"Are you marrying soon?" Felipe asked. "Maybe we can travel together."

"That's a possibility," James said, "but Maria does not care for travel, but we'll see. In any event, I must go back to Saint Louis soon."

*****

Three weeks later, on a cloudless day in early May, the priest and his assistant rode their burros to the Montez *hacienda*. They went immediately to the chapel to prepare for the wedding ceremony. Every crucifix and holy picture in the chapel shone from vigorous rubbing. The crocheted altar cloth gleamed white and pure as a baby's soul, and new beeswax candles flickered on the altar.

Felipe and Alondra went separately to the chapel. They knelt in the confessional and asked forgiveness for any sins they may have committed, so that they could enter the holy state of matrimony with a clear conscience.

Aunts, grandfathers, cousins, and friends filled every room in the house. Unmarried men and young boys slept in the stable. Families camped in the guard tower.

For three days, the women had cooked and baked. Two steers and a hog roasted on spits over outdoor fires. Pots of beans bubbled on every fireplace in the house.

Seraphina, Christina, and Grandmother took charge of Alondra. They bathed her with perfumed soap and rinsed her hair in rose water. They massaged her hands and feet with scented oil and gave her delicate cotton undergarments to wear. She hesitated only when Seraphina insisted that

Alondra remove her dagger and leave it in the bedroom.

The women dressed Alondra in the white silk dress and draped the lace *mantilla* over her black curls.

Ready for the wedding ceremony and with Clory beside her, Alondra walked the path to the chapel. Her stomach fluttered and her knees weakened. She touched her leg, wishing she had her dagger. She clutched Clory's hand. "I can't do it, Clory. I'm scared."

"Shoot, Alondra. There ain't nothing to it. I did it. You can too."

"Everyone treats me nice now, but what if they change their minds?"

"That's what's good about getting married. The priest said that Lalo and me are tied together for life, and no one can tear us apart. Once you and Felipe are married, it don't matter what anyone says, you'll be together forever. That's what you want, ain't it?"

"Yes, but Clory, I haven't seen a shooting star or a rainbow in days. Last night, I heard an owl, and this morning three crows pecked at something right outside my door. Maybe those are bad omens, and it means that Felipe and I won't be together forever."

"Felipe says he don't believe in that kind of stuff. Maybe you should listen to him. If you love him enough, it don't matter. It's better to be together for even just a little while than not at all."

Her love for Felipe overcame most of her fears and Alondra took a deep breath. "You're right, Clory. I'm ready now, but I feel naked without my dagger."

Clory laughed. Her blue eyes twinkled, bright as the clear spring sky. "You won't need it today. And I bet you won't ever need it again."

Guests crowded outside the chapel door. Smiling, they opened a path for the bride and her attendant.

All fears and doubts left her when Alondra saw Felipe

waiting for her at the altar. He held out his hand and, as in a dream, she went to him. They held hands throughout the ceremony, and Alondra scarcely heard the priest's words.

Since the chapel was too small to accommodate all the guests, the priest agreed to perform the final blessing outdoors. Alondra and Felipe followed him to the courtyard out into the fresh air. Under a smiling sun, with green cornfields and cottonwoods as a backdrop and surrounded by family and friends, the couple made their vows to cherish one another until death parted them.

"*Para siempre jamás,*" Felipe whispered in Alondra's ear. "Forever and ever and all eternity, *querida.*"

Happiness filled her heart and glowed in her eyes.

He touched her lips with his in a kiss that filled her soul with gladness and her heart with love.

And Alondra knew that he spoke the truth.

ABOUT
ATMOSPHERE PRESS

Atmosphere Press is an independent, full-service publisher for excellent books in all genres and for all audiences. Learn more about what we do at atmospherepress.com.

We encourage you to check out some of Atmosphere's latest releases, which are available at Amazon.com and via order from your local bookstore:

Shadows of Robyst, a novel by K. E. Maroudas

Dying to Live, a novel by Barbara Macpherson Reyelts

Looking for Lawson, a novel by Mark Kirby

Surrogate Colony, a novel by Boshra Rasti

Á Deux, a novel by Alexey L. Kovalev

What If It Were True, a novel by Eileen Wesel

Sunflowers Beneath the Snow, a novel by Teri M. Brown

Solitario: The Lonely One, a novel by John Manuel

The Fourth Wall, a novel by Scott Petty

Rx, a novel by Garin Cycholl

Knights of the Air: Book 1: Rage!, a novel by Iain Stewart

Heartheaded, a novel by Constantina Pappas

The Aquamarine Surfboard, a novel by Kellye Abernathy

ABOUT
THE AUTHOR

Olivia Godat has enjoyed reading her entire life, and has often said, "I've never met a genre I didn't like." After retiring from her professional career, she had time to pursue her other passion—writing. Over the past twenty-five years Olivia has written several novels, novellas, short stories, essays, and poems.